A Republic

of Shadows

Andrew Clawson

This book is a work of fiction. The character, incidents, and dialogue are drawn from the author's imaginations and are not to be construed as real. Any resemblance to actual events or persons, living or dead, is entirely coincidental.

Cover design and illustration by Books Covered

Get Andrew Clawson's Starter Library FOR FREE

Sign up for the no-spam newsletter and get two novels for free.

Details can be found at the end of this book.

Epigraph

A throne is only a bench covered with velvet.

—Napoleon Bonaparte

Prologue

London, England
July, 1702

The two most powerful people in the world stared at each other in silence.

Only one would survive this conversation.

"Good afternoon, cousin."

"And a good afternoon to you, Your Majesty."

Anne didn't blink. Queen of England, Scotland and Ireland, Defender of the Faith. Yet this impertinent toad wished to steal the throne upon which she sat. Her cousin, a man whom she should have held dear, plotted against her.

And she could do nothing about it.

"Bring the Queen her tea." George turned to one of the myriad attendants lining the room.

"No, I'm—"

Except the girl vanished, obeying this man above her sovereign.

Unsurprising, considering he'd corrupted every last one of her ladies-in-waiting. Money, gifts, mercy, whatever it took. George coerced those around his cousin the Queen into obeying him, bringing that most valuable of commodities.

Information.

Where she went. What she did. Who kept her company. George knew it all, and had maneuvered so carefully, so masterfully, that Anne could do nothing about it.

"How fares your health, Your Majesty? I cannot imagine the pain you must feel at the loss of your son."

Though I can imagine the joy you felt at his loss, you wretched viper.

1

"I am strong, George. Strong for my son, strong for our nation. A queen must not waver in her duties, no matter what she faces."

He lied to her, feigned interest and care with others present, but she knew the truth. George could not have been happier for her loss. Prince William, Duke of Gloucester and heir to the throne, gone. Taken during a hunt some months ago, his entire retinue of bodyguards killed save one, left alive to deliver a message. Unfortunately for him, the man told Anne his horrid tale in the presence of her cousin, and George saw to it that this brave guard didn't live to repeat it.

"He is mourned every day, dear cousin."

The lying bastard. How she wanted to shove a dagger through his throat, cut that toxic tongue from his mouth and shout to the world of his deceit. Except he'd outmaneuvered her, parlayed her son's disappearance into the perfect coup.

It did not take much. Admittedly, Anne did not fare well at the news, the shock overwhelming. In the short time it took for her to recover, George spread the lie of Prince William's death at the hands of highwaymen. She woke to find this falsehood accepted as truth, all her trusted attendants and personal guards either murdered or turned against her, and an unstoppable movement in parliament to pass the Act of Settlement.

"I understand your legislative endeavors have settled the matter of succession at my passing," Anne said.

"Merely a precaution, my Queen. May you live a long and full life, filled with joy. And who is to say there will not be another prince forthcoming?"

Her eyes narrowed. George knew by now that her time for bearing children had passed. Any one of the physicians attending her could tell him that, for she knew his coin lined their pockets, buying her closest secrets. And with her line, the Stuarts, holding title to the throne, her husband would never become King.

And to this end, George orchestrated passage of the Act of Settlement, ostensibly to provide a lasting peace for England and her territories should Anne die without further issue. However, the true rationale lay open for all to see.

The act barred any Roman Catholics from occupying the throne. The Stuarts were Roman Catholic, every last one. Her cousin, however, did not follow that faith. George of the House Hanover practiced Protestantism, and based on the act, this religious affiliation alone could occupy the throne.

A perfectly played usurpation.

"And your scouts, cousin George. Have they brought any news of my son?"

"Your son is dead, Your Majesty." Unblinking, unmoving, uncaring. And utterly convinced he was right. "We still pursue his killers and will never cease. At the moment, though, they have not located the scoundrels."

With a great groaning, the door eased open to reveal a servant bearing tea. Pastries and biscuits topped the silver platters, a steaming pot the centerpiece. As usual, the servant presented these refreshments to Anne first.

"In a moment, dear." The silver platter clattered on a table between them, and the girl scurried away, taking her place among the dozen others lining the walls.

"My cousin and I require privacy," Anne said, rising from her chair. For a second, no one budged. "You will all leave at once."

Steel edged her words, and the young women vanished in a rustle of lace.

"That includes you as well," she said, pointing to the Yeoman Warders standing guard. Normally only on duty at the Tower of London, these two were part of the group assigned to protect her at all times, a team assembled and deployed by her cousin while Anne recovered from the loss of Prince William.

"Your Majesty, we must assure your safety at all times."

"If you do not leave, I'll have you beheaded."

Even though they worked for George, took his money and reported on her every move, a queen's threat was too much. Both men vanished without so much as glancing toward George.

She turned to find her loathsome cousin grinning. "The Queen commands with an iron fist."

"Now that we're alone, I suggest we dispense with the pleasantries." Her need for privacy was twofold. First, she needed George to loosen his tongue. Without witnesses, she suspected he would speak freely. Second, what she planned to say would give even the most impartial observer reason to question her sanity, and given George's successful plotting to date, she had little doubt this conversation would be used against her.

"Where is my son?"

Instead of answering, George leaned over and filled her cup. "This tea will be cold soon," he said. "You should drink. A warm cup to keep the cold from your bones."

"Answer the question."

"Your son is dead, my Queen. God rest his soul."

"That is a lie." Spittle flew, her jaw clenched so tightly each tooth ached. "You heard what the guard said." An arrow in his arm, the man had come straight to Anne, telling her everything. Unfortunately, George had overheard. "William was kidnapped, taken by a group of Irishman."

"I'm worried about your health, dear cousin." George set the saucer in front of her, nudging it as he spoke. "Take some tea to calm your nerves."

"I do not want—"

Why did he push it so? George cared not a bit for her well-being, yet he urged this soothing tonic on her again and again. He did nothing without considering his own gain first.

"Perhaps I shall," she said, effortlessly changing tone. "Won't you join me?"

The servant controlled by George. His insistence on tea. It cried out to her, a beacon of distrust. Had he the gall to poison her?

"I'm not thirsty," George said, leaning back. "But please, go ahead. It will raise your spirits."

"I insist." Again, Anne's tone brooked no argument.

Halting in his chair, George returned her gaze. A moment passed, and then another.

"As you wish." He poured, setting the saucer on his leg.

"What do you know of William? Have you found any sign?"

At first she thought he would deny it, as he had every time she'd asked, each instance only adding to the rumors swirling that Anne's fragile nature had cracked, that a weak-willed woman sat the throne.

He surprised her. "I have not. The trail is cold, and William lost. Even you must realize he is dead." George leaned closer, the untouched tea clattering as he moved. "Once the brigands who stole William learned their demands would not be met, they killed him." Her lips quivered, and Anne raised a hand to cover them. "Do not fret," George said, his snake-like tongue offering false comfort. "Alive, William would only lead to their downfall. You know how this game is played. When a bargaining piece becomes worthless, it must be cast aside."

"If this is so, he is murdered by your hand. Had you not told my court that William died in the assault, I would have met their terms and regained our future king."

"And encourage further attacks? You must be mad." He leaned back, contempt dripping on every word. "Capitulation is a sign of weakness, and in times such as these, our monarch must be strong. A leader without compare."

Fresh scents wafted from the cup in front of her. Perhaps this is what nightshade smells like. Sweet, floral, and deadly.

"And I assume you believe you will fill that role?"

"That is for God to decide," George said.

"And as my closest Protestant relative, it seems the good lord has decreed it so." No reason to argue with the man. Anne knew what he'd done, and cared not. The return of Prince William is what drove her now. George could have her empire.

"I am but a mere servant to His whims." Blowing on his tea, he peered at her over the rim. "This smells wonderful."

And then he drank deeply, emptying the cup.

Apparently George did not plan to poison her today.

"I trust you have my uncle continuing the search for William?"

"Fruitless though it may be, of course he is, my Queen. Laurence Hyde is your representative in Ireland, Lord Lieutenant and your personal envoy to that nation. I would be remiss in my search were he not to take a leading role."

Except Laurence couldn't possibly know the truth, not with George keeping her locked in this castle. Ostensibly for her protection after the recent period of weakness, though both knew she lived in confinement, not under protection.

"He must know the truth," Anne said. "Otherwise his efforts will be wasted, will end too soon."

"As we've discussed, dear Anne, that cannot be. The monarch cannot be seen as weak, not with the French and Spanish growing ever bolder. England, above all, must be strong."

The icy demeanor Anne allowed George to see stood at odds with the fire burning inside her. "I will see your head removed, dear cousin. You may count on that."

An empty threat, and George knew it well. With his turncoats surrounding her, Anne's power had diminished too far to comprehend.

"You are my Queen. My head and my heart belong to you."

Taking one of the hot biscuits, she imagined biting through his neck as easily as she did the flaky treat. Except George would overpower her, twist the incident to benefit him. Perhaps she could draw him in, use her dagger to end this?

She finished the biscuit and her tea, considering how to best parry George's attacks.

"I'll take another cup." She set the saucer down, coughing into a gloved hand. The dry biscuit had parched her throat, leaving it dry as dust.

George didn't move.

"More tea," she said. Another cough, harder this time. And each breath burned, the air hot as she struggled against the dryness creeping down her chest.

"I don't believe you'll find that to help. You really should not have dismissed your food taster."

She opened her mouth, but the words wouldn't come. An invisible fist tightened, her throat crushed in its embrace, ragged gasps failing to fill her lungs.

"I was told this poison works quickly, my Queen." He leaned toward her as she flailed about, falling into the table, the service set crashing all around. George leaned closer, whispering in her ear. "You've suffered enough, dear cousin. I only want to reunite you with your son. And to thank you. For giving me your throne."

Then he jumped out, shouting and running for the door. People rushed in, servants calling for a physician, but Anne didn't hear. Dark spots clouded her vision, each breath more shallow than the last.

As she lay on the cool stone floor, a final thought pushed through her mind, a last hope better than any breath of air.

The painting. Laurence would see it, would uncover her true message and carry on where she had failed.

And then the world went black.

Chapter 1

Dublin, Ireland
Present Day

Cotton clouds dotted the Irish sky, lazy puffs hanging far above the National Gallery of Ireland, a centuries-old institution that housed Ireland's finest collection of national and European artwork, all situated in the heart of bustling Dublin.

Alongside pieces by Caravaggio and Monet stood a collection of offices and work studios for the dedicated men and women overseeing the operation, and in one towering room a talented young restoration specialist repaired one of her treasures.

Michelle Berks stood over a damaged portrait, planning her attack. At least the custodian whose broom handle went through the painting told them about his mishap. Last time this happened it took months to uncover the damage. Regardless, the painting stood in Michelle's studio, in need of repair.

Slipping cotton gloves over her hands, the outside world fell away and it was with a mother's care that Michelle inspected the torn canvas.

She had no husband, no children, and didn't particularly want either. These masterpieces were her children. She'd relocated from America to work at the prestigious facility upon graduating from her doctoral program, and an art lover such as herself couldn't dream of a better job, her heart fluttering every time she tended to a damaged piece. Something about the historic brush strokes she repaired sent a tingling up her spine. Michelle loved her work, and was proud that her hands helped preserve these masterpieces for generations to come.

The small tear didn't affect the central figure, Queen Anne of Great Britain. A simple fix, as Michelle only need determine how the canvas attached to the frame before beginning. With any luck, this girl should be back on display within days.

Tweezers in hand, she adjusted the bright overhead light, her face inches from the tear. Just as she suspected. Tiny iron nails bound the canvas and frame. Simple, really. Remove the slim nails, patch the damaged area, and Queen Anne is good as new.

An American radio station streamed on her phone as Michelle dove in. She loved Ireland, with its storied history and breathtaking scenery, but there were some things she desperately missed from home. Real ketchup, for one.

Nails rattled on her stark glass examination table, and with a soft hand, Michelle pulled the canvas away from its frame. As it moved, something grabbed her eye.

Ohmygod.

She'd ruined it. Destroyed the painting.

Wait a second...what in the world?

A thin envelope fell from inside the painting.

Her fluttering chest flipped from panic to intrigue as she laid the fallen item on a glass examination table, the lights underneath bursting to life. Thick and rough, the envelope lit up like an x-ray. Across the flap, a splash of red wax sealed the vessel shut.

Michelle leaned in closer. There was a design in the wax, some type of intricate seal. The image exploded under her Sherlock Holmes style magnifying glass. It *was* a shield, with heraldic symbols in each of the four corners. A fleur-de-lis in one, a harp in the other.

A door creaked open behind her, crowd noise suddenly competing with her streaming radio.

"Morning, Michelle. How's old Anne doing?"

It was Kris, a colleague who specialized in sculptures.

"You okay?"

"Yes," she stammered. "I'm fine. The tear isn't bad, an easy fix."

Her ruse worked as Kris kept his distance, headed toward the coffee pot. "Good to hear. Want any coffee?"

"No, I'm headed out for a quick bite. Forgot to eat breakfast this morning."

"I'm sure Anne won't mind. Good luck with the repairs," Kris said as he disappeared through the door.

Why was she acting like this? She felt a desperate urge to keep the finding to herself, at least for now. That was okay, wasn't it? Properly investigate the envelope first, and then share it with colleagues. Nothing wrong with that.

Using a thin blade, she broke the wax seal, lifting the dry paper to reveal a single ivory sheet. Elegant handwriting filled the page.

As she read, the outside world faded away. Lost in her find, she didn't hear her phone alarm buzzing until it clattered off the table.

Erika.

Her former grad school classmate arrived in a few hours. Michelle had been ecstatic when her friend called a few weeks ago to announce that she and her significant other were coming to visit.

And talk about perfect timing. An Ivy League history professor, Erika had forgotten more about the past than most people ever knew. She loved this kind of stuff.

Could Erika get emails on the plane? She hoped so.

With tingling nerves, she dashed off a brief message, enough to whet Erika's appetite. After tucking the letter and envelope back inside the portrait frame for safekeeping, Michelle rushed out the door, struggling to process a tale of treachery, death and deceit.

Chapter 2

London, England

Dim halogen lights hummed on the ceiling, the office buried inside a building darkened by age and the past. Feet on his desk, a man stared at five oversized computer monitors, eyes flicking from one screen to the next, a phone pressed to his ear.

"Shouldn't have had that last round, mate. My head's foggier than a moor."

He and a few colleagues shut down the pub last night, and now they were paying for it.

"Same here. How's the endless watch?" his mate asked.

"How do you think? Same as always. Nothing to be seen, only nonsense running across the screen."

Among the men on their team assigned to rotate at this desk, they referred to the eight-hour shift as 'the endless watch'. Twice per week each of them had to sit here, watching the screens blink, listening to nothing at all, because their boss had decreed that this room be soundproofed to ward off any distractions. The boss wasn't a total slouch, however. He'd seen to it that the poor bastard on duty sat in a top flight desk chair and had their own coffee machine. Important, both of them, for whoever found themselves at this desk needed all the caffeine and comfort possible.

"You'll be worm food before they ever find anything," his friend said.

"Probably. I heard this search has been going on since before we were born."

"Wouldn't be surprised if that were true," his friend said. "You think they'd have better programs to search for it now, though. Must have been the first computer code ever written when they started searching."

Both men chuckled at that. On the monitors, an alert pinged.

"Damn. I'm backed up on these alerts, and you know I'll catch hell if Chief finds out we're not reading every bloody one of these the moment they come in."

"Let's see what we have here," he said to himself, hanging up the phone. The keyboard clicked, clearing the message. None of these damn things were ever important. Not a single one, and he'd been doing this for going on two years now.

The parameters were simple. A search algorithm scoured the globe for a combination of phrases. Phone calls, emails, text messages, social media. You name it, this program searched for it. And in over a hundred languages. Were the searches legal? Maybe. But with this project grouped under the catch-all "national security" tag, elected officials didn't ask too many questions.

And so it went for decades. Long before he'd ever thought about his career, before he had any notion he wanted to be a part of Her Majesty's government.

Another ping, this time tagging a phone call in Australia. Again, no dice.

Some of the stuff that came up wasn't even close. The specific items they searched for were listed in front of him, taped to the desk. As if he needed it any longer. He'd stared at the phrases and word groupings so many times he could recite them in his sleep. If he ever found any part of a message matching the list, he went to the boss for further review. Only twice in two years, resulting both times in scarcely a peep from his superiors. Only a "thank you, but it's nothing." And so it went, shift after bloody shift.

"Time for another cup." The fancy machine went to work (it even made espresso) and a minute later a double steamed in his hands.

His running shoes returned to their post on the desk, chair creaking as he leaned back.

A new message dinged for attention.

"Can I have a minute off, please?" He tapped the keyboard, pulling it up for review.

Five seconds later, espresso splashed across the floor, the cup bouncing as he raced down the hallway.

Chapter 3

Dublin, Ireland

There are 666 licensed pubs in Dublin. A betting man could do worse than to wager that most were rather dim, cramped, and populated at all hours of the day and night. This was one of those pubs, an anonymous place where men who didn't want to be bothered with other people came for as many drinks as needed to forget their troubles. The barkeep didn't specialize in small talk. He offered plenty of whiskey, neat if you don't mind, and a long memory for good tippers.

One of the regulars sat at the bar now. Nothing wrong with a few beers while the day was still young.

On the lacquered bar top, a cell phone rumbled. Only one man had this phone number, and when he called, it never went unanswered. No matter how delicious that Guinness looked.

"Roy here."

"There's a job."

Two minutes later sunlight assaulted his eyes as he stepped outside, phone pressed to an ear.

"Where the hell are you?"

"On the way, Roy my boy. Rounding the corner now."

The car arrived, both passenger and driver staring straight ahead as Roy slipped into the rear seat, passing a note to the driver. "Head there. We need to retrieve something. And a girl needs taken care of."

Silence abounded while they drove through Dublin. Metal clicked on metal as each man inspected magazines and actions, and ten minutes later the three-man team pulled to a stop near the apartment of Michelle Berks, art historian with the National Gallery of Ireland. Roy didn't know her,

12

didn't care to. He cared about one thing. Doing what the man who'd called needed to have done.

And today that man needed something Michelle Berks had. And then he wanted her to die.

Affiliated with the British government in some way, a way Roy didn't care to know about, the man paid in cash and on time. He kept Roy and his two mates on retainer, paying them to be ready for service at a moment's notice. Whatever they needed, the voice on the phone provided. Guns, drugs, a quiet place to bury bodies. He asked for two things in return. Follow orders and never ask questions.

"The girl lives alone," Roy said. "Should be home from the office by now, and she should have a letter with her, very old. We get in and out before anyone else shows up, so don't muck about."

Both men grunted. It wasn't the first time they'd handled a situation for the caller, not by a long shot. One woman? They'd be back at the pub in a flash.

"Looks like she's home," the driver said. As they watched her apartment, curtains parted and a window opened. Roy compared the woman to a picture on his phone.

"That's the girl. Remember, we get this letter and take care of her. Make it look like a robbery." Both men followed his lead, strolling toward her apartment, eyes roving as they walked. "Street looks quiet enough," Roy noted. "Let's do the package routine this time, boys. I'm knocking."

Without a word, the men spread out, one on either side of her door. Roy glanced around and found the street empty. Go time.

Knock knock knock.

Footsteps, and the front door opened. Like most of the people he killed, this girl trusted too easily.

"Package for Michelle Berks." They never looked, never noticed his empty hands, tucked out of sight.

"That's me," the woman said. "What is it? I don't believe I ordered anyth—"

Cold steel punched her in the face. "Inside. Now."

Roy shoved her, his mates shutting the door behind them. She didn't even have time to think, let alone scream.

"Now listen here," Roy said. "I'm only going to ask once. If you scream, you're dead. Understand?"

Michelle nodded, her milky skin flushing.

"Where's the letter?"

The diminutive art expert took small steps back, away from the barrel. He let her go. The farther from the door, the better.

"What letter? I get a dozen every day."

"The letter you just found. The old one."

Shock spread across her face like a sunburst.

"How... how do you know about that?" They were in the kitchen now, and Michelle bumped against a counter, her retreat halted.

"I'm asking the questions. Last chance. Where is it?" Her breath came in ragged gasps. "Focus!" he shouted, spittle flying. "Where's the letter?"

"At my office. I left it there."

"Where?"

Michelle's hand covered her face, fingers quivering. "In the painting. I didn't take it out."

Not good. Now they had to go to her office, where people might ask questions.

"What painting? And who else knows it's there?"

"Where I found it today, in Queen Anne's portrait. And I didn't tell anyone else."

"What about the email?" Roy asked, following orders.

"The what?"

Roy jammed his gun against her leg. "Don't piss with me, girl."

"*Wait.*" She looked out from between shaking fingers. "Wait, I remember. Yes, I told Erika. That's the only person, I swear."

That's all I need to know.

He took a swift step back. "I appreciate your honesty, my dear."

Michelle backpedaled to no avail, trying to burrow through the kitchen island. An apple sat there, diced and ready to eat.

"Why do you want that letter? How did you know about it?"

He ignored her. "You've been a big help, miss. Sorry about this. Nothing personal."

His pistol spat fire, and Michelle crumpled to the ground.

Chapter 4

Dublin, Ireland

Detective Wes Conroy drove after a long graveyard shift. Birds fluttered about, a late morning sun reflecting off shiny windows. Both welcome sights after a long night investigating assaults and robberies.

As a member of the Garda Siochana, Dublin's police force, Wes Conroy knew gunfire when he heard it.

So when a shot rang out from the unassuming flat behind him, he stopped in his tracks.

Gunshots didn't belong in this neighborhood. He should know, considering he lived down the block. He and his wife chose this area because it was close to work and, more importantly, peaceful and dull. At least as dull as any part of Dublin could be. There was little crime, nothing more serious than graffiti artists.

Pigeons took flight, squawking as they rose.

The stainless steel Sig Sauer P226 slid from under his shoulder as he darted toward the flat. With his back pressed to the stone wall, Wes risked a look through the open window.

Three men inside. A woman lay on the kitchen floor, blood pooling around a hole in her chest.

A detective for just over a year, Wes never had to use his firearm, not even in his secondary role on the emergency response team.

Time for that to change. He lived here, and this couldn't happen in his neighborhood.

"Detective Wes Conroy requesting backup at 9 Chancery Lane," he whispered into his phone. "Shots fired, possible fatality."

"Roger that, detective. Backup is en route. ETA, two minutes."

Deep breaths. You know what to do.

15

The thundering heartbeat clouding his mind slowed, and his hearing returned. He looked through the window again.

The thugs walked toward the front door.

Three men, no visible weapons, though he didn't doubt they were close at hand.

In the distance, tires squealed and an engine roared, backup on the way.

The door creaked open. Wes backed off to the corner, the pistol in his hand leveled head high.

One face appeared. Short and narrow, his neck craned forward as he walked, a bird bobbing along.

"Drop your weapon!"

Bird man turned, with a scowl. Steel flashed from a pocket, but the pistol caught, tangled in his shirt.

Wes didn't hesitate.

Two blasts and bird man slumped over. As Wes expected, a new gun slid around the doorframe, firing wildly.

Wes darted around the corner, bullets pinging off the stonework, shards of rock whizzing past his face.

Crouched low, Wes glanced through a side window as he ran. The second intruder stood in the main hallway, his gun pointed at the front door as the third man disappeared into the kitchen.

Wes Conroy had pledged to uphold the law, to protect the citizens of Dublin. Normally, he'd do his best to ensure these men were arrested to face trial.

Not today. Not in his neighborhood.

The guy in the hallway never saw it coming.

Wes took aim through the open side window and fired twice. Two slugs slammed into the second thug's back, sending him down. He wouldn't be getting up again.

The third man was gone, lost in the depths of the house.

Screams ripped the air, coming from inside the house. A man's voice, though his cries quickly faded to nothing.

Wes turned back and darted through the front door, only stopping when he went past the kitchen.

The third gunman lay slumped over in the kitchen, next to the girl, a knife handle protruding from his neck. The girl's hand clasped the handle.

As tires screeched outside and sirens filled the air, her hand slipped to the ground, never to rise again.

Chapter 5

London, England

History weighed heavily on these stone walls, dark with age and centuries of feeble torchlight. Modern electric lights did little to quell the sense that time had stopped in this place. A man paced over the stone floor with purpose, his path worn smooth over the centuries by millions of footsteps before.

A subordinate passed, headed the other direction. "Hello, Chief Rose," he said, offering his superior a nod. The man returned it, though his stride never wavered through the dim halls. Logan Rose had more on his mind than most. Today his world changed forever.

This building, where he reported for work every day, stood as a testament to one nation's greatness, an enduring legacy spanning nearly a thousand years.

Chief Keeper Logan Rose worked in the Tower of London. The same place where hundreds had been imprisoned, tortured, and even murdered. But such sordid activities were in the past, left behind as the world turned into a more caring place.

Or maybe people just got better at hiding things.

Either way, Logan had a problem. It wasn't new. Quite the opposite, as he'd known of it for a decade, ever since he'd been promoted to Chief Keeper following his time in the Keeper ranks. Prior to that he'd spent twenty years in Her Majesty's Armed Forces, retiring as a Lieutenant Commander in the Royal Marines. During his time in the armed forces, Logan learned that the government kept a group of men on their payroll to handle the more *unsavory* aspects of governing. When you were trying to keep over sixty-four million people safe, hands got dirty. The kind of dirt you didn't talk about publicly.

"Sir." A Keeper saluted as Rose passed. He nodded, his thoughts elsewhere. One of their junior officers had paid him a visit earlier today, arriving at the Chief Keeper's front door in jeans, coffee all over his shirt.

"Sir," he'd said, out of breath. "I think you need to see this."

Logan knew the man came from a soundproofed room he'd ordered staffed around the clock. He knew the men hated it, that they thought he was a daft bugger with nothing better to do than make them waste a shift in that dark hole. Which was fine. A veteran of the trenches, during his time in the ranks one of the favorite pastimes was cursing the commanding officer. Times may change, but people stay the same.

"At ease," he said to the man, eyeing the coffee stain. "What is it?"

The salute went down, but this fellow stayed ramrod straight. "The program, sir. There's an exact match."

"Send it over immediately."

The kid turned and ran, crashing through the stone halls. Logan watched him go, his thoughts turning to a conversation ten years past, when the outgoing Chief Keeper handed his command to Rose.

"Rose, there's something I need to tell you," the old codger had said. Lines creased his weathered brow, but his eyes shone with a razor-sharp intellect. "Now that you're Chief Keeper, there is one final duty you must undertake."

"Certainly," Logan had said. "How may I be of service?"

The last thing he'd expected was for the old guy to launch into a story three hundred years in the making, a tale surrounding the truth behind their founding. At first, Rose kept a straight face. The story couldn't be true. Maybe the old guy had lost it. But as the words poured forth, Rose's jaw fell open as he became privy to one of the realm's most fiercely guarded secrets, facts that could never see the light of day.

His mind racing with the memory, Rose turned a corner and slipped into his spartan office, finally alone with his thoughts. First, the over-sized hat came off, freeing a luxurious mane of salt and pepper hair. For his entire adult life he'd been forced to wear his hair like a disease. Now retired, Rose let his thick locks grow until they nearly brushed his shoulders.

A folder sat on his desk. Inside, the message he never thought he'd see.

Steady knocks sounded on his door. "Come in."

The door creaked open, revealing Keeper Oliver Moore. Service mates from day one, Logan trusted this man with his life, the only living person besides Logan Rose who knew the entire truth they were sworn to hide.

"Sir, we have a problem."

Lines creased Rose's brow. "I thought it was contained."

"It is, sir." Oliver's shaved head gleamed in the office lights. "Or I should say it *was*. There may have been complications."

"What kind of complications, Mr. Moore?"

Oliver took a seat. "I think the team is dead."

"What?" Rose said. "All of them?"

"I'm afraid so, sir. There are reports on the Dublin police scanner of shots fired at the residence, and *four* people are dead."

Four. Three too many. Per Rose's instructions only Michelle Berks died today.

Unbeknownst to most members of Parliament, Logan Rose and his men operated outside the law. Most officials never heard of the Keepers of the Realm. And with good reason. Their existence came about slowly, evolving over time, an off-shoot of the famous Yeoman Warders. The Beefeaters, like the Keepers, were stationed in the Tower of London. However, the Keepers weren't men who spent their days dealing with tourists and telling tales. Their duties were simple. Protect the realm at all costs.

"Do you want a second team to the flat?" Oliver asked.

"Yes," Rose said. "That letter could be anywhere, and I need eyes on the scene immediately. If our team is dead, the best lead is the woman Dr. Berks emailed regarding her find, the message that alerted us to the discovery." Logan consulted one of the oversized monitors on his desk and set a printer to chattering. "Find out everything you can about this girl. I'll expect a report within the hour. Once we know who we're dealing with, I'll advise the second recovery team on how to proceed."

Oliver Moore snapped off a crisp salute and disappeared through the office door, leaving Rose alone with the message.

Anne of Great Britain. King George. No living heirs.

Such disparate words found together cannot be coincidence.

He studied the computer monitor, reading a message intercepted earlier, the message which sent his men to kill Michelle Berks. As he read Michelle's last communication with the world, a twinge of sorrow flashed through his heart, sorrow for Dr. Erika Carr. Thanks to Michelle's email, the Keepers of the Realm were interested in Dr. Carr.

And that often proved fatal.

Chapter 6

Dublin Airport
Fingal, Ireland

A bubbling stew of languages filled the air as passengers disembarked, blending with the waves of travelers filling Dublin Airport. Images of lush green countryside replete with stone castles tempted visitors, the rich history and fabulous natural beauty of Ireland on display for all to enjoy. Down one hall, a young couple hurried toward the taxi queue, the first step on a dream vacation.

At the luggage carousel, Parker Chase hefted a bulky bag from the track. His girlfriend must have brought every single pair of shoes she owned.

"Hurry up. Look how long the line is." The aforementioned girlfriend gave orders, marching ahead as he lugged their bag.

"Don't get me started," Parker said. "If you didn't bring so much crap, we'd be out of here already."

Erika Carr ruffled her hair, stretching away the last remnants of a seven-hour flight.

"Stop whining." She never turned around. Parker hurried to catch up, grumbling all the while.

In truth, he was thrilled to spend the week in Ireland, an itinerary of his own creation already lined up. Though Erika certainly didn't argue.

An assistant professor at the University of Pennsylvania, Erika Carr had brains, and the inside track to tenure. As an undergrad, she studied with Parker's uncle, a world-renowned historian more than capable of unleashing her potential. Now a respected scholar in her own right, Erika had continued to shine even after her mentor's untimely death not long ago.

As they passed under the glass airport entrance and walked outside,

Parker got his first breath of the famed Irish air.

Exhaust and acrid smoke filled his lungs. So much for the Irish Spring commercials.

"What's wrong, pretty boy?" Erika tapped his wrinkled nose. "This lovely air too rough for your tender lungs?"

Parker sniffed again. "It stinks."

Parker spent a good amount of time in Philadelphia, where the pollution from millions of people living close together didn't do much for the air quality. The only grassy fields most Philadelphians saw were in magazines.

"Did you talk to Michelle and see if she's at home?" Parker asked. "I don't want to lug all this stuff to her office."

"I'll call her in a second. Aren't you excited?"

Erika squealed, her long arms encircling his chest. Their first trip abroad together, she'd talked of nothing else for weeks. As an added bonus, one of her former classmates lived in Dublin.

"Where to, lovely lady?"

A stooped cab driver tipped his flat cap to Erika, the accent so thick you could bottle it.

Erika gave the driver Michelle's home address, and they rattled away, diesel engine coughing out smoke.

"Isn't he the sweetest old man?" she whispered, her head nestled on his shoulder.

The cabbie hummed as he drove, veering in and out of traffic to the beat.

"He's a peach," Parker said. "What did Michelle say? I'm starving, by the way. Airplane food stinks."

"When aren't you hungry?" Erika pulled out her phone. "Don't worry. I'm sure we can find a place to eat."

Parker rolled the window down, air washing over his face as they cruised toward Dublin. A bright sun warmed the breeze, brilliant against a cloudless sky. He looked over and saw a curving river follow the road, a raft of ducks landing as he watched, their feathery bodies cutting through the sparkling water.

"That's odd," Erika said. "She didn't answer. I'm sure she's at home."

"I don't mind waiting if she's not. Just don't tell if I raid the fridge. I'm up for anything as long as I don't have to sit on my rear end for another seven hours."

Parker rubbed his posterior for emphasis, a stiff back and aching knee humming for attention, both ailments as much from his collegiate football career as the flight.

Erika laid a hand on his as she took in this new land. His mind flashed back ten years, to the first time he'd seen her. When he first glimpsed this girl in the sports complex, he'd soaked in her beauty and never stopped looking. Both on athletic scholarship, their paths crossed several more times before he worked up the nerve to ask the leggy blonde volleyball player on a date.

"Tell me how excited you are for some authentic fish and chips with a pint of Guinness?"

Erika grinned. "I'll start with the beer. Michelle told me about a pub close to her apartment. It's been in operation since before America was a country. And," her eyes lit up. "They have a band."

"I hope they open early."

As their cabbie wove between traffic with practiced ease, Parker slid a hand into his pocket, just to make sure.

It was the hundredth time he'd checked since they left Philadelphia.

Unbelievable that something so tiny could bring such large changes.

So far Erika seemed oblivious to his plan. Beside him, she held the phone to her ear again. "Michelle isn't answering. I hope she's not still at work."

Out of the countryside and into the urban jungle, Dublin now surrounded them, ancient whitewashed stone buildings standing their ground against more recent structures, the dichotomy a symbol of the city's storied history. Pedestrians filled the sidewalks, the slow paced Irish life nowhere to be found.

Erika's phone beeped. "Michelle just sent me an email. I wonder what—"

"Here we are." The cabbie pulled to the curb, quaint row homes lining either side of the street.

Parker stepped onto the cobbled street, dodging a row of double-parked police vehicles as their luggage rattled.

"I think her place is over there," Erika said. "Near the yellow tape."

Police tape cordoned off part of the sidewalk. A half-dozen police officers stood inside the yellow barrier, dark blue caps bobbing as they spoke.

"I thought European police didn't carry weapons," Erika whispered in his ear.

"You're right," Parker said. "Only emergency response teams carry weapons in Ireland. And these guys are packing serious firepower."

Nearly the entire block had been roped off, with an officer standing every few feet. The compact automatic weapons they held were in stark contrast to the nightsticks that dangled from the belts of the traditionally uniformed beat cops.

"Those are Heckler & Koch submachine guns, MP7s. Serious weapons." His nerves woke up. "Something's not right here."

Her hands came together, twisting and turning.

"But I'm sure everything is fine now," he said. "They wouldn't let us get this close if it were dangerous."

Erika nodded, though he saw concern in her eyes. "Come on, let's find Michelle." Erika followed the numbered doors until she ran into the yellow tape. Michelle's flat was in the off-limits zone.

"Excuse me, sir?"

An officer glanced her way, elbowing the man beside him.

"Miss?"

"We've just arrived from America to visit a friend, and I think her house is on this street."

"What's her name, miss?"

"Michelle Berks." When Erika rattled off her address, the police stood a little straighter.

"Give us just a moment, if you would," one officer said before they both disappeared.

Parker looked around, a hollow pit in his gut. Erika hadn't noticed the cops all stood around one flat.

Michelle's.

He sidled up to Erika, roller bag grinding.

"I need you to stay calm."

Her azure eyes narrowed. "Did the police tell you something?"

"No. I don't want to alarm you, but I think that's Michelle's place they're standing in front of."

Behind her, the dour policeman reappeared. "Miss, how do you know Dr. Berks?"

"Yes, we went to school together. I'm supposed to meet her at her apartment."

The young officer glanced at his partner. "I'll need you to come with me."

23

"Is something wrong?"

The officer didn't reply, one hand holding the yellow tape high so they could pass under. Asking questions that went unanswered, Erika ducked below the fluttering barricade, Parker right behind her as the officer led them to the open front door. A grizzled man with captain's stripes on his shoulder emerged from within.

"I'm John Peterson. Did you know Dr. Berks?"

Erika didn't catch the phrasing. "Yes, we're friends. We just arrived from America to visit her."

Parker laid a hand on her shoulder, ready for what came next.

Captain Peterson removed his hat. "I'm afraid I have bad news."

Chapter 7

Dublin, Ireland

As they worked the crime scene, detectives and officers gave Erika a wide berth, well-versed in the process of death and grieving. Captain Peterson knelt beside them as Parker held her, sitting on the sidewalk. Parker and Erika told the police what little they knew about Michelle's routine, her habits, and anything else they thought of.

"Can you think of any close friends? A colleague or neighbor, perhaps?"

Erika sniffled into a tissue. "I'm sorry, but no. She never mentioned anything in particular about coworkers."

"What happened to her?" Parker asked.

As the captain laid out a sanitized version of the murder, Parker started digging, looking for an answer that likely didn't exist.

"Captain, do you have any idea who did this?"

His head shook. "I'm afraid not. No identification on the bodies."

"What made them pick Michelle's house?" Parker asked. "What's here that's worth killing for?"

"I don't know, but my team will get to the bottom of this. Thank you for your time," Peterson said, holding the yellow tape up for Parker and Erika. "If either of you think of anything else, here's my card."

The cop answered his ringing phone. And that jarred a memory loose.

Cell phone.

"Erika, didn't Michelle send you an email?"

"You're right. I completely forgot." Erika fumbled through her purse. "Just before we got out of the cab. I should tell Captain Peterson."

"Read it first." The detective hadn't been open with them. Let him wait.

"Found it," Erika said. "It's only an hour old. She must have sent it just before…"

A minute passed, and Erika said nothing. *How long was this email?*

"What did she say?" Only when he stopped studying the surrounding buildings did Parker noticed her staring lasers through the phone. "What's going on?"

Erika pulled him down the street, farther away from the bustling police activity.

"I think I know why Michelle died."

Outside the National Gallery of Ireland, acrid exhaust fumes wafted by as Parker wondered who the hell he'd pissed off to deserve this mess.

"Let me get this straight," Parker said. "Michelle repaired a painting of Queen Anne and found a letter the woman wrote three hundred years ago?"

"Correct. But that's not the important part."

Of course not. As if this happened every day.

"What matters," Erika continued, "is what the letter *said*. Do you realize the implications if this is true?"

Her phone changed hands, and Parker studied Michelle's final email.

Erika,

This sounds crazy, but hear me out. I'm restoring a painting of Anne, Queen of Great Britain, and today, I found a letter inside the frame. Why does that matter? I'll tell you. Anne's reign ended at the beginning of the eighteenth century, and when she died, she left no living heirs, making Anne the last monarch of House Stuart, a Catholic line.

According to the 1701 Act of Settlement, Anne's closest living Protestant relative inherited the throne. George Hanover was that man, even though Anne had Catholic blood relatives who were closer to her. Fast forward to today, and there is a direct familial line from George I to Elizabeth II. Why does this matter?

It's possible that Elizabeth II is not the rightful monarch of Great Britain. And this comes directly from the Queen's letter I found hours ago. Hand-written by Anne, as best I can tell.

Think about that. I'll meet you at my place, and we'll inspect this together.
-MB

"It sounds enticing," Parker said. "But how are we supposed to find the letter now? It's probably in her purse, and the police aren't going to give that to us."

Erika played with her hair, twisting and turning strands as she spoke. "Michelle wouldn't bring a letter like this to her house. There's no way of knowing what kind of condition it's in. Paper that's kept away from light and moisture for several centuries can deteriorate rapidly when exposed to the elements."

"So you think it's still at her office?"

Erika nodded. "That's where I'd keep it. Wait for a qualified person to assess the situation."

"And I assume you're qualified to do this?"

"I am trained to handle fragile artifacts," Erika said. "It's the smart thing to do, and Michelle was nothing if not smart. No way would she make a rookie mistake and risk destroying the letter."

Four pillars festooned with square decorative blocks framed an archway, all of it lording over two massive oak doors. A trickle of tourists moved in and out of the National Gallery, all types of people taking advantage of the free admission.

"I hope you can bullshit your way into her office."

Confidence bubbled on Erika's face as she grabbed his wrist. "I can charm my way past a few guards. Just keep quiet. We're supposed to be academics, after all."

She left him to lug their single bag, tiny wheels grinding over the paved roadway. Through the doors and past a pair of guards, Parker craned his neck at the soaring ceiling. Light fell on the bright stone walls, one bearing a map.

"This way."

Erika led him down a wide passageway, past a collection of Jack Yeats sketchbooks. Around the corner, they found a smoked glass door with *Restoration* stenciled on it.

"Here it is." Erika tapped a name plate marked *M. Berks, Ph.D.* "If anyone stops us, let me do the talking."

The office resembled a warehouse, the ceiling stretching at least twenty feet overhead. Desks and workbenches dotted the interior, and a number of academics hunched over computers or peered through microscopes.

"That must be it," Parker said, pointing across the room. "It's the only portrait in here."

"You're correct. And this is Michelle's work area."

Parker's arm fell over her shoulders as Erika stood at the desk, one finger touching an empty chair.

"The news hasn't reached them yet." Parker glanced at the employees. "No way we're allowed in here if it did."

"You're right," she said, taking in the barn-like room, high ceilings and workstations sporadically staffed with restoration specialists. "You take her desk, and I'll take the painting."

Erika walked to the painting as Parker studied Michelle's desk. A few museum employees looked their way, more curious than anything. Dr. Berks was an organized woman. A single notepad, detailing the damage to Anne's portrait. Parker opened her drawers and found pencils and stacks of paper, but no letter.

Across the room, a rail-thin man stared their way. His beard looked like someone had glued handfuls of black cotton to his face at random intervals.

First rule of trespassing, act like you belong. Parker waved and smiled. Suddenly the guy didn't look so concerned, offering a half-hearted wave and losing interest.

"Find anything?" Parker opened another drawer and found a stack of glossy photos. All of old paintings, none of hidden letters. "Erika, did you hear me?"

Erika still didn't respond. What was she doing?

Parker eyed a few of the other academics, none of whom were paying them any attention. Fortunate, but their luck wouldn't hold forever.

"Got it," she said.

He turned to find an envelope pinched between her thumb and forefinger.

"Move." Erika shoved him aside and laid her prize on Michelle's desk. A magnification lamp came to life, Erika peering through the oversized lens.

With Parker looking over her shoulder, a fantastic story came to life.

Chapter 8

A pair of reports landed on Logan Rose's desk within the hour, delivered by Oliver Moore.

"Give me the short version," Logan said. Settling into the seat across from Logan, Moore summarized the contents, revealing Erika Carr to be more than a pretty face.

"Ph.D. in American history from the University of Pennsylvania," Moore said. "Summa cum laude, Fulbright scholar. Attended undergraduate school on an athletic scholarship and is currently in line for tenure at her alma mater."

"An impressive woman."

A hint of a smirk crossed Moore's lips. "She is a looker, sir."

"If only that were the limit of her attributes. What do you think, Oliver? Is this one history buff chatting with another, or is there still a problem on our hands?"

"I don't believe in coincidences," Moore replied. "Although there's no indication Dr. Carr is different from any other professor. She and Dr. Berks roomed together in graduate school. Carr purchased tickets to Dublin months ago, and all emails and texts between the pair prior to today are benign."

"*Tickets*, Mr. Moore. Plural. What do you have on her traveling companion?"

Oliver cleared his throat. "Parker Chase. Early thirties, lives in Pennsylvania. Founded a wealth management and investment firm this year with offices in Philadelphia and Pittsburgh."

Logan raised an eyebrow. "Founded? So Mr. Chase is a man of means?"

"Affirmative. Prior to developing an entrepreneurial spirit, Chase worked at a larger investment firm for several years. We cannot determine the source of his capital, as the business is privately held."

"Any indications Mr. Chase is more than an ordinary citizen?"

"None, sir. He played American football while attending undergraduate college with Dr. Carr. No living relatives, and no criminal history."

A dull ache settled behind Rose's eyes. "I hope that's all there is to be found, Mr. Moore." Logan's file flipped shut. "What's the status of our replacement team?"

"Due to arrive in Dublin within the hour, sir."

"Too late to catch Dr. Carr while she's still at the scene. Any idea where she and Mr. Chase are staying?"

"Prior emails indicate Dr. Berks' apartment, sir."

Damn. With no eyes on the ground, electronic surveillance had to suffice.

"Chase and Carr are now on the national watch list, with any hits routed directly to me," Rose said. The database tracked all electronic payments in the U.K., credit cards, bank cards and the like. "When we get one, we follow them. I doubt anything drastic is necessary, but I'd prefer to know where they are until we acquire that letter."

"I directed the Belfast team to head straight to the dead woman's office. They'll contact us once they arrive."

Dismissed, Oliver Moore saluted and marched out the door. Right now it was imperative that they secure the letter. Should the contents ever become public, political chaos would ensue.

The type of chaos not seen in England for over three hundred years.

Chapter 9

Dublin, Ireland

Amid the restoration wing's controlled bustling, Parker leaned over Erika's shoulder, the world forgotten as an ancient tale of treachery and deceit unfolded.

10 March, 1702

Dearest Laurence,

My beloved uncle, I write to you in this, my direst hour. I pray you will receive this plea and act to save my kingdom, for you have been falsely told of the death of my son. Prince William is not dead. However, this lie serves to hide a terrible truth. One suppressed by Protestant factions within the realm, those traitors who are responsible for the Act of Settlement that will end the line of Stuart's time on the throne. My cousin, George of Hanover, has begun a bloodless coup, intent on usurping the throne from beneath a sitting Queen.

I believe William is not dead. He is kidnapped, stolen away to be used for bargaining. The kidnappers wish to see Ireland freed from the Crown's rule, and plot to trade William's life for Irish independence.

I have only just received these outrageous demands, and now prepare to find my son. Should I fail, the rain-soaked green isle will be freed. Any demands will be met so long as my son is alive and returned. Before that fate befalls me though, I will chase these unworthy devils and attempt to retrieve William on my own.

Dear uncle, I need your aid. As I prepare to depart for Ireland and chase William's captors, I've learned that my traitorous German cousin found members of my own court willing to shadow my every move.

I speak of the Beefeaters, the Yeoman Warders charged with guarding my tower. They are joining this journey, acting as guards. However, I know their true intent. These men, proclaiming to act as my protectors, will prevent any action on my part to recover William so that George may steal the throne.

This letter is my safeguard should I fail. If you're reading this, my faith in your ability to spot the clues left in the painting is founded. If my son is not found by years end, or if any ill befalls me, I beg you to continue my quest. To aid you, I offer this.

There are steps in the rock close at Blarney Castle that I know to be most peaceful, for upon resting there I cleared my mind. With luck, the same inspiration will strike for you.

Anne

"Michelle didn't exaggerate," Erika said. "This is huge."

A good story, sure. Almost too good, Parker thought. "Listen, if this letter is real, it's pretty amazing. But all of this happened three hundred years ago. Does anyone care anymore?"

He may as well have dumped ice water down her back.

"A kidnapped prince and potentially illegitimate monarchy is a big deal, Parker. The entire world will care."

She had a point. "Look, we can talk about this later. It may be a coincidence, but Michelle died within an hour of finding this letter. Let's not hang around here any longer than necessary."

"Are you suggesting I steal this letter?"

"I'm sure Michelle wouldn't mind."

"Parker, this is a fragile artifact. I've already risked damaging it."

"Fine. If you want to know what killed her, we need the letter. If you don't, then put it back."

After a moment's hesitation, she snapped a photo of the text and slid the letter into an envelope for safekeeping. Safely tucking it in her purse, Erika followed him out of the hangar-like office into an emptying hallway, as closing time drew near.

Even with the tragedy of Michelle's death, Parker was glad to be getting on with the vacation. He reached into his pocket yet again, and once more, the ring failed to disappear.

"The police told me Michelle's family won't arrive for a few days. Do you want to stay in town?"

Sandstone walls sparkled in the sunlight, the spacious museum growing quieter by the minute. "The funeral won't happen for at least a week. Until then, we should enjoy ourselves. It's still the trip of a lifetime."

Parker squeezed her hand. He felt the same. Having recently realized a substantial return on his professional and personal investments, two first-class tickets to Dublin had been one of his first purchases.

"Agreed," he said. "So what's first?"

"I say we start in Cork, visit Blarney, and then make our way back north."

"And this has nothing to do with that letter?"

Erika swatted his arm. "Of course not."

"Right," he said. "We'll poke around, and once you see there's nothing to it, we get on with our vacation. Remember, we're supposed to be relaxing."

Ahead, a smartly dressed greeter wished them a good day, tipping his cap to Erika. Outside, two men in dark suits pushed past the crowd, one meaty shoulder jostling Parker.

Parker turned and froze, a sarcastic comment dying in his throat. Outside the front door stood a third identically-dressed man, a phone pressed to his ear.

"We're at the gallery now, headed to her office. We'll see if it's still there."

He grabbed Erika, pulling her deeper into the crowd.

"Put your head down and keep walking," Parker said.

"What's going on?"

"That man we just passed said something about going into an office to see if it's still there. And he's British, not Irish."

"If what's still there? What are you talking about?"

"Trust me on this," he said. "We need to get out of here."

A line of taxis waited ahead, and they hopped inside one of the black vehicles. Parker turned around and saw the third man still outside the door, phone pressed to his ear.

"That guy right there, with the shades. He's the one I'm talking about."

"Do you think he's looking for us?"

"I doubt it," Parker said. "No one knows we're in Dublin except for the police." None of this made sense. "But why else would anyone want to search Michelle's office? And more importantly, if what you suspect is true, why kill her for a letter?"

Only when the thick Irish brogue rolled over his ears did Parker remember the driver.

"You two going anywhere?" the cab driver asked. Staring ahead, he never turned around.

"Know anywhere we can rent a car?"

"That I do."

The driver motored away, never once looking back. Years behind the wheel must have imparted a sense of when to keep his mouth shut, and the guy stayed silent as a statue the entire ride.

The small lot at which he deposited them sat filled to bursting with rentals. Parker inspected the nearest vehicle, the door handle barely reaching his knees. "Look at these clown cars," he said.

Fiats and Minis, hardly a single roof climbed far beyond his waist. His knees ached just thinking about the hours of cramped driving.

Erika walked toward the rental office. "Stop complaining. Think of all the money we'll save on gas."

"I'm not buying any insurance," Parker said. "Won't be around to collect it if we wreck anyway."

Ten minutes later he walked out holding the keys to a brand new Land Rover. He'd upgraded to the larger model, gas mileage be damned.

Erika consulted a brochure for Blarney Castle that the salesman had provided.

"This isn't so bad," Parker said. "Other than the steering wheel being on the wrong side."

"Three hours to Cork," Erika said. "Let's move."

Chapter 10

Dublin, Ireland

The National Gallery of Ireland framed him, a man talking quietly into his phone as leaves rustled on the breeze.

"The photos are on the way now. Check back when you have an update."

His crew of three had arrived minutes ago from their base in Belfast. To what purpose, he knew not. A former warrant officer, Billy Wall served Her Majesty for eight years in Kosovo and Afghanistan. After leaving the service, he drifted around, growing disenchanted with civilian life until a retired commanding officer contacted him with a most unusual offer.

In exchange for his willingness to follow orders from an unknown source without question, he earned a hefty salary and a rent-free flat in Belfast. A no-brainer for a man in his shoes.

Initially instructed to sit tight outside the museum, that all changed when Billy read the message, the nature of this exercise revealed.

Their photos were sent, his targets. Both were American.

A woman named Erika Carr, accompanied by a male, Parker Chase. If located, he needed to follow them, nothing more. The message didn't say why, and Billy didn't ask questions.

His two companions burst through the museum door, one barking into his mobile.

"How long ago? Damn. All right, we're on it."

The man hurried past, never breaking stride. "Chase used his credit card twenty minutes ago at a car rental."

Billy nodded and followed him to their vehicle. Minutes later, a small rental lot came into view, a pimple-faced salesman standing out front by a double wide trailer. The guy couldn't have been more than twenty.

"How's it going? If you gents need a car, you've come to the right place."

A glance from the boss told Billy to keep watch while he handled this. "It's about a bill," Billy's mate said. "Can you help me?"

"Come on in," the kid said. A minute later he followed Billy's boss back out, looking dazed and disoriented. Billy's friend had that effect on people.

"We missed them by forty-five minutes. They're in a blue Land Rover, and they asked for information about Blarney Castle."

"Three hours to Cork," Billy said. "Less if we move fast."

Rubber smoked as Billy motored away, leaving behind a car lot manager who'd recently gained an appreciation for the small things in life.

Unbroken kneecaps, for one.

Surrounded by speeding traffic on the M7 highway, Billy didn't notice the black Audi sedan trailing behind them. The Audi tailed its quarry, never losing sight of Billy as he drove toward Blarney Castle.

Chapter 11

Dublin, Ireland

Hot coffee steamed on the dining room table, a man watching intently as his flat mate stumbled into the room, squinting in the sunlight.

This must be serious. Sipping his coffee, Gavin Rooney wondered what it could be. Anything that got a booze-soaked scoundrel like Harry Moran moving this early had to be.

"Good morning to you," Gavin said, blowing on his coffee. "How's your noggin?"

"A tad rough, you pious bastard. Stop pissing about and get ready to leave. You left your iPad in my room, and it woke me up. The QM sent a message."

He swiped the coffee from Gavin's grip. "Get Brin," Harry mumbled, gulping the pilfered black gold.

"It's about time." He found Brin Stewart, in his room, their third team member cleaning one of his guns.

"I heard that booze-soaked moron Harry up and about just now. Figured we got a message."

"We're leaving soon," Gavin said. "Get that thing back together."

Metal clicked as Brin put the Smith & Wesson back in working order.

"Something's going on," Harry said once they'd gathered around the kitchen table. "The Quartermaster is in a state." The Quartermaster, their direct leader, was not a man prone to overreaction. "A little birdie told him those Keeper bastards sent men into Dublin, and guess what happened? The pricks got themselves killed."

"Did we do it?" Brin asked.

"No, we weren't the triggermen. The Keeper men broke into a flat and the local authorities showed up, had themselves a shootout. An American lived there, and she's dead too."

"Too bad about the girl," Gavin said. "At least we didn't kill the Keeper men, though." Despite all the progress over this past decade, a single misstep could hurtle them back to those bloody, troubled times.

And this dead crew of Keepers presented a problem. "How solid is this intel?" Gavin asked. "Is the Quartermaster certain the Keepers sent this crew?"

Harry nodded. "He is."

"And there's no indication our group had anything to do with this?" Brin asked.

"Positive," Gavin said. "The QM's certain."

Not all Irish Republican Army members moved about as freely as Gavin. The English authorities knew certain members of the IRA, including their Quartermaster General, which is why he operated out of Northern Ireland, well away from London's prying eyes.

Their faces unknown, Gavin's Dublin-based field team utilized this anonymity to move about the city at will.

However, working in two different nations caused problems.

One being that in the northern part of their island, the Quartermaster constantly struggled with his more violently disposed brethren. This predisposition to extreme force splintered the group, nearly leading to an insurrection. After decades of bloody struggle and incessant fighting, a younger IRA faction argued for a more diplomatic approach, tired of constant bloodshed during The Troubles. Gavin's father had been a former IRA field leader, and his death at English hands convinced Gavin outright aggression caused more harm than good.

Like all their members, Gavin wanted an independent Northern Ireland, free from the United Kingdom, and to see the territory reunited with Ireland in a single nation.

He knew first-hand that horrific loss accompanied any war. Having seen tragedies their struggle caused, Gavin knew peaceful resistance, not violence, would best accomplish their goals. Discourse triumphed over bullets in today's world. A country filled with graveyards testified to the IRA's past failures. Now they must move on.

All sentiments with which the Quartermaster General agreed.

"May I see the message?" Harry handed him the iPad, the QM's message on-screen.

He recognized the gist of it. An assignment, orders to be followed through to completion. In truth, he searched for something else, a unique phrase known only to the two of them the QM used to indicate the Northern extremists in their group had forced his hand.

Ten minutes later, the trio of freedom fighters hustled outside, a brilliant Irish morning greeting their arrival. Trees in bloom lined the street, a green canopy providing cool shade for another hot day in Dublin.

A gym bag landed in the boot with a metallic *thunk*, enough weaponry to see them jailed for decades if the authorities found it. In consideration, Gavin kept under the speed limit as their black Audi motored through the streets toward the apartment of one Michelle Berks, recently deceased art historian and restoration expert. The ride passed in silence, and minutes later Gavin took in an active crime scene.

"I don't see anything," he said, "and we can't hang around here."

"No Keepers that I can see," Brin said. "Harry?"

"Bastards aren't here," Harry said. "We should try the art gallery, see what we can find there. Maybe the dead girl had some friends who'll talk to us."

Apparently the whiskey hadn't drowned all his brain cells.

"Agreed," Gavin said.

"Why kill this girl?" Harry asked. "The QM mentioned a painting, but didn't say which one, and this place must be flush with art."

"Could be the English will lead us to it," Brin said. Scarcely a minute passed before he pointed through the windshield. "And would you look at that. I do think we found our man."

A pale man stood outside the towering doors, his suit stretched to the breaking point.

"Damn fool might as well wear a sign on his neck. And here's his crew," Harry continued. "They're triplets."

Two more men in dark suits joined their friend. When their forest green Mercedes peeled out of a handicapped spot, Gavin merged well behind them, out of view.

"Didn't see any painting with them," Harry said. "What the hell are they interested in some blasted art for?"

Silence met his question. For now, Harry and Brin remained in the dark on certain aspects of IRA operations. To them, chasing Keeper thugs over a painting seemed strange indeed.

For Gavin, though, this mission meant so much more. Elevated to field commander after his father's death, the bittersweet moment brought truth to temper his pain. For once promoted, the IRA's most dearly held secrets were revealed, shared in a private conversation with the Quartermaster General himself. The foundation of the Army, for one. Most members believed it originated with the struggles at the start of the 20th century, but in truth, the origins lay much earlier in the history books, a fact known only by the QM and a few of his most trusted allies.

Bound on a length of wizened leather around his neck, a pendant was all that remained of Gavin's deceased father, a family heirloom passed on far too soon. He wore it at all times, a reminder of the best man he'd ever known.

This mission and the events that preceded it stretched back over three centuries, to the beginnings of a movement that became the IRA and impacted the course of British history.

Chapter 12

Driving south, Erika battled spotty cell phone service while researching Anne's letter, unable to render a verdict for hours.

Finally, she set the phone down and started talking. "Here's what I verified. Laurence Hyde was Queen Anne's uncle, which jives with the letter. Queen Anne's mother was Anne Hyde, Duchess of York and wife of King James II of England. Laurence and Duchess Anne Hyde were brother and sister, and more importantly, Laurence was the Lord Lieutenant of Ireland."

"Why can't English people just have one name like the rest of us?" Parker asked, only half-joking.

"Because that wouldn't do for royalty. Ancestry is important to them. However, what matters to us is her uncle didn't live in England. Instead, he resided in Ireland as the British monarch's official representative."

If they believed Anne's letter, it made sense. "Which meant he wasn't in Britain, and as such, wouldn't know about the Beefeaters shadowing Anne's every move and essentially imprisoning her in her own castle."

"Exactly," Erika confirmed. "If Anne sent word of her plight to Laurence, he'd be in a position to carry on the search for her kidnapped son, Prince William. Laurence had access to considerable resources, and if the prince survived and was in Ireland, Laurence was her best bet to find him. Not to mention the only person she trusted."

Parker maneuvered around a slow-moving tractor-trailer, unnerved by this driving on the wrong side of the road stuff.

"Considering her cousin staged a coup, you're probably right. Which leads to the next question. Why didn't Laurence ever receive this letter?"

"One mystery at a time," Erika said. "We're almost there."

A sign indicated their destination lay just ahead, and a few short minutes later, a majestic structure appeared.

Built in 1446 on the ruins of a stone fortress, Blarney Castle stood through countless wars, its gray stone walls never faltering over the centuries. The main castle keep and tower burst from the rolling hills, an elegant, dark window to the past.

Crunching down a stone pathway, Parker passed dozens of vehicles and tour buses. Groups of people milled throughout the grounds, guides regaling their charges with tales of Castle Blarney's colorful past. Overhead, the late afternoon sun cast vibrant light, liquid gold beams riding a soft summer breeze.

Parker lucked out when a spot opened as he rolled past, his tires barely stopped before Erika hopped out.

"Excuse me," Parker said, following her toward the entrance. "We're supposed to be on vacation. No need to rush around here. Let's enjoy ourselves."

The gleam in her eyes shattered any notion of serenity. "First we solve this riddle. Then we have fun."

Parker paid for two passes and pushed through the turnstile. Ahead of him, stone walkways branched off in all directions.

"Look at this." Erika held a map out. "The stone close. We should head there."

The area sat west of the castle, outside the sturdy walls.

"Why do you want to go there? The letter pointed us to this castle."

"Wrong. Read it again. Actually, just listen to me."

Erika closed her eyes.

"There are steps in the rock close at Blarney Castle that I know to be most peaceful, for upon resting here I cleared my mind. With luck, the same inspiration will strike for you."

Her eyes snapped open.

"Rock close, verbatim. According to this map, inside the close we'll find something called the *Wishing Steps*. Sounds like a good starting place to me."

A tour group passed, their guide's heavy brogue leading the way.

"First of all, what is a rock close? A cave?"

"I have no idea," Erika said. "Maybe this gentleman knows."

Parker turned to find one of the most impressive beards he'd ever seen.

Fire red, bushy and thick, and all the more grand given the bald and freckled head it framed.

"Afternoon to ye," he said. "Welcome to Blarney Castle." Clad in a massive tan windbreaker bearing the Castle logo, he offered a meaty hand.

"Thank you," Erika said, her hand lost in his. "I have a question." When Erika batted her eyelashes like that, watch out.

"The name is Seamus, and I'll do my best, young lady."

"I'm Erika. We're interested in the Wishing Steps, but don't know much about them. Would you enlighten us?"

"A fine question indeed. The Steps, one of the better secrets within our humble cottage, are a sight not to be missed. Shall we walk?"

Damn, this guy was good. Parker fell into step with the round man, following a path through the castle grounds, past towering walls and over rolling hills surrounding the castle.

"Our rock close is a gift. It is a magical place, and not only in your mind's eye."

Over a rustic bridge, beneath which a crystal clear stream twirled. Shadows danced on the ground, thick trees twisted with age throwing cool shade all around.

"Once there was an altar in this rocky respite, a pagan house of worship meant for Druidic sacrificial offerings. Some say that at night you can still hear chanting echo through the woods."

Dirt hardened by time and millions of footsteps led them to a boulder surrounded by foliage. When their guide halted, Parker craned his neck back, taking in the moss-encrusted rock blocking their path.

"Oh my goodness," Erika said. "I didn't see it until just now."

Parker opened his mouth, but then it happened. His eyes adjusted, and as a shadow in the fog becomes a speeding car, an entrance appeared. Cut through the rock, a narrow staircase descending *into* the ground.

"The wishing steps," Seamus said. "Follow me, and use the handrail."

Damp walls swallowed their group as the Irishman plunged into darkness.

At the bottom he stepped out of the shadows and into the light, a stream trickling alongside the path, hard by a wooded copse, eventually disappearing under a bridge ahead.

Erika turned to their guide. "Have you ever heard of Queen Anne visiting the castle? I read that she journeyed here during her reign, but I haven't been able to verify it."

43

"I can do one better than that," Seamus said. "Turn around."

Parker twisted, his back to the steps. Ahead, leaves hung low over the empty, unremarkable path.

When they stood rooted to the ground, Seamus said, "Off the path, note the bench. The perfect resting spot on a hot summer day."

"Is it connected to Queen Anne?"

"More than that, Miss Erika. The Queen herself brought that bench when she visited Castle Blarney. So taken by our natural beauty, she believed all should stop and enjoy the sight."

"I understand why she'd fall in love with this place."

"'Tis a place of wonder, miss."

"You know," Erika looked at Seamus as she took Parker's hand, "I think we'll take her advice and rest here for a while. Thank you for the tour, it's been wonderful."

"A fine idea, my friends. Enjoy the day."

Once Seamus vanished into the trees, Parker turned to find Erika kneeling by the bench, running her fingers over the stone slab.

"I think this is granite," he said, joining her. "And it's definitely made of several sections joined together."

White and gray streaks accented the stone, crystal specks reflecting the sunlight.

"Do you notice anything?" Erika's nose nearly rubbed the stone.

"No." He poked and prodded, twisted and turned. "It's a bench."

"The letter led us here," Erika said. "Do you think it's a coincidence she commissioned this bench?"

"No, but there's no writing or inscription of any kind. What's a bench supposed to tell us?"

Erika scampered behind the bench. "Maybe another message? Anne made this. Maybe it's not only for sitting on. Maybe it's a container as well."

"You think she hid something in here?" He smacked the stone. "Looks solid to me."

"Look for any marks or masonry work that seem out of place," she said. "It wouldn't do any good to make it obvious."

Warm stone met his touch, smooth and unyielding. Each piece fit seamlessly with the others, a rock solid three-hundred-year-old bench, built to last.

Cool grass under his back, Parker studied the underside. Darkness limited his vision, so out came his cell phone, the improvised flashlight showing nothing but smooth stone.

"Parker, get up. Someone's coming." Her foot found his posterior, and he wriggled out.

Searing pain sliced through a finger, and he promptly smacked his head on the granite.

"I think something bit me," he said. "Look at this."

A couple emerged from the wishing steps, chatting in German, their camera flashing at anything and everything, including the American couple.

"Look at this." Blood dripped from a cut on his finger. "There's something sharp under there."

"Ouch. How'd that happen?"

"I don't know. There wasn't a sharp corner on that whole thing, but I cut myself on something. Unless there's an unfinished edge down there..." He scrambled under the bench. "Get down here."

Erika joined him, Parker's phone light focused on where he'd sliced his hand.

"Hold this," he said.

"Are you sure there's nothing dangerous under here?"

Parker ignored her. "Unfinished granite edges are sharp. This bench is exquisitely crafted, and there are no sharp edges anywhere else. Why would there be one under here?"

"Because someone did work down here," Erika said. "Hidden work." Her words flew out. "Where'd you cut your hand?"

"Right here."

She illuminated the area, his fingers running across the stone.

"I knew it. Feel this."

He guided her free hand, and Erika jumped when she felt it. A razor-thin opening on the inside of one supporting leg.

The rental keys rattled in his hand. "It just fits in there," he said.

Centuries of grime crumbled onto his face, Parker worked the tip of the key into what looked like a panel. "I think it moved." When Parker twisted the knife back and forth, the piece shifted. Six inches wide and half as tall, he wriggled and worked the piece until it jiggled loose.

Dirt dropped into his eyes as he wriggled the granite piece, and a moment later it fell free.

"Nice work," Erika said, seizing his prize and stepped into the sunlight. Eyes stinging, gritty dirt in his teeth, Parker scrambled into the sunlight.

"What is it?" A sweaty hand wiped debris from his face.

He barely caught her breathless reply. "Look at this ring. It's beautiful."

His chest went cold. *Had the engagement ring fallen from his pocket?*

Only when his eyes cleared did he realize. It wasn't his diamond in her hand.

"Look at the size of this thing."

Erika held a tiny granite drawer which contained a small scroll bound with string. In her other hand, held aloft to catch the afternoon rays, a stunning ring.

The center gem sparkled as brightly as the pair of diamonds surrounding it.

"It's a sapphire," he said, taking the ring in his hands and glancing around to find nobody else in sight. "A huge one."

"Take this." Erika shoved the granite drawer his way. "That ring must have belonged to Queen Anne. Which means this paper is the first clue she left behind in her search for William."

"Are you going to read it?"

Erika shook her head. "Not here. We've been through this before. I don't want to risk damaging the paper, and we have zero privacy right now. Let's get back to the car before we do anything."

As she spoke, voices filtered from inside the Wishing Steps.

The scroll disappeared as Asian tourists clustered around the bottom of the steps, speaking rapid Mandarin. One man gestured behind them, pointing up the steps.

"Let's get out of here," Parker said. He reached for Erika's hand as the Asians scattered.

Three men in dark suits stepped into the sunlight.

The same three from the National Gallery.

"Put your head down and walk fast." Parker grabbed Erika's shoulder and whipped her around, but it was too late.

They'd been spotted.

Chapter 13

Blarney Castle
Cork, Ireland

Rooted to the ground, Erika stood frozen. How had these men found them?

Parker took off down the path, dragging her along. Racing toward the castle, the three suits thudded behind them at full speed. Parker pushed past the German couple, their camera flying into the woods as Erika went by.

Around a corner, and a fork in the road waited. Blarney Castle to the right, an open field and stables to the left.

Parker veered left. "The castle is a trap. We can hide over here."

A low-slung stone bridge took them over one of the streams crisscrossing the estate. Parker leapt the stone barrier, and Erika landed beside him on the grass at the water's edge.

Hidden under the bridge, footsteps echoed like gunshots, their pursuers halting right before they reached the crossing.

"You two go right," one of the men said. "To the castle. I'll go straight. Remember, we need the girl."

They were after *her?*

Two sets of feet pounded toward the castle, slowly fading. Head tilted to catch any sound, Erika heard nothing at all.

Parker touched a finger to his lips as a soft breeze rustled through the leaves. The man above didn't make a sound, a ghost floating in the air.

Parker grabbed a rock, used two fingers to simulate someone walking, and then he hit the finger-man with his rock.

A crude plan, but effective if it worked. When the man came into view,

Parker would attack, knock the guy out, and then they'd make their getaway.

Looks like they weren't going to kiss the Blarney Stone after all.

Birds whistled, and nothing moved. No footsteps, no sign of their pursuer.

And then he appeared. Crunching over tiny stones, he didn't look their way until he'd taken several steps on to the bridge.

Parker jumped, crashing the rock against the man's jaw.

Down he went, a wide gash leaking blood. And then the handgun came out.

Parker threw the rock, a direct hit to the forehead. The guy fell, and Parker tossed his gun into the stream beneath them.

"Come on," he shouted, grabbing her arm and running toward an open stable gate. Fifteen stalls lined each side of the open-air structure, filled with snorting, chewing animals.

A perfect hiding place.

Behind them, the man rose on unsteady legs, glistening blood covering his face like a mask.

"We'll be trapped if we hide in a shed." Erika resisted as Parker moved to enter one of the smaller buildings surrounding the stables. "We can hide with the horses."

Whinnying and moving about, the massive beasts covered any sounds she or Parker made, their footsteps lost in it all.

"Grooms and riders must come through here often. He can't hang around once they show up."

Parker nodded, moving silently over the rich dirt floor. Horse enclosures lined each side, all under one long roof. Nearly all of the bays were full, the animals indifferent to these human intruders.

Bent low, Parker led her past several stalls before ducking into one. Erika followed, slipping on a slick patch of straw.

Scrambling to stay upright, she slapped a warm, velvety soft rear end.

Well over six feet at his back, the black stallion barely reacted, whistling and flicking his tail.

"His ass is rock solid."

"Be careful," Parker said. "You wouldn't want him to kick you."

She crept beside him, ducking behind a feed barrel. Wooden boards lined three sides of the stall, with a gate on the fourth.

Parker peered through a gap in the boards. "He's coming this way. And he found another gun."

Erika shoved him aside. Carrying a pistol in plain sight, he didn't seem to care if anyone saw him, but right now this part of the grounds remained empty.

"Time to go," Erika said, grabbing the gate latch.

Parker snatched her arm. "Get back here. First of all, if we run now, he'll see us. They want to take you alive, but they didn't say anything about me."

He had a point.

"So what do we do? We can't sit here all day."

"You're right," Parker said. "We wait here until he walks past. He'll assume we kept running. Once he's gone, we head back to the wishing steps. There will be people there, which means guards, and Irish Santa had a radio. We find one of them, we can call for help."

"Fine. Now be quiet."

Erika slid further behind the barrel. Parker scooted beside her before turning back around. "Don't make any – oh no."

She followed his eyes, looking past the horse.

Damn.

She hadn't closed the gate.

The black stallion stamped his feet, dust flying, the massive hooves pounding the straw-covered floor.

Those enormous hooves, inches from her face.

Erika reached out and found Parker's hand. "I have an idea. Follow me."

Scurrying around the horse, Erika put his bulk between them and the approaching gunman.

Except now Erika could no longer see the man approaching. Her hands ran across the floor, searching. She needed something sharp.

And straw didn't cut it.

A saddle hung behind her. Straps dangled from the device, straps of leather designed much like a belt, with a length of metal hanging from one side.

As she grasped it, the horse stamped again. Footsteps scuffled outside the stall.

Parker pointed beneath the stallion. A pair of legs headed their way.

Two more steps.

One foot paused, and then moved ahead, now directly behind the horse. One more step, and he'd see them.

Now.

Erika jammed the pointed metal clasp into soft black underbelly.

Screaming, one hind leg shot out like a missile.

The dress shoes vanished, and a thunderous crash broke the air.

Glancing around the angry beast across the aisle, she spotted their quarry slumped on the ground, his neck twisted grotesquely.

Erika dropped the belt buckle and darted through the gate.

"Holy shit." Parker scrambled out to join her. "Nice aim."

I didn't want to kill him.

Oblivious to her shock, Parker retrieved the dead man's gun, slipping it into his waistband. Frisking the corpse, he came up with a wallet.

"You're stealing his money?"

"He can keep the money. I only need this."

Parker held up a driver's license and replaced the wallet. Leaving the body behind, they ran over the still-empty path, eventually joining a passing tour. "Do you still have the scroll?"

Erika couldn't shake the image of the man's broken neck. She only wanted to stop him, knock him out. Not kill him.

"Hey, did you hear me?" Parker said.

Erika reached into a pocket, the dry paper crackling. "Yes, it's here."

"Good," he said. "Keep your head down. The exit is ahead. I'm sure there's a guard stand nearby where we can get help."

But I killed that man. They'll arrest me.

And right now, sick as it made her, a tinge of pleasure tickled her spine. No, not pleasure. More than that.

Vengeance for Michelle.

"Forget the guards," she said. "Head to the car."

Parker nodded, and they passed through the castle gates, never glimpsing either of the remaining men who'd been after them.

Safely on the highway, Parker's fingers drummed across the wheel. "How did those guys know us? We only landed a few hours ago."

"I have no idea. Nobody but Michelle knew our plans," she said. "But I'll bet you anything this is related to the letter."

"You're probably right, if only because nothing else makes sense." Parker stared out the windshield, creases on his forehead. "Where to now?"

"I don't know. Maybe this will tell us."

Unrolling the scroll, Erika found a hand-penned message in an elegant, familiar script.

"It's from Queen Anne," Erika said. "And I have no idea what it means."

Chapter 14

Blarney Castle
Cork, Ireland

Gavin Rooney jogged through the Blarney Castle entrance gates with Harry and Brin behind him, scanning the crowds. Those Keepers could be anywhere in this mass of humanity.

"Spread out," Gavin said. "If you see anything, call me."

"I'll take the castle," Brin said. Harry headed in the opposite direction, and Gavin went straight ahead.

Jagged walls loomed above Gavin as he searched for any sign of the Englishmen. Moving deeper into the estate, he chanced upon the stables when a scream pierced the idyllic scene.

Gavin raced toward the source, making his way inside to find a woman backed up against a stall gate, hands covering her mouth.

One of the Englishmen lay crumpled on the ground, his neck bent at an angle normally reserved for hairpin turns. Only a few other people milled about, but more arrived every minute.

"It's alright, miss. I know CPR." While the woman quivered, Gavin bent down, checking for vital signs and rummaging through the dead man's clothing.

A wallet, cell phone, and under one arm, an empty shoulder holster.

"Don't worry," Gavin said, patting the woman's arm. "Help is on the way."

Pilfered goods in hand, Gavin put his head down and walked, cell phone at his ear.

"Harry, get Brin and meet me at the entrance. Right now."

When he made it back, Brin and Harry stood waiting, each surveying the crowd.

"I found one of them in the stables with a broken neck." The cell phone and wallet appeared. "He had these on him, but no gun. Did either of you find his friends?" Brin and Harry both shook their heads. "Then we wait. If they're here, we can follow them once they leave."

"Looks like the phone is our only lead," Harry said. "Best get on it."

To do that, Gavin needed to call for help.

"I'll take care of it," he said. "Keep your heads down and eyes open."

Lost in the crowd, Gavin walked to a quieter part of the grounds. The dead man's phone held promise, but to properly utilize it he needed to bring other IRA men into the fold.

"This is Rooney. I need to speak to the QM."

Moments later, a grandfatherly voice came through. "Gavin, my boy. What's on your mind?"

Quartermaster General Connor Whelan projected a calm authority over their group of nationalists, a steadying influence in times both good and bad. Beneath this gentle demeanor lurked a fervent, focused desire to see Ireland and North Ireland united, and woe unto any man trying to stop him.

"I found a Keeper at Castle Blarney with a broken neck. No identification, but I found a cell phone I thought might be of use."

"Well done, Mr. Rooney. I'll have our technical team contact you at once."

All were more hard-line members than Gavin or the QM, prone to overreact, to incite damaging retribution at any opportunity.

Given this, Gavin and Quartermaster Whelan first tried solving any problems on their own. Involving others always upped the chances of violence.

Connor Whelan's safety depended on cooperation from all IRA members, and he couldn't afford to alienate any faction of their membership.

Neither of the remaining Keepers made an appearance before Gavin's phone buzzed.

"Rooney, what do you have for us?" It was their I.T. arm, a group of younger recruits, downright wizards with technology.

"A Keeper's phone. I need you to find anything dealing with an American, name of Michelle Berks. Also, send me everything on here from the past twenty-four hours."

"No problem, I'll have it right away." The techie recited a number, which Gavin dialed into the stolen phone. "I suspect the QM will call you when we have it. Hang tight."

True to their word, someone rang back within minutes.

"Our tech team found something," QM Whelan said. "A calendar on the cell phone indicates the team you're following is to meet with one of their superiors." Connor cleared his throat. "Some of our men want to launch an attack on this gathering."

How unimaginative, as always. No thinking, no long view, only killing.

"I suppose there's no way to avoid this?"

"Not entirely," Whelan said. "I convinced them a warning strike is more effective than an outright attack. At least this way we avoid any deaths."

Until the next attack.

"There's something else you should know. We discovered an email Dr. Berks sent to a former classmate of hers. That friend and a man arrived in Ireland today. We believe they have information about why Dr. Berks died."

Silence.

"Anything else, sir?"

"Yes, there is. I believe this American couple is involved with centuries-old events and they don't realize it."

"So Queen Anne is reaching out from the grave?"

"Listen to me, Gavin. Right now you need to find those two Americans. Contact me once you do."

"Understood." Connor Whelan once told him a tale of the IRA's beginning, a story most believed lost. Except today a long-buried ghost rose once more.

Looking for the two Keepers, he walked back to where Brin and Harry waited. "New assignment. Let's move."

Hustling to their car, they mixed with a stream of tourists leaving the Castle grounds, the sun falling hard against the horizon.

In the rear seat, Gavin linked to a portable printer which produced photos of the American tourists along with the dead girl's email.

"We need to find these two." Gavin passed the photos up front. The email stayed with him. "Top priority."

Harry let out a low whistle. "We supposed to take them down?"

"Locate them for now, and then follow up with the QM." Brin started the car, the engine humming smoothly. "Right now we wait and see if the other Keepers show up. If they do, follow them. Odds are these Americans will be nearby."

Brin maneuvered their vehicle to face the castle entrance, offering a full view of everyone leaving. As they waited, Gavin read the email, parsing every word.

Talk about unlucky. For centuries the myth lay dormant, no more than a ghost tale. And then a letter, a royal letter, nonetheless, falls out from a painting and within hours two people die, and these tourists have the Keepers and the IRA after them, both desperate to control this narrative, to hell with the rest.

A fate Gavin wouldn't wish on his worst enemy.

Chapter 15

The man stood silent as a wall, and Chief Keeper Logan Rose only noticed him when the office door clicked shut.

"Have a seat, Mr. Moore." A welcome intrusion on the paperwork threatening to overwhelm his desk. "What's the matter?"

"One of our men died at Blarney Castle. They found his body in the stables with a broken neck. We're uncertain if it was intentional or accidental. Local paramedics and authorities are currently at the scene."

"Which means we can't contain this, and the police will eventually identify him," Logan said. "Is there any way to trace him to us?"

Oliver Moore shook his head. "No, sir. Everything was off the books, all cash."

"Good. Send the surviving team members to Waterford, specifically to Reginald's Tower. Have them call me when they arrive."

Moore turned to leave, and then stopped. "Do you really believe it's out there? After so long?"

"I guess we'll know if those two Americans show up in Waterford."

"If Dr. Carr goes to Waterford," Oliver said, pacing, "that could mean she *did* locate a message somewhere at Blarney Castle." He stopped, eyeing the framed picture of England's current monarch, Elizabeth II. "Perhaps this situation calls for more direct oversight."

The man had a point. "Agreed," Logan said. "You'll lead the search for Dr. Carr and her companion while I'm gone. It's nearly dinner time now. I don't anticipate being gone for more than twelve hours. Contact me if you discover anything."

Logan dismissed his subordinate, and picked up the phone. Minutes later, he had a military helicopter ready to ferry him to Waterford, a two-hour journey by air.

Changing into civilian clothes, Rose unlocked his safe, revealing several thousand pounds, passports of varying nationalities, and a Smith & Wesson .40 pistol.

Donning a shoulder strap, Logan holstered the gun and slipped two extra magazines into his pocket.

On the bottom of his safe, tucked under the stacked currency, was a folder containing a Keeper intelligence report prepared three centuries ago. Written by Queen Anne's Beefeater escorts on her tour of Ireland, it contained every scrap of knowledge they'd gathered during their journey. Counting on this information, unverified and impossible to corroborate at all, seemed the height of stupidity. Unless, of course, it proved true. If it led him to the Americans, who Rose believed to be following in Anne's footsteps, then everything changed.

Assuming all went smoothly, he'd be back in London tomorrow morning, Queen Anne's letter in hand. And should Dr. Erika Carr and her associate prove to be an issue, he would do what a good soldier always did.

Protect the realm, consequences be damned.

Chapter 16

Highway N25
North of Cork, Ireland

"I think we're clear," Parker said.

Checking their rearview mirror ever since they left Blarney Castle, found no signs of pursuit. The winding country highway aided his efforts, making it impossible for a tailing vehicle to remain hidden while they wound through the open fields, with grazing cows often outnumbering the cars.

Erika looked up from the scroll, gazing into the distance.

"We were right."

"Right about what?" Parker asked.

"This," she held the scroll aloft, "is the same handwriting as the letter we found at Michelle's studio. This proves Anne visited Blarney Castle, and she left another breadcrumb. But I have no idea what she's trying to say."

"Are you going to tell me what it says, or do I have to guess?"

As a scholar, Erika easily became engrossed in whatever she studied. If Parker didn't speak up, they'd be back in Dublin before she said anything.

"It's a story. About two people I've never heard of."

Parker kept one eye on the rearview mirror as Erika recited Queen Anne's cryptic message.

I find myself in the footsteps of Strongbow, set on a path by the promise of the lovely Aoife. After his conquest, this brave lord united with his love in the fallen city. Now I too will journey to recover what is mine from this towering loss.

"That's it?"

"The scroll's not very big," Erika said. "Whatever Anne is trying to tell us involves this Strongbow and Aoife pair."

"You're the history professor. Any ideas?"

"None. But my specialty is *American* history, not English. Give me a second."

Erika's fingers raced across her phone's keypad. If she didn't find anything soon, they should find a small town and hide. No point in driving aimlessly.

Scarcely a mile passed before she smacked his leg. "I think I have it."

"A destination too, I hope."

Erika threw him a look. "I'm getting there. First, I needed to figure out who Anne is talking about. I'm not well-versed in Irish history."

Parker said nothing. He knew better than to interrupt again.

"When Anne wrote this message, these allusions were an excellent cover to keep most readers from understanding her message."

"Which is?"

"Right, sorry. The pair mentioned in her message, Strongbow and Aoife, were a couple. Aoife was the daughter of..." here Erika consulted her phone, "a local Irish king, one Dermot McMurrough."

"What do you mean, local king?"

"In the twelfth century multiple kingdoms composed Ireland, with regional borders and rulers. Ireland didn't band together under the rule of a single king until the sixteenth century. The King of England, but that's not important. Strongbow was a lord and warrior. The local king, McMurrough, needed help to reclaim part of his kingdom lost in battle. He recruited Strongbow to help, and in return, agreed to have his daughter Aoife marry Strongbow."

An interesting story, but it didn't give them a direction. The longer they drove aimlessly, the better the chances those men from Blarney Castle found them. "Which means we need to go where?"

"They were married in the town of Waterford."

He knew that name. "As in Waterford crystal?"

"Correct. The town is now known for crystal, but what we're concerned with is the last line of Anne's message. She said, *'I will journey to recover what is mine from this towering loss'*. Strongbow and Aoife were married at Reginald's Tower. It dates from the time of the Vikings, and still stands today."

"That makes sense. One problem. Once we get to the tower, if that's even possible, what are we looking for?"

Erika shrugged. "I have no idea. Anything associated with Queen Anne."

This didn't seem to trouble her much. "You think it'll be that easy? Just ask a tour guide about Queen Anne, and he'll show us a secret stone with her initials on it?"

"It worked at Blarney Castle."

Erika and her stupid logic.

"Waterford is less than two hours northeast of here. I keep forgetting how small this place is compared to the States."

"That should give us just enough time to look around before it closes."

As they rode, a shadow seemed to envelope the car, draining their energy. Erika put her phone away, shrinking into the seat, both arms wrapped around her chest. "How did this happen? I mean, we're supposed to be on vacation. Now Michelle is dead and someone's trying to kill us."

Most people would go to the police now. One problem, though, is that Erika didn't think like most people. A murdered friend made this personal, and the historical bent made it irresistible. Trying to change her mind would be like moving mountains. Right now Parker could only hang on and enjoy the ride. Not that he minded.

"Whoever wants that letter isn't kidding around," Parker said. "Which to me indicates there's something big in all of this." In all the excitement, Michelle's death fell off the page. But he couldn't change that, couldn't bring her back. And Erika needed to know that. "Let's look at this logically."

"All right," Erika said, perking up. "Where do we start?"

"First, who today cares about a three-hundred-year-old letter from Queen Anne discussing a kidnapping? Is what Michelle suggested even plausible?"

"The first one's easy," Erika said. "The British government cares. The monarchy is an integral part of their national history, and the most visible aspect of what it means to be English. As to Michelle's suggestion Prince William may have lived to adulthood, I doubt we'll ever know the truth."

"This situation is important enough that someone sent armed men after us." Parker consulted the dead guy's identification. "Whoever this guy worked for wants Anne's letter, and they want it badly." Between them sat the dead man's gun, which Parker found to be fully loaded. "You know how strict gun laws are in Ireland and the United Kingdom. Not just anyone can carry a handgun. Maybe we should see if Nick can tell us anything about this Carrick guy. If he has a criminal record, or if he works for any government."

Through a unique set of circumstances, CIA agent Nick Dean and Parker recently became strong allies. As tough as they came and with access to government databases, Nick was the kind of friend you needed in hard times.

"I'll shoot him a message," Erika said. "Do you think we should tell him everything?"

"I do," Parker said. "Who knows what details will mean more to him than to us."

Settling in for the drive, checking his rearview all the while, Parker's thoughts drifted to the pending proposal. Right now a Queen and her mystery kept getting in the way, but it wouldn't stop him from popping the question, no matter how many twists this mystery took.

Chapter 17

For the second time that day, a black Audi followed the green Mercedes through Ireland's interior, this time headed northeast from Cork, with the Audi hanging well back as they wound along the scenic highway. In the rear seat, Gavin Rooney sat lost in thought.

Soon after receiving the photos of Erika Carr and Parker Chase, Gavin and his men had spotted the two surviving Keepers leaving Blarney Castle. Snapshots of each man went to headquarters, so now Gavin's team followed the Englishmen, waiting on further instructions.

Harry's phone rang, breaking the silence.

"What do you have? Right." He clicked off. "Just what we suspected. Two Keepers, both ex-military."

Behind the wheel, Brin shook his head. "Why are the Keepers involved with this?"

"Who knows," Gavin said. "The QM will call later with an update. Maybe he can shed some light on it."

And you two will hear the story of a lifetime.

"Hold on." Brin slowed as the Mercedes exited ahead. "Looks like we're headed to Waterford."

Over a sloping hill, the ancient city appeared, modern buildings pushed up against the stately River Suir, the oldest city in Ireland picturesque as ever on this early summer evening.

Located in the southeast portion of the country, Waterford dated back to the ninth century, established when Vikings settled the area. This city contained the oldest urban civic building on the island, a circular Viking defense structure known as Reginald's Tower, the first Irish building to use mortar. Over time, the tower had been used as a mint, prison, and military store.

Brin kept well behind the Keepers, hidden in the flowing city traffic.

The Englishmen's Mercedes headed into the heart of the city, running along tiny John's River, which fed into the River Suir. At the confluence of the two waterways, their target turned toward the city center, eventually stopping near Reginald's Tower.

Brin swerved into an open spot one block behind them.

Neither man emerged from the Mercedes, two immobile heads visible through the rear window.

"What's going on, Gavin?" Harry asked.

A soldier followed orders, even when he didn't like them. "I'm not sure, but this is top priority. The QM said he'll be calling soon, so until then, we wait."

As traffic flowed past, they watched the Englishmen sit. Ten minutes later, Gavin's phone buzzed.

"What's your status?" QM Whelan asked.

"Still watching the Keepers. They're stopped in the middle of Waterford, by Reginald's Tower."

"Any idea why they chose to stop there?"

"None. There's nothing unusual around, just commercial buildings and apartments, an old statue."

"Are you with Harry and Brin?"

"We're all here."

"Then please allow them to listen in. It's time they learned about certain events far removed from today."

Gavin put the QM on speaker. "Gentlemen, I'm sure you're curious as to what the Keepers are doing, and why I've assigned this mission. To understand, it's necessary to go back to the Act of Settlement in 1701. To refresh your memory, that's when the bastards in the English Parliament decreed the throne of England and Ireland could only be occupied by a non-Roman Catholic. Meaning that Queen Anne, a Roman Catholic, had to produce an heir or see the crown pass to one of her Protestant relatives."

Brin and Harry shared a glance, unaware of Gavin studying their every move. "Around the time this Act was passed, Queen Anne's only son died. Eleven years old, Prince William proved to be the last of her offspring to survive past infancy."

The other two finally looked back. Where was the QM going with this?

Gavin shrugged. Another lie.

"Now why am I giving you a history lesson? The answer lies at the very foundation of our organization, specifically in the death of Prince William. You see—"

"Look at that," Gavin said.

An arm sprouted from the Mercedes, pointing across the street.

Reginald's Tower loomed high above the cobblestone street on which they now sat. Atop the circular structure, stone walls protected the rooftop, obscuring it from view. Only the pointed roof's apex stood above the walls, stretching toward the sky.

Right now a man held on to the spire, feet dangling over the roof's edge, sixty feet in the air.

"There's a man on top of Reginald's Tower, QM. Wait a second." Gavin squinted at the guy. "I think it's the American."

"And the Keepers are getting out," Harry said.

"To be continued," Whelan said. "I suggest you stay back at first, observe what happens. Whatever you do, don't let the Keepers take either American with them."

"Understood. We'll update you on our progress." Gavin ended the call, and looked up to see both Keepers dodging through traffic toward the Tower entrance. "The Americans may have information the QM needs. We'll stay put for now, but get ready to move if the Keepers go inside. We can't risk losing sight of them."

Harry and Brin settled into a well-rehearsed routine, both men checking firearms and counting bullets.

Each Englishman darted across the street toward the lone entrance, an arched wooden doorway at ground level. Without hesitating, both disappeared inside.

"Time to move," Gavin said. "We need eyes on those two Keepers, and I want to know what the hell that daft Yank is doing on the roof."

Gavin led the way through traffic, horns blaring as they ran toward the thick, weathered entrance. He pressed an ear next to the door, listening for anything. It was a futile effort. This wood could withstand a direct cannon blast.

"Ready?"

Brin and Harry both nodded.

With one hand on his gun, Gavin opened the door.

Chapter 18

Waterford, Ireland

Through the entrance to Reginald's Tower, Parker and Erika found a gray-haired attendant seated behind a low desk, her bespectacled eyes focused on an e-reader. When the front door jingled, she looked up, a kindly smile creasing her wise features.

"Welcome to Reginald's Tower."

"Thank you," Erika said. "I assume you're the resident expert?"

"Any questions you have," her arms moved in a circle, encompassing the stony interior, "just ask. Here's our literature, and you'll find information at every display. Is this your first time here?"

"It is," Erika said. "It's more beautiful than we'd imagined."

Parker paid the entrance fee for them both, leaving a generous donation in the collection box as well. It never hurt to grease the wheels.

"I'm wondering," Erika said, her nose in the pamphlet. "Is anything associated with Queen Anne of Great Britain in here? I'm a history professor, and I have a special interest in her."

"Queen Anne herself blessed the very capstone which rests atop this tower. She visited while on a tour of Ireland and attended the ceremony."

Erika glanced at Parker. "That's interesting. Is the rooftop accessible?"

"I'm afraid not," their hostess said. "Only the interior floors are open to the public. It can be quite windy up there."

"I understand. Thank you for the information," Erika said, grabbing Parker's hand and practically dragging him away.

"Enjoy yourselves. I'll be here if you need me."

Erika pulled him through a narrow archway and up the slick stone staircase. Much as it had been at Blarney Castle, Parker's shoulders nearly touched each wall.

"How did people ever walk in here?" His fingers ran along the cool stones, worn smooth by the passing of centuries.

"This staircase is narrow for strategic reasons," she said. "Think about it. A few men could stop an army in here if they held the high ground."

"Good point." Anyone assaulting these steps faced a host of problems, most fatal.

Up the winding staircase, they passed a glassed-in slit only inches wide. Designed to provide protection for archers, they allowed defenders a wide firing range through the openings along with significant protection.

Open doors welcomed visitors to each level, lacquered boards with iron supports clearly more recent additions. Parker spotted cases displaying artifacts, though there didn't seem to be any other visitors around.

"Looks like we have the place to ourselves."

Erika moved on a direct path to the top floor. "This place closes in an hour. Right now, most tourists are out looking for a good restaurant or pub. We don't have much time to find what we came for before that guide comes looking for us."

To the top floor they went, four landings in all. Parker walked under a low archway and found display cases lining the room's perimeter. Glass-encased, each contained medieval weapons and tools. He didn't read the little cards, but all the weapons looked like sticks of metal as likely to cause death by gangrene as anything else.

"There's the roof access door." Erika stood in front of a wide doorway across the room, conveniently labeled *Roof Access-Employees Only*. "It's locked." To further emphasize the point, a large padlock secured the door.

"Do you think we can break this off?"

"Not a chance. Even with the right tools, ripping those screws out would make enough noise to wake the dead."

Around them, warm light filtered through several windows, each set in a recessed alcove and offering amazing views of downtown Waterford. Erika checked them all, her feet pounding across the wooden floor.

"Damn. No fire escape. We can't climb to the roof." She whizzed past, checking each window again. "There must be another way."

He recognized the signs, the desperation. Too focused to consider their safest and most reasonable option, Erika needed to remember what brought them to this beautiful country in the first place.

"You do realize that we can walk away from this? Maybe start our vacation? Better than looking over our shoulders for those guys from

Blarney Castle all week." She stopped racing around, turning to face him. "Speaking of that, did Nick ever get back to you?"

"No. He hasn't responded yet."

Erika stalked over her eyes narrowed.

Oops.

"One, I agree these are awful circumstances, but if you don't think this is an amazing opportunity, I'm dating the wrong guy. Two, Michelle started this, and we're going to finish it. Who else will do it, considering she's dead? And three, could you live with yourself if we walked away from her discovery?"

That look again.

"This could affect history," she said. "Who knows what we'll find next?" Arms crossed, she stood inches away, daring him to disagree.

Unfortunately, Erika didn't know the meaning of the word surrender.

His hands went up. "Fine. But if we run into anybody else with a gun, we're getting Nick involved. No arguments."

"Deal." She wheeled around and went back to the roof access door. "Now get over here and figure out how to open this door."

Like a man facing the gallows, Parker trudged over. "Erika, these walls are made of stone."

"You're the one with all the muscles. Figure it out."

Despite her assertions, Hercules he was not. This problem required power of the mental variety.

Studying the lock, he recalled sharing a house with several teammates in college. Parker occupied the largest room, situated away from the main living area, offering peace and quiet. And the only working air conditioner, which meant his room remained cool while the rest of the house grew insufferably hot. To keep unwanted guests out, Parker installed a locking hasp and hinge on his door. It worked until one of his more enterprising roommates realized that although he couldn't unlock the deadbolt, it *was* possible to unscrew the hinge from Parker's door frame, thus freeing it to be opened.

"You don't happen to have a screwdriver, do you?"

With the rooftop access secured in the same fashion as his college door, Parker only needed to bypass several steel screws the size of his finger to get outside. A sturdy screwdriver may do the trick.

"Why yes, I packed one with my hairdryer," she said. "In case I needed to build a house."

"Those displays have tools in them. Might be a screwdriver in there."

"I'll bet these cases don't even have locks," she said, fiddling with a tiny latch. "Told you." Erika beamed, lifting the display case cover to expose an ancient and rusted metal tool set.

"I need something narrow, like this." One of the metal sticks had a tapered point, narrow and flat. "This may work. Keep an eye out for anyone coming up the stairs."

With Erika posted as lookout, Parker went to work. A few minutes of twisting and turning, and four screws rolled on the floor. The latch remained bolted to the hasp, which was securely fastened to the stone frame. The wooden access door, however, stood free.

"Got it."

"I don't hear anyone downstairs," she said. "And it's thirty minutes to closing time."

With that, she pushed the door open and stepped through.

Parker pocketed the metal screws and followed her into a narrow stone passageway. They stood inside the Tower walls, but the sky was visible overhead. A short stone staircase brought them to roof level, where cool evening air blew crisply over the rooftop.

Encircled by a chest-high wall, an inverted cone jutted from the roof's center. The capstone sat atop it, supporting a spire pointing to the clouds.

"Did you bring the screwdriver?"

Parker gave it to Erika, who knelt at the cone's base. Composed of stone and mortar, the rocks offered plenty of purchase for an ascent to the capstone ten feet above. "We may need that tool to access whatever Anne left behind. Hand it over."

He ignored her outstretched hand and scurried up to the capstone himself, crawling on his hands and knees. "You stay down there and catch me if I fall."

Even in this breeze, he felt safe enough to stand, always keeping one arm on the spire. Made of slick metal, it was probably a lightning rod, as the tower was the tallest building around.

A blaring car horn caught his attention, and he realized he was exposed for all to see. Including any authorities who happened past the tower.

Gripping the metal spire, Parker studied the capstone, lying at a forty-five degree angle.

"What do you see?" Erika said.

"Nothing yet. I'm going to circle around."

Wind swirled, the short surrounding walls too close for comfort, the perfect height to trip him if he fell from the capstone. As Parker slid around the spire, a gust of wind knocked him off-balance. His feet slid out, and both hands locked onto the lightning rod.

Which sent the medieval screwdriver sailing over the upper wall and out of sight.

Erika ran over and looked to the streets.

"You're lucky," she said. "It's a grass lot down there. You didn't hit anything, but we'll have to sneak it back up here."

I nearly fall off the roof and she's worried about that damn screwdriver.

"Keep moving," she said. "We're running out of time."

Two hands on the spire, Parker slid further around, looking for anything. A broken block, cracked seam, he'd take either. Gritty dust brought tears, blurring his vision. Parker pulled one hand free and wiped the salty liquid away.

And he found it.

He blinked fiercely, his nose inches from the rock.

A single weathered letter, cut into the capstone, scarcely two inches high.

A

"Erika, you need to see this."

She scrambled up to join him, one hand locked on his shoulder in a death grip. "What is it?"

He outlined the faded letter, Erika traced a finger over the small carving, the wind blowing her hair all about like Medusa's snakes.

"It's true." The wind took her words in a flash. "Anne left this letter for her uncle to find. Why else would Queen Anne care about a tower in Waterford?"

Cars moved about beneath them, the city alive as they stood high above, in plain sight if anyone wanted to look.

"What does it mean?" Parker asked. "Is this pointing us somewhere else?"

"We're on top of a tower. I bet this is the beginning and end of this step in her trail. That, and the fact that it's the only building left standing from when she visited. It better be up here, or we're out of luck."

"Good point." Hands running over the capstone, he found only rough, scratchy rock. "I can't find a seam for a drawer or chamber in this rock. My guess is she put something inside."

He could really use that screwdriver right now. "We have a problem. I can't break this rock open without any tools."

"What about this?" Erika grabbed the lightning rod. "It's not drilled into the rock, and if you pull on it hard enough, the capstone may break."

A professional historian, advocating the destruction of a national treasure?

"Are you serious?"

"We're running out of time," Erika said. "What choice do we have?"

Parker wasn't about to argue. The longer they stayed up here, the more likely a night in jail became.

"Stand back, and if I slip, catch me."

Erika slid away as he tugged the spire. Bolted to the capstone by way of a metal plate, it barely moved.

He pulled harder. The metal creaked, giving a bit further.

What the hell.

He got on both feet and ripped back as hard as he could. The metal screeched, went almost parallel to the roof, but didn't break.

Then it snapped back into place.

Parker never let go and found himself airborne, staring at a red sky.

Arms flailing, totally out of control, only when his torso rotated did he see the roof.

Hard rock smashed into his face, leaving plenty of skin behind when he smacked the knee-high wall, inches from going over.

"Parker!" Erika ran over, her angelic face blocking out the falling sun. Fire rolled down his cheek, the gusting winds like icy needles on his raw flesh.

"That was stupid of me."

"You are such a jerk. I thought you were dead."

Blood rolled down his lip, a salty taste of his mistake. "But I think you did some damage. Look at the pole."

No doubt about it. The lightning rod now listed to one side atop the cracked capstone, jagged breaks on every side.

"Get behind me again," he said. "I'll roll with the whiplash this time and crack it open."

Grabbing the rod, he leaned back, and then let it pull him forward. Dust shot from the capstone, the cracks growing. Back and forth once more, the pole now noticeably looser. On the next pull, a bolt shot into the air, zipping past his face.

"You almost have it."

Erika stood behind him, one hand on his belt. Feet planted, he ripped the pole again. A screeching death cry filled the air as the plate gave way. Dust bloomed as the capstone split in half, the entire rock falling to pieces.

Scrambling, flailing, Parker fell ass over elbows onto the roof, still holding the lightning rod. Debris choked his throat, dry particulate rough in his eyes. Only once he'd sneezed away the ancient allergen did he realize Erika stood in his place, crouched over the ruined stone.

"It's hollow," he said.

"I knew it."

A metal box sat in front of her, rusted with age.

"Whoever laid the capstone hollowed it out and set it on top of the metal box."

As vehicles hummed beneath them, Parker glanced at his watch.

Closing time.

"Grab that thing and let's go," Parker said.

With the precious box in hand, Erika followed him back inside. Try as he may, the screws wouldn't turn into their recently vacated holes. Without the medieval screwdriver, it was useless.

"We'll have to grab the tool I dropped and come back up," he said. "Tell the attendant you left your purse."

Hustling after her down the steps, he kept a step behind until she screeched to a halt at the third floor.

"Someone's coming."

A door stood open behind them, and Parker pushed her through, finding more display cases set against a circular wall, identical to the floor above.

"Hide behind one of those. When they pass, we'll make a break for it."

Erika ducked behind an interactive display case about life in the Middle Ages, Parker squeezing beside her, invisible to anyone walking by the door.

Footsteps sounded outside. Two sets, two different voices.

"They sound British," he said, his mouth scarcely moving. "Like the guy at Blarney." British voices could be a coincidence, but would he bet his life on it?

A gruff voice rumbled in the hallway. "Check that room." Footsteps shuffled through the doorway. Parker's heart pounded, the silence deafening.

"They're not here. Let's check upstairs." Two pairs of feet disappeared upstairs.

Erika's eyes were stretched wide. "They're talking about us. No one else is here."

Hard to argue coincidence on this one. "Follow me," Parker said. "And forget about that tool. It's staying outside."

With Erika on his heels, Parker darted into the hallway. Down to the second level, and they were halfway home, Parker reaching for his car keys when he heard it. A quick squeak, like shoe rubber catching on stone.

When he suddenly stopped, Erika slammed into his backside.

And dropped the box.

Screeching and clattering, it fell down the steps, bouncing to the second floor landing. Voices thundered from above.

"Did you hear that? Go check it out."

Parker took off, scooping up the partially-opened box. Inside, green sparks flashed like lightning.

"That can wait." Erika grabbed the other fallen item, another scroll, similar to the one from Blarney Castle.

Past a stunned visitor with squeaky shoes on the second floor, pounding footsteps chased them to ground level, where the elderly attendant sat reading.

"It was really great," Erika said as she ran outside.

Parker grabbed the massive entrance door and pulled it closed. Maybe it would buy them a few seconds.

Erika pushed past a group of pedestrians, who were then sideswiped by Parker as he barreled past.

Dodging traffic, Parker jumped in their car, Erika right beside him. As the engine turned, two men burst from the Tower entrance.

"Take this." Parker tossed the metal box onto Erika's lap. Tires smoked as he peeled away, roaring through a cacophony of horns past the British guys climbing into a green sedan.

"They're right behind us," Erika said. Parker glanced in the rearview and spotted the green vehicle gaining ground.

"Watch out!"

Parker shot through the red light, cutting off a motorcycle. The driver skidded and went up on the front wheel, speeding off an instant later as the green Mercedes barreled through.

"Who the hell are those guys?"

Parker shook his head, swerving around a stopped delivery truck. "They sounded English, like the guy who died in Blarney Castle, so I bet these two knew the dead guy and somehow followed us."

"They followed us?" Erika asked.

Did they tail us from Waterford and I missed it?

"How else could they find us? Unless they read the scroll at Blarney Castle, they must have followed us."

Two pedestrians ambled across an intersection, oblivious to their impending doom.

"Hold on." Fighting the steering wheel, they went left, tires squealing as the top-heavy vehicle nearly rolled.

They needed a bigger road.

"We can't stay in the city. We'll kill someone or get trapped in an alley."

"There," she said. "The M9. That's a major highway."

A blue sign ahead indicated an exit, traffic backing up at the red light, with parked cars blocking any move to the left.

Out of options, Parker swerved into oncoming traffic as the traffic light turned green.

Headlights raced toward him. As traffic beside them began rolling, Parker swerved back over, an oncoming vehicle clipping his bumper.

The green sedan didn't fare so well, stopped in the oncoming lane, no openings to move through and no way to follow.

"They're stuck," Parker said. "And here's our exit."

Erika twisted around. "Here they come."

Behind them, the powerful vehicle smashed through stopped traffic, Renaults and Peugeots pushed aside like toys. With only one broken headlight, the roaring German beast followed Parker onto the highway.

"Any ideas?"

"Go faster." And for some reason, Erika decided to investigate their haul from atop Reginald's Tower.

"We have people trying to run us off the road and you're doing inventory?"

"No, I'm trying to determine our destination. What do you want me to do, faint?"

Hard to argue with that.

"So what's in there? The necklace looked promising."

Parker swerved around a slow-moving box truck, the Mercedes following suit and gaining ground.

"Hang on. I can't outrun them in this thing."

Directly in front of the box truck, Parker slammed the brakes. The truck did too, horn blaring as tires smoked under the bulky vehicle.

The truck fishtailed into the passing lane, but defying the laws of physics, it veered back and failed to tip over.

"Damn. Almost had him."

"Are you trying to cause an accident?"

"That's exactly what I'm aiming for," he said. "If I can flip the truck, those British guys are stuck. They can't go around the concrete median on our right or the guardrail to the left."

"There's another truck up ahead with lots of cargo in the back."

Another box truck rumbled ahead of them, the flat bed uncovered. Wooden boards fenced in dozens of stacked steel pipes, a chain latching the wooden tailgate shut.

"Is anything tying those pipes down?" Erika asked. "They look like they're just wedged into the back."

Gunfire split the air, sparks mushrooming on the asphalt.

"He's going for the tires," Erika said.

More bullets sparked on the asphalt, inches from their wheels.

Swerving back and forth, Parker kept the shooter off-balance, though his luck wouldn't hold forever. A shot ricocheted and took out his mirror.

"Hold on," Parker said. "You're not going to like this."

"Like it less than getting shot at?"

Accelerating next to the pipe truck, on their left, he looked at the driver, an oblivious older man singing as he drove.

Empty road stretched ahead. A good thing, because this was about to get messy. Parker fell back, pulling even with the box truck's rear.

Here goes nothing.

He swerved, slamming the truck's rear end to send it bouncing onto the shoulder. Wobbling precariously, the driver regained control, muscling back onto the roadway.

Exactly what Parker hoped for.

Behind him, the Mercedes loomed large, a pistol sticking out the window.

Metal crunched and screamed as Parker smashed into the truck's rear again to send the wide back end fishtailing. For an instant, the truck swerved back, aiming straight ahead.

And then it happened.

The back end slid around, rubber streaking the road as it skidded. Parker veered far away, nearly scraping the concrete median as the truck careened out of control, flipping over and sliding against the metal guardrail.

Engine roaring, Parker gunned it, missing the overturned truck by inches.

Pipes filled the air, metal javelins bouncing on the asphalt. Parker sped past the unfolding disaster, gaining speed as he watched.

The Mercedes had no chance, skidding sideways before flipping one hundred eighty degrees onto the roof. Metal shrieked as the upended car slid, scattered lengths of pipe bouncing off the spinning car as the box truck ahead came to rest on the passenger side.

When it did, the Mercedes slammed into the upended truck, glass and metal exploding.

Gavin Rooney stared at the destruction. It was like a bomb had gone off in the middle of the M9.

"That was the damnedest driving I've ever seen," Harry said.

Brin tried to reverse, but traffic piled up behind them. Several drivers were out of their vehicles, moving toward the accident.

"Move, damn it." He laid on the horn, waving at bystanders.

"Right there," Gavin said. "We can slip through."

Brin pushed through an opening in the wreckage, bumping the Mercedes to send a loose length of pipe rolling.

Movement caught Gavin's eye. "Look there. The truck driver."

As they wheeled past, the man crawled out of his cab. Dazed but moving, he appeared to be in one piece.

"Hit it, Brin. Don't lose the Americans."

Theirs was the lone car to make it past the wreck, Brin pushing their speedometer to over one hundred fifty kilometers per hour.

Gavin drummed his fingers on the leather seat, only leaning back once the dented Land Rover came in to view.

If they lost the Americans now, the truth might disappear with them.

Chapter 19

"You can slow down now."

Parker glanced at the speedometer, currently hovering at one hundred kilometers per hour. "My fault."

Engine settling, Parker slipped into traffic, the twisted cars and burning roadway well behind them. Overhead, red sunlight colored the sky, fading gently into the green pastures below.

"Now we can see what this box is about." Erika said, all business. "Based on what I know about metalworking, I estimate it's fifteenth or sixteenth century, which is Queen Anne's time."

Set atop the glove box, the rusted piece begrudgingly opened, the lid protesting like a newborn being baptized.

"My goodness, this thing is heavy."

The necklace gleamed in her hands, golden loops holding a green gemstone the size of a silver dollar, every facet reflecting a shamrock's fire.

"Judging from the weight and lack of discoloration, this chain is gold, befitting a queen. I'm certainly not a gemologist, but this stone is stunning."

"Why do you think we're finding jewelry with these letters?" Parker asked. "First the ring, now this necklace."

"To establish authenticity. Who else but a queen has jewels like this? If her uncle followed this trail, these are a dead giveaway the messages are real."

"Anything in there that tells us where to go?" She may be caught up in the wonder of discovery, but he needed a destination.

"Right." As the necklace settled back inside the box, Erika flipped the stone over. "There's an inscription here."

"What's it say?"

"*From Charles, with love*."

"Who in the world is Charles?"

"No idea." She unfolded the scroll, revealing a familiar script.

"That looks like Anne's writing," Parker said.

Erika read in silence, the crackling paper scarcely larger than a playing card. "Her son went to Reginald's Tower, but she missed him. Listen to this."

"William was within these walls, but was taken away. He is gone to Ormonde's, held by his Irish captors. I know not if Charles is part of this treachery, but will carry on to his castle."

"I've never heard of *Ormonde's*," Erika said, "but if there's a castle involved, we should be able to figure out what she's talking about."

"The sooner, the better. For all we know I'm headed in the wrong direction."

"Hold on, Mr. Impatient. Let me see what I can find."

Erika tapped her cell phone, searching for answers while Parker considered how this trip had morphed from a vacation into a race for survival. Gunshots and dead bodies accompanied that first letter, and now this. A queen's hidden trail, all stemming from an old painting. It made no sense, but whatever lay at the end of this path must be worth killing for.

And all I want to do is get engaged.

Personal mission aside, what was it about this ancient history that made bullets fly and justified murder? And who was pulling the trigger? Prince William died centuries ago.

Another angle could be Queen Anne's jewelry. The stones were worth a fortune, and people had died for much less.

"Listen to this," Erika said. "Ormonde isn't a name, it's a title of Irish nobility involving a line of dukes. Duke *Charles* Butler, to name one."

"So you think Duke Charles knew Anne?"

"That's possible," Erika said. "The Butler line included earls, dukes and other nobles. They ruled parts of the country for hundreds of years from their base of operations at Kilkenny Castle."

"And there's the castle Anne mentioned. Any chance it still exists?"

"The property is now owned by the people of Kilkenny, a town in southeastern Ireland."

"Southeast? We're in that general vicinity."

"Better than that. Kilkenny is on the M9, and only forty kilometers ahead. We can make it there tonight."

The Land Rover's GPS confirmed Kilkenny lay one hour ahead.

"It's about time we catch a break," Parker said, the speedometer inching higher. "Question is, what are we looking for in the castle?"

"I'm working on it. Only Anne's uncle is supposed to know this trail exists, so chances are her next marker is obscured like the other, just enough to hide the true reason for her Irish visit from George's spies."

"So she used gifts as markers," Parker finished. "The spies wouldn't know they were actually breadcrumbs for Laurence to follow."

"Exactly. She found the best place to hide anything. Out in the open."

Fragrant air slipped through the car, scented by the rolling fields stretching in all directions. Parker urged the Land Rover onward, following Anne's trail and racing to stay alive.

Chapter 20

A thousand feet above southern Ireland, an iron demon burst through the thin curtain of misty clouds. Heavy rotors beat the air, the *whump-whump* drawing stares from below. On loan from the Royal Air Force, the Puma HC1 transport bird carried two crew members and a single passenger. In the rear hold, Logan Rose watched the terrain scroll past.

His headset crackled to life. "Sir, you have a call."

"Patch it through."

Oliver Moore's voice came through. "Chief Warder Rose, are you there?"

Rose glanced at his watch. Ten minutes to Waterford. "I'm here. What is it?"

"There's a problem. The remaining members of our team at Blarney Castle are dead."

And the plot thickened. "Are you certain?"

"Positive, sir. A traffic accident on the northbound M9, near Waterford. Witnesses reported shots fired. A box truck overturned, and our two men crashed into the wreckage. Neither survived."

"How'd you hear about this?"

"I'd flagged the plates, sir. The locals notified me at once."

"So we no longer have eyes on the Americans." Not ideal, but not fatal either. "Any hits from our surveillance net?"

"No credit card or passport usage, and no intercepted phone calls either."

So they'd deal with this a different way.

"We did intercept an email from Dr. Carr sent to one Nick Dean. I can't find him in our database, but based on the message, it seems that he's with the American government in some capacity."

"Erase the email, government or not. I don't want this Dean fellow sticking his nose in our affairs. The Americans headed north from Waterford?"

"Correct."

Which meant whatever Anne left in Waterford was gone or never existed. So be it. On to the next stop. "Change in plans. I'm going to Kilkenny. Contact me if there are any further updates." Rose switched channels to speak with the crew. "Gentlemen, we need to change course. Take me to Kilkenny."

The two pilots didn't flinch. "Understood, sir. Updating the flight plan now."

Rose's stomach dropped as the chopper banked, red sunbeams warming the cool cabin. His most precious possession in this chase sat beside him, pages of first-hand notes on Anne's journey. He pulled one free, the archaic script a window to the past, Yeoman Warder reports of three hundred years earlier which Logan knew to be a map of the future.

Until they'd intercepted the email to Erika Carr, none of the Keepers, Rose included, knew of the clues the Queen had laid on her journey. She had done well to hide her tracks, and only through the redundancy of government record-keeping did Rose have these records. Otherwise, he'd have been out in the cold without any advantages over the tourists.

Anne's journey carried onward from Waterford and went straight to Kilkenny. Given the M9 ran directly to Kilkenny as it wound its way northward, the odds were in his favor that the Americans traveled in Anne's footsteps, the same path laid out on these pages.

Logan even knew *where* the Americans would go. As to what awaited them, though, he knew not. Regardless, one thing remained true.

Their journey's end drew near.

Chapter 21

Kilkenny, Ireland

Set a stone's throw from the River Nore, Kilkenny Castle guarded the vital waterway, an impregnable stronghold standing since 1195 when four stone towers rose from the dirt atop a rounded hill. Ever since, the waterway served as both a trade route for moving goods and an indispensable source of life for villages along the sloped banks.

Of the four original towers, three still stood, and alterations over the centuries added dozens of rooms and other structures necessary to sustain a thriving household in medieval times. Today the people of Kilkenny owned the castle and property, the beautiful stone fortress one of Ireland's most-visited tourist sites.

Turning off the town streets, the estate's entrance bisected ornamental gardens and manicured fields. Beyond the gardens, Kilkenny pushed up against the water, built on both banks of the River Nore and home to twenty-five thousand Irish souls.

"Parker, this is beautiful."

Erika's window lowered as they rolled by a rustic stone fountain spraying sparkling water through the day's final rays. Lush roses lined the pavement, a roundabout leading toward visitor parking.

"Let's keep moving," Erika said. "We can't afford to let anyone catch up."

Parker whipped their Land Rover into a parking spot, and after tucking the Englishman's gun into his waist, he followed Erika under a canopy of foliage to the main castle area. Several dozen visitors milled about the grounds, most near the gray stone walls rising toward a darkening sky.

"Where are we headed?" Parker asked as they walked inside.

"I don't know. Anne didn't specify, and nothing on here jumps out," Erika said, studying a tour map. "We don't have time to wander."

While Erika made inquiries with a front desk attendant, a chart on the wall grabbed his eye. Arrows pointed every which way, including one aimed toward the Butler Gallery.

Charles Butler, perhaps?

"Erika." She turned and headed his way. "Check this out."

"We have a problem," she said, ignoring his outstretched finger. "The attendant informed me Queen Anne is well-represented on the walls. Apparently the original proprietors treasured their relationship with her and filled this place with her artifacts."

"That's odd," Parker said. "Considering she didn't know whether or not to trust Charles Butler. Speaking of him, I found a good place to start."

She took in the sign. "Agreed. The front desk attendant suggested I start with either the Butler or picture gallery."

With that, Erika walked off, Parker scurrying to catch up.

Hand-wrought wooden beams stretched from floor to ceiling, the petrified rib cage supporting untold tons of stone. Underneath the gazes of long-dead nobility, Erika studied a guide book as Parker trailed behind, the sheer audacity of the wooden beams drawing his eye as they soared, an Irish Sistine Chapel in whittled wood.

"What's carved on those beams?"

"The arches are actually made of stone, and those carvings reflect nature's role in supporting this estate."

Sure enough, when he squinted, the animals and birds came into view.

"Without the surrounding forest and wildlife," Erika said. "This place wouldn't exist. From wood for building and warmth, to the animals harvested for food or labor, Kilkenny Castle depended almost entirely on what nature offered. Those carvings symbolize this connection."

"I'm not so sure the animals liked it. Their slaughter is Kilkenny's gain. Not to mention that all these carvings are a bit macabre."

"To each his own. I think this is it."

A sharp turn, and they arrived.

Fading sunlight fell through skylights, stretching the hall's length. Exposed beams boasting detailed carvings kept the roof floating high above, while smooth walls festooned with paintings stretched into the distance, longer than a football field and nearly as wide. Rows of chandeliers hung from the rafters, electric lights burning.

A hell of a lot safer than candles.

Few guests were around, only a pair of gray-haired women scanning the walls and a seated younger couple.

Despite this cavernous area's natural beauty, icy fingers tiptoed on his spine.

"There are dozens of paintings in here. Where do we start?"

Erika glanced at the guidebook, back at the walls, then the book once more. A moment later, the book smacked shut.

"We'll do a circuit of the room. You go left, and I'll take right. Look for anything related to Anne, including Charles Butler."

Watched by lords and ladies long gone to dust, Parker took off in search of Anne's next marker. So far the Queen left them concealed within a painting, tucked in a hidden compartment, and buried under a rock. Perhaps he should look for a painting once again.

Portraits and landscapes stretched out on all sides, two and three high. Smaller canvases hung closer to the floor, while the larger portraits, and some were much larger, sat above. Period tables and furniture hugged the long walls, and one of these first grabbed his eye.

A weathered bureau, elegant lines and polished wood, with only a few drawers. Nice, but not remarkable except for the plaque hanging above it stating this particular piece belonged to Charles Butler. One drawer sat open, an inkwell and quill inside. Given Anne secreted her first clue in a hidden drawer at Blarney Castle, why not a writing desk now?

No guards in sight, so the top drawer rattled open.

To reveal nothing, not even dust. Felt-lined and immaculate, without cracks or tiny fissures to be found. Pulling it completely out, the underside proved to be as solid as the rest of it.

Four additional drawers offered more of the same, and only when he noticed Erika glaring at him did he move on.

Glancing above the unpleasantly sturdy furniture, a familiar face cast her gaze about the room.

Queen Anne, heavy brush strokes surrounding her soft features, the husband at her side no more than an afterthought.

Was this the next clue?

"Erika." She rushed over when he nodded toward the painting. "Look who I found."

"This painting is from 1699, a year before her son was kidnapped. It's dated in the corner."

He marched on, undeterred. One down, a hundred others to inspect. You can't be right all the time.

Thirty minutes later he stood at the far end of the massive room, out of paintings to inspect. Several had grabbed him, all of Anne, but none with anything to offer. Another set of table and chairs belonged to the Queen, but Parker's spirited inspection revealed they were rock solid and completely devoid of any secret compartments or clues.

"Excuse me, sir?"

A porter stood behind him. "Yes?" Parker said.

She must have seen me trying to tear apart the table.

"Please begin to make your way to the exit. The castle will be closing in ten minutes."

The lady moved on with nothing more than a smile, repeating her message to the next person she saw, the only other person left in the gallery.

"We certainly will," Erika said. The attendant nodded and walked out, leaving them alone.

"I didn't find anything," Parker said. "We need to find a hotel and come back tomorrow." After desecrating a national treasure in Waterford and narrowly escaping a car full of armed villains, he needed a break.

Get some food and shuteye, and come back tomorrow with a clear head. Jet lag and adrenaline crashes didn't mix well. With how he felt, Parker could easily miss the next clue, could walk right past it.

"Let's get out of here." Halfway toward the exit, Parker had the distinct sensation he traveled alone. Erika had vanished.

Scratch that. She'd run to a darkened corner, partially hidden behind a pillar.

"Erika, we have to leave."

With an outstretched finger, she beckoned him to join her.

"This better be good," he said, grumbling as he walked.

Only when he rounded the pillar did he realize she'd found another room. Not a room, really, but an alcove. And inside, softly lit by recessed spotlights, another painting.

"That's Queen Anne," Parker said. "And I'll bet you that's Prince William on the lawn behind her."

"Two points for you," Erika replied. "Why didn't you see this before?"

He must have walked right past it. "This is a poor place to hang a painting. It's practically hidden behind that massive plank." Parker pointed at the beam. "I'm surprised you spotted it."

"Do you recognize where Anne is standing?"

Modest in size, the painting measured less than five feet tall and half as wide. Anne stood in front of a two-tiered set of stone steps, steps Parker knew at once.

"That's outside, in front of the castle."

"Those steps lead to the main entrance we walked through earlier," Erika said. "And that's Kilkenny Castle behind her."

Luscious green grass stretched on either side of the steps, and on this colorful carpet a young boy ran, brown hair fluttering in the breeze.

"I can't recall anything about Prince William joining Anne on a trip to Ireland," Erika said, arms crossed. "And William is her only child to survive infancy. So I'd say you're right about the Prince. But that begs another question. Why is he in this painting?"

"This isn't just a painting. It's the next stop on Anne's journey."

"What does it mean?"

Closed on three sides, the alcove had a single exit back into the towering hall. Behind them, an enormous floor-to-ceiling window looked over a grassy patch of land between two wings, the stone walls no more than fifty feet away.

"I'll take photos of this, and when we come back tomorrow we might have a better idea of her message." Parker used his phone to capture the aged brush strokes, paint he hoped contained the next clue. "Ready?"

Erika gazed at the portrait, chewing her lower lip. "We're not leaving."

"Why not?"

Hands on her hips, she turned to face him. "We can't take the risk that whoever came after us in Waterford is still on our tail. We need to figure this out *now*."

"A sentiment I agree with wholeheartedly, but that's impossible." He knew how Erika got when an idea took hold. Only a fool tried to change her mind. "The castle is closing, and they're not going to let us stick around to investigate."

"Who said anything about asking?" One corner of her mouth bent up. Without another word, Erika grabbed the painting and leaned it against the wall.

Why not? "Better than getting killed," he said. "Try not to break it."

"Stop being such a worrywart," Erika said, hands running along the rear of the canvas. "It's not alarmed, and there aren't any cameras back here."

She flipped the framed painting around to the blank rear side, just a length of scratchy canvas.

"Other than Prince William, I didn't notice anything unusual in the painting itself," Erika said, poking and prodding the frame. "No writing, or anything unusual in the background."

Parker took a deep breath. Too late now. A glance around the corner revealed no guards or other tourists.

"This is a terrible idea." Bargaining might work here. "However, if you promise to put that back on the wall, I'll humor you."

"Agreed," she said. "Please go on."

He didn't believe her for a second.

"I didn't see anything unusual in the painting either. Nothing in the woods, on the grounds or the castle itself." Parker studied the high-resolution snapshots on his phone. "My guess is the same as yours, that William is the clue, hidden in plain sight."

Erika nodded, and stuck her hand out. "Keys. Now."

Only once they jangled into her hand did he realize.

"No, Erika. This is too far. We can't un-damage that painting."

"Think about it. Anne already hid one message in a painting, and if William is the next marker, where else would it be? I've seen enough artifacts to know this canvas is original. In all likelihood, everything about this picture other than the hook on the back is too."

And with that, the key turned into a knife, ripping through the canvas.

"If I'm wrong, all we do is hang it back on the wall. I'm only cutting open the *rear* portion. No one will know until we're gone."

Given she'd already damaged another Irish national treasure today, Parker shrugged. "Hurry up."

Tearing canvas reverberated off the ceiling. Parker tore his eyes away and leaned around the corner, again finding it empty.

When he looked back, a jagged tear ran down the backing. Erika slit the three remaining sides, and set the ragged fabric aside. Dim light did little to illuminate the murky interior behind the canvas, all of it lost in the dusty depths.

"Give me your phone," Erika said, and a steady beam of light flooded their small corner of the hall.

Erika shifted the portrait, white dust blooming like a cloud, particles dancing in the light. Once the haze cleared, Parker hovered over her shoulder, curiosity getting the better of him.

"It looks like… nothing."

Unless Queen Anne used invisible ink, the rear side of this painting contained nothing more than centuries-old dust.

"No obvious writing, though that isn't conclusive. William's disappearance pre-dates Anne's visit to Kilkenny, her only holiday in Ireland. There's no logical reason for him to be in here other than to draw our attention."

"Erika, think about it. The painting is hundreds of years old. The dating may easily be off by a few years. Even if it's not, who knows why William is in it? Maybe the artist wanted to make Anne happy, or to ease her heartache. There are a hundred reasons why this painting isn't Anne's next clue, none of which we have time to investigate right now." They'd tempted fate long enough. "Hang it on the wall and let's go."

If he didn't make her leave, she'd stay here until security showed up. They'd damaged enough Irish history for one day.

"But why would William be here? It's the only reason that…"

Her voice trailed off. Parker peered around the corner, expecting to find trouble bearing down.

"Erika, stop messing around. Hang it on—"

"Look at this."

Low, soft, he barely heard it. Like someone stole the air from her lungs. Parker turned and found her hunched over the painting.

"There's a patch on here. And it's very, very old."

A piece of canvas, the same color and texture as the rest of the backing, pasted on the rear. From a few steps back it looked identical, but a closer look revealed the patch didn't match exactly.

"Is that a repair?"

"No," Erika said. "Because," she flipped the painting around, "if it was, you'd see it on the front. Even the best ones aren't invisible, and with a piece this old, perfectly blending the original and new paint is impossible."

"Then what is it?"

Erika grabbed one corner of the patch and pulled. At this rate they'd be breaking apart the Blarney Stone by mid-week.

The patch held fast. And then without warning, the entire piece ripped away in a flash, the noise like buttons popping from a shirt. Parker didn't even bother looking around. If the castle staff showed up now, they were toast.

"Is that—"

"*Writing*," Erika said.

Concealed words emerged into daylight, the black ink, haggard and misshapen on the rough surface.

Shadows played across the letters as Erika read a centuries-old plea.

Dearest Laurence,

William is just beyond my grasp, his Irish captors only days ahead of me as I follow their warm trail. I learned from the villagers that Irish brigands traveled through Kilkenny less than a week ago. A young boy was in their company, fair of skin with flowing hair and hazel eyes.

It can only be William, forced along this treacherous path by his captors! Laurence, please hurry, and trust no one. This struggle for Irish independence turns brother against brother, a reprise of the dark O'Carroll legacy known so well in this land. Seek guidance from our holy father that you will not tarry in your quest, for the Bloody Chapel awaits, and William cannot be left in this place forgotten.

Parker spotted more ink beneath the writing.

"At the bottom, what is that? It looks like a design."

A circular mark in place of the signature. Intricate lines filled the interior, dividing it into four quadrants.

"It's a shield design," Erika said.

Shield.

"A coat of arms."

"That's a harp in the lower left," Erika said. "With three birds above it. No, those aren't birds. They look more like lions."

"The Three Lions. England's coat of arms."

Erika glanced up. "How do you know that?"

"You weren't the only person paying attention in history class," he said with a wink. "Plus that's the English national soccer team's name."

"Watching sports finally pays off. You're correct. This is the Royal coat of arms.

Confirmation Anne wrote this message."

A door slammed behind them, shattering the quiet.

"Quick, take a picture of this."

Parker snapped away before Erika re-hung the portrait. The canvas she'd ripped free went into a trash can, and Parker rounded the corner, an excuse on his lips. Except the hall stood empty. "Must have been down the hall," Parker said as they started jogging toward the exit.

"We still have five minutes," Erika tapped her watch. "Let's find a hotel and get to work on this next clue."

"First we get away from here. Then we worry about that."

Around a corner, they headed toward the exit, one wing ahead.

"What's that noise?" Erika asked.

Soft at first, so faint he scarcely heard it, a heavy mechanical thumping grew in volume. Parker knew what kind of bird flew on those beating wings.

"It's a helicopter."

"And it's coming here," Erika said.

She pointed through a window, and his stomach twisted.

Grass flattened in all directions as the metallic beast settled, branches shaking and dust flying. A moment after the skids touched, the cockpit flew open and two men exited, bent low beneath the twirling rotors.

"Look at the door," Parker said. "That's a military transport. Keep your head down and *move*."

Running through the next hall, the exit lay just ahead. Several porters gathered around the door, pointing at the strange sight on their front lawn. A trio of visitors stood near the reception desk, chatting with the attendant. One of them looked their way, face hidden under a ball cap.

Then the two helicopter men walked through the front door.

Something isn't right.

"Hold on." He grabbed Erika's shoulder. "Let's hang back for a second. No need to rush out right now."

As they ducked behind a wall, Parker noticed that the three men talking to the receptionist moments earlier had vanished. The one with the hat on had taken an interest in him, more than a casual glance. Almost like the guy recognized him. Which was impossible. He needed to chill, not get paranoid.

"What's going on?" Erika asked. Hidden behind a thick column, she couldn't see anything.

"I'm not sure. The staff is looking at something the helicopter guys gave them." Parker leaned around further, squinting. "It looks like a picture of two people, but I can't... uh-oh."

He recognized that porter. The one who told them closing time was coming not ten minutes ago, and how one wrinkled finger pointed toward the picture gallery wing. The same wing where Queen Anne's desecrated portrait hung.

"Move it," he said. "They're headed this way."

"What happened?" Erika demanded as he propelled her deeper into the castle.

"I think those helicopter guys are showing the staff our pictures."

"*What?*"

"Quiet," he said. No one chased them, at least not yet. "We need to worry about escaping first."

Which, despite the countless halls and alcoves they passed, proved difficult. Though the place had literally hundreds of doors, the only ones leading outside all had alarms.

As they passed yet another corridor, she pulled him close. "Both of the helicopter guys are coming this way."

So far the path he'd taken led toward the Butler Gallery, but a directional sign overhead sparked an idea.

"This way."

Now moving away from Anne's painting, he raced for the castle's rear. If those two men truly were after them, perhaps he and Erika could exit through the rear, circle around the grounds and get to their Land Rover.

A corridor appeared ahead, hard to see in the gloomy castle. Most of the lights weren't on yet, and with the sun dropping so quickly, the castle's interior grew darker by the minute.

"This leads to the rear. If we can get—"

A man grabbed Parker, pulling him into the black archway and silencing his cries.

Chapter 22

Kilkenny, Ireland

A military helicopter on Kilkenny Castle's front lawn. Gavin Rooney didn't need to see the passengers to know who it carried. Only one man had both a reason and the pull to make this happen.

Chief Keeper Logan Rose. The man in charge.

After narrowly avoiding the massive crash on the M9, Gavin and his team headed straight to Kilkenny Castle, spotting the American's Land Rover as soon as they pulled in. Gavin decided on a passive approach, first checking for any unexpected threats lurking in the castle depths before moving in. The site closed soon, so he'd just as soon let Parker and Erika come to them.

However, it wasn't long until repeated protests about "sitting on our bloody arses" convinced Gavin it was only a matter of time before the Keepers showed up, so he went against his better judgment and headed inside.

A baseball cap tucked over his eyes, Gavin chatted with a guide when a muted thumping began beating the roughly-hewn walls. What the hell was he going to do now? Logan Rose wouldn't recognize him, but with the Englishman around this operation got complicated in a hurry.

A man locked eyes with him from across the castle's cavernous entryway. Backed under a doorway, dim interior light cast his face in shadows. Wait a second. He looked to be the right age...

When the guy stepped back and headed deeper into the castle, a shaft of light flitted across his features.

"Come on," Gavin said. "I found them."

Brin and Harry fell into step. "Where are they headed?" Harry asked, head down as they passed under a security camera, a network the Keepers could access within minutes.

"That way," Gavin pointed down the hallway. "Can we loop around and cut them off?"

Brin eyed a map on the wall, took the lead and a hard right. "This passage runs parallel to them."

Imposing wooden doors passed on either side, black with age. Past several corridors and then he stopped.

"Hold still," he said, back flat against the wall in a short hallway. A pair of electric lights shaped as medieval torches offered only the faintest hint of illumination.

Brin glanced around the corner, jerking back as though hot air filled the corridor, fingers flashing back and forth.

Two people coming. Brin takes the first one, Harry the second.

An instant later, Parker Chase appeared, Erika Carr a step behind.

Scrambling and cursing, Parker fell into the gloom, Erika following without a sound.

"Easy," Gavin said, one hand on Parker's mouth. "Be quiet. We're here to help you."

The American ceased struggling, his chest heaving.

"Don't make any noise." Parker nodded and was set free. Beside him, Erika darted free, Harry jumping out of range to avoid her fists.

"Who the—"

"Keep your voice down," Gavin said. *A lot of fight in this girl.* "Follow us, and we might make it out of here."

"Not until you tell us what the hell is going on." Arms crossed, feet planted like trees in the stone floor, Erika dared them to challenge her.

Gavin glanced over and his mates shrugged. *May as well be straight with these two.*

"We're a field team for the Irish Republican Army. We followed you from Blarney Castle. The man who just landed outside is Chief Keeper Logan Rose, and I suspect he's here to kill you."

"Nice work on that Keeper in the stables," Brin said.

"I didn't try to do that," Erika said. "The horse kicked him."

Parker Chase spoke up. "Why are you following us? And how do you know who we are?"

"You have Erika's friend to thank for that," Gavin said. "The art professor who died this morning emailed Erika about a letter she found in a painting. The Keepers intercepted that email, killed your friend, and now they're after you. Or to be precise, after the letter."

"And how do you know all this if you don't work for them?" Erika asked.

Gavin cracked a wry grin. "Excellent question. The Keeper you killed, we hacked into his phone. They killed your friend, not us. My superiors gave two directives; keep you safe and find out why that letter has the Englishmen up in arms. So if you don't mind," he peered around the corner and found an empty hallway. "We need to leave."

Erika reached over, and without taking his eyes off Gavin, Parker took her hand. "First, how do we get out of here?" Parker asked. "And second, what the hell is a Keeper?"

"We're working on the first one," Brin said, leading the way. "Follow me, and once we get out I'll explain everything."

Gavin brought up the rear, and they soon found themselves in a long hallway, portraits and displays on either side, ribs of wood supporting the sloped ceiling overhead.

"There are doors at the far end, but they're locked," Parker said. "We found... we were in here earlier."

The look on Erika's face would melt steel.

What did Parker find here?

"We'll see about that," Brin said, pistol in hand. Even in soft whispers, their voices bounced off the plaster walls and marble floors, echoes too easily followed.

Through the cavernous hall, Erika led them into a small alcove where French doors stopped their progress, thick glass plates set in modern steel frames. Gavin turned around and looked up at Queen Anne, her portrait set against the majestic backdrop of Kilkenny Castle.

The doors rattled. "Shut tight," Brin said. "Take a step back, please. This might get messy."

Brin smashed his gun against the glass door, the heavy metal handle bouncing off with barely a sound.

"Damn, that is thick." The gun bounced off again with the same result. Not even a scratch.

"The hell with this. Take cover."

Gavin scarcely pulled the Americans to safety before Brin fired, a cannon blast in the confined space. Gavin peered through the haze.

"It's bulletproof," he said. "Bloody hell, why does this castle have bulletproof doors?"

"Do you have any idea how much these paintings are worth?" Erika asked. "You're foolish to believe that locked doors keep thieves away."

"I don't give a damn about the paintings," Brin said, walking to another pair of doors. "We need to get out of here before—"

Sparks rained on his head. Supersonic metal pierced the air, bullets bouncing off the thoroughly bulletproof windows. Across the hall, two Keepers raced toward them, guns out and firing.

Plaster dust coated Gavin as he ran for cover. Crouched low behind a corner, he returned fire along with Brin and Harry, their bullets sending the two Keepers behind a thick stone bench.

"Is it the pilot and Chief Keeper?" Brin asked, still firing as he ducked behind Gavin.

"Damn right," Gavin said. "And you know what that means. Where there's one of those bastards –"

"There's another," Harry finished.

Surrounded by stone walls with no exit in sight. Only another set of those damn bulletproof glass doors, and a wide stairway leading to parts unknown. Renewed Keeper fire cracked the walls and sent shards flying. No sense in staying here to die.

"Up the stairs."

"Do you have any idea where you're going?" Parker asked.

"Away from here," Gavin said. "Those have to lead somewhere."

"Were there only two men in that helicopter?" Erika asked.

"That's right. The pair trying to blow our damn heads off," Harry said. He glanced around the corner, and two shots sent him scurrying back into the dead-end hallway. "Those stone benches are along every wall and they're perfect cover for them to keep moving."

"Then as long as we keep running, we'll stay ahead of them," Erika said, one foot on the first step. "No one else is here to trap us."

"For now," Gavin said. He liked the way her mind worked. "Though you know they'll have back-up on the way."

A renewed barrage gave the Keepers something to think about, and then everyone darted up the wide staircase, scattered lights casting lengthy shadows ahead. Gavin bolted down the narrow hallway at full speed. They couldn't stop, not after they'd started to run. If the Keepers crested those stairs now, the hallway turned into a shooting gallery, and they were the targets.

Past a drawing room and a library, they stepped ahead in time several hundred years, running past newer rooms, the modern architecture in stark contrast with the medieval designs found one level below.

The hallway ended, branching off in either direction. Gavin never slowed, taking the left corridor. Stairs lay ahead, leading up.

Except they needed to go down. Gavin hit the brakes, only to have Erika bounce off his back, and then Parker slam into her. "Sorry," Gavin said. "We need to go down."

Brin and Harry rumbled down stone steps, Gavin raced after them, pistol tucked in his coat. Parker flew past the intersection, dragging Erika as he ran. Wind rushing past his ears in the eerily silent halls, Gavin glanced down the central hallway for any signs of pursuit.

Two men were at the top of the stairs, guns in hand. Both fired.

Snowflakes of plaster filled the air as the bullets whizzed past, so close he could *feel* their force. Gavin didn't bother shooting back. He just ran.

Down the curving stairs, Gavin urged the Americans to follow. Standing at the top, he looked behind them.

The Keepers appeared, guns blazing.

Bullets vibrated the air around him, gouging the walls and floor. Gavin didn't bother shooting back.

Down the curving stairs, Gavin followed the Americans, twisting and leaning until they spilled into a wide room where towering tapestries stretched from floor to ceiling.

"The front exit's this way," Brin said. "If we get on the road before those Keepers get airborne, they'll have a hard time spotting us in traffic."

Past the brooding portraits and detailed battle scenes they ran, marble fireplaces on either side, beyond which the front entrance waited. As Gavin made it to the entryway, a bullet shattered the stones beneath his feet.

On either side of the front door, employees cowered in fear, hands covering their faces. A woman shrieked when Harry burst into the room, gun at the ready.

"Stay down," he said. In an instant, quivering staff lay flat on the floor. Harry raced to the front door and ripped on the handle.

The door didn't budge.

"Keys. Who has the keys?"

"Here they are." A head appeared from behind the reception desk, tufts of gray sprouting from beneath a tweed cap. "It locks automatically after closing hour."

Gavin grabbed them and tossed the jingling set to Harry. "Sorry about all this. We'll be out of your hair soon."

Gavin's Irish lilt matched that of the keyholder, and the lines on his aged face deepened for a beat. "You're not English," the man said. "The helicopter pilot was English."

"No, sir. That's who's after us."

"Then Godspeed." Like the sun slipping from behind a turbulent sky, a thin smile pierced the old man's cragged features. "Keep 'em. It'll lock behind you."

Bullets whistled into the room, stone shards flying, and every head vanished once more.

"Might want to hurry," Brin said, returning fire.

"Got it." Harry whipped the door open, arm windmilling. "Everybody out."

Parker and Erika ran past as Gavin wedged it open with his foot.

"Get the car and come back for us," he told Harry. "We'll hold them off."

Harry's feet churned as he bounded down the wide steps outside, headed for the distant parking lot. Once he returned, Gavin planned on visiting the helicopter to empty his weapon into the controls grounding the Keepers.

Across the room, Brin poked his head around the stone archway. A bullet smacked beside him, blood flowing from above one eye.

"Just a scratch," Brin said. "They're holed up behind the fireplaces, one on each side. I can't get a clean shot."

Gavin risked a glance. In the room through which they'd come. Thick pillars framed each fireplace, more than wide enough to offer cover. A pistol appeared from behind one and fired twice.

Gavin ducked out of sight. "Harry's getting the car and swinging round for us. I'll put that helicopter out of order before we go. If we beat the other Keepers to the highway, we'll be in the clear."

"How much ammo do you have?" Brin asked.

Gavin tapped his pocket. "Full mag. Never leave home without it."

"Unload the rest, and I'll take the pilot out. Unless Chief Keeper Rose knows how to fly, he's stuck."

Even under fire, Brin never stopped thinking. "Ready?"

Brin nodded, loosing a shot, and Gavin swung around the archway, firing until the hammer fell with a soft *click*. Stepping back, he watched Brin eye his target.

For a few beats, nothing. Then Brin fired twice.

A muffled curse followed. Something metallic clattered across the stone floor. Gavin leaned out to see the pilot lying in plain view, his gun out of reach.

"He's done. Two in the chest."

"Nice work," Gavin said, looking through a window at Harry ripping through the manicured lawn. Chunks of thick grass and rich soil flew as he skidded to a halt, destroying some very nice rose bushes in the process.

Gavin reloaded and kept firing, forcing Logan Rose to take cover.

"Let's go." Once Brin made it outside and Gavin shut the door, the Chief Warder would be locked inside.

He turned as Brin stepped from behind the archway. Crimson sunlight spilled through the front door, warm on his skin. He stepped back so Brin could pass.

Only he never made it. Halfway across the room, he stopped moving. Arms akimbo, Brin stood still, his face eerily calm. Red seeped onto his shirt as Brin stood, suspended in time. And then twisted violently when a third shot slammed home.

No.

Gavin raced to him, shooting aimlessly. The incoming fire ceased, Gavin dragging him to cover.

"Come on, Brin. Let's go." Shaking him, slapping his face.

It was too late.

Kneeling with Brin held in his two numb arms, the silence surrounding them fell apart.

The Chief Keeper, firing again. With a final glance at his fallen mate, Gavin gained his feet and took aim.

Rose must not have seen him, because he walked right out. The first shot winged his shoulder, spinning him around. Gavin's second shot missed by inches.

The Chief Keeper hit the ground and rolled, slipping behind a wooden desk and out of sight. Gavin hesitated a second too long. Vengeance would have to wait.

Iron dragging his heart down, he bent to one knee and touched Brin's bloody forehead. "Until we meet again, my friend."

And then he ran, the castle door slamming shut behind him. Sparks flew and smoke filled the helicopter when he emptied his gun into the control panel. *That should slow the Keepers down.*

As Gavin jumped into their car, Harry looked back, his face ashen.

"Is he—"

"Yes."

No one spoke as Harry slammed the accelerator, tearing through the grass and down Kilkenny's entranceway, the rear seat one passenger short.

Chapter 23

Inside the locked front door of Kilkenny Castle, Logan Rose ignored the bullet in his shoulder. He'd been shot before.

The dark sedan sped away, taking with it any hope of finishing his mission.

These damn Irish.

Stuck here with a dead pilot while those terrorists escaped with the Americans. Given that Dr. Carr and her companion made it this far, they were capable of following the trail to its end.

"I need a phone."

Once his government credentials came out, everyone stopped looking at him like a potential terrorist and started cooperating.

Logan dialed the home office in London. "This is Rose," he said. "What's the status on my backup?"

"A team should be on site within fifteen minutes, sir."

"Too bloody slow." Logan gave a description of the sedan, though with their head start, it wasn't much use. With no air support, the chances of locating a dark-colored sedan were practically nil. Especially when his only lead lay cooling on the stone floor.

With his pilot dead, Rose had found himself trapped behind the fireplace pillar with nowhere to run and no chance of surviving a full-on assault if the enemy came after him. But a non-stop barrage of fire gave him a chance. Such a blatant waste of ammunition meant they were making a run for it. Once the withering storm ceased, Logan lined up his shot, anticipating the mad dash. He killed one of them, and nearly sealed his fate in the process when he foolishly ventured into view and took one in the shoulder.

Lesson learned. Now he needed to figure out who the three men were, the ones helping the Americans.

"My colleagues are arriving shortly," Logan told the castle staff. "That door needs to be open by then."

Amid a flurry of activity, no one else ventured close to the corpse Logan knelt beside. Red hair, skin fearful of the sun, the hallmarks of an Irishman. If it weren't for the two ragged holes in his chest, the man could be napping.

Logan's hand first went to the front pockets, finding his cell phone. In the rear pockets he uncovered a few hundred pounds, but no wallet. Nothing to identify him, where he lived, or why he died in Kilkenny Castle shooting at a senior member of Her Majesty's government. As expected, the phone didn't contain a single shred of information.

No identification, a brand-new phone, and a Sig Sauer P229. Exactly what Logan carried. Which begged the question of who stood between him and the Americans? And why?

The answer to his first question lay in the second. Other than Logan Rose and Warder Oliver Moore, no Keepers knew the true story about Prince William. In fact, only one other organization could possibly know.

The Irish Republican Army.

Though they weren't called that at the time, Rose strongly believed the men who conspired to capture and release Prince William in exchange for Ireland's independence never faded entirely, carrying on their efforts through successive generations and various incarnations, all of which led to the current group of terrorists hell-bent on securing the Emerald Isle's independence from British rule. And lying at his feet, the latest fair-skinned lad in a long line of Irishmen to give their lives for the cause.

To Logan, they were criminals, every last one.

"Sir, we've disarmed the locks." The frantic castle employee returned, his mission a success. "The front door is open."

"Have all the employees wait outside. We'll need to interview everyone. This is a crime scene."

The man turned, herded his fellow workers outside. Freeing Logan to make a call.

"Oliver, it's Rose."

"The men will arrive at any moment, sir."

"Not important. I need your help. I got one of them, IRA from the looks of it. I'll send you a head shot and fingerprint scan when our team arrives. I want you to handle this personally. Search the Interpol and Garda Siochana databases, and run it through our internal programs as well. Even if he doesn't have a record with Interpol, the Irish police may have him on file for non-criminal activities. If not, let's hope we've identified him as a suspected militant in the past."

Her Majesty's government cast a wide net in regards to categorizing and logging information about anyone suspected of affiliating with the IRA, both guilty and innocent alike. At times like this, Logan appreciated the overzealous pursuit, and more importantly, his unfettered access to these terabytes of information.

"I'll handle it," Oliver said. "A new pilot is en route. He'll fly you back to London immediately."

"I have another destination in mind. If you confirm the man I shot is affiliated with the IRA, contact our friends at the BBC. A terrorist attack is something people should know about."

"Understood."

If the IRA killed his pilot, a public pronouncement of their actions upped the pressure on the two now with the Americans, cutting off resources and tightening his net.

From outside the castle door, a medley of blaring horns and slamming doors heralded the reinforcements arrival. Guns drawn, the cavalry stormed the castle entrance.

A uniformed policeman approached. "Chief Warder, are you injured?"

"I'm fine," he said. "Lock down and process this scene. My associate, a man named Oliver Moore, will supervise remotely. Contact him at this number," Logan said, handing over a business card. "Have him linked to view your progress. A British government official is dead, and this crime scene is under my control until further notice." When you had the Queen's ear, things like jurisdiction weren't a problem. A phone call on his way over to the Minister for Defense assured all courtesies were extended to Logan and his men. Now, to more important matters. "Where's my pilot?"

From behind the grizzled veteran emerged what appeared to be his newest recruit.

"Lieutenant Gruver, sir!"

Logan's eyes pinched nearly shut. "How much flying experience do you have?"

"Graduated from flight school three weeks ago, sir."

I have boots older than this kid.

"Prep my bird for immediate departure. I'll be outside in twenty."

Gruver darted outside. Given he stood hours from the nearest true city, a go-getter like Gruver probably wasn't so bad. Even if he didn't have to shave yet.

Approaching the front desk, Logan said, "I need your security tapes."

"Heather can help," the attendant said, nodding to a pale girl beside him. Heather looked like she could use a little sunlight.

"I handle electronics, sir. Our camera system is mostly on the ground floor."

"See him?" Logan indicated the corpse. "I want to see every step he and his associates took in this castle. Now."

Looking as though she found Logan rather frightening, Heather scurried deeper into the castle. She passed through an arched hallway, and then stopped at a narrow wooden door.

"We keep an eye on the castle in here," she said. Inside the surprisingly spacious room a dozen monitors flashed and flickered, each covering a different area of the castle.

"How many cameras do you have?"

"Thirty-six in all, the majority positioned near high-traffic areas."

Not bad for a small town. "Start with the main entrance, two hours ago."

Heather fiddled with a dial, tapping the keyboard. "Let's see. Two hours ago, right here."

On the central monitor, Logan found a bird's-eye view of the entranceway. A trickle of people moved in and out, but not the Americans.

"Speed it up." Digital figures jumped across the screen as a clock spun rapidly.

"Stop. Those two." He tapped the screen where Parker Chase and Erika Carr stood frozen. "Show me where they went."

Heather took Logan on a high-level tour of the castle, following the pair. Through several display rooms and down a long hallway, they eventually emerged in the towering hall where Logan's pilot first fired at them. As if he stood a chance in hell of hitting them from across the room.

"We don't have any cameras in that alcove," Heather told him as they watched the footage.

Parker and Erika disappeared into a secluded corner of the room, out of sight, their shadows moving while they remained hidden.

"What's back there?"

"A portrait of Queen Anne in front of this castle."

Of course.

Rose bolted back through the crime scene, his footsteps echoing across the cavernous hall before Heather caught up, huffing and puffing. "Is anything wrong?"

"I need to see that alcove."

Around a corner, and Logan came face to painted face with a very old, dark, and above all uninteresting painting of Anne. Well done, yes, and certainly a part of Ireland's storied past, nothing about it seemed worth two men dying.

"Heather, is this work alarmed?"

"No. Only a few items in our castle have that level of security."

Just what he wanted to hear.

"I need to speak with whoever handles artifact preservation."

She scampered off. As soon as she rounded the corner, he grabbed the painting. What did Dr. Carr see? The front revealed nothing more than aged paint. And then he flipped it around.

Now that's more like it.

A short paragraph, the letters haggard yet elegant, written in the flowing script of a bygone era. The handwriting, Logan knew, of a queen.

He snapped a picture, re-hung the painting and headed toward where his helicopter waited.

Bloody Chapel?

Logan didn't need centuries-old intelligence reports to know where to find the Americans.

Amid the controlled chaos, Logan grabbed the local police chief. "Have Heather show you the painting of Queen Anne, and take it into evidence immediately."

Through the now-open castle door, Logan stopped when he found his new pilot waiting outside. Whatever enthusiasm this new flyboy displayed earlier had vanished.

"Ready to leave, Lieutenant?"

"Bad news, sir. The cockpit controls have been rendered inoperable, because somebody put a half-dozen bullets in them."

Adapt and move on. That's how you played this game. "Secure the fastest vehicle on the premises, Lieutenant. You're now my driver."

The kid snapped off another skull-rattling salute before racing away. If he drove half as fast as he ran, the two Americans and their newfound Irish protectors were in trouble.

Chapter 24

North of Durrow, Ireland

Surrounded by empty countryside, running under a star-filled sky the dark sedan kept to the speed limit. The two Irishmen in the front stared at nothing. In the rear, the pair of American tourists pondered a long-awaited vacation turned deadly.

Quite a few miles passed before Erika's impatience boiled over. A foot smashed Parker's leg, her blazing eyes conveying in no uncertain terms that he better speak up or he'd be sorry. The two up front may be armed, but Parker knew bullets weren't the most dangerous thing in this car.

"Listen," Parker said, "I'm not sure why you're doing it, but thanks for helping us. I have no idea why anyone is interested in that email, but I'm guessing you do."

No response. "Care to tell us just how deep we're in it?"

Face hidden under a baseball cap in the passenger seat, the one Parker assumed to be the leader tapped the armrest, a staccato beat rolling like a horse down the track.

"My name is Gavin. This," he pointed to the driver, "is Harry. The two shooters at Kilkenny were Keepers, agents of the crown who handle the dirtier aspects of governing the U.K. The one who survived is the Chief Keeper, a man named Logan Rose. I'm guessing you two never saw him before today?"

"Never," Parker said. "Maybe I'm missing something, but why does the British government want to kill us over an email?"

"An email?" Gavin said, turning to face them. "A simple email doesn't send you two running all over Ireland, does it? I've been straight with you, Parker Chase. Return the favor."

Parker glanced at Erika. *Why don't you take this?*

104

She took the hint. "Michelle was an art historian specializing in restoration. We're here on vacation, but when we arrived at her apartment, the police told us she'd been killed. I didn't read the email until after I knew about her murder." Erika paused, glanced at Parker. "You're not going to believe what it contained."

"Try me."

"Michelle was restoring a painting of Queen Anne. Inside the painting she found a letter written by Anne discussing the alleged death of her son, Prince William."

Parker noted Harry stiffen.

"According to the letter, which Michelle believed to be genuine, Prince William did not die of disease as history tells us. A group of Irishmen kidnapped him for use as a bargaining chip to secure Irish independence. Anne claimed her Protestant cousin George suppressed the truth in order to steal the throne. His plan worked well, as he became George I. Which doesn't happen if Prince William is alive."

"And how the hell did George keep this quiet?" Harry asked. "She's the Queen of England, for God's sake."

"A Catholic Queen without a male heir," Erika said. "And an unprecedented groundswell of support for Protestantism existed at the time."

"An interesting story, Dr. Carr." Gavin fingered a pendant around his neck as she spoke. "Harry raises a valid point. Unless George has a small army at his disposal, keeping Anne quiet is impossible."

"He had one better than that," Erika said. "He controlled one of the world's most elite military squadrons. Men you should know. The Yeoman Warders."

"The Beefies?" Harry said. "You're a loon, miss. Those buggers *worked* for the Queen. Plus," he looked back, "they're closer than you think."

"A lame-duck queen if there ever was one," Erika said. "Think about it. Her only son is supposedly dead. George has the public behind him. If you're a Beefeater, what would you do? Support Anne and find yourself in a shallow grave once the dust settled, or keep your mouth shut and follow orders from your soon-to-be-boss? If George instructed the Beefeaters to transition from champions to captors, you don't argue."

Erika may be fired up, but Parker didn't miss what Harry had said. "What do you mean? Who's closer than we realize?"

"The men trying to kill you are only one step removed from the

Beefeaters of whom you speak," Gavin said. "In fact, the men who originally kept the Queen under surveillance, the Yeoman Warders, eventually became the Keepers we speak of."

"So the Tower of London guards are really a hit squad for the U.K. government?"

"No," Gavin said. "But they're much more like their Beefeater forefathers than the ones who prance around in tall hats today. The original Beefeaters were true soldiers. Killers who protected the realm at all costs. Over time, the two groups split, and today Keepers handle lethal enforcement, while the Beefeaters are more for show."

"And how do you know this?" Erika asked.

"Suffice it to say the IRA has a long history with the Yeoman Warders and Keepers both." Gavin said, studying the darkness outside.

"So about George and the Beefies," Harry said. "You're telling me they kept the Queen under control until she died?"

"It's better than that," Erika said. "Anne mounted a search for her kidnapped son, but George undercut her when he sent the Yeoman Warders to spy on her. Watched every minute, Anne sent a letter to the only person she trusted. Her uncle, Laurence Hyde."

"The Lord Lieutenant of Ireland. The highest-ranking British official on Irish soil," Gavin said.

Harry cocked an eyebrow. "How in the name of St. Patrick did you know that?"

Something made Parker reach out, his hand brushing against Erika's thigh, keeping her reply on the tip of her tongue.

"Harry, there are certain… aspects of our organization of which you are unaware," Gavin said. "Do you remember earlier today when the Quartermaster told us about Waterford?"

"Sounded like he was about to tell a story, but then we see this Yank almost fall off the bloody building," Harry replied, nodding at Parker.

"That's right. What QM Whelan spoke about involves Queen Anne."

"So what the hell's going on, Gavin? Brin's dead, and if you think it's because of some legend and a dead queen, I'd like to know."

"It's not a legend. It's real, and it's back to haunt us."

"What's real?" Harry barked. "That story about the Prince being kidnapped?"

"Prince William," Gavin said. "And yes, it happened. The Irishmen who took him founded a group that became the IRA." Moonlight washed through the car as he spoke, soft shadows falling across Gavin's face. "You didn't know what your murdered friend sent you this morning," he said to Erika. "And neither did my team. I received a report that men working with the Keepers were killed this morning, and my team went to investigate. We didn't know the killings were related to one of our most closely-guarded secrets, or that the Keepers would go to such lengths to obtain this information."

Gavin wasn't explaining a part of the puzzle, and Parker didn't like it.

"How did you know what the email said?" Parker asked. "Erika didn't see the message until after we knew Michelle died, after the police interviewed us."

"Our organization is not without resources."

"No," Erika said, and Parker sat back. Gavin didn't know it, but this would not end well for him. "Granted, you saved our lives in Kilkenny Castle," she said. "Thank you for that. But that doesn't change the fact that my friend is dead and you're partially responsible. We're involved in this, with no choice in the matter. It's happened, and now you're stuck with us. If we're going to work together and stay alive, you have one option, and that's complete honesty."

A sigh escaped Gavin's lips. "As you wish. We discovered this information from an informant inside the Tower of London where the Keepers operate. Our Quartermaster learned of the email and subsequent deaths associated with your deceased colleague and sent us to investigate. The Keepers intercepted that email and they have the full weight of the British government behind them."

"What would draw their attention to that specific email?" Parker asked, though he had a good idea of the answer. "There must be *millions* of emails sent every minute of every day in Great Britain. Why would the Keepers be drawn to this specific one?"

"I assume that the contents caused a government tracking program to flag the message," Gavin replied. "What did it say?"

Erika passed her phone up to Gavin, Michelle's final message on display.

"My guess is they look for any mention of Queen Anne combined with Prince William, and filter messages as they're identified," Gavin said. "This fit their parameters."

"Hold on a second," Harry said, looking to Gavin. Parker noted his knuckles were white on the wheel. "You're telling me the Army began as kidnappers? How can you be sure?"

"There are several letters in our archives, scraps of paper really, discussing the plan. Only the QM and one other member know of their existence at all times. Mainly for security purposes, but also because if the story gets out, it's likely to be twisted and warped to fit an agenda. And then the truth vanishes."

"And you're the one other guy who knows?"

Gavin nodded, turning to face Erika. "I am. And until today, the only proof we had were those scribbles written centuries ago. Now everything's changed. Our founding patriots knew Queen Anne followed them through Ireland, and even mentioned it in their records, but never talked about a conspiracy within Anne's court to stop Anne from succeeding. No one in the IRA knew about George trying to steal the crown."

"So what happened to Prince William?" Erika asked.

Gavin shrugged. "No one knows. Nothing in our records indicate the Prince's ultimate fate. The last knowledge we have about their path with the prince ends at Kilkenny Castle. We suspect the Keepers may have their own records regarding these events, but as to what they say, your guess is as good as mine."

And with that Gavin fell silent. Erika glanced at Parker, the question on her lips visible only to him. Should they share what they'd found at Kilkenny Castle? Parker shrugged. One of these guys died to save them. They owed them one.

Erika agreed. "We know where the IRA took Prince William after leaving Kilkenny Castle."

Gavin spun around. "How?"

"Do you remember the alcove, where we tried to break the windows?" Gavin and Harry nodded. "The painting hanging there."

"Queen Anne," Gavin said. "What does it have to do with this?"

"That painting is the next step on a path laid out by Anne hundreds of years ago." Erika summarized their movements since receiving Michelle's email, beginning with the letter recovered from Michelle's office, to the hidden drawer at Blarney Castle and the destruction wrought upon Reginald Tower, finally ending with their discovery in Kilkenny Castle.

"First of all," Gavin said. "Thanks for sharing. You're the first people to uncover her trail, so kudos to you. But I must know, where does Anne's message point?"

"I'm glad you asked," Erika replied. Parker handed his phone to Gavin, displaying a snapshot of the hidden poem.

"O'Carroll's legacy… Bloody Chapel. Do you recognize these phrases?" Gavin asked.

"Not yet," Erika said. "I haven't done any research. I'm certain I'll unravel her clues given the proper resources."

"We can do you one better," Harry said. "There's little mystery to be had in those words, so long as you're asking an Irishman."

"Do you know what she's talking about?" Parker asked.

"Not only that, but I also know we're headed in the right direction," Harry said.

"Every Irish lad knows the story of the Bloody Chapel," Gavin said. "That dark room still stands to this day, a grim reminder perched atop Leap Castle of how power can corrupt even the closest of allies."

Alone on the highway, Harry nudged the speedometer above one hundred thirty kilometers per hour, which according to Parker's questionable estimate equated to eighty of the non-metric units. Apparently wherever they were going, they needed to get there fast.

"Where exactly is Leap Castle, and how do we get there?" Parker asked.

"West of Dublin," Gavin said. "About thirty minutes away."

The short distances between cities in Ireland relative to America amazed him. However, that meant the Keepers wouldn't be far behind.

"The Bloody Chapel got its name from a bitter dispute between two brothers in the O'Carroll clan, the family who built Leap Castle," Gavin said. "One of the brothers was a priest, and he presided over services in the castle chapel. One day, while he was preaching to his family flock, another O'Carroll brother crashed through the doors, sword in hand, and murdered his brother in front of their entire family."

"Talk about bad blood," Erika said.

"Most of which spilled all over the altar when the priest died," Harry said.

"And was this tale widely known in Anne's time?" If it hadn't been common knowledge, their theory about Anne relying on it to surreptitiously communicate with her uncle took a hit.

"Damn straight it was," Harry said. "Those clans warred among themselves a long time before Queen Anne ever came to our shores."

"Any idea if Anne ever visited this castle?" Parker asked.

"I don't know," Gavin said. "But I'd wager a month's pay Anne pointed Lord Hyde to Leap Castle. The grounds," and here Gavin consulted a cell phone. "Open at eight o'clock in the morning, and closed an hour ago."

"We'll need a hotel for the night," Parker said. "Somewhere to lay low in case those Keepers show up."

"Why wait?" Gavin asked. "I say we pay the haunted chapel a visit tonight, see if any O'Carroll ghosts are wandering around."

Parker stared at the back of Gavin's head. *Was he joking?*

"What are you talking about? I'm not breaking any more laws tonight."

"Don't worry about that, Mr. Chase. You have to remember. You're on *our* island." Gavin turned to face Parker, one side of his mouth curled up. "Let me make a call."

A burst of Irish Gaelic ensued, Gavin's poetic words spoken in hushed tones. A minute later he set the phone down, and Harry hit the gas.

"A friend of a friend knows the caretaker at Leap Castle. Seems as though he's forgotten to lock the door tonight, so we'll need to stop by and make sure all is in order."

Parker grinned. Apparently rumors of the IRA's demise had been greatly exaggerated.

"As to what we're looking for when we arrive, I have no idea. Any thoughts on the matter?" Gavin asked, looking to Erika.

Leaning against the window, she searched the night sky.

"Erika?"

"What?" she said. "Oh, yes. What to look for. Given that Anne explicitly mentions the Bloody Chapel, I say we begin searching there."

"No argument here," Gavin said. "You and Parker picked up this trail when no one else had, so I'm following your lead."

"It wasn't just us," Erika said, looking over the dark landscape. Eyes once again on the lush landscape, so green in bright sunlight, now glowing a cerulean blue black under the rising moon. Parker knew Michelle's death weighed on her mind.

Landing in Dublin felt like a lifetime ago, and he touched the velvet-smooth box stowed in his pocket. For now, the box stayed put and the future waited.

Chapter 25

Kilkenny Castle
Kilkenny, Ireland

While Logan's newly-promoted driver secured a vehicle, the Chief Warder walked over the lush front lawn, lit up like the night sky by dozens of headlights. Night's arrival bathed the stately grounds in soft moonlight, and green fields turned to rolling waves of purple and black.

"Sir?" Oliver Moore's voice rumbled in Rose's ear, the phone pressed tightly to his skull.

"This situation is still open, Mr. Moore. I'll need your assistance to end it."

"What should we do, sir?"

Men with urban combat experience and a local's knowledge of the land now aided the Americans, so Logan needed to turn up the heat. An attack on multiple fronts, orchestrated without revealing the truth behind his actions to anyone else.

The original Beefeater intelligence reports from Anne's journey mentioned she stopped at Leap Castle. Coupled with the poem found, Rose felt confident enough to act.

"First, draft a press release about my pilot's murder at Kilkenny, hinting at IRA involvement. Nothing too overt. Second, contact the local police in Roscrea and tell them you suspect Leap Castle is being utilized as a hub for this group's operations. Again, don't be specific, but dangle enough bait to get some men up there. Given that none of our men can make it there anytime soon, it's the best option we have."

"Understood, sir. Do you require any further backup?"

"No. And get moving with this press release. We need the Irish on their heels."

Opportunity came with the pilot's murder. Suggesting that terrorists killed him gave Logan more than enough reason to chase them anywhere across the country. Once Oliver warned local police the suspects may be in their vicinity, the situation became all hands on deck.

Which it had to be. If Erika Carr somehow managed to infiltrate Leap Castle and uncover Anne's next message, a dead pilot became the least of Logan's worries.

Chapter 26

Outside of Roscrea, Ireland

A low set of headlights washed across the roadway, broken streaks of paint flashing white amid the black asphalt sea. Eyes shut to the world, Gavin Rooney considered every factor in play, each person or group affecting their foray into Leap Castle a moving piece on the chessboard filling his mind's eye. And then his phone rang.

"It's the QM," Gavin said. "He'll need to be told about Brin and Dr. Carr's discovery."

Gavin laid everything out for the QM, from the moment they grabbed the two Americans through their hasty escape, one man short. Only once he fell silent did Connor Whelan respond, each word measured.

"Brin will be missed, but we cannot afford the luxury of grief with the Keepers so close behind."

Gavin expected nothing less. QM Whelan knew in war each side must press every advantage. "We already secured entrance to Leap Castle."

"I wouldn't expect the Chief Keeper to tarry. The death of one of his men does not bode well for us. If you cross his path again, don't try to fight."

More guerilla tactics, the end result only the promise of more death. He preferred diplomacy to bloodshed, but soldiers followed orders.

"What do you think the Keepers will do about their dead man?" Gavin asked.

"Even absent proof, our name will surface in the aftermath of Kilkenny."

"Which will only incite action," Gavin said.

"Unfortunately, you're right. Some of our men are pushing for a more drastic response to the Warders invading Ireland, and Brin's murder may be the last straw. I won't be able to stay them for long. Just remember what we discussed."

In the event IRA hotheads decided to carry out an attack on the English, the QM would warn Gavin with a phrase only the two knew. A secret code to give Gavin as much warning as possible should any action be imminent, IRA action which could put his team in danger. Not much, but seeing that field teams weren't always notified of other teams missions, at least Gavin and his team would be prepared for the fallout.

"Keep me apprised of your situation," Whelan said. "Remember, you're dealing with a man who carries the full support of a nation. Don't try to be a hero. If this starts to go south, get out. You're no good to me dead."

With that cheerful directive, the QM clicked off.

"New orders," Gavin said. "We get in, find whatever Anne left in the Bloody Chapel, and get out." He turned and met Erika's gaze. "I'm counting on you to uncover her secret, Dr. Carr. You managed to come this far on your own. Now the IRA is in your corner, and we're seeing this through to the end."

The American didn't appear worried in any way, her mouth a hard line. Though he didn't like it, circumstances dictated the fate of his mission now lay in the hands of two tourists who, he suspected, had more than a few tricks up their sleeve.

Chapter 27

Belfast, Northern Ireland

Antrim is one of six counties comprising Northern Ireland. Contained within its borders are some of the nation's most vibrant areas, including the capital city of Belfast, oftentimes ground zero for the battle between rival paramilitary groups plaguing the United Kingdom to this day. Despite the Good Friday Agreement in 1998, the specter of death still lingered over this city, a haze that didn't dissipate no matter which direction the winds blew.

And right in the middle of Belfast, those who pulled the strings of this war hid in plain sight. Every day thousands of people passed within steps of the weathered metal door concealing the IRA's senior leadership, who through determination, devout belief and a bit of luck survived the blood-soaked Troubles.

A social club in the city, one of many, sat one block from a rambling campus which housed the University of Ulster administration. A slowly fading relic of decades past, passerby looked at the place every day, but never truly saw it. The aged façade, the repainted exterior, all hallmarks of a place where old men came to escape their wives and relive the glory days.

Appearances can be deceiving. Depending on who you asked, this three-story brick structure housed many of the most wanted criminals in Europe. Others might call it a safe house for freedom fighters. Either description fit, but whatever your preference, the fact remained the IRA's top brass resided here after one of them realized the second largest city in Ireland was a good place to remain anonymous.

As long as you didn't go around setting off bombs every week.

Standing outside this humble headquarters, the IRA's current leader stood rock-still, bright stars twinkling overhead, his flowing silver mane fluttered on the cool breeze.

These damned fools don't know how tenuous peace is. They're willing to risk everything we worked to build only to prove their foolishness.

The tobacco in Connor Whelan's pipe smoldered, a red-hot furnace of guilt shining like a beacon on this moonlit night. Deserted sidewalk stretched in every direction, no dusty academics or harried students to be seen. Connor's shadow flowed across the concrete, slicing through the yellow haze cast by sodium streetlights overhead.

As QM, he needed to tell his fellow leaders about the field operative's death. Brin's passing came far too soon, a casualty Connor must ensure was not in vain. However, Connor feared that while his colleagues shared his anger; they'd fail to keep a level head in their response. He needed to direct their unbridled enthusiasm for destroying the British, control the appetite for vengeance and manage it so the headstrong fools didn't run themselves into an early grave.

Red embers floated on the evening wind, Connor blowing the last bits of burnt leaf from his bowl. A muted *click* sounded when the front door locks disengaged, Connor nodding to the spotlight overhead, which concealed a miniscule camera lens, the feed monitored around the clock by IRA guards in the operations room several stories underground. The place looked like NASA's mission control center, with over a dozen live feeds streaming from around the country, state-of-the-art electronics for their younger technical team to monitor practically anything in the world. In private he referred to these lads as *Q's*, the fictional quartermaster who supplied 007 with all manner of sophisticated weaponry.

Seated behind bulletproof glass, the guard on duty saluted as Connor Whelan walked in. Through another steel door, this one reinforced and guarded like the last, he looked around the IRA's more informal gathering area, a room rivaling even the most exclusive clubs in London.

Chestnut brown mahogany lined the walls, vertical slats dulled to a soft shine by decades of smoke. A single blackball billiards table stood to one side, across from the bar, a lacquered surface polished to perfection by an endless supply of often unsteady elbows. Seats of rich leather faced a fireplace, currently unlit in the summer heat.

"What's it about, Whelan?"

The speaker sat around a smallish wooden table, five chairs on the circumference. Four of those chairs supported the collective leadership and controlling council of the Irish Republican Army, now gathered to hear about their latest mission. As far as these men knew, Gavin Rooney's team now investigated the Keepers' interest in a pair of American tourists, shadowing the Englishmen through several cities. Interesting, but nothing extraordinary.

"Grave news, Arden." Whelan joined his fellow leaders, settling into the head seat. "Brin is dead, shot by the Chief Warder."

Battle-hardened though they were, the entire group flinched. Connor knew what to expect, and like a key grip on the curtain call, Arden Flanarty rose to the occasion.

"Those damned Keeper bastards!" he thundered, bulbous nose glowing like Connor's pipe embers. "How'd it happen? Shot him in the back is my guess."

Connor relayed the encounter at Kilkenny Castle and their team's subsequent escape.

"So you're telling me the damn Keepers are up in arms over a pair of tourists?" Arden asked. "What gives?"

Connor met his eyes, black specks tucked under two unruly hedges of white. Slim as a rail, red veins crisscrossed his face like a map of their green land. Arden Flanarty may look like the town drunk, even acted like it at times, but a razor sharp mind and burning hatred for all things British hid behind the crusty exterior.

"I don't know," Connor lied with ease. "It all started with an email from Dr. Carr's friend, who's now cooling in the morgue. Whatever this is, the Tower's on full alert."

"A doctor, is she? I like the smart ones," Arden said, winking to his mates. Two of the other men chuckled, each ardent followers of the Flanarty school of thought.

Unfortunately for Connor, those two tended to vote with Arden in most matters, which put him and his mate on the leadership council at a significant disadvantage. He battled constantly to avert a potential catastrophe at every perceived slight sent their way by the British.

Plainly speaking, those three men harbored more *violent* ambitions than Connor, and sought any excuse to do battle with the English government. Brin's death provided the perfect opportunity for them to advocate an attack, the kind that ended with limbs flying and men dying. If he did anything tonight, he'd talk at least one of these men down from the pride-built ledge they surely intended to ascend.

"What do we know about the pair of tourists?" Connor's staunchest council ally asked.

"Dr. Erika Carr is a historian, traveling here with her boyfriend to visit a classmate employed by the National Gallery of Ireland. And today, through what looks to be coincidence, that classmate made a discovery." He recapped how she uncovered a letter from Queen Anne, and then sent an email which eventually embroiled their men in the entire mess. "It seems the timing of her discovery is coincidence, and Dr. Carr had no knowledge of what was in that painting before receiving the email."

"Which put the Keepers on their tracks and got our man killed," Arden said, a bony fist tapping the table.

"Her companion is Parker Chase," Connor continued. "He's in the banking business, and from what I understand they're a formidable team." Connor sketched out how the couple disabled a Keeper at Castle Blarney and eluded their English pursuit during a high-speed chase, causing a serious pileup in the process.

"Not bad," one of Arden's companions said. "Why do you think the Keepers are interested enough to send their Chief out of his cushy Tower to get these two tourists?"

Maybe he'll listen to reason tonight. He only needed to convince one of them to get three votes, enough to stop Arden from unleashing vengeance.

"I don't give a damn about what Queen Anne left behind," Arden said. "We're fighting our battles today, not blundering about the island chasing ghosts. They killed one of our boys."

His words spilled out, hot and peaty whiskey for a thirsty Irishman's tongue. And as the world knew, no man from this Isle ever had just one drink.

"We cannot forget Brin," one of Arden's allies said. "Wouldn't be right, letting this go."

Time to stop this smoke before it burst into flame and burned everything.

"And his sacrifice will not be in vain," Connor said. "However, it would be a disservice to his memory if we didn't use this chance to learn why the Keepers are so interested in these tourists. Right now they're on the defensive. If we stay on their trail and keep out of sight, either the Keepers or the Americans will lead us to the answer."

"Must be big, whatever it is," the man replied.

"Which is all the more reason to stay in the shadows."

Arden's hand shot out, pointing at Whelan's jaw. "Piss on that, Connor. We cannot be seen as weak. It's time to kill some English."

"To what end?" Logic rarely worked with a true believer, but Connor spoke to the ears which might actually listen. "Why should we conduct a rash operation? Say we do put something together on short notice, murder a few of the enemy. What do you suggest? Any action we take would have no purpose, doesn't further our cause beyond stoking the will of those already loyal. The best we could hope for is none of our men are captured or sent through St. Peter's gates."

It might have been his old age, but Connor thought he saw one of Arden's mates nod.

"You've lost your spirit is all," Arden said, dismissing him with a wave. "This won't be a suicide mission." Like a puppet dancing on his strings, Arden rose from the table. "While you spend your time talking and hoping for scraps from the Queen's table, some of us have moved ahead. Planned for the future, for when we need to be strong."

Connor turned, packing his pipe with deliberate care. Only once a hot coal bloomed did he respond. "What are you getting at?"

A grim smile creased Arden's ruddy visage. "There are certain targets that *ask* to be taken out. One of them isn't far from here, a few miles up the road." Arden sat down, sipping whiskey with care. "Barclays, the oldest bank in England."

"You can't be serious," Connor said, smoke spewing from his nostrils. "You want to rob a bloody bank? That's your big plan?"

The yellow teeth cracking Arden's face grew longer. "Not rob it, Quartermaster. I intend to destroy it."

Bring down a bank? Pure lunacy.

"Our computer wizards downstairs have been workin' their magic," Arden said, on a roll now. "They uncovered a crack in the bank's armor. You see, the powers that be over in London decided their bank needs more than one way to call for help in case of a robbery. Not a bad idea, right?" The men all nodded, eyes on Arden weaving his tale. "So these buggers installed dedicated phone lines to be used in the event of an emergency. If one of the villains is smart enough to cut the main phone line, there's a backup to call for help, a line only for use in such an emergency."

"What does that have to do with murdering English bankers?" Connor asked.

"*Everything,* Quartermaster," Arden said. "You see, the phone lines leading out of the bank are ranked in a certain fashion, with this private line being on top. Which means any calls made on this line supersede all others, because only the bank employees are supposed to know it exists."

One of Arden's cronies jumped in. "If the crooks got control of the public phone line and made the teller call in to say it was a false alarm. The employees could still call in the truth on the other line."

"Correct, sir. That line is treated as the gospel truth, to be believed above all others," Arden said, rising to his feet. "And fortunately for us, our technicians can not only hijack that line, they can jam all cell signals in the area to prevent any unwanted calls."

"Interesting, but I fail to see how controlling a single land telephone line will allow you to do much of anything."

In truth, Connor knew what Arden drove toward, but he needed to hear everything from the old snake's mouth. A showman, Connor knew Arden's tongue loosed when facing an audience.

"Allow me to enlighten you," Arden said. "The second piece of our puzzle comes from outside the bank, twice per week to be exact." Throwing back the dregs of his glass, Arden found the bar and poured a healthy measure. "One of our boys, a loyal soldier, recently took on a side job to supplement his income. This enterprising young lad now works for the armored car service contracted to deliver and retrieve money at the main Barclays branch here in Belfast. Once we give him the word, our man will supplement a delivery of currency with several bombs."

"And kill a few old grannies depositing their pension?"

"Now, now Connor. You know me better than that. I have no intention of harming any of our Northern brethren. This isn't another simple explosion. What I have in mind is a targeted assault."

"So what are you getting at?" one of Arden's mates asked.

"You probably don't know that while this Barclays branch employs locals for most positions, they also retain an emergency security team in Belfast. With ten branches in the area, the head office in London decided a group of *native* Englishmen should be shipped out to our city to provide the very best security their blood-soaked money can buy. Gentlemen," Arden said, draining his glass, "those Brits are the target."

"So you're going to hang our deliveryman out to dry?" Connor asked. Even Arden wouldn't stoop this low in his quest for revenge.

"Far from it. I'd rather swear allegiance to that old bag Elizabeth than sell out one of our own. The only people going down in my plan are the blasted British security team. Most of them are ex-military."

Grumbles came from throughout the room. Even Connor could deem such casualties acceptable.

"Here's the rub, QM," Arden said. "As soon as our delivery man arrives with the cash shipment, we call the bank's private security force and claim a robbery is in progress. The line's been tapped for several days, and we have the proper codes to convince the private guards to race over. No customer or employees inside will be any the wiser until the cavalry shows up. When they do, the customer and employees clear out and those British buggers head in."

"And then you detonate the bombs," Connor said. "No one will see it coming."

"That's right, Mr. Whelan," Arden slapped the QM's shoulder, practically bouncing across the floor. "All the Irish get out, the Brits get blown through the wall, and dear Brin can rest in peace."

Around the table, Connor noted mixed reactions. Arden's closest ally barked a laugh, raising his glass to the plan. Connor's man stayed silent, one hand on his chin. The wild card, Arden's red-haired companion, seemed to be in favor, one ruddy finger tapping the smooth wood.

Connor laid his pipe on the table. One shot to stop this. "Not a bad plan, Arden, I'll give you that. One question though."

Arden leaned against the billiards table, arms crossed. "And what's that?"

"I have no doubt our man can get the bombs inside. And I'm sure you'll set them off at just the right time, once those British lads swarm the lobby. However, what happens to our operative *after* the explosion? Unless the blast destroys the bank's security system and any backup hardware they have, his face will be on camera, and it won't take long for the coppers to discover how the bombs made it inside."

"Good points all," Arden said, rolling a black ball over the felt-covered table. "And each considered. As to the coppers finding out those bombs came in with the money, we aren't worried about that. The money arrives sealed at the truck. All our man does is put it in the bag while his partner watches."

"And what does that mean for us?" Connor asked. "All he'd have to do is slip the bombs into a bag."

"Which means we can't be that stupid. The bombs may be in these delivery bags, but that's not the only thing in them."

"What are you saying?" Connor's mate asked, his eyes narrow.

"This will hurt, but we're going to hide the bomb inside *our own* bag of money. You see, each package of currency is sealed in a plastic shell, vacuum-packed and triple-wrapped. We're going to add a sealed bag of currency to the delivery satchels, each containing bricks of C-4. No one would ever suspect a bomb wrapped entirely in money. Once it goes off, the explosives experts can investigate all they want. I hope they do a bang-up job." Arden rolled a ball away before rejoining their seated group. "Once they find the bombs were inside sealed packages of cash, our man walks. How could a lowly armed guard ever have known the money package also held a bomb?

"This might be the most expensive bomb package we've ever had," Arden said, "but it'll be worth it to see British blood spilled across the marble floors of their dear bank."

A great plan, Connor had to admit. But he spotted one weakness even Arden couldn't account for, an intrinsic part of each man at this table Connor would use to stop this disaster.

"How many pounds will be in the package?"

Like an unseen right hook, the question stopped Arden in his tracks.

"A decent amount, but what's it worth compared to the chance to kill Englishmen?"

Arden knew it, just as Connor did. One trait every man here shared is they grew up far from any silver spoons. All their fathers were IRA men, some killed in service. But they all knew poverty intimately. Truth be told, desperation and destitution were two of their best recruiting tools.

"I'm no banker, but there have to be thousands of pounds in those delivery bags. At least."

"Are the bombs already wrapped for delivery?" Connor's mate asked.

Arden looked around, found silence on all sides. "Yes. We're ready to move at once."

"So how much is in the package?" the redheaded one asked.

Arden rubbed his nose. "Fifty thousand quid."

The words dropped like lead weights. Connor couldn't thank the man enough for being so foolish. "That's per bomb, correct?" Arden nodded, seeing the writing on the wall. "And how many bombs did you make?"

"Three," he replied, the hubris gone.

Protests filled the air, with even Arden's closest mate joining in. One hundred and fifty thousand pounds was far too much to waste on killing such low value targets as a private bank security team. IRA leaders needed to grasp the long-term ramifications of any actions, for this promised to be a lengthy war.

"Gentleman," Connor said, calling for quiet. "Though now may not be the time for such action as this, this is not an option to be discarded entirely. Our I.T. team did a fine job cracking the bank's secure phone line. We should keep this in our arsenal to be deployed at a more opportune time. Right now, however, I counsel we avoid such direct and expensive action and instead bide our time."

Fists tapped the table in agreement, and Arden's face went to stone. "As you wish, gents. I'll have the bombs dismantled immediately."

Low voices buzzed through the room, chair legs scraping as everyone migrated toward the polished bar. One switched on the television, a news podium flashing on-screen.

Amber whiskey, aged eighteen years, lolled around the bottle in Connor's hands like golden sunlight, heavy with the promise of peat and fire. As a reporter onscreen began to talk, two fingers splashed out, plenty to celebrate his small victory.

"...joining us at this late hour. And now we go live to the Historic Royal Palace's press office, where the special contingent of Her Majesty's Yeoman Warders have called a conference."

"Turn that up," Connor said. "This may be about Kilkenny."

A man ascended the stage, his clean-shaven head sparkling under the lights. Clad in a dark suit, he looked nothing like the spectacularly-dressed Warders known throughout the world.

"Good evening. My name is Oliver Moore, of Her Majesty's Government, Special Operations Contingent. I've called this conference in response to the events that transpired this evening at Kilkenny Castle in Ireland, which is managed by the Office of Public Works. As a publicly maintained structure, the castle falls under the protective charter of the special contingent unit of Yeoman Warders."

"You're nothing but a damned Keeper!" one of the IRA men shouted. None disagreed.

Flashbulbs lit the man, flanked on either side by the flags of Great Britain and Ireland.

"Several hours ago our office learned of a disturbance at Kilkenny. Two warders responded, and upon their arrival, identified multiple suspects wanted for questioning in connection with a murder committed in Dublin this morning."

"That's not what happened," Connor said. "Gavin's crew didn't make any trouble. The Keepers showed up and started shooting."

"When the response team attempted to detain the suspects, one of the men wanted for questioning opened fire. The pair of warders returned fire, and during the ensuing exchange one warder was shot and killed. A single suspect also died, though two additional suspects escaped. We also believe this incident is related to a suspicious death from earlier today at Blarney Castle, which is currently under investigation."

"Lies, all of it," Connor's mate shouted, beer soaking the floor.

"The deceased criminal in Kilkenny has not yet been identified. However, I can say that at this juncture, evidence recovered leads us to believe the events in Kilkenny are an act of terrorism, conducted by a large group of nationalist dissidents well-known to British authorities."

The speaker paused, pitch black eyes boring through the screen. "Our investigation into this cowardly assault on the British government is ongoing, and we will not stop until these murderers are brought to justice. I encourage anyone with knowledge of this attack to contact your local authorities immediately. Thank you."

Shouted questions filled the air. "Mr. Moore, how do you know this was the IRA?"

Moore paused, studying the reporters off-screen.

"We cannot confirm who is behind these attacks, but indications are that this is a terrorist strike. However," and he paused again, letting the silence carry on, "I cannot confirm responsibility for the murder at this time."

This time Oliver Moore walked off-screen with purpose, ignoring the pleading mass of journalists. Once another network talking head came on-screen and began recapping the statement, Connor shut the television off.

"None of that is true," Connor said. "The Keepers fired first. Gavin tried to run, and only shot when the Keepers opened fire."

A tidal wave of anger drowned him out.

"You heard his lies," Arden railed, stoking the fire. "Using Brin's murder to justify coming after us. We can't let that happen."

Voices rumbling in agreement.

I'm losing them.

"Now's the time to take the fight to them," Arden said. "One thing I've learned in my life is to never let those English bastards get the upper hand. They won't stop until we're all in pine boxes."

"Wait a minute," Connor said, hands up. "We mustn't do anything drastic. That's a good way to get someone killed."

"Damn right it is," Arden said. "Some Englishmen."

Connor felt his hard-won victory slipping away. "What are you saying?"

"The English brought this on themselves," Arden replied. "We move ahead with our plan and take out those bastards, destroy a wretched symbol of British rule. All is ready for tomorrow. You just give the word."

Fiery support spewed forth from the third council member, sealing Connor's fate. Three to two in favor of attacking the bank.

I have to warn Gavin.

Connor walked outside, leaving the smoky, stale air behind. He'd been so close, had it all under control, and then the Keepers twisted this to their advantage and destroyed Connor's leverage with his men.

On a deserted sidewalk he punched Gavin's number, and the call went unanswered. He tried once more without result. Chances are the Keepers didn't know how to find Gavin's team, but Connor didn't take chances when lives hung in the balance.

Every policeman on the island had an itchy trigger finger right now, and Gavin might be walking into an ambush.

Ice crept into Connor's veins as the phone rang unanswered again.

I hope I'm not too late.

Chapter 28

None of the buildings stood taller than three stories, a nearby church steeple the highest point to be found. Two headlights passed through the sleepy market town of Roscrea, anonymous in the sparse traffic. A pair of American tourists occupied the rear seats, each staring out the window, Ireland's beauty lost on them both.

Parker cracked his window, the warm night air replete with wheaty grass and a touch of wildflower touching his nose as they rumbled over cobbled streets into a storybook landscape. Maybe they'd be here when the sun came up, and this fairy tale setting truly came to life.

In the front seat, Gavin ended his phone call.

"Rear service entrance," Gavin said. "Our friend left it open. The only request is we lock up when we're done."

"What about the local coppers?" Harry asked, accelerating out of town, the road winding north toward Leap Castle.

"Afraid we don't have any pull with them," Gavin said. "We move quickly tonight and get out of the castle before anyone knows we're here. Erika, you're the best chance we have at uncovering why Queen Anne points us to the Bloody Chapel at Leap. You're in charge, but be mindful of our time constraints."

"No pressure, huh?" Erika said. Right now her nerves were strung tighter than a miser's purse strings, but Parker knew inside the castle she'd be in her element. If Anne left a clue on her trail, they'd find it.

"There it is," Harry said.

The stone bridge ahead traversed a dry gulley. Down the narrow road, they veered in a looping half-circle, stopping in front of an arched wooden

126

door. Matching windows framed the door, two dark mirrors revealing nothing.

Stretching skyward in a jagged display, a tower of stone loomed five stories overhead, the rock glassy and black, reflecting patches of scant moonlight like a shimmering wave. An additional tower leaned in on either side, both with battlements along the top. A rock and mortar wall that had seen better centuries extended along the circular drive, flowing out to meet a freshly-cut swath of grass, the green lawn now a rolling field of black glistening in the moonlight.

"We'll park under the bridge," Gavin said. "I doubt anybody will be around this late, but if someone does show up, they won't see our car down there."

Harry completed the loop, the bridge enveloping them in a dark embrace as they rolled underneath. Anyone driving across would never see the car ten feet below.

"Follow me," Harry said flashlight in hand. "And stay close."

They took a wide berth around one side of the castle, jogging past a derelict stone house several hundred feet from the main structure. Open fields stretched behind the castle, running into a heavy forest of stately trees.

Light ran over the castle walls until Harry found a small doorway tucked into one corner.

"That must be the service entrance," Gavin said. He took the lead, the wooden barrier opening into darkness so absolute it swallowed the pitiful flashlight beam at once.

"If you've never been here before, how do we find the chapel?" Parker asked.

"This might help." Harry grabbed something from the wall and gave it to Erika.

"A tourist map," she said, flipping the pages. "Follow me."

Chilly air nipped at his ankles, bracing after the summer breeze outside. His fingertips scraped the walls on either side as they walked, the narrow passageway even tighter when it couldn't be seen.

Following Harry's bouncing beam, Erika stepped ahead, her footsteps silent on the cool stone floor. Faint moonlight crept through a tiny window overhead, scarcely larger than an arrow slit, the light distorted by thick, bubbled glass.

"The chapel is upstairs, in this center tower," she said. "Be careful on the staircase. I don't think it's up to code."

Dirt and construction debris crunched underfoot as they ascended. Parker trailed a hand along the stone wall, keeping close to that side. Given the other side dropped off into darkness without handrail or banister, slipping on the dirty steps promised to bring more than a sprained ankle.

"They must be preserving the entire hall," Erika said as they reached the second level. An open room devoid of ornamentation came to life under the flashlight, gothic arched ceilings cast deep shadows in every direction, the only other illumination provided by a single window.

"Keep that thing down," Gavin said. "We can't let anyone know we're in here."

"The chapel is through there," Erika said, pointing to the steps ahead. "Be careful when you get inside. There's an oubliette where the O'Carroll clan threw their victims, dead or alive. If you fall in, you'll be lucky to only break one of your legs."

"O-what?" Parker asked. He couldn't see five feet in the dim light. "Is that some kind of dungeon?"

"You're not far off," Erika said. "Oubliette is a French term. But it's really just a hole, usually deep and narrow. Once you find yourself at the bottom of one there's no way to get out. If the fall didn't kill them, anyone thrown down there eventually died of dehydration. Not a pretty way to go."

"A good hiding place for Anne's next marker, perhaps?" Harry asked.

"I doubt it. According to this guide"—Erika tapped the paper—"there used to be a full chapel up here. The chapel in which one brother killed another in front of the entire family."

And with that morbid tidbit, Harry ascended the final step, ducking the chapel. Two rounded panes of clear glass fronted the room, a mirror image of the floor beneath, with no other exits. Only an empty window, the stone wall cut away, leaving a ledge several feet off the ground. Once Parker oriented himself, he realized the strange window couldn't possibly offer a view of the hills surrounding these ancient battlements, because the opening was on an internal wall.

"Stay away," Erika said. "That's the oubliette. Three cartloads of skeletons were taken out during the last renovation."

Harry whistled, his flashlight stuck on it. Strong though the beam was, it simply disappeared into the empty depths, all brightness stripped from the air in the presence of such an evil place.

"Why would they put something like that in their chapel?" Harry asked.

"To remind worshippers of what happened to those who sin," Erika replied. "And considering that some of the skeletons taken out bore evidence of arrow wounds, anyone thrown in who made too much noise got a crossbow bolt for their trouble."

"Nasty business," Harry said. "If you please, Dr. Carr, hurry up and find Anne's message so we can get the hell out of here."

"With pleasure." Erika shoved the map in Parker's hands. "Now, how do you suppose this chapel's oriented?"

Crumbling mortar fell from the walls, leaving bare stones between plaster patches, the fallen chunks mixed with bits of straw scattered about the floor.

"Search the walls," Erika said. "Look for any type of sculpture or drawing. A chapel should have a cross etched into the wall, along with pictures of saints or biblical scenes."

"Do you think Anne used one of those as a hiding place?" Gavin asked, face deep in shadows cast by his phone's light.

"Not likely. I want to determine which parts of the room are front and back. Like most Christian churches, the congregation sat facing the priest. My assumption is Anne hid her message in an area unlikely to be touched. Given the sanctity of religious symbols like the cross or altar, that's where we begin."

Parker began sweeping the loose rock and straw from the floor. The others joined him, and soon the edges were piled with pebbles and dusty straw, particles of dirt forming a hazy curtain in the still air. Sweeping and kicking, Harry loosed a ferocious sneeze, his flashlight swinging wildly.

"Get it together," Gavin said. "I can't see anything with you flailing about."

"Damn dust. Parker, you find anything yet?"

He stood near the room's lone window, bent over at the waist. "No, but I have an idea. Given that this is the only natural light in the room"—he pointed to the window—"the altar table should be located nearby. If I'm the priest, I want my altar by the window."

"Shine that light over here," Erika said.

Dust particles sparkled as his beam played across the floor. Gavin stood in front of the window, his back pressed to the glass. "I can't block all of it, but we need to keep the light from getting outside. Anyone can see in as easily as we see out."

Under Parker's hand, dust and dirt fell away as the others followed suit in an organized assault on grime. Several minutes later, sweat beaded on his forehead and stung his eyes, though he scarcely noticed.

"Look at this," he said. One dirty finger outlined a slightly depressed part of the floor. "This used to be covered. Maybe a bench or pew." The rectangular depression sat slightly lower and rougher than the surrounding floor, darker in color and the size of a bench's support column. At least that's what he thought.

"There's another one over here," Erika said. "Harry, do you see anything?"

The Irishman scrubbed away behind Erika. "I do. Same shape and color."

"Two rows of pews, and this is the center aisle." She outlined the seating arrangement, a long aisle separating her side from Parker's. "And if Parker's right about the window being a focal point, the altar should be in front of Gavin."

"My markings are about three feet behind Erika's," Harry said. "But it doesn't look like there's anything in front of it."

"That makes sense if the altar is up here," Gavin said, stepping away from the window. "Keep the light down."

"You know," Parker said. "Not to be a pessimist, but if all that's left of the altar and pews are these outlines, anything Anne left is long gone."

"It depends on what she hid and where she put it," Erika said. "There's no way of knowing why or when the altar disappeared, so our chances of finding anything are slim. But remember the other breadcrumbs."

"One inside a bench at Blarney Castle," Gavin said. "And another in the capstone of Reginald Tower. Are you thinking another hollowed out spot here?"

"One way to find out," she said. "Start searching the floor where the altar stood. Look and listen for crumbling mortar, hollow bricks, anything to indicate a hiding spot. Remember, what we're searching for could be as small as a stamp. Look for any opening where you could hide a piece of parchment."

With Harry's light shielded, the walls turned to black. Each of them took a corner of the altar outline and began searching. Knuckles, and in one case, a gun barrel, tapped the stones. Tiny pebbles of mortar rolled around as each crevice and crack revealed whatever secrets they held.

It didn't take long to realize there were none to find.

Erika jumped to her feet, undeterred. "So she didn't use the altar. The next most likely spot is a religious symbol or an icon on the wall."

They repeated the search in vertical fashion, uncovering several etchings and the faint outline of where a cross once hung, though no hiding places. Fingernails caked with grime, Parker turned to see his despair reflected in the eyes of everyone around him.

"Perhaps we need to reconsider Anne's message," Erika said, lifting a strand of hair and smudging dirt on her cheek.

"Let's see the message again," Gavin said, grabbing Parker's phone. After reading it again, he said, "There's little doubt Anne pointed to this castle. The O'Carroll and Bloody Chapel references are unmistakable."

"Is it possible someplace else fits the clues?" Harry asked.

"Unlikely," Erika said. "These clues are for Laurence only, in the context of Anne's search. Anne needed to obscure the truth of her meaning, not bury it."

"Anything else useful in that pamphlet?"

"Not that I can see," she said. "It's basically an outline of the grounds, which aren't very extensive. The Bloody Chapel legend is recounted in detail, claims about this being the most haunted castle in the world, and a few other tidbits. There's a nice picture of the oubliette and a dark reference to how dozens of people died in it." Parker scarcely caught her next words. "I don't think the answer is here."

Soft light bathed Gavin's face as he studied Parker's phone. "This last line. After Anne mentions the O'Carrolls and the Bloody Chapel. She says *William cannot be left in this place forgotten.*' Do either of you speak French?"

Neither did. "I take it you do?" Erika asked.

"Yes. We may have missed Anne's true intent." Gavin handed the phone to Parker.

What about this grabbed his eye?

"Erika, do you think Queen Anne and Laurence Hyde spoke French?"

"I'd bet a year's salary on it," Erika said. "Members of the royal family learned French, Spanish, and Latin, all necessary to interact with other European ruling families." Erika's head cocked to the side. "Why do you ask?"

"What are you getting at, Gav?" Harry asked.

"Would you turn that damn light off?"

"Sorry."

"Don't ask how I remember this, but in French—"

A booming crash split the air, and footsteps echoed through the castle.

"Don't move." Gavin crept to the door, where a faint light slithered up from the lower levels.

"It's the Garda," Gavin said. "Two of them, headed toward us."

"Roscrea Garda," a disembodied voice shouted. "Come out with your hands up."

Parker looked around, found one option, and he didn't like it. "Come on," he said, grabbing Erika's hand. "And don't scream."

Only when they stood in front of it did Erika realize.

"Not a chance," she said. "I'd rather go to jail."

The utterly black hole stole light from the air, a portal to another dimension.

"You Yanks are all nutters," Harry said. "We might as well jump from the roof."

"Look inside."

Earlier, Parker had noticed a tiny ledge *inside* the opening. Not even a ledge, really, but something to stand on where bricks shifted out and mortar rotted away. Less than a brick's width at ground level, below the knee-high opening.

"You're out of your mind," Erika said. "I am not getting in there."

"At least three of us could stand on it," Parker said as his phone light played over the uneven row of bricks. "Harry on one side, you and Gavin on the other. And the rotted mortar gives plenty of handholds."

Harry's wide shoulders would take an entire side of the ledge.

"What about you?" she said. "You can't just vanish."

"I'll squeeze with Harry. Now stop arguing and get in there."

Erika hesitated, leaning away from the darkness.

"Parker's right," Gavin said. "Those Garda will have quick trigger fingers if the Beefies sent them. This is our only option." He stepped past Erika, one foot on the oubliette's ledge. "I'll go first."

With debris falling into the void, Gavin inched his way behind the wall until only four clenched fingers remained, white as snow.

"It's tight, but we can do it."

Flashlight clenched between his teeth like a pirate's sword, Harry disappeared around the other edge.

Rapid-fire footsteps sounded on the stairwell outside.

"Go ahead," Parker said. "I'll be right behind you."

Erika's hand tightened on his bicep, and she stepped into the darkness, slipping her slender frame behind the wall.

Parker now stood alone in the chapel. But not for long.

The footsteps grew louder, echoing all around. They'd be here in seconds.

No time to be afraid now. He stepped over the ledge as Harry flicked on the flashlight, shielding it so only a sliver of white escaped.

Just enough light to see no room remained.

Footsteps stopped on the landing outside.

Maybe a foot of room remained open on the ledge, less than half of what Parker needed to be hidden. Which left only one option.

Parker stood on the ledge, turned to face the chapel, and squatted down. With images of broken bones and dusty skeletons in his mind's eye, Parker let his feet drop into the void, hanging from the ledge with a death-grip.

Harry's flashlight went dark. An instant later, the oubliette's entrance lit up as the police flashlights swept through the room.

Chapter 29

Roscrea, Ireland

"Unit two-seven, over."

"Unit, this is dispatch. What's your current location?"

"Passing Roscrea Castle, dispatch. What can we do for you?"

Roscrea Garda officers Robbie Clark and Marc Ward cruised past the stone castle in Roscrea's center. A quiet night so far, not even so much as a traffic stop to break the monotony.

Six men comprised the entire Roscrea Garda force, as small-town as it came. All born and bred in this market town of County Tipperary, and each loved his hometown fiercely. With crime in short supply these days, Robbie figured his friend Liam for a bored man, stuck behind the dispatch desk tonight.

"It's ten in the evening and all is well," Robbie said. "We're thinking about stopping by to see yer Mum. We all know she's the only good one of the bunch."

"I'll have her get the hunting rifle out, tell her to shoot on sight. There's plenty of forest around here," Liam replied. "I'd dig the holes."

That got a chuckle out of Marc, slouched in the passenger seat.

"On the straight though, something's come up. A call from the Kilkenny Garda. They asked us to look over Leap Castle, make sure everything's clear."

"What's the problem?" Robbie asked. Tires squealed as he whipped the squad car around.

"Property damage at Kilkenny Castle from the sound of it, and they're asking we check our castle. There are even a couple of suspects," Liam told

134

them. "I sent them to your phones."

Marc flicked through the images. "Any idea why these two want to invade Leap?"

"They didn't say, but there's one other thing you should know. I saw on the news they think the Provos might be involved."

Robbie glanced at Marc, easing off the gas. "That so? What's the IRA doing destroying their own heritage? Doesn't make sense."

"Got me," Liam replied. "Just thought you'd want to hear that. Be safe out there and keep me in the know."

"You got it," Robbie said. "Two-seven out."

Scarcely five minutes passed before Leap Castle came into view. Far from the castle entrance, Robbie flicked a switch, dousing the headlights, long shadows from the tree-lined roadway melting into the black grass underneath. Guided by only the soft running lights, their cruiser slid to a halt fifty yards from the front entrance.

"You see that?" Marc said, stepping from the vehicle.

Robbie went still, one foot on the grass. "What're you looking at?"

"Up there," Marc said. "There it is again. A light on the top floor."

Birds cawed and a lone owl hooted as Robbie followed the flashing light. Like a lighthouse turning round, the light burst into existence, murky through the thick glass, only to vanish in a flash.

"That's the chapel," Robbie said, though Marc knew it too. Every lad in Roscrea knew the Bloody Chapel. An entertaining legend, but the tales were only ghost stories, more useful for drawing tourists than educating kiddies. Whoever was up there now was made of flesh and blood. And he had just the remedy for that.

"Make sure you have a full mag," Robbie ordered. "They're trespassing, for one. Let's see what else is going on in this pile of stones."

Marc grabbed the lockbox from beneath his seat. Moments later, a gleaming handgun reflected under the moon, with a second one right behind. Roscrea Garda officers rarely carried firearms, but with the IRA involved, no need to show up empty-handed.

High above them, the mysterious light reappeared once more as Robbie led Marc to the front door, their looping path following the castle walls, shadows blending with the darkness to render the pair virtually invisible.

The front door failed to open under his touch. "Must have snuck in another way," he whispered. Marc put a finger in the air, swinging it around.

Circle around, find how they got inside.

Around back, a small door facing the surrounding woodlands opened when Robbie tested the lock. Voices bounced about inside, disembodied in the still air.

"Announce ourselves?" Marc asked.

"Better than getting shot," Robbie replied. Startled criminals tended to shoot first. "Let's follow the book on this one."

Turning to shout at the intruders, his knee slammed into the reception desk, rattling loud enough to wake the dead and sending a chair crashing to the ground.

Only once the echoes faded did Robbie look at his partner. Marc flashed a thumbs up.

"Roscrea Garda. Come out with your hands up." Robbie's voice echoed through the hall. A beat passed with no response. "Let's go," he said, taking the lead.

Past the first landing, with only silence above them. At the second landing, Robbie slowed beside the chapel entrance, a narrow opening cut in the gray stone.

Leaning against the wall, Robbie cocked an ear toward the chapel.

Nothing. Not even a peep.

Hand on his gun, Robbie floated around the corner, and looked into an empty room. No burglars, thieves, evildoers or ghosts inside. A sliver of moonlight cut across the gray floor, dust dancing on the beams.

Where'd they go?

He didn't imagine those voices, sounds made by flesh and blood human beings, not shapeless ghosts drifting through walls. The earthly denizens of his town caused enough trouble without worrying about some long-dead bugger.

Nonetheless, his eyes didn't lie. Moving slowly, Robbie started along one side of the room, and Marc took the other. A minute later they met near the lone window, where a summer wind snuck through the centuries-old glass.

"What the hell?" Marc said. "I heard them up here."

"We both did," Robbie said. "And this room's emptier than your head. Any other way out of here?"

"The roof access is from a different room," Marc said. "And there's only one door. Unless we were hearing things."

Just as Robbie started to second guess his ears, the Bloody Chapel's eerie calm shattered.

Someone sneezed.

Arms screaming, fingers sliding precariously closer to the edge of his handhold, Parker tried to ignore the sweat dripping down his nose.

Come on cops, leave now. I can't hang on much longer.

Each step the police took echoed down the shaft, the acoustics remarkable, like a concert hall. Fading footsteps mapped their progress, circling to a point across the room. The moonlight blinked out when they stopped, a low voice suggesting they head upstairs.

Electricity coursed through his aching fingers. If the police went upstairs, they had a chance. Slip outside, hide in the darkness, not spend their vacation in jail.

And then Erika sneezed.

Their safe haven evaporated, dust coating Parker's face and hair.

"Come out now, hands up!"

A pale-faced eclipse loomed overhead. The cop looked left and right, mouth agape. Then gravity won and Parker's hand slipped, pebbles skittering into the gloomy depths.

"Bloody hell… how many of you are in there?"

"Four," Erika said. "Stand back so we can get out of here."

The cop's flashlight came on, blinding in the dark shaft. Arms screaming, his nose scraped the stone wall, the rough rock like sandpaper. Blinking away tears, he saw it.

Chiseled into the stone, inches from his face.

A

Gavin and Harry leapt out, each grabbing one of Parker's arms in an iron hold to lift him. It was a good thing they did, because he didn't trust his shaking limbs.

That's it.

Anne's next clue. Except right now two more pressing problems stared them in the face, guns drawn.

Massaging the life back into his aching hands, he studied the cops, one a full head taller than his partner.

"Any of you armed?" the short one asked.

Gavin glanced at Harry.

"Hands up," the cops shouted, and the first officer, short and fair of skin, relieved them of their guns.

"You're looking at some serious jail time," the shorter officer said.

"Why are you breaking into an empty castle? There's nothing but dirt and rats in here."

Silence met his questions, the IRA men standing firm.

"Whatever your reasons, someone else knew you were coming and talked." Parker saw Gavin flinch, his face pinching up. The cop noticed too.

"You didn't think your friends would sell you out? Well, you're wrong. We got a call saying Leap Castle was in harm's way, that some terrorists intended to wreak havoc. And look what we find. You."

"We're not terrorists," Harry said, calm as could be.

The shorter officer turned to face Harry, his gun now pointed at the ground. "I never said you were."

"We don't take kindly to thieves destroying our heritage," the tall cop said. "But sometimes that depends on your point of view."

"We heard the Provisionals may be causing this trouble," the short one said. "You wouldn't know anything about that, would you?"

Wind whistled through the ancient stones. The silence stretched out, filling the room, until Gavin spoke. "I don't know anything about the IRA, but it seems to me Irishmen have little cause to destroy their own heritage."

The short cop looked up into Gavin's eyes, his own a blank mask. "I'd have to agree. What's your name?"

"Gavin Rooney."

What the hell? No need to make it easy on these cops. Who, by the way, just ruined their chances at getting Anne's next message.

"Well, Mr. Rooney, you look and sound like an Irishman. Are you here to destroy Leap Castle?"

"No, sir."

"And are you part of the IRA?"

"I'm not part of any terrorist group, and neither are my friends."

"Then you won't mind, if you'd please, telling me what in the name of Sainted Patrick you're doing here?"

"We have guests in town," Harry said. "They couldn't wait to see the castle."

"And you felt the need to carry firearms during your visit," the short cop replied. Harry's grin vanished under the stark flashlight beam. "What's your name, funny man?"

"Harry Moran."

"You two." The shorter one pointed to Parker and Erika. "Not from around here, are you? Americans would be my guess."

How did Europeans do it? They spotted Americans from a mile away.

"That's correct," Erika said. "We're here on vacation. I'm a history professor in the States, which—"

"Save it," the officer said. He didn't seem the least bit interested in either of them.

"Mr. Rooney, a moment ago you said an Irishman has no reason to destroy his past." The short cop moved toward Gavin, hands looped on his belt. "In my mind, that man has even *less* cause to do so if he is part of the Provisionals, the new brand of IRA man. Wouldn't you agree?"

"I would," Gavin said, his reply measured.

The short cop stared at Gavin, one eye nearly closed. "Do you think there are many IRA men in Ireland?" he asked.

Gavin's forehead wrinkled. "I wouldn't know."

"What do you think, funny man?" he shot back, the words aimed at Harry.

With all of the attention on their Irish caretakers, Parker caught Erika's eye, and she shrugged.

"My guess is no," the cop said. "Secrecy is prized in a group like that."

"IRA men are tight," the taller cop said. "Close as fleas on a dog."

"Right," his partner replied as a cell phone came out. "You keep an eye on this group, Marc. I'll call dispatch."

Tall Marc's gun remained up when his partner left the room, headed far enough down the stairs so Parker didn't catch the conversation. Officer Marc didn't drop his guard, but he didn't threaten to shoot them either.

Wind whistled through the ancient stones as they waited, dust dancing across Marc's flashlight beam. Everyone waited until footsteps smacked on the staircase and the shorter officer reappeared.

"Dispatch is happy to hear it," the shorter man. "No sign of intruders, IRA or otherwise. Leap Castle is safe on this quiet night."

"Good news indeed," Marc said. "Have to note that in our report."

Both policemen started toward the stairs, not even looking at the four intruders as they left.

"Oh, dispatch did mention one other thing," the shorter man said. "Apparently the British called in that tip about criminal activity here at Leap. Word is they're sending a team to investigate, should arrive shortly."

Outside the chapel entrance, the officer paused. For the first time since he'd stepped out to make a call, he looked at one of them, his eyes locked on Gavin.

"I strongly suggest that when those men arrive, you and your companions aren't here. If you are, I won't be able to help." His back turned, the officer stepped away. "One more thing, Mr. Rooney. Our day will come."

With that, he vanished down the staircase, the rear castle door crashing shut, leaving four supposedly non-existent and thoroughly confused criminals in their wake.

"We need to move," Gavin said. "Someone's watching out for us."

Erika darted in front of Gavin, poking his chest. "Just a minute. You don't think this is a setup? How do we know there won't be a dozen officers outside waiting to shoot? You can't expect me to trust a crooked cop."

"He's not crooked," Harry said.

"And how would you know that?" Erika asked.

"Because he's a sympathizer," Gavin said. "Did you hear him? *Our day will come.* That's an IRA rallying cry."

Fascinating stuff, but Parker could do them one better. "I found it."

"Bobby Sands wrote those very words the day he died in prison," Gavin said. "Sands was a commanding officer and Member of Parliament. When—"

"Did you hear me?" Parker said. "I found it."

Erika finally looked over. "Found what?"

"Anne's next marker. It's in the oubliette."

Chapter 30

Belfast, Northern Ireland

Alone in his office, Connor Whelan's silvery mane shook back and forth.

The vagaries of fate are mysterious indeed.

Knocking interrupted his thoughts. "Everything alright, QM?" one of the men asked.

"For the moment," Connor replied. "What is it?"

"Just so you know, Arden's planning more than one operation," his colleague said. "And a couple of the boys are gettin' curious about Gavin's team."

"Come on," Connor said, walking out. "I'll share the good news and see what we can do to corral Mr. Flanarty."

Connor found Arden leaning over the polished bar, their fellow councilmen hanging on every word as he tapped a tablet computer depicting a map of Belfast, a red line following wherever his finger trailed.

"...and the British private security thugs are based here, a couple blocks away. They'll arrive in under five minutes. Once the evacuation is complete and the security team's inside, we start the fireworks."

While Connor's anger mellowed as he aged, Arden's seemed to have only intensified, blinding him to what the IRA could achieve if they put down their guns and picked up a pen.

"What do you think, QM?" Arden asked. "Any suggestions for tomorrow?"

Votes were cast, the decision made. He couldn't go against his men now.

"Just make certain our man cannot be tied to this at all."

"No chance of that, QM. He's safe as can be."

Connor nodded. "Gentlemen. A word, if you please?"

Curiosity, and in one instance, suspicion, surrounded him, the map under Arden's finger suddenly forgotten.

"I received a call from one of our men near Dublin. He hails from Roscrea, and has a cousin in the Garda." The chattering died away, all eyes on Connor. "The Roscrea Garda received warning about members of a *terrorist* group who wished to desecrate Leap Castle. Which is where Gavin and Harry headed after they left Kilkenny."

"Damned Brits," one man muttered. "Of course they call us terrorists when they keep us under their boot."

"Why did they go to Leap?" Arden asked. "Nothing in that old pile of rocks is worth stealing. Unless those Americans have them chasing that Queen Anne rubbish."

Connor didn't rise to the bait. "I believe we should pursue this as far as we safely can and have Gavin and Harry stay the course."

Arden Flanarty peered at him from beneath twin white hedges. "As you say, QM."

"What exactly are they after with all this Queen Anne business?" another council member asked.

Connor turned to face his closest friend on the council. "Other than following young William's trail, I couldn't say." The lie came easily this time. None of the men here knew the secret, and for now, that wouldn't change.

"Which we can't even say is real."

"Correct," Connor said. "Though someone at the Tower of London believes the dead American professor was on to something."

"A terrible fate for her," Arden said. "But I hope there's plenty of room at the morgue. We'll be filling that place full before long."

"Can't be more than a dozen you'll take out at the bank," Connor said.

"Which is why we don't stop there. Tomorrow is just the beginning."

Right now he couldn't win this battle, not after Brin's murder, so Connor Whelan curtly nodded.

"The English want to play dirty and make saints of our soldiers," Arden said. "More than just a bank will be going up in smoke in the coming days, QM."

"I'll expect a full briefing." Safely inside his office, Connor called Gavin, relief blooming when he answered.

"QM, you need to hear this."

"Are you safe?"

"Yes," Gavin said. "We're on the M7 now, headed east."

The M7? "Good news. Two things I must tell you. One, I spoke with Stoker. We're on for tomorrow, with another engagement to follow."

Silence, which meant Gavin heard him loud and clear. Their private code for imminent danger, chosen in honor of Ireland's famous literary giant, the author of *Dracula*.

"I'll keep that in mind," Gavin said.

"Second, one of our men called earlier. He claimed his cousin called him, a Roscrea Garda officer, saying he'd found a couple of Provisionals snooping around Leap Castle. Even knew their names."

Gavin whistled. "So that's it. I'll be damned."

"Once I confirmed you're a proper Provisional, all seemed to be well."

"A close call," Gavin said. "You won't believe what we've found."

Chapter 31

Harry kept moving through sparse traffic, staying a touch under the speed limit. In the night's darkness, few tail lights dotted the endless expanse of black around them.

"This is gold," Erika said. "It could even be one of the crown jewels."

She held a ring, the band a dull yellow. A lovely piece, though the ruby it held grabbed the eyes, a flaming crimson stone sparkling with fire even in dull moonlight.

Inside the ring, however, lay the true treasure.

"Was that common practice?" Gavin asked from the front seat.

"Yes," she confirmed. "Likely given as a gift, and the giver wished to be remembered."

She referred to a carving on the inside of the band.

Anne

"This ring gives credence to the story," Parker said. He studied the sheet of paper sitting between them, running a finger along the tarnished box which protected both ring and letter over the centuries.

Once the Garda officers vanished with a cryptic statement Erika didn't comprehend, Parker dragged her to the oubliette in Leap Castle.

"I found it," he said, nearly tumbling over the low ledge in his haste. "Anne's next clue is in the oubliette. A brick with her initial."

Fingers snapped behind her. "I knew it," Gavin said.

"What are you talking about?" she asked.

"Right before the Garda showed up, I started to tell you. *Oubliette* is French for 'forgotten place'. Do you remember Anne's message at Kilkenny?"

Of course she did. *William cannot be left in this place forgotten.*

144

"That phrasing isn't a coincidence," Gavin said. "Anne must have known of the oubliette and decided in advance to use it if Prince William wasn't found at Leap Castle."

The brick proved to be loose, coming free with a bit of coaxing, to reveal this metal box. Hidden inside, a stunning ruby ring engraved with the same initial. And lying next to the ring, Anne's next message.

Gavin's phone chirped. "It's the QM," he said. "He needs an update."

Voice low in the confines of their vehicle, Gavin described the events at Leap Castle, ending with an account of what they'd found.

As he spoke, Erika read the letter, the next chapter in Anne's quest to save her only child.

Laurence,

I can thank the Lord that you have followed my path to Darby's estate. I sense William's presence, but my son remains out of reach.

But all is not lost. William sat inside these very walls not ten days past. As you know, I may not be long for the throne, so my son's safe return means all.

It is rumored that one of the Irish captors is a man of learning, and that he is leading the group to Trinity College. It is to Dublin that I now travel. I will leave word within the book that separates my family and nation.

Anne

Gavin's voice ripped her back to the present. "Understood, sir. I'll provide an update once we arrive."

"What's the QM say?" Harry asked. "Any idea why they let us go?"

A wave of light washed over the interior, shadows chasing each other as a car flew past on the right, headed toward Roscrea.

"That we've friends all over. Turns out that Garda man has a cousin in our group. Once QM vouched for us, the copper said he had no interest in interfering with our affairs."

"So he let us go, even gave us a warning," Harry said.

"Why would a police officer let us break the law?" Parker asked. "Even if his cousin is your friend?"

"Many people are sympathetic to our cause," Gavin said. "Just because they don't take up the fight like we two doesn't mean they're loyal to Elizabeth. There are quite a few folks who'd like nothing more than for

Ireland to break free, to grab her independence like the Scottish tried. And like another former colony once succeeded in doing."

Erika felt a smile touch her lips.

"Point taken, Mr. Rooney. As long as the officer and his partner keep quiet we'll be ahead of the men from Kilkenny," Erika said. "Given we have Anne's message, I suggest we keep moving."

"We're forty miles from Trinity," Gavin replied. "And parts of the college open with the sunrise. We should grab a bit of sleep while we can, and then figure out what book Anne is talking about."

"Do you think we can get a hotel room at this hour?" Parker asked.

"No need to worry. I have a place in mind."

"What do you mean?" she asked. Sleeping in this car did not appeal to her, no matter how heavy her eyelids grew.

"The party keeps a number of houses for our use."

"You mean a safe house?" Erika asked.

"You could call it that," Gavin said. "The QM said it's ours for as long as we need it."

Erika's hand found Parker's, gave it a squeeze. Apparently he wasn't as intrigued as she, yawning widely.

"There's one other item," Gavin said. "I don't know the details, but QM Whelan used our code word and warned me Arden's group is planning an attack tomorrow."

"He doesn't know where?" Harry asked.

"I don't think he could say," Gavin said. "Our team won't have anything to do with it, but there's no doubt the heat will be turned up on us."

Despite his demeanor, she knew that under the cool exterior a fervent belief boiled, one for which he'd kill and die for.

"What code?" Erika asked.

"The QM told me he spoke with Mr. Stoker, that they're on for tomorrow, with another engagement to follow."

"As in *Bram* Stoker?" Erika asked.

"Yes," Gavin said. "An Irish writer who created one of the most fearsome literary icons to haunt your dreams, and who also attended Trinity College."

"The author of *Dracula* is your code word for impending death?" Parker asked. "Not a bad choice."

"There's going to be more than one attack, and the QM doesn't know the second target," Gavin said.

"We need to decode Anne's message," Erika said. Eyes closed to the world, Anne's elegant script materialized like shapes through a fog. "She said she would *'leave word of my steps within the book that separates my family and our nation.'* So we need to determine what she's talking about. It could be literal. Or Anne might be speaking metaphorically, and the book she mentions isn't a physical book at all."

"What else could it be?" Harry asked.

"If Anne used a phrase or reference that only her uncle recognized, or if she and Laurence had a shared experience, there's little chance of us deducing what she's talking about. For all we know the book she refers to could be a town or village, or a tapestry."

"So we can't worry about that," Gavin said, rubbing his hands in front of an air vent. "What about the second half of it, the separation of family and nation? That sounds more like an idea than a book."

"Or it could be an idea *contained* within a book," Parker said. "Something like Martin Luther's ninety-five theses, or Thomas Paine's *Common Sense*, which helped start the Revolutionary War."

She knew she liked this jock for a reason. "That's what I thought," she said. "Given what precipitated Anne's search for her son, I think I know what she's talking about."

Gavin's fingers snapped together, a whip cracking in the silent vehicle. "Of course. The whole reason she had to call for help. Her cousin George wanted to steal the throne, to use her family's Roman Catholic faith to prevent any relatives from succeeding her."

"As a Protestant, George was next in line," Erika finished. "It was religion that divided her family and their nation. We're looking for the original bestseller."

"The Bible," Gavin said. As they climbed a short hill, the surrounding fields of inky black fell, and a shaft of white hit his face, lighting on the dark circles beneath his eyes. "Which one? Are we searching for Laurence Hyde's bible? Anne's bible? Or any bible, and then for a specific passage?"

"My instinct is to locate one at Trinity with ties to Anne. So far she's incorporated a number of her clues into items left behind during the journey through Ireland. It's likely any items she donated or used would still be part of their collection."

In truth, anything could have happened to Anne's next message, even if they were on the right track. Despite this, Erika took heart in the progress they'd made. So far, Anne's path continued to unfold.

"The safehouse isn't far from here," Gavin said. "And Trinity College will be open early. Sleep while you can, because I don't know how long we'll be able to stay ahead of the Keepers. The Chief Keeper is one pissed off man right now. He'll be after us like the hounds of hell."

Lights dotted the horizon as they crested a rise and accelerated, the capital of Ireland glowing brightly in front of them.

Chapter 32

Roscrea, Ireland

The oppressive halogen lighting common in every police station stung Logan's eyes. A cup of steaming coffee, bitter and weak, did little to brighten his mood. He leaned against a filing cabinet, one arm draped over the top.

"And you found nothing at Leap Castle?"

The two men in front of him stood motionless, arms behind their backs, eyes focused on a point just above his right shoulder. The universal blank gaze of policemen facing a superior with only bad news to report.

"That's correct, sir. We searched the castle, top to bottom. Nothing but dust."

The shorter one did the talking, his vocally-challenged partner content to stare a hole through the wall. The Roscrea chief trusted these men, and as much as Logan believed the two Americans and their IRA guides should be in custody by now, he couldn't blame this failure on this pair of Garda officers.

"Her Majesty thanks you for your service. Dismissed."

Rose had full use of the Roscrea Garda conference room, a humble affair with room for no more than ten around an aged conference table. Logan sat alone, studying the Yeoman Warder intelligence reports from Anne's journey.

"Where'd she go?"

These sheets traced their path, the movements of a woman long since dead outlined in meticulous detail. So far these reports had enabled Logan to trace Dr. Carr's movements. For the first time, the past did not foretell the future.

"So you left Kilkenny and came to Leap Castle," Logan said, re-reading the report. "And then on to Dublin. But where?" Had the Queen managed to slip away from her protectors, or did her minders simply not find her movements noteworthy? Whatever the reason, Logan now needed to find four people in a city of nearly two million. He damn well couldn't pull all of the warders from their normal duties without providing a good reason, and right now he couldn't share that reason.

The clock struck midnight, Logan's eyelids fighting a losing battle with gravity, every blink a task.

"Come on," he barked at his new driver. The man looked how Logan felt, slumped over in a chair outside the conference room. "Find a hotel, grab some rest. We'll get back at this first thing in the morning."

Logan thanked the chief on his way out, and as he climbed into the undercover sedan, felt the first tinge of doubt take root in his psyche. Those Americans had no idea who they helped, or of the catastrophe awaiting them.

Chapter 33

Soft amber sunlight crept over the horizon, the promise of a warm summer day greeting each inhabitant of Belfast. Cobblestone streets came to life, the first early risers joined by a trickle of businessmen, with a tide of students and professors soon to follow. Inside a building across from the University of Ulster, the inhabitants began to move about, more than a few shaking off the Irish flu with powerful cups of dark coffee.

"What's the word, lads?"

Arden Flanarty stood over a trio of seated technicians, each young enough to be his son. Though short on years, these were the IRA's best and brightest on anything electronic, a new breed of freedom fighter.

"Our courier just boarded the truck, and we expect him at Barclays in ten minutes. It's the first stop on their route."

"Be ready to call in the robbery alert once our man is in the vault."

"Will do. There's a tracking device on the detonator, that blip you see right here." The young tech pointed at a green dot on the screen, his finger trailing the blinking light as it moved. "They just left the currency storage facility. We also have the bank schematics, and we've overlaid a map of the city so you can tell where the bomb is at all times."

"And our triggering mechanism is working?"

"It is," the tech said. "I tested it earlier, but as a precaution we haven't activated it yet. Once the threat is called in, I'll turn it on and be certain he's well outside before we detonate."

Tiny waves rippled across the coffee in Arden's mug as he blew on it, steam wafting up his nose. "It's a beautiful day, lads. And it's only getting better."

As Connor Whelan walked into the control room, brief snatches of conversation flitted on the air, one of their masterful technicians speaking in that reserved, almost reluctant manner Connor noted in so many of today's youth. Maybe he feared Arden Flanarty. If so, good for him. You didn't trifle with Flanarty lightly. He'd spilled more than his share of blood over the decades, revered in IRA circles as a freedom fighter who showed no mercy. Connor only hoped he could limit the damage done today, Arden's rash response to Brin's murder a threat to all the Provisionals had built. Realizing lasting peace in a free Northern Ireland didn't happen by bombing banks.

"Good morning, men. How are things?"

"Going as planned, QM," the young tech said. "I'm updating Mr. Flanarty as to our progress."

Connor learned that two tracking devices were in play, one on the bomb and one on their man.

"Carry on then." Connor studied the monitors, marveling at the image of downtown Belfast projected on the wall, each street and building laid out in vivid detail. Keyboards clicked, signals went on their way, and men died.

"A word?"

Connor stood at Arden's elbow, his voice low. Arden nodded, following Connor away from the rapt crowd.

"I don't suppose I can convince you that this is a bad idea."

"Come now," Arden said. "You know better than that. We can't let this go, not when one of our lads is dead."

Arden spoke in a level tone, his words even. To an outsider, they might be discussing Celtic's latest football match, not the impending murder of a dozen people.

"You know how this will affect us," Connor said. "There'll be no doubt who set this up, and the Queen's wrath will come down on our heads. I don't see the upside."

"That's because you're not looking at it properly. Pride is the lifeblood of our movement, Connor. It's necessary to keep it alive."

"Killing twelve people isn't something I'm proud of."

Arden didn't blink. "Maybe you're right. Maybe I am a monster. I really don't know anymore. We've tried diplomacy, made a run at it with the Good Friday Agreement. You call that progress. Not in my eyes. All we've done is line our yoke with velvet."

Which didn't surprise Connor in the least. A killer, sure, and some called him evil, but Connor knew Arden didn't kill for spite.

Arden *believed*.

The hardest kind of man to break, the worst kind of enemy. Arden possessed unshakeable faith in their cause. And he always thought two steps ahead.

Which worried the hell out of Connor.

"You say this is more of what we went through thirty years ago," Arden said, steam rising from his coffee. "You're right. I remember when they took limbs off the street in buckets. I was there. I did some of the killing. Just never got around to the dying part. What has changed is that we can do this. We can have our freedom, but we must *take* it."

"And this bank job, you think that's what we need to rouse the troops? To get people on our side, screaming for independence? I can't say I agree."

One of the technicians approached, studying his shoes. "Five minutes, QM and Mr. Flanarty. That's when we'll make the call."

"Thank you," Connor said, and the boy scurried off.

"I remember when I was that age," Arden said, reaching into his pocket. Connor caught a hint of soft, peaty smoke as whiskey mixed with the black coffee. "Thought I had the world ahead of me, would make it my own. At least this part of our island, anyway. Little did we know."

"We were fools," Connor agreed. "And we needn't make those same mistakes again."

"The only mistake is going halfway," Arden said. "That's one I won't be making."

With that, Arden headed toward the waiting group, all eyes on the bright displays.

Going halfway?

Joining their small circle, Connor stood behind the technicians. The blinking dot wasn't moving.

"He's entering the bank," a technician said. "Pulling up internal schematics now."

On the wall, the image swept from a bird's eye view, through the front door of the bank and into the lobby, a virtual blueprint with room labels and dimensions.

"Now they have to wait for the vault to be opened," the tech said. "Okay, he's inside. Time to call it in."

A button clicked and the call went out.

"There's a robbery in progress at the Barclays," the technician said.

"Yes, downtown. The security code is green, green, two, seven. There are three of them, and they have guns. Please hurry." The tech clicked off. "That should get them moving."

Moments later, the tech pulled his headset back on. "You see them? Good. How many cars?" He swiveled around to face Connor. "That was our man outside the private security building. Two trucks just headed out, and in a hurry."

"Perfect," Arden said. "Our courier is still outside the vault. Let's hope the security team arrives on time."

"They're right on schedule," the tech said. "It takes at least ten minutes inside the vault to do a cash exchange, and the security team will be there in two."

Several tense minutes later, a call came in from another man stationed outside the bank, currently walking his dog in circles.

"The trucks are here," he reported. "A dozen officers kitted up in combat gear, swarming all over."

"Copy. Let us know when you see the courier."

The tech fell silent as all eyes locked on the green tracking dot.

"The currency delivery team just walked out," the tech relayed. "Only one of the British guards is with them. That leaves eleven inside."

"That's good enough," Arden said. "Ten seconds. Then set it off."

When his count hit zero, the young man at the controls reached out. His hand stopped, hovering over the red button.

He glanced to Connor Whelan.

Christ forgive me.

Chapter 34

Roscrea, Ireland

A fitful night's rest did little to improve Logan's situation. When the first rays of dawn slipped through an open window curtain, tiny claws of pain squeezed his eyes. Sleep had proven elusive, thoughts of Prince William and Queen Anne haunting the darkness.

The hell with this. If those dead royals were going to keep him up, he may as well get some work done.

The centuries-old Warder's intelligence report of Anne's journey came out, the words burned in his memory by now. Except this time they failed him. Anne's every move laid bare, from London onward. The reason he stayed one step ahead of the IRA team, except the leg from Leap Castle to Dublin didn't follow suit.

Leaving him with nothing. Three centuries ago Dublin over sixty thousand people, with countless building and sites for Anne to visit. Assuming she chose a secure hiding spot for her next clue, he immediately suspected a landmark, lasting and secure. Which left hundreds of options spread across the city.

On top of this, Dr. Carr and her minders may locate Anne's most recent missive or map. The Roscrea town guard hadn't found the Americans, but that didn't mean they never made their way to Leap Castle.

For the first time, Logan found himself on the defensive, the intelligence reports failing him.

"And this is the last stop on your journey," Logan said, thumbing through the pages. "After Dublin, you returned to London, back home, your son lost. You should have killed your cousin George." History showed that force kept you in power, a lesson Anne never learned.

Logan knew that life wasn't in the business of giving things away. Success isn't owned, it's leased, and the rent is due every day. Fortunately for George of Hanover, Anne failed her son and lost the throne.

His phone buzzed. "What is it, Mr. Moore?"

"Turn on the television. I think we have their attention."

Chapter 35

Dublin, Ireland

Pain sharp as knives stabbed Parker's back, both knees aching. One arm, stuck under his head, tingled with invisible needle-pricks, and each joint ached as though his tendons were wound too tightly. To top it all off, a fist hammered his door, rattling the thin wood.

"Go away."

The door swung open, revealing the culprit to be Gavin Rooney. "We leave in ten minutes. Breakfast is on the kitchen table. Erika's already downstairs."

Parker glanced at his watch. Exactly four hours earlier they'd walked into this nondescript rowhouse in Dublin, two stories of blandness blending perfectly with the endless blocks of urban dwellings all around.

He still wore the clothes they'd traveled in, every joint protesting as he rolled out of the narrow bed. Erika slept in the room next to his, in a bed just as small. Splashing water on his face, one knee mashed against the toilet crowding behind him, and Parker stood ready to face the day. Well, not actually ready. His back ached, his neck creaked, and a persistent fog filled his brain.

"I hope you're hungry," Harry said as he stumbled into the kitchen. "We've an Irish breakfast, and you have eight minutes to eat."

Strong coffee, hot bacon fat, fried eggs and toasted bread met his nose, piled high on his plate, a cup of black gold steaming beside it.

It only lasted five minutes. Enough time for his back to loosen, and as he scraped the last bit of grease off his plate, Parker felt like a new man. A tired one in a foreign country with people trying to kill him, but what the hell?

"The college library is open now," Gavin said. "And as Erika believes it's the best place to begin our search, we're heading over."

"Given Anne's last message, we're likely searching for an object containing writing. This suggests a book, of course," Erika said as they climbed into Harry's vehicle. "There's a chance she wasn't referring to a book, but right now we have to move on that idea. No telling when the Keepers may show up."

"Will, Dr. Carr. Not may," Gavin said. "They have resources and men. Crowds are our friend."

"We shouldn't be long here," Harry said. "Find the Bible or whatever we're looking for. I hope this is the last stop and we can figure out why these Brits have their knickers in a twist."

"Do you see that?" Erika asked, pointing to a cluster of buildings ahead.

"That's the college," Gavin said.

"Correct. And I'm pointing to the tallest building."

"What about it?"

"That's the Old Library Building. It's where we'll search for Anne's next message. It's the largest library in Ireland."

Silence filled the car.

"Just how big are we talking here?" Harry asked.

"Roughly six million volumes. Give or take a few hundred thousand."

"That's a lot of books,"

"One of which is the Book of Kells. Written nine centuries before Anne lived, so we can count that one out at least to start. We have an enormous amount of material to review and not much time in which to do it. We have to narrow things down before we start. First, cut any books published after 1700."

"How many do you think that will eliminate?" Gavin asked, fiddling with the amulet around his neck.

"If it even is a book she's talking about," Parker said.

Big mistake.

Her eyes narrowed. "We start with that assumption. There are so many books because it's a legal deposit, which means the library receives all material published within Ireland, England and Scotland."

"So this library gets a copy of every new book published in the United Kingdom?" Harry asked.

"It does," Erika confirmed. "Most of which can be eliminated right now. But that still leaves us with thousands of possibilities."

"So search for anything associated with Anne?" Parker asked.

"I'll talk to a librarian and see if they have anything Anne owned," Erika said. "If we don't get lucky, we'll see if anything related to the Stuart dynasty fits the bill. Beyond that, we'll make an educated guess."

"Let's make sure that doesn't happen," Gavin said. "The longer we spend in one place, the more likely the Keepers catch up. Even in Dublin."

Rumbling over cobblestones, Parker leaned over and craned his neck, the massive quadrangle filling the windshield.

Damn, that's one big library.

"We have to walk from here," Erika said. "The Old Library is open to the public, and I'd like to avoid using my academic credentials."

"Good call," Gavin said. "If you must, we can be your graduate assistants. Fake names, of course. I've no idea if the Keepers can access Trinity's internal network, but it's not a risk worth taking."

Inside the square, Parker found lush green amid concrete walkways. Students hurried past, most with their nose buried in a phone, a few in actual books. Windows lined the library's front, in columns stacked three high.

Through a front door thick enough to withstand a battering ram, Parker leaned over the front desk, straining to catch a word the attendant said.

"Good morning." Curly black hair fell over his eyes. "May I direct you in any way?"

"I hope so." Erika leaned in close, flashing her brightest smile. "It's my first time here, and I'm a bit overwhelmed."

The young man ran through his hair, trying and failing to contain the unruly locks. "I certainly understand. How may I help?"

"I need to find anything related to Queen Anne of Great Britain. I'm a fan of hers."

"You've come to the right place," he said, walking around the reception desk. "We have two million volumes on display, with twice that number in our reserves. If you'll follow me, I can show you how to use our database."

"That sounds wonderful. But before we start, can you tell me if you have anything here which belonged to her or her family?" Erika's eyelids fluttered. "It's silly, I know, but it would be wonderful to study a piece intimately connected to her."

"Part of what I love about this place is the chance to be so close to our past," the attendant said with a smile. "Did you know the oldest harp in Ireland is in this building? I'm a bit of a musician myself, and having one of the symbols of our country nearby inspires me."

"That's exactly what I mean," she said, her fingers running across the kid's hand. Parker bit his lower lip, stifling a grin. She wasn't pulling any punches. "I'd truly appreciate if you'd help me search."

"It'll be just a moment. Feel free to inspect the Long Room while you wait, but I won't be long."

As he darted away, Erika led them toward the room, shoes squeaking on marble floors. When Parker rounded the corner, he suddenly felt very small.

Bookshelves stretched for acres, set atop wood polished by millions of footsteps. Row upon row of shelves, a continent's worth of knowledge, theirs for the taking. Sunlight fell onto the center aisle, each color of the rainbow courtesy of the stained glass windows overhead. Paper rustled and chairs squeaked, a soundtrack for this most imposing avenue of learning.

"I sure hope that kid can help us," Gavin said. Erika led them into the hall, stopping in front of a marble bust.

"Who are all these guys?" Parker asked. Dozens of busts stretched in a line, one at each bookcase, a stony honor guard running the length of the hall.

"This is Jonathan Swift," she said. "And Gavin should know the one beside him."

"Bram Stoker," Gavin said, reading the nameplate. "It is his alma mater, after all."

"There's no chance we can search this place in one day. Probably not even a week." Parker stood in front of a glass display case, one of many placed along the main thoroughfare. "And what if the book we're searching for is on display? I doubt even your Ivy League credentials will get us access."

"Worry about that later," she said. "Our conquering hero has arrived," she said as the attendant reappeared.

Eager was an understatement for the attendant as he reappeared, fully under Erika's spell. "I have good news," he said. "We have an abundance of resources directly related to Queen Anne. A few of which may surprise you."

Reverently clutched in both hands, the young man offered her a manila folder. "This is a list of all relevant tomes. Should you require any further assistance, I'm at your disposal."

Never the shy girl, Erika pulled him in for a hug. "Thank you," she said, the young man too pleased to respond.

"You're a devil, Dr. Carr." A wolf's grin creased Harry's face. "That lad's putty in your hands."

"If I can't handle a bookish college boy, I'm in trouble. This is where we start," she said heading toward an empty table. Shelves of books rose on each side, the volumes packed together from floor to ceiling.

"I suggest we split up and everyone take a section of the list," Gavin said. "If you approve, that is."

"I do," Erika said. "And we might need another table."

The list ran multiple pages, single-spaced.

"The kid's thorough," Gavin said. "But hold on. This one's about the entire Stuart dynasty." He shuffled through the pages, lines creasing his forehead. "Every one of them from the looks of it, not just Anne."

Gavin tapped the title in question. *A History of the Stuarts, Monarchs of Great Britain, Scotland and Ireland.*

"Maybe he was too helpful," Erika said. "I'll go through this and cut out the extraneous works. For now, Parker and Gavin search for Bibles related to Anne, and Harry can gather whatever I find that's relevant."

Harry moved among the stacks, Gaelic curses in his wake as he navigated the endless shelves. Parker worked a computer, searching the entire collection of six million volumes. His search parameters returned nearly one hundred pages of results.

"We're never going to find this thing," he muttered. Not too loudly, though. Erika sat close by.

"Here's the revised list," Gavin said a short while later. "I thought we were buggered at first, but then one of the front desk aides helped me sort by publication date. There aren't nearly as many from Anne's time, and almost all of them are stored in this room."

"Nicely done. I'll take the bottom," Parker said, ripping the paper in half. Now he needed to figure out where everything was. Labels bearing both letters and numerals adorned each shelf, none of which made sense. He needed a map.

And as luck had it, the information desk offered them.

"Thank you," he said.

The snowy-haired attendant touched her lips. "You're welcome. But please keep your voice down."

Parker flashed a smile and ran for it. Book one resided on the bottom floor, not far away. Only when a dry cover crackled in his grasp did he realize. *This book is over three centuries old. It's in a protective cover, sure, but I can pull it off the shelf and read it.*

"These Irish sure trust us," he said, sliding the tome free.

In short order, Parker balanced a pile of books in both hands, the tower leaning Pisa-style against his chest. With his nose hovering above the shifting stack, he dodged through the shelves and made it to their table without a single book hitting the floor.

"Two trips would have been silly," Erika said as the piles landed on her desk.

"Out of the question." Covered in books, the table was a library unto itself. "I see we have quite a few candidates."

"Start searching," Erika said. "Look for anything linking to Anne. It may be a note, a symbol, or an underlined passage. The most likely option is anything hand-written."

With Gavin and Harry flipping pages. Parker grabbed a book from the closest stack. It snapped shut ten minutes later, no traces of Anne Stuart to be found.

Crossing more titles off the list, books slowly migrated from their table to the returns cart Gavin procured. The cart's top row filled in no time, and two hours flew past before Parker glanced at a clock.

What were the chances that the Keepers could find them? Slim, but possible. If the Keepers did show up, these stacks became a maze, and they the rats trying to escape.

"Wake up." Erika smacked his arm. "What's so interesting about the front door? We can't leave until we get through all these books."

"I'm worried." Without thinking, one hand reached to his pocket, checking the ring. A sparkling secret, currently on hold.

"You having any luck?" he asked Gavin.

"None so far. These bleeding bibles are all the same. I feel a bit holier than I have in a long while," the Irishman said. "Maybe the good Father will notice and shine a light on Anne's next message."

Shadows grew small as they searched, the sun rising overhead. In turn the two IRA men stepped out, stretching their legs and taking stock of the area. As more time passed, several rounds of coffee came and went with no sign of the Keepers or a message from Anne.

"Do you know what these guys look like?" Erika asked, rolling her neck.

"Yes and no," Gavin said. "Even if they blend in well, anyone hanging around will stick out. Conducting surveillance in a place like this is hard."

"We'll sweep again in an hour. If anyone's watching, Gavin and I will notice," Harry said. "Remember, if we see them, it's probably too late."

Running in this maze did not appeal to him one bit, and if they escaped, then what? Trying to hide in a city where he didn't know his way around the block. "Let's find this damn message and get out of here."

Another hour flew past, the crowds thinning before noon. One minute visitors clogged the aisles, the next, only silence walked past.

"That's it for my list," Parker said. "Over a hundred books and nothing to show for it."

Harry and Gavin reported identical results.

"We need to do another security check," Gavin said. "See if you find anything in the last book before we get back."

The lone remaining option sat in front of Erika. Thick as a phonebook, the cover measured a foot wide and the spine stood twice as tall.

"What is this?"

"A monstrous bible," Erika said. "It must be illuminated."

"A picture book? Right up your alley."

"Funny." What little darkness remained in this room found a home on Erika's face. "You realize what happens if we don't find anything?"

"We'll find it," he said. His arm settled on her shoulder, pulling her in, fragrant hair tickled his nose, alive with the scent of lilacs. "Don't worry. Michelle started this, and I know you want to finish it."

This wasn't just about them. Michelle and Brin dead, both at the hands of shadowy government agents. They couldn't walk away, not after that.

"Let's find some answers," Parker said, opening the beastly book and revealing a page more brilliant than any he'd ever seen. "That looks like real gold."

Elaborate etchings ran around the edge, framing a towering cross.

"It's beautiful, but I promise you it's not the prettiest volume they have. That particular work is at the end of this corridor." She pointed to the main walkway running between each towering row of shelves. "The Book of Kells is on the far side of the Old Library."

"Book of Kells?"

Erika cocked an eye. "Parker, I'm disappointed. The book is one of Ireland's national treasures, arguably the most amazing illuminated manuscript on the planet." As she spoke, they studied the pages, searching and eliminating one after another. "The Book of Kells is illuminated, similar to this, though far more intricate. It contains the four Gospels of the New Testament."

"How old is it?"

"Around twelve hundred years."

That was *old*. Under different circumstances, not to be missed. With a group of killers breathing down their necks, however, he'd take a rain check. "Very neat," he said. "Unfortunately, what isn't are these clue-free pages. I don't see anything."

"Neither do I," Erika said. "And we're halfway through. Maybe Anne scribbled in the back."

By the time Gavin and Harry returned, the final page folded over without result, and the front and back covers revealed nothing beyond a couple of loose threads.

"What else can we look for?" Parker tried to stay upbeat. "The Bible angle is wrong, and Anne didn't leave her personal diary here. Is there anything we missed? Other books or artifacts here that might work?"

As four puzzled and frustrated people searched the floor for answers, Erika's admirer appeared.

"I see you've moved quickly," he said. "I'll take these books away for you if you're finished."

Erika gave a half-hearted reply, and the young guy twisted the cart around, wheels squeaking. As he did, Parker glimpsed a folded pamphlet jammed in his rear pocket. From its cover, Jesus Christ stared back.

"What's that?"

The kid saw Parker pointing at his backside and spun around, a dog chasing his tail. "What?" The pamphlet came out. "It's new promotional material for the Book of Kells. We're having an event during which the pages are turned every ten minutes based on audience requests. Really a neat opportunity to see different images from all parts of the New Testament."

"But the book isn't a Bible, is it?" Parker asked.

"Not in the traditional sense of the word," he said. "Or at least not a complete version. However, the text is believed to be based on the Vulgate, which is the Catholic Church's official Latin version of the Bible."

"What do you mean, *official* Latin version?" Erika asked. "Why would the Church call it that?"

"Excellent question. Would you like the short answer or the long one?"

"Short one." Parker, Gavin and Harry spoke in unison.

"It stems from the Reformation, when a designated reference for scripture was required. Church leaders chose the Vulgate translation."

"Which would make the Book of Kells quite biblical indeed," Erika said. Her fingers tightened around Parker's arm. "Were any additions made to the book since it's been here?"

"Not as you're suggesting," he said. "It's been re-bound, and the original single volume became four." He looked toward the ceiling, one hand scratching his unkempt hair. "I believe the folio numbers were also added later."

"Who did that?" Gavin asked.

"An Irish bishop."

Parker saw the hope fading from Erika's face. The overloaded book cart rumbled away.

"Wait a second." The cart stopped. "I almost forgot." The attendant said, turning to face them. "One alteration didn't actually make it in. More of an attempted alteration, really. Queen Victoria and her husband, Prince Albert, signed what they believed to be the book. Turns out they actually signed a more modern addition, and those pages have since been removed."

Erika nearly slid off the edge of her chair. "And those are the only royals who signed it?"

"As far as I'm aware, but I'm not positive."

"Would we be able to look through the book?" Harry asked. "For research purposes."

"The Book of Kells? I'm afraid not, sir. Only our most senior librarians are permitted to handle the book, and even then infrequently. But the entire manuscript can be viewed online. You may use the computer over there if you'd like."

The words scarcely left his mouth when Erika brushed past him, speed-walking to the nearby workstation. Parker pressed against her chair, Gavin and Harry at his sides.

A few clicks and Erika looked at the front cover of the Book of Kells.

"Just because no one's seen it yet doesn't mean it's not there," Erika said. "We're going to find it," Erika said.

The image doubled in size, and then again. Parker squinted, looking for anything out of place as Erika toggled, eliminating one grid at a time.

It didn't take long.

"What's that?" Gavin pointed to the third page, five illuminated golden columns rising to support windows beneath a curved dome. Letters fit between the columns, Latin of course, forming narrow paragraphs which filled the space between each column.

"What are you talking about?" Parker asked.

"Under these letters," Gavin said. "Do you see it?"

Faint, so soft as to be nearly transparent, but he saw it. "It looks like some letters are underlined," Parker said. "A specific part of the passage."

"Or it's a crease in the page," Erika said. "Or age discoloration, maybe a darker part of the calf skin used to make the page."

Possible, but it sure looked like ink under the letters. "I think he's right," Parker said. "The line's just below the letters, and it starts and stops abruptly. But more importantly, what's underlined? I can't read Latin."

"I think I know who might," Erika said. "Excuse me." Several aisles away, the most helpful desk attendant in town cheerfully shelved their discarded books.

Erika tapped his shoulder. "Would you come over here please?"

He ambled over to their group. "How may I assist you?"

"You wouldn't happen to speak Latin, would you?"

His face fell. "Not very well, I'm afraid. I'm a bit better at reading it, but can't speak much other than what we hear in mass every Sunday."

"That's perfect," Erika said. "Look at this line. Can you tell me what it says?"

"Let's see." His lips moved, no sound coming out. "I think it's along the lines of *'Cast thine eyes upon the heavenly light. God's wrath shall smite the demons of hell'*. Or something to that effect."

"Thank you so much for your help," Erika said.

"Assuming this is her next message, to what kind of *light* would Anne refer?" Gavin asked once the kid walked away. "Do you think she means knowledge or wisdom?"

"I hope not," Erika said. "If she's referring to an idea, our journey just got much harder."

"So it's something physical, an item you can actually touch?"

"We'll work with that idea," she said. "Maybe she's leading us to another book."

"Damn these books," Harry mumbled.

Parker didn't agree. "Anne hasn't played any games so far. Remember, she left these breadcrumbs while her cousin's spies watched over her shoulder. Most of the clues so far have been hidden in plain sight."

"And what's this business about *God's wrath*?" Gavin asked. "Sounds like another Biblical reference to me."

I should have paid attention in church. Struggling to recall his scripture, Parker squinted, sunlight bouncing off the table, spots dancing in his vision.

Sunlight.

"What if she means sunlight?"

"Actual sunlight?" Erika said. "It's an idea, but I'm not sure how Anne would use that to send a message."

"And if it's cloudy outside?" Harry asked.

They were missing it. "Not actual sunlight," Parker said. "Think about it. What do you see when you look up? When you *cast thine eyes upon the heavenly light?*"

"You'd see the sun, the sky, maybe clouds or trees." Gavin tried, but he didn't see the forest for the trees.

"Wrong. Well, you're right, but you're not." He pointed to the windows above them. "Look at the sun right now. Do it."

All three of them stared at the answer. Or *through* it, to be precise.

"It's almost directly overhead," Gavin replied. "I can't see it because there's no glass dome above us."

Erika finally got it. "You think she's talking about a window," she said, smacking his backside. "Not my first choice, but worth checking. Nice work."

"I do my best," he said. "Yes, I'm talking about windows. Look at this page from the Book of Kells. What else is on it? Above the pillars."

"A curved roof," she replied. "And below that are windows. Stained glass windows."

Four of them, each boasting an intricately detailed scene.

"Tell me that's not something you'd use to kill demons," Parker said, his finger tapping one of the windows. On it, a polished silver blade gleamed, a red cross-guard bisecting the yellow blade.

"That's a damn fine sword to smite demons," Gavin said. "But why is Anne pointing us to it?"

"Get that guy back over here," Parker said, his skin tingling. The sword could be here, on display between the aisles. Trinity's library boasted a famous harp. Maybe this blade resided here as well.

"Have you ever seen that?" Parker asked.

The shaggy-haired librarian leaned over Erika's shoulder. "Oh my goodness."

"What is it?" Erika asked.

"Earlier you asked about anything in our library associated with Queen Anne. Though we have many books on Her Majesty, I neglected to consider other options. And given it's no longer on the grounds, it slipped my mind."

"What slipped your mind?"

"A magnificent stained glass window. One nearly identical to this window." He tapped the screen. "Donated by Anne during a visit to Trinity College."

The rest of the library faded away, Parker leaning toward his new best friend.

"Where is the window now?"

"It's in Dublin Castle. Straight down Dame Street, not five minutes away."

Erika stood, planting a kiss on his cheek. "Thank you for all your help today. We couldn't have done it without you."

Not bothering to inquire as to what wouldn't have been possible without his aid, the rosy-cheeked young man wandered off, his cartload of books forgotten.

"I'll admit this looks promising, but how can we be sure?" Gavin crossed his arms. "It can't hurt to check Dublin Castle and see this window. Just remember we aren't positive about this. We need a backup plan in case things get hairy."

"Speaking of that, I'm overdue for another sweep," Harry said.

"Get on it, but you only need to check the front entrance. We'll be leaving shortly."

Harry vanished in the increasing flow of foot traffic, more people returning from lunch.

"Parker, look at this."

He followed Erika's outstretched finger to the stained glass window in question, specifically the wicked sword. "What about it?"

"What does that look like to you?"

A sword. Even a child knew that. When he opened his mouth, she cut him off.

"Look on the blade."

Then he saw it. "I'll be damned. Looks like we're on the right track after all."

"What are you two getting on about?" Gavin asked.

"Anne underlined those words," Erika said. "You know how I can tell? She signed her work."

Gavin whistled softly when he saw two letters tucked under the cross guard. "You'd never see that if you weren't looking for it. Even after a thousand years."

Two tiny letters, hidden in plain sight.

A S

"*Anne Stuart.* She left this note," Erika said. "And a real stained glass window for emphasis."

Behind them, shoes slapped the marble floor.

"Time to leave." Harry's head never stopped moving as he spoke. With one hand he pulled Erika from the chair, the other on Parker's arm. "They're here."

"What? Who's here?" Parker swiveled around, searching for anything out of place.

"The Keepers," Gavin said, hustling away. "They found us."

"There's only one I can see," Harry said. "He's out front, casing the place. And in no hurry from the looks of it."

"How do you know he's one of them?" Parker asked.

"All these side doors are alarmed," Harry said. "And there aren't any doors in back. We'll go through the lobby and out one of the front doors."

"Harry, how do you know the guy is a Keeper?" Erika asked as Gavin hustled them along.

"There's a man standing near the front entrance, looking around, holding a sheet of paper and checking out everyone who walks past him. It didn't sit right, so I circled around until I could see the paper." Harry tapped Parker on the chest. "It's a picture of you and Erika."

"What kind of photo?" Parker asked.

"Headshots, probably from your passports. Another reason I can tell he's bloody government."

Other visitors walked past, jostled aside by their group. They reached the edge of the Old Library's central walkway, and ahead lay the main entrance.

"You see him?" Gavin said.

Harry took a few steps out, stooping over and tying his shoe before returning.

"He's around the corner to your right." Harry stood in front of Erika, his bulk shielding her from view. "Not twenty feet away."

"You go out, get eyes on him," Gavin said. "When he's looking the other way, touch your ear. We'll slip out the other entrance."

Whisked away in the stream of visitors, Harry vanished. A beam of sunlight fell on Parker, the rays warming his neck.

"Once Harry gives the signal, keep your heads down and don't stop walking no matter what happens." Gavin's phone chirped. "Sorry, QM," he muttered, silencing the call. "Bit busy right now."

Tucked against the wall, Parker couldn't see the Keeper on their tail. Erika stood beside him, her hand in his. Across the suddenly never-ending expanse, Harry looked at his watch, and then toward where the Keeper stood.

He scratched an ear.

"Go," Gavin said. "I'll cover your back."

Eyes down, feet moving, Parker led the way. One shoe in front of the other. What he wouldn't give for a hat right now.

Halfway toward the far entrance, and no sounds of pursuit.

"Is he coming?" Erika asked.

"He's headed this way, but I don't think he's spotted you yet," Gavin said. "Keep those blonde locks hidden if you can."

A wall of shimmering glass rose beside them, their reflections nearly lost in the crowd, flashing out of sight every other step. A burst of yellow caught Parker's eye as Erika pulled her hair back, banding it into a ponytail.

"Shit." The curse fell like a hammer strike. "Don't look back and don't panic." Gavin said. "He's headed this way."

Fighting the urge to flee, Parker reached for the door. "Where to now?"

"Head west," Gavin said. "Keep moving. He's coming."

Parker looked back, noted a disturbance in the crowd.

"Come on," Erika shouted. Seconds later, the door through which they'd exited crashed open.

A river of humanity flowed ahead, people only moving aside as Gavin cleared a path, shoulder first. Erika stayed behind him, with Parker bringing up the rear. At least he did, until running headlong into a guy on his cell phone.

"Sorry," he shouted as the man tumbled. Not far behind, the Keeper sped up. For a moment, his eyes locked on Parker, eerily calm as he barreled through the crowd, leaping over the fallen.

"Watch out!"

Parker smashed into a postal delivery girl. Letters filled the air like snowflakes, red hair sparking in the sunlight as she fell.

Gavin juked down a side street, more crowded than the one they'd left. Restaurants and cafes whizzed past on either side, stunned diners watching as a three-person demolition crew laid waste to everything in their path, their shock doubling when the Keeper barreled past, only steps behind.

An empty chair sat ahead. Inspiration struck Parker as he grabbed the metal seat and pulled it down, clanging and clattering on the cobbles. In any good movie, the man running behind them should fall. Only he'd seen this trick before, hurdling the chair with ease.

Gavin swerved again, back toward the main street, Erika now matching him stride for stride.

"What if he's leading us into a trap?" Erika asked.

"I haven't seen him on the phone," Gavin said. "Worry about getting away first."

"He's catching up." Parker accelerated, nipping at Gavin's heels.

Now back on the main thoroughfare, Gavin dodged between pedestrians and leapt a fire hydrant. An alley loomed ahead. Gavin raced past as a car crept out, headlights giving scarcely enough warning for Parker to slide across the hood.

"Hurry up," Gavin said, glancing back at them. "We need to—"

He never saw it coming. Another car darted out from the next side street, nearly running the stop sign, Gavin slamming into the side as tires screeched. Broken shards of window fell like diamonds, glittering in the sun. Flipped up and over the roof, the Irishman disappeared down the other side of the low-riding Fiat.

A string of sputtered Spanish filled the air, coming from the driver. Erika skidded to a halt, but Parker grabbed her as he passed, pulling her along.

"Get up," he said. Gavin lay on his back, one hand covered in blood and a gash on his cheek, but that seemed to be the worst of it. "Can you move?"

Gavin stood, stumbled, and then righted himself. "I'm good."

"Freeze!"

A gun hovered inches from Parker's face. The screaming Spaniard driver had masked the Keeper's approach, only falling silent when the weapon came out. Pedestrians stopped, mouths hanging open before they fled in all directions beneath fluttering pigeons, gray wings clawing the air as they climbed.

"Hands up." The pistol never wavered as the Keeper dug through his pocket. "Chief Rose is gonna love this. Trinity College, of all places."

Inside the Fiat, the Spaniard stared slack-jawed, one end of his emerald scarf hanging out the open window. For some reason his hands were up as well.

Like a vengeful wraith, a dark shadow rose behind the Keeper. Outlined by the sun, Harry jumped over the Fiat's hood with both fists out and smashed the Keeper's head.

Direct hit. The Keeper fell and didn't get up.

"About time you caught up," Gavin said. From the Keeper's pockets he removed a cell phone and wallet as Harry grabbed the fallen gun. "Getting a bit out of shape, aren't we?"

"You had a mighty head start," Harry said. "And I wouldn't be talking much if I was you, seeing as how that car tripped you up."

Parker turned and found the Spaniard had finally come to his senses and taken off running. Halfway down the block and accelerating, the old geezer could really move.

"Not sure if we need it, but that guy left his keys for us," Parker noted. "We could put this one"—he pointed at the unconscious Englishman—"in the trunk, make it harder for him to find his friends once he wakes up."

"Excellent idea," Gavin said. "You take his feet."

It took some prodding and twisting, but as Harry and Erika ran interference on the road, they stowed him in the trunk, two hundred pounds of dead weight tucked neatly out of sight. The Keeper wasn't dead, but he'd have one hell of a headache when he woke up.

"You drive," Gavin told Harry as they all jumped into the vehicle. "I have to call the QM. Park close to Dublin Castle if you can, on a side street. Wouldn't want our friend back there to be found too easily."

A flow of foot traffic moved around them, this Fiat with a broken window not even registering on any pedestrian's radar.

"The cops will be here soon," Erika said. "We should get this car off the streets."

"Agreed," Harry replied. "There's a parking garage ahead. A spot way in back should work for us. The question is, what do we do in Dublin Castle?"

He glanced at Erika, tucked beside Parker in the minuscule backseat.

"There should be an information desk near the front door, so we'll try the employees first, see if they can direct us to the window. It worked at Trinity."

"Any chance we could get a disguise?" Parker asked. "Maybe a baseball cap? There are bound to be cameras there. Keeping our faces hidden may pay off later."

"There's a street vendor ahead," Harry said, pointing. "We'll stop on our way out. No time now."

The Fiat lurched as it left the roadway, bouncing over a speed bump and into the parking garage. Twice Parker's shoulder smashed against the door, and twice he hoped Italian engineers built a sturdy car. Buried in a corner spot on the top floor, they twisted out of the thing, except for their new English friend. He stayed in the trunk.

A phone pressed to Gavin's ear. "I see. Thanks for the update. I'll call when we have news." He clicked off, his mouth a hard line. "Time's running short. We need to move quickly."

"What's happened?" Parker asked.

"It's the rest of the leadership council. They organized another attack."

"Killing more people while we're trying to stay alive," Erika said. "Looks like your leaders only care about their cause, not their men."

Gavin didn't flinch, but his face softened. "There are times when I couldn't agree more, Dr. Carr. However, the decision is not mine to make, though this attack isn't meant to kill. The more aggressive council members decided to conduct a symbolic attack, to detonate a bomb at the statue of Queen Elizabeth here in Dublin. There should be no casualties."

Parker didn't like it any more than Erika. "In the city? The last thing we need are more police on the streets. Where's the statue and when is the bomb going off?"

Gavin silently led them down the parking garage stairwell and onto a crowded sidewalk. Dublin Castle loomed ahead, a rounded stone and mortar tower jutting skyward, protected by a low-slung crenellated rock wall.

"Near St. Stephen's Green."

"Damn." Harry started walking faster.

"Is that bad?" Erika asked as they passed under a metal gate, the castle entrance ahead.

"It's only a few blocks from here," Gavin answered. "And the bomb's going off any minute."

Chapter 36

Belfast, Northern Ireland

Inside IRA headquarters, QM Connor Whelan listened to Arden Flanarty discuss his latest scheme.

"Wait for my call to detonate," Arden was saying, a phone pressed to his ear. "Oh, and do your best not to kill anyone."

Arden Flanarty clicked off, his tumbler rising. A smile tugged at the corner of his mouth, though whether from the whiskey or the thought of destroying another English landmark, Connor couldn't tell.

"I appreciate your consideration," Connor said.

"This is your show, Quartermaster," Arden replied. "As they say, our time has come."

The whiskey put fire behind his words. Barely past noon, the man was drunk with success and more than a bit tipsy on booze. Worst of all, his reckless plans placed Gavin in danger. Connor did what he could and warned him, but the boy wouldn't have an easy time of it after this bombing.

And for what? To destroy a statue of Queen Elizabeth. It carried symbolic value, no argument there. But for Gavin and his team, the timing couldn't have been worse.

At least Flanarty agreed not to kill anyone. Or to *try* to avoid it. Hot ash lit Connor's face as he puffed his pipe, smoke swirling across his vision. Not only did this statue nonsense muddy the waters, but Connor knew Arden Flanarty, and success only emboldened the man.

"How are Gavin and Harry doing with their American friends?" Arden asked, digging like an old operative always did.

As if Connor would reveal the truth. Do that, and a desecrated monument became the least of their worries.

"They succeeded at Trinity, and are moving on to Dublin Castle. A bit of a scrape at the college, nothing serious. Gavin's calling with an update when they unravel the next piece of the puzzle."

Another IRA man walked over to them. "Any idea what in the hell has these Keepers so fired up?" he asked, a cigarette dangling from his lips. "Maybe our little diversion will keep those bastards off their case, buy them some time."

"No idea, other than what we discussed about Queen Anne. And while I hope you're correct," Connor said, eyeing Arden. "I fear it may not be so."

"Don't worry," Arden said. "This battle has only just begun."

Exactly what the QM worried about. Arden would burn it all if he could, even if it left no one to remember his name.

"It's about that time," Arden said. "Gather round, boys. The fun's starting. That old bat Elizabeth can kiss her arse good-bye."

Amidst the cheers and roar, QM Connor Whelan clasped both hands behind his back, lines creasing his forehead. Gavin's hunt carried on in secret, and Connor had to make sure it stayed that way, doing all he could to guide them safely through.

Chapter 37

London, England

For one thousand years and counting, the Tower of London guarded this city, perched on the banks of the Thames. Like any great leader, she held secrets close to her strong heart, and often her enemies closer than that. And through it all, the Tower kept her endless watch, always at the ready.

Consider her now, bustling with a level of activity not seen since the end of World War II, men working around the clock in the lowest levels deep underground.

From these guarded rooms, Deputy Chief Keeper Oliver Moore orchestrated a manhunt, a group of Keepers assembled in his office. "Do not underestimate the enemy. Terrorists have co-opted these Americans, brought them into the fold," Oliver said. "That's all for now. I'll provide an update shortly." Once they left, Oliver fell into a chair, finger rubbing at his aching temples.

Logan Rose suspected the two IRA terrorists were in Dublin with the Americans, but gave no reasons for his suspicion. The original Yeoman Warder reports gave little insight into Anne's activities in the city, so his motivations must have stemmed from elsewhere. Fine with Oliver, but now he needed to comb through over a million Dublin residents to find four people, two of whom blended in like natives.

"Might as well throw darts at the bloody map with my eyes closed."

A fan twirled softly overhead, shadows chopping through the room. Oliver kicked his boots up on the desktop, his eyelids growing heavy. Five minutes, that's all.

And then his cell phone clattered for attention.

"Moore here," he said, rubbing a bloodshot eye.

"Did you find them yet?" Logan Rose asked.

"Negative," Oliver said. "Every resource at our disposal is in the field. Our men are deployed to potential landmarks, with photographs of the targets. Given we only have low-quality surveillance images of the two terrorists, the Americans will be easier to recognize."

By the book, exactly what Logan wanted. Except watching their manpower disperse so thinly, Oliver realized this plan reeked of reaction, of playing defense. Winning a war took decisive action, not a scattershot approach.

And so, for the first time in his life, Oliver questioned his commanding officer.

"Sir, perhaps we should consider concentrating our efforts. As it stands, we have one man for every three possible locations. The chances of missing our targets are higher than I'd like."

"That's not possible, Deputy Moore. What information I have is limited. Between the two of us, I'm not even certain we're looking in the right place. I'm thirty minutes outside Dublin now. If we don't have any success in the coming hours, we'll regroup and bring city law enforcement agencies into the fold, people we can trust to keep things buttoned up. With those agencies comes access to closed circuit cameras and private security systems, and a greater chance of spotting them."

"How do you know we can trust the locals?"

"I don't. But it's our best shot. This debacle must end now. Should these terrorists continue down Anne's path…"

Logan didn't have to finish. They ventured into unknown territory, amplifying the risks. Anything could be out there, and centuries of experience proved the unknown to often be far more dangerous than any flesh and blood enemy.

"Understood, sir. We'll locate the terrorists and their American associates in short order," Oliver said as another phone rang. "A field agent is calling, Chief. I'll report back as soon as I have news."

Oliver clicked off and put the agent on speaker.

"Deputy Chief Moore, are you there?" Shouting, his words nearly lost in background noise.

Were those *sirens*?

"Speaking," Oliver said. "What in blazes is that racket?"

"It's gone, sir. It's just gone." Static howled on the speaker, as though the caller stood in a windstorm.

"What's gone?"

"I'm across from St. Stephen's Green," the field agent said. "I only left the Royal College of Surgeons a few minutes ago when it went off."

Oliver's knuckles went white around the phone. "Are you talking about an explosion?"

"Affirmative. A statue of Queen Elizabeth outside the Green. There's nothing, sir. It's a great bloody hole now."

Those crazy bastards blew up a statue? "How many injured?"

"None, sir. Doesn't look like anyone was near the statue when the bomb went off. There were sawhorses around it, but they're all burnt up now."

"Are you sure it wasn't an accident, maybe a generator explosion?"

"Definitely not, sir. No work vehicles in the area, and I don't see any construction men around here. Hold on a second." Garbled conversation mixed with the racket. "A lady here says she took pictures of the statue when the explosion happened. She didn't notice anything going on near the statue, no workers or equipment. Just the barricades around it."

"Confiscate her camera. Get to a police station and have any images transmitted directly to me."

"Understood, sir."

His cell phone noted two missed calls before it started ringing again. Which meant he faced an onslaught of men with information and in need of direction. Before they came, though, he needed a moment to think.

If the IRA did this, why blow up a statue? These Northern Irishmen loved to maim, to kill. Symbolic destruction wasn't their M.O. Unless, of course, they'd only just begun.

A Keeper knocked, pushing the door open. "Deputy Chief, a word?"

"Gather everyone," he said. If the IRA meant to divert Oliver's resources, he couldn't take the bait. "Bring them to the central office."

Sixty seconds later every available Keeper stood in the expansive main room, which alternately served as a central office, gathering area, and in times such as these, a situation room.

"Fellow Keepers," Oliver said, his voice reaching from wall to wall. "Terrorists have surfaced in Dublin. Less than an hour ago, they destroyed a statue of Queen Elizabeth. We suspect this is a precursor to additional attacks, so most of you are being mobilized into the field."

High fives and battle cries filled the air. All former military, these were men of action. Wherever these terrorists now hid, the full weight of the Keepers followed.

"Locations and plans are being finalized. You'll be notified shortly of your destination, but for now, plan on leaving for Ireland before the day is out."

Controlled pandemonium erupted, music to his ears. He'd taken a few liberties with that announcement. After all, the Chief Keeper, not Oliver, made the final call. With the men sufficiently roused, Oliver hustled to his office and rang his superior.

"What's going on?" Logan Rose asked by way of greeting.

"An explosion," Oliver said, recounting the details. "The men are preparing to leave now. All we need is a course of action."

"No injuries at the scene? That's perfect," Logan said. "Those fools gave me the reason I need to send the cavalry. How many men are ready to go?"

"Out of our thirty, twenty-five are available to leave immediately. The other five could go as well, but I suggest leaving them behind to man and secure the Tower. Five men are the minimum we can use to keep our operations running."

"I agree," Logan said. "Now, where to deploy them."

"No progress on identifying possible targets?" Oliver asked.

"I've been through the original intelligence reports over and over. There's nothing. All we know is Anne headed to Dublin, and after a time there she returned to London. It's as though the Yeoman Warders no longer thought her movements were worth noting."

"Maybe Anne ran out of options?"

"Or she gave them the slip and they didn't want to face George's wrath. Our reports disappeared over the past three centuries. Whatever happened, we're running blind now. Our best move is to post men at every historical landmark from Anne's time, places a queen might visit," Logan said. "The list can't be long,"

"We'll keep monitoring for any sign of the Americans," Oliver said. "Credit cards, passports and the like."

"If word gets out, what happens next will make a few dead Irishmen look like child's play. The Queen will have our heads. There's a reason we keep secrets."

"We'll find the terrorists and silence them."

"It must be done quietly," Logan said. "Check your email. I sent the list of locations to monitor. Can you think of any I missed?"

"Looks good to me," Oliver said, scanning the message. "I suggest assignments in pairs, rotating between locations. That way we cover more ground and keep the men safer."

"Agreed. Work out the logistics. Put one experienced and one newer man in each group. Keep a few solo to pair off with the men already in Ireland."

A car horn ripped through the phone. "I just arrived in Dublin," Logan said. "Get those men airborne within the hour. I'll meet you at the airport."

Logan clicked off, leaving Oliver with cold chills on his spine and a steely resolve. Their enemy didn't hesitate to kill, so Oliver planned to return the favor, and if those Americans got in the way, so be it.

Chapter 38

Dublin Castle
Dublin, Ireland

In Dublin Castle, the past lived on, ancient towers standing beside modern conference centers in the heart of Dublin. An active government complex and bustling tourist attraction, parts of the sprawling architectural mix surrounding Parker dated from the thirteenth century. This included the record tower where Erika finally located someone who knew of the window they sought. The blue-haired attendant even offered to take them there.

"I love when people take notice of our past," she said as they crossed the courtyard. Birds flew overhead, a warm breeze following their path. They passed another narrow tower rising from the ground like an angry fist damning the heavens, gray stone topped by a pointed turquoise dome. "You know," their guide said when she caught Parker looking. "The Irish Crown Jewels were stolen from that tower one hundred years ago."

"Is that so?" Parker said. "How did that happen?" Getting out of here with all the guards around couldn't have been easy.

"No one knows," the guide said. "The jewels are still missing, and the mystery remains unsolved."

Harry let out a low whistle. "Never heard that tale. Damn shame to lose so much of our history." To Parker's ears, the words rang sincere, those of a true believer.

"Mankind is the greatest destroyer of his own past," Erika said. "More history is lost through men's treachery than through any natural disaster or the passing of time. We're our own worst enemy."

"Amen," the guide said. "It warms me to know young folks like you care enough about our heritage to visit and learn. And here we are. I promise you won't be disappointed."

Pillars fronted the building, stretching out to either side, three pairs of double doors in their way, the center set thrown open.

"There's a spot of magic here. Every seven years an ordinary man enters these doors," their guide said, "and emerges a President. The inaugurations of our nation's leaders are held in this building."

Through the front doors, their group passed a guided tour headed outside, schoolchildren screaming and shouting.

"There is much to learn in our beautiful complex, though you four have chosen one of the lesser-known artifacts to review. Of course, that doesn't make it any less fascinating," the guide said. "In my opinion, the Throne Room is the most beautiful portion of the State Apartments."

Inside the apartments they found a room dominated by white and gold. Gold curtains, gold paint, even gold inlay on the carved ceiling, layer upon layer of molding welcoming visitors to the royal confines. A gold and crystal chandelier provided modern lighting, and even the electrical outlets sported gold-plated covers. A rustling fire warmed his legs, though what stood across the hall blew him away.

"The throne of a king," their guide said. "Built for a visit by George IV in 1821, elegant in its simplicity."

A frame of gold plating formed the surprisingly simple chair, with sable velvet lining the backrest and cushion. A single red rope reminded visitors this cultural treasure was hands-off. Not the kind of warning Parker or Erika tended to heed.

"That's not what most people think of when they picture a throne," Erika said. Parker noted her eyes barely touched on the piece. "But I must confess I'm excited to see the window."

"Then you're in luck," their guide said. "It's right behind you."

Exquisite paintings hung throughout the room, accenting other artifacts or fireplaces. On one side of the elongated square, however, windows stood sentry, golden rays of sunlight tinted every hue of the spectrum falling through to paint the marble-tiled floor. Atop a display of period weaponry, the next step in their search waited.

"Commissioned by Queen Anne during a visit to Ireland, this wonderful piece resided in Trinity College for several hundred years before being transferred to Dublin Castle in 1900. Each color in the piece is symbolic, representative of Anne's hopes and dreams for her country."

A window identical to what they found in the Book of Kells. A brilliant green background surrounded the sword. An elongated silver blade, white in the window pane, cut through the green glass like a mythical dagger.

"The green background symbolizes Anne's love for Ireland and the freedom our association with England allowed us to maintain. Gold represents the wisdom Anne possessed in ruling over the most powerful country on earth." As she spoke, the guide looked up, the sparkling panes reflected in her eyes. "And at the top and bottom of the handle, the red grip symbolizes passion for her country."

Parker caught something in her eye, a twinkle of wit.

Why did that sword look familiar?

"Wait a second," he said. The answer sat in front of them. *Literally.*

"Is the sword in Anne's window in this room?"

"Well done, young man. Quite observant of you, though we did try to make it so. If you look closely, you'll see a sword on display which closely resembles the glass weapon in the window. We believe them to be one and the same."

Beneath Anne's window, five swords fanned out against a red felt backdrop. The one Parker now thought to be Anne's next clue held center position, inverted and unsheathed scarcely an arm's length away.

"What can you tell us about it?" Erika moved so fast she seemed to materialize in front of the display without having to burden the floor underneath.

"It belonged to the Lord Lieutenant of Ireland, and we believe the Queen presented it to him."

"Laurence Hyde owned this sword?" Gavin asked.

"Few visitors are so well-versed. You four are a welcome exception. Yes, it did belong to him."

This presented a puzzle. If Anne left this trail for the Lord Lieutenant to follow, why leave a path of shadowy clues for the man when she could have told him the truth face-to-face?

Erika beat him to the punch. "I suppose Anne gave Laurence this sword during her visit, at the same time she commissioned the window?"

"One would think so. And you're testing the limits of my knowledge, young lady. But alas, one would be mistaken. In the Dublin Castle archives it is noted that Laurence traveled north to quell a rebellion when his niece visited, not returning until well after she departed."

And just like that, back in business.

"Those campaigns could go on for years," Erika said. "Similar to the Troubles."

"Very true. Though I believe a lasting peace will prevail on our island." Their guide's eyes weren't on them as she spoke, instead on Anne's vibrant window. "But enough about my thoughts. Please, feel free to enjoy this room and all the others here at Dublin Castle."

Their hostess departed, leaving them alone, all the other tourists gone as well. Parker turned back to the display to find Gavin hadn't wasted a moment.

"What are we looking for?" Hovering over the sword, his head twisted back and forth, darting from the window to the wall.

"Take it easy," Erika said. "This display may be alarmed, and even if it's not, you can't damage the artifacts."

"It's a bloody sword," Harry said. "It's meant to kill people. A few fingerprints won't hurt."

"Don't do it," Erika said. "Do you see those cameras?" Parker spotted a half-dozen black circles on the ceiling. "They're not here for show."

Polished steel sparkled with reflections, all gold flashes and sparks. Slender strips of metal coiled round and round a red grip abutting a rounded golden pommel at one end and cross-guard at the other. Upon closer inspection, Parker noted imperfections on the pommel.

"Look at this," he said. "There are designs etched into the gold. It looks like the Jewish thing they light candles in."

"A menorah," Erika said. "Which holds either seven or nine candles, depending on what it's used for." She brushed past, a hint of lilac tickling his nose. "This does resemble the Jewish version, but with fewer candles."

Four candle holders topped a central spire, one jutting out horizontally in each cardinal direction, tiny etched candles perched on all four ends.

"Mean anything to you?" Gavin asked Erika.

"Not in this context. However, these are more familiar."

Tapping the blade, Parker noted markings along its length, fine lines snaking over the steel.

"That's a snake," he said. "Look, it even has fangs and a forked tongue." Running along the shaft, a slithering serpent darted toward the blade's tip, tongue flicking the air. Beyond that, no other motifs adorned the blade. Which didn't make sense.

"Aren't swords normally covered with designs or drawings?" Parker asked. "I thought this would be a little flashier. You know, the kind of gift a queen would give."

"You're right," Erika said. "Look at these other swords. Most are

184

ceremonial, but not this one," she tapped a particularly nasty-looking blade. "It's meant for battle, and there are engravings on the blade." Nicks and scratches cut along the edges, a weapon that had seen use.

"What about the other side?" Gavin asked. "I can't tell. It's pressed up against this fabric."

The fanned-out display hung tightly to the wall, each sword less than an inch from the dark cloth backing. As he poked and prodded, Parker noted Harry sidling behind them, scoping out the doorways.

"Go ahead and give it a pull," Harry said. "I'll run interference for the cameras, and if our guide shows up, we'll say it was an accident. She likes us, remember?"

Before anyone argued, Gavin went for it. Metal shrieked as the blade bent, but the display held. Again he pulled, again without result.

"Give me a hand."

Parker obliged, two hands on the cross-guard. "This thing's coming down, intact or in pieces."

"On three," Gavin said, chuckling. "One."

A deep boom welled in Parker's chest, his entire body vibrating as thunder smacked off the walls. Glass rattled above them, a dark cloud passing across the sun.

And then silence, utter and complete. The absence of noise lasted for one thudding, confused heartbeat before a shrill alarm ripped through the air.

"What was that?" Erika asked, cringing.

"An explosion," Gavin said. "Trust me. Security will be here any second. Let's get this thing down."

Shouting filtered from down the hallway, footsteps and panicked shouts coming from all directions. For the moment, they were still alone.

Either the blast loosened the sword or adrenaline filled them both, but this time it came away.

Erika snatched the sword from his grasp. "You were right, Parker. There's a cross on the reverse side."

A pair of crossed lines, the shorter length bisecting a longer one off-center.

"That's it?" Gavin asked. "It's a cross. Like a hundred others. Why would Anne leave this sword and no clues?"

"A cross is all it needs to be," Erika said. "Look at this."

She tapped the cross-guard, where a trio of letters had been etched on either side, repeated to the right and left.

"Time to go." Harry stood in the doorway as frenzied tourists raced past outside.

"What does it say?" Gavin asked, guiding them to the door.

"It doesn't say anything," she said, fumbling with the weapon. "They're not letters."

A blue hat burst around the doorway, blocked by Harry's unyielding bulk and the gold-framed doorway. "Is anyone injured in here?" Another officer leaned in, pushing past Harry.

"No," the bull-headed Irishman said, one hand covering his eyes. "I'm just dazed is all. We're trying to leave."

"Then get moving." Shielded by Parker and Gavin, the officer didn't notice Erika drop the sword.

"Oh my goodness. That fell from the wall." Flailing about, Erika hopped from one foot to the other. "What's happening?"

It did the trick. "It's alright, miss. There's been an explosion. Follow everyone outdoors and get away from the buildings."

"Thank you," she said. "I think other people are trapped down the hall."

The officer raced away, his partner a step behind. Harry took off, pushing through the frantic crowd, all of them sliding along in the wake he left behind. Backed up at each exit, they shuffled through the doors before bursting out into the sunlit courtyard, following as Harry shoved his way to the far exit.

"I hope that damn sword is bloody worth it," Harry said. "This is a castle. Which means they have walls to keep people out." He pointed to a stony example surrounding the courtyard. "Great bloody walls that also keep people *in*. We don't want to be stuck in here, waiting for the Keepers to show up."

"Let's get out before they lock it down," Gavin said.

They made it through the gates with only moments to spare. Blue lights flashed, bathing the phalanx of officers descending on Dublin Castle from all around.

Outside the gates, the crowd thinned as they pushed through an onrushing horde of first responders. Onlookers gathered across the street, held at bay by harried policemen wielding batons and nightsticks. Once they melted into the growing mass of humanity, Erika grabbed his arm.

"Stop moving," she said. "I found it."

"Found what?" Parker asked. She had that look, that fire burning inside her.

"The sword is Anne's next clue."

"Were you able to decode it?" Gavin asked, eyes darting back and forth. "If you know where we should go, say it. If not, I need to figure out what's going on and how we can keep out of it."

"The snake is the first part," Erika said, drawing their circle ever tighter. "Alone, it's a nice etching, but not much else. Then the cross. That's the second part." She looked to Harry, who, like Gavin, studied the crowd around them. "As you said, it's a simple cross, notable only in that it's on the sword. Anne chose those designs for her uncle."

"Why?" Parker didn't see where this led. What did she see that he'd missed? "Unless you know of a holy place associated with snakes."

"Right idea, wrong question. We're not talking about a place right now. This is about a *person*. And Anne led us right to him."

"This has to do with those numbers on the cross-guard." Numbers he didn't see clearly after the blast. "What were they?"

"Roman numerals. Three, one, and seven."

Added together they made eleven. *Or is it three hundred seventeen?* Possible connections flashed through his mind. A deep booming intruded, the clock tower striking above. And then the light bulb went on.

"*Time,*" Parker said. "You're talking about time. The numbers are a date."

"Correct. March seventeenth."

"St. Patrick," Harry said. "Who drove the snakes from Ireland." Erika nodded. "And the patron saint of Ireland who has the most famous church in the country named after him, here in Dublin."

"Well done," Erika said. A shrill police whistle cut through the air, but couldn't silence her words. "Standing since the twelfth century, long before Anne's reign. The next step is St. Patrick's Cathedral."

Chapter 39

Dublin Airport

A seventy-ton bird soared overhead, Rolls Royce engines roaring as the jet clawed for altitude. Burnt fuel shimmered high above as Logan Rose drove onto the highway, Oliver Moore sitting beside him.

"What did you tell the locals, sir?" Oliver asked.

"We're working as consultants, monitoring this situation for the Crown," Logan replied. "Wasn't hard to sell them on a few dozen helping hands after I mentioned terrorism."

Arms were twisted, favors called in, but Logan eventually secured operational control for his unit. No one questioned the Queen's men in times of crisis, the vague cover of *national security* concerns scary enough to put him in charge. Right now Logan needed to locate the two Americans, which meant access to surveillance feeds, increased patrols at landmarks, and loads of people searching for them.

"Our men have their assignments and will report in when they're in place," Oliver reported. "All buildings and locations on the list are covered, and each pair of Warders has photographs of Dr. Carr and Mr. Chase to distribute." Tires humming on asphalt, they darted through traffic, heading into the city. Twice Logan saw his subordinate's lips part, and both times no words escaped.

"Out with it," Logan said. "No time to dance about now."

"I can't figure why they blew up a statue," Moore said. "Makes no sense. Not only do they run the risk of getting caught, but there wasn't a single casualty. It looks like they went out of their way to keep people safe. It doesn't add up."

"I've learned not to question a terrorist's motives. Whatever they're doing, it won't end well for England. We must stop them." In truth, this scared the hell out of him, though he'd never admit it. Uncertainty spread quickly in times of crisis. Every single Keeper needed to be at the top of their game, and a frightened leader didn't inspire confidence.

"You and I will coordinate the search," Logan said. "Dublin Garda have a mobile command at the bomb site and we've been given private quarters inside, with a communications and video network ready to go. Closed circuit security cameras, traffic and municipal feeds, all of it live. If those Irishmen are in Dublin, we'll find them."

Never mind that he had little idea where to look and even less of a notion as to their next destination. All his info came courtesy of an ancient intelligence report better suited for a museum. He didn't have a damned clue where to find Erika Carr. Which made Logan Rose a desperate man.

"Once we locate the four of them, how do we proceed? The men will need instructions for their detention or elimination."

"For now, we try to take them alive," Logan said. Heavy rumbling filled the car, smooth asphalt giving way to cobblestones. In the heart of Dublin, a sea of blue lights flashed like an underwater laser show in the clearest of oceans. "However, I want every man armed and aware their targets are willing to kill to evade capture. You and I alone know what is truly at stake here. We contain this threat by any means necessary."

"Does that apply to the Americans as well?" An armada of Ireland's finest milled about outside their vehicle, disciplined chaos with a smoking metal hulk in the epicenter.

"Without question," Logan said. "National security will not be compromised. If that requires a few dead Americans, so be it."

Chapter 40

Inside the IRA's headquarters, Connor Whelan's grasp on his organization slowly slipped away. A breeze of his rival's success now grew beyond anything he'd imagined. The winds carrying Arden Flanarty now gusted with storm-like intensity, all manner of reason and rational thought blown away. Even their senior members, battle-hardened and weary of death, felt the stirrings, a longing for the type of action not seen in decades. How quickly these men forgot the horrors of what they'd wrought, the memories of their past successes so easily blinding them to the costs they incurred.

Gavin and Harry were the day's lone bright spot. Emboldened with news of their continued success, Connor slipped back to the bar, listening to the chants and joyful exultation at the symbolic destruction inflicted upon Elizabeth. Inane, but nothing dangerous. The true danger lay with Arden Flanarty, with the man's misguided desire for a better land, an anchor dragging them into the vicious past. Unless, of course, Connor stopped him.

"I spoke with Gavin," Connor said. Only those closest to him heard the soft words.

"What'd he say?" one asked. "Still out with those Americans, tryin' to find whatever the damn Keepers wanted?"

"Aye," Connor confirmed. "He's given them the slip." Conversations fell silent, more IRA men drifting over, catching wind of Whelan's tale, and his summary of Erika's discovery in the State Apartments drew them in. He always delivered a gripping story, a skill honed as he rose through the IRA ranks. The muddle around him grew in size until he noted Arden Flanarty look their way. Connor Whelan with an audience was not a welcome sight.

A question came from the group. "What blasted secret could Anne have hidden?"

"I couldn't say." Actually, he could, but he chose not to. And wouldn't even if Gavin found the end of this royal trail.

"So the treasure hunt continues?" Flanarty's words broke through the circle, cold water to dampen any sparks of allegiance Connor cultivated. "Maybe he'll find the Irish Crown Jewels and we'll all be heroes."

Growls of laughter followed.

"One can hope, Flanarty. I trust all is well with your bloodless attack? Congratulations. An explosion free of casualties is never easy."

Arden nodded, suspicion in his eyes. "For our freedom, of course." The frigid gaze vanished as he turned to the men around them. "And it's a great sight, that old bag blown to dust. Wouldn't you say so?" Glasses filled the air. "And we aren't going to stop there."

What is he talking about? Connor didn't know of any additional plans. A cold wave clenched in his guts.

"Enjoy the victory, boys. There's much to be discussed before we pull back the curtain on the next step."

Arden met Connor's gaze, nodded to the building's rear. Seems he won't completely blindside me this time.

"Before we make any further moves," Arden said, closing the door. "I'd like to hear your thoughts." Arden accepted the whiskey, taking one glass from the pair Connor filled. "You're the QM, after all."

"I want what's best for us all, same as you," Whelan said, biting his tongue. "Demolishing the statue rallied our men's spirits. These walls haven't heard such excitement since you and I ran the streets, mystified at what went on behind the QM's door." Smoky whiskey rolled down his throat. Arden had an angle. He always did. Now Connor needed to figure out what it was and where he stood on the matter. "How times have changed."

"That they have," Arden said from across the vast expanse of Connor's desk. Shouts erupted from down the hall. Sounded like the boys found the Celtic match. "Fortunate for us we pull the strings now," Arden said. "We have a chance to finally achieve our goal."

"Every step must be considered," Connor said. "The old ways may no longer work." He didn't need another lecture, another try at turning his mind. Arden chose his path long ago, taking a dark road Connor did not walk.

"Though you agree we should always consider all options. Which I've done, and which led to today's success." He finished his glass, grabbed the bottle and poured two fingers more. "And I believe our next step is already in place."

"Care to enlighten me?" Connor asked, keeping his tone neutral.

"Time and again our field agents prove to be our most valuable members, both in intelligence and productivity. Scattered throughout the United Kingdom are skilled men and women ready to act at a moment's notice." Another small sip, whiskey rolling around Arden's mouth, as languid as his words. "I believe these resources are under-utilized."

"Theirs are operations in the shadows, Mr. Flanarty. Except in the most dire of circumstances. You acknowledge a large portion of their value stems from anonymity?"

"I do," Arden said. "However, an unsharpened blade loses its edge."

"You propose we activate one of our field teams," Connor said. "To what end? There are no pressing matters which come to mind."

"That's because you only think *defensively*, Quartermaster. It's time we take the fight to them."

"We do, every day. No destruction or death does not mean we're standing pat." The whiskey swirled in his glass.

Maybe this is the time Arden finally hears me.

"This is a war, Arden. I haven't forgotten. Good people are dead, those we grew up with, fought beside. There will be no decisive battle, no final charge. Victory is as much in the realm of public opinion as on the battlefield. Our field agents gather intelligence, conduct surveillance. As a last resort, they confront the enemy. We're outgunned and outmanned. Head-on attacks are a fool's errand."

Arden nodded as he spoke, his normally expressive countenance blank. When he finally spoke, Whelan strained to catch it.

"I agree. But you assume we must play by their rules." Arden stood, his gaze lingering on the William Wallace statue atop Connor's desk. "An assumption I don't make. We *will* take the fight to the British. For too long they've pushed their boot on our neck while telling us to be grateful. I do not, as you may suspect, have a death wish. My goal is the same as yours, to see our country free from English rule. I intend to make that happen."

"I suspect your plan is more than thought."

Arden favored the QM with a wicked grin. "You are correct." One hand went up as Connor's jaw grew tight, his teeth grinding. "Don't worry, no orders have been given. I know only you authorize operations, and I wouldn't dodge your authority. However, as a leadership council member, I have a plan I hope you will consider."

Arden had momentum right now, but did he over-estimate his influence? If he recruited the other council members, Connor couldn't stop him.

"What have you in mind, Mr. Flanarty?"

"The statue is only a taste," Arden said. "Now we go for the kill. Metaphorically, of course."

"Another deathless assault on the Crown."

"As you require," Arden said, pacing back and forth. "We have several teams in London. I've alerted them to a possible mission."

Connor knew of no such mission, and told Arden so.

"Consider yourself aware, Mr. Whelan. I've laid the groundwork, much as I did for bombing Elizabeth's statue. All that remains is to take a vote."

"And this ground work. What might it be?"

Flanarty stopped pacing, laying both hands on Connor's desk.

"We're striking at their heart. I propose we bring down the Tower of London."

He nearly choked on his whiskey

"As in Her Majesty's Royal Palace and Fortress? You propose to destroy a thousand year old castle?"

"Not the whole bloody thing. We'd never get enough explosives inside. We only need destroy a part of the tower to succeed. As you said, this battle is as much for hearts and minds as for territory. Striking such a recognizable symbol of English power will never be forgotten."

"You didn't plan this yesterday."

"It's been in the attic for years, waiting for the right time. That time is now. Elizabeth and her hounds are on their heels."

Connor's antique grandfather clock ticked off the seconds.

How to play this? Not a bluff. Arden knew too much to fall for it. And throwing his weight around would only embolden the man. He needed more time.

With great care he refilled Arden's glass, topped off his own.

"Let's say I consider this. What's your plan?"

With each word, Flanarty's guard fell. Connor needed details, for in these lay his best hope of thwarting this disaster.

"Simple and straightforward, like all good plans." Arden leaned close, his face brimming with delight. "Those lads outside. In my eye, they're the valuable ones. You know why? They've forgotten more fantastic weapons than we could dream of."

On this, at least, they agreed.

"Their most recent concoction? A device to rain destruction on English soil from afar. They've crafted a *drone*, Connor."

"A drone. As in a miniature fighter jet."

"The very same!" Arden's fist boomed on the desk. "Not as large or with as much range, but capable of delivering an explosive to level houses."

"Or the Tower of London."

"We can't bring it all down, but we identified where to strike for maximum damage." Arden threw back his glass, arms out wide. "The White Tower. The keep, home of the lord of the manor. Which in this case is the Queen herself."

"The strongest and most secure portion of the castle," Connor said. Arden certainly had a flair for the dramatic. "A message to ring loudly across the kingdom and around the world." One finger tapped his lower lip. "How do you propose we deliver this device? No doubt the airspace around the Tower is restricted. Security will be tight."

Arden's hand washed through the still air. "Launch the craft within fifty yards of the castle walls. Even if the top Keeper marksman is standing watch, he'll never be able to react before the drone is airborne and inside the perimeter. And be honest, the chances of even an expert marksman hitting such a target are remote," he continued. "On top of that, the Keepers have their hands full chasing our American allies who, according to Harry, left one bloke in a boot."

"That they did," Connor said. "How will the drone get so close to the perimeter before launch? Even with so many resources devoted to the search, the Tower is still well-defended."

Amber liquid poured into Arden's glass before he replied, though Connor shook his head at the bottle. If the whiskey helped loosen Flanarty's lips, all the better. "The value of central London real estate solved that problem for us. Roadways surround the Tower on all sides, except for where the Thames stands guard. All we need do is park a vehicle in the closest handicapped spot and walk away. There's even a legitimate placard ready to go."

Walk away? Connor arched an eyebrow.

"This drone is truly a marvel," Arden said. "No larger than a briefcase, with propellers on either side facing up and down, and rotors on the central portion. Which leaves room to spare in the backseat of a four-wheel-drive with the top down. All we do is park on the street and walk away. Our lads here take care of the rest, and we watch in high definition from this very building."

"Just ram into the Tower and set off the explosives? That will only blacken the stones."

"It's a hot summer. So hot the Tower staff open upper floor windows on sunny days to allow a breeze inside. The windows are off-limits to tourists and may be watched, of course. But that's just to be sure no foolish visitors fall out. No one will expect anything to come *in to* the room."

Connor's hopes faded. Arden clearly learned from his past failures, from when Connor either reasoned with or cajoled his fellow leadership members into vetoing Flanarty's merciless attacks. Now, however, he had it all. A sound plan, recent success, and a weapon to enthrall the warriors outside.

"How will you ensure no one is killed?" Connor asked. A last, desperate shot.

Leaning back in his chair, a scowl covered Arden's face. "We'll do our best to avoid any casualties. The main target is a barracks on the upper floors, private quarters for Beefies. However, nothing is guaranteed. A lesson with which you are intimately familiar."

He spoke the truth. Years ago, Connor orchestrated missions which killed British soldiers. Attacks, once set in motion, tended to have a mind of their own. More than once innocent bystanders died as well, and overbearing grief, a black stain on his heart, finally convinced Connor there had to be a better way.

"Admitting we made mistakes in the past does not excuse us from our current responsibilities," Connor said. "Perhaps the assault could be launched after the Tower is closed? That way only the Beefies will be inside. No civilians."

"Grand idea," Arden replied, the flippant tone at odds with his words. "But bright as those lads are, headlights are one thing they didn't install on their toy. This must be a daytime mission, and also because we need the Tower windows to be open. They shut them after closing."

How can I stop this?

"This drone, they crafted it from scratch?" Connor asked.

"Not entirely. It's actually a device anyone can purchase, modified to suit our needs."

"And you're certain this can't be traced back to us?"

"I've been assured the purchase is untraceable. With what they can do, hiding their identity on the internet is no challenge for those boys."

Connor couldn't argue there. Couldn't argue much of anything, with no obvious holes to poke in this plan. Only one option remained.

"I'll need time to consider all options," Connor said. "We don't want to rush into anything."

"I assure you this has been thoroughly reviewed," Arden said. Lines grew on his forehead, his eyes narrowing. "All that remains is to put it to a vote."

A losing vote, Connor knew. Even with his closest associate on the council, Connor had two votes to Arden's three, and the political blowback from his opposition could easily be seen as obstructing their cause. Which is exactly what he wanted to do. Unfortunately for Connor, not every IRA man felt the same way as he about needless killing.

"I know you think I'm soft, that I back down from confrontation and have forgotten the old ways," Connor said, running a hand through his silver hair. "I believe times have changed. We must adapt or risk alienating our supporters. Not the base," he said as Arden tensed in his chair. "The less demonstrative. Men and women who agree with us, who wish for a free and united Ireland, but who lack the conviction to act on those beliefs. Those are the ones who need to be swayed, whose favor we must curry, for without their numbers we are lost. This war will be won—"

"—in the court of public opinion, yes, I know. Christ, you've said it enough times to drill holes through my skull." Any semblance of camaraderie vanished. Never one to expose himself, the tiny spark of understanding from moments ago now blazed into loathing. "If it is as you say, then why, after nearly a decade of peace, do we still fight in virtual anonymity? Ours is a dying cause, Connor, and men like you will be the final nail in our coffin." Arden spat at the ground. "It's my right to have a vote on this. I'll damn well have it now."

And ten minutes later, he did. By a vote of three to two, Arden's scheme commenced immediately. As the men celebrated, or in a few cases, rued the upcoming assault, Connor retreated to his office. Arden won this round, and Connor couldn't stop him. Right now he needed to bring Gavin in from the fray, to keep him out of the ensuing firestorm sure to erupt once this drone detonated inside England's most venerable castle. The IRA would survive, like it always did. That didn't concern him. The idea of what they stood for, their true cause, that's what scared him now. He only hoped their soul didn't go up in flames with the Tower.

What Connor wasn't certain about was the lasting damage that would be done to the *idea* of the IRA, of what they stood for.

The IRA existed for many reasons, represented a host of ideas or beliefs to different people. To Connor Whelan, one stood above all others. A truth held close to Quartermasters' hearts for centuries, knowledge passed from man to man, too volatile to share any further. Gavin Rooney held the key to this dark knowledge, and his safety stood above all else.

Arden may blow up the Tower of London and destroy in a single blow all the goodwill Connor had worked so hard to build, but above all else, he must keep Gavin safe. The QM picked up his phone, cheers rumbling outside his office. Another Celtic goal, most likely. Dialing, a profound sadness filled him, for Connor knew what lay down Arden's path.

That, more than all else, rattled Connor Whelan to his very core.

Chapter 41

St. Stephen's Green
Dublin, Ireland

Dozens of officers surrounded the Irish Garda mobile command center, a great metal box on wheels, with wires and saucers haphazardly patched on as though Victor Frankenstein had set about crafting a murderous toaster oven. A helicopter buzzed overhead as men in full combat gear streamed about, thick boots stamping over the cobbled ground. Half a stone's throw away the smoking shell of Queen Elizabeth peered accusingly, a desecrated ruler demanding justice.

Logan Rose peered at one of the dozen monitors, a Rubik's cube of digital data flowing in from around the city. Just as he suspected, any cameras around the statue offered nothing of value. And the more he learned, the less he suspected the tourists or their companions of any involvement. Running for your life left precious little time to orchestrate a bombing. This pointed to something else entirely.

The door cracked open to reveal Oliver Moore.

"Anything?"

"No reports so far," Oliver said. "Warders are spread around the city." A pair of mirrored sunglasses clattered onto the table. "And you know as well as I do the chances of finding them are practically nil."

At least he kept his voice down. Several Garda technicians were hunched over the monitors nearby, keyboards clacking as they worked. If word got out the Chief Warder didn't believe, how could they expect the men to?

"Keep that to yourself, and keep the faith, Mr. Moore. Often it's all we have."

Oliver nodded. "Understood, sir. In regards to this mess," he looked through a window at the ragged Queen. "Seems like a shot across the bow to me."

"I agree. Those Irish bastards didn't want anyone to die here. Which worries me." Logan spun a pencil, yellow wood flipping through the air. "It's not often the IRA organizes an attack without dead Englishmen as the goal. I fear this is either a distraction or a one-fingered salute. Reminding us that for all our advantages, they're still out there, watching and waiting."

"You think it's related to the Anne situation?"

"My gut says no," Logan replied, instincts which kept him alive all these years. That and a ruthless streak lurking beneath the surface. "Did we ever get confirmation on the one I shot in Kilkenny?

"Name is Brin Stewart. Born in Belfast, moved to Dublin as a young child. No arrests, though he's known to associate with several terrorists, one of them a cousin," Oliver said. "Certified paramedic, but no indication he ever worked in the field. Bank records indicate he did consulting for a marketing firm based in Edinburgh. As best we can tell it's an empty office."

Exactly the nondescript background he'd seen countless times before. Small pieces, possibly pointing to something larger, but nothing conclusive.

"My money's on the IRA," Logan said. "Which we already suspected. If that's the case, why would these three, excuse me, *two* now, work at odds with the central office? Whoever set this bomb off certainly didn't do the two surviving IRA men and the Americans any favors," he said, gesturing around. "Dublin's thick with police now, right when they're trying to escape."

"Perhaps they're flying solo, outside the chain of command."

"But why?" Logan rubbed his bloodshot eyes. "No one alive knows what's at the end of Anne's trail, or even how to get there. The only two men who have a clue are standing here talking about it. And even we aren't sure."

"The American professor, Dr. Carr. She's a historical scholar. A fortuitous profession in this case."

"Except she's here with her boyfriend," Logan said. "And until she received an email from her deceased friend, nothing suggests she knew of Anne's letter. The discovery and her arrival coinciding seems to be chance."

"And now those two run with the IRA and lead their hunt?" Oliver shook his head. "That's not logical."

"Remember what started it all," Logan said. "Those fools you sent to retrieve the letter. They should have ended it then. Three hundred years we search, and when the time comes, it all unravels." Fire burned in his chest, threatening to cloud the detached demeanor Logan so desperately needed right now. "But it's done. If we hadn't killed that art restorer, Dr. Carr would have no idea Anne's letter was important."

Guilt hung heavily on Oliver's face.

And blaming anyone got them nowhere. "We can't go back," Logan said. "So worry about fixing this before anything comes out about Anne or what brought her to Dublin."

A thunderous bang ripped the air as a Garda officer shoved the door open, not bothering to knock.

"Chief Warder Rose?" Logan nodded. "There's a man on the line who claims he works for you saying he's been assaulted."

Logan grabbed the cell phone. "Rose here."

"Chief, this is Warder Shick. Dr. Carr and Mr. Chase are in Dublin."

The man sounded groggy, almost dazed. "Where did you see them?"

"Inside the Old Library at Trinity College."

"Where are they now?"

Shick paused. "I'm not certain, but they can't be far."

"You lost them." A deep breath, cooling the fire. "How?"

Logan listened in silence, with pursed lips. Only when the man described waking up in the boot of a parked vehicle did he respond.

"Sounds as though the other IRA bloke caught up to you. Remember this. Never turn your back on the enemy. And be thankful for the boot's built-in escape lever." Logan didn't give the man a chance to argue. Better to let him worry for a bit. "Are you able to carry on?"

"Of course, sir."

"Good man. Events are unfolding." Logan summarized the destroyed statue before ordering Shick to report to mobile command.

"I'll have Shick disciplined," Oliver said. "Failure is unacceptable."

"You'll do no such thing." Failure should be handled in various ways, and always with a purpose. "Use your head, man. What will his mates think when Shick comes back and the first thing you do is send him to the brig? Throwing away resources is short-sighted and serves no purpose."

"As you wish, sir."

Paper crinkled as Logan spread a map of Dublin across the table. "Warder Shick spent no more than an hour in the boot," Logan said. "He spotted Dr. Carr here"—one finger tapped Trinity College—"and chased them to this intersection. Given the explosion occurred not long after Warder Shick's attack, Dr. Carr's group is likely still carrying on their search."

"Do you believe they'd be foolish enough to stay in the area?"

"I think they'll go where Anne's path takes them," Logan said. "The IRA doesn't know it, but they're nearing the end of Anne's journey."

"How can you be certain? Anne's records indicate she returned to London after leaving Dublin."

"With no other stops on the way," Logan said. "Which leads us to believe her quest ended in Dublin. However, the truth may have been lost, hidden, or deliberately altered for all we know." Red circles sprouted on the map as Logan highlighted all major landmarks within walking distance. "Dr. Carr's success cannot be discounted as luck or coincidence. She's not giving up the hunt now."

"And you believe Anne's journey through Dublin didn't end at Trinity College?"

"I don't." Logan hurried to the door, ripped it open. "Analysts, get in here." The Keeper technical team streamed inside, a half-dozen of their best technicians. "I need all the CCTV footage from these streets over the past two hours, starting with this intersection." Logan indicated the route Warder Shick covered from Trinity College to his encounter. "They attacked one of our men at this very spot. Your work is what will catch the terrorists responsible. Not only for this assault, but for the smoking ruin outside."

The lads couldn't have responded any faster if he'd pulled out a gun. Not five minutes later one of them shouted.

"Chief Rose, I found them."

Peering over the man's shoulder, Logan watched Warder Shick face down one of the terrorists, his gun drawn, only to have the other Irishman come from behind and knock him out. Into the trunk he went, eventually ending up in a parking garage.

"Smart move," Oliver said. "Stuffing him in the boot like that."

Logan grunted. The IRA men weren't fools. His technical team worked the cameras, following Dr. Carr and her entourage from inside the garage to their next destination.

"Dublin Castle," Logan said. "Mr. Moore, get ten men and head over there now. And try not to spook them," Logan called as Oliver walked out. "No need to announce the cavalry has arrived." Logan tapped the tech seated in front of him. "See if we can get a close-up of the two men with Dr. Carr and Mr. Chase. If they're IRA, they'll have some kind of record."

Every pair of eyes studied their prey as the noose tightened, four doomed souls facing a reckoning with Logan Rose. Perhaps he'd open the Tower dungeons in their honor. They wouldn't be the first group of criminals to walk through the infamous doors, and never come out.

Chapter 42

Dublin, Ireland

"A *drone*? How in the bloody hell did Flanarty pull that off?"

Gavin turned down yet another side street, trailing behind Erika and the others as they looped through Dublin's back alleys, staying as far away from St. Stephen's Green as possible. With all the authorities milling about, the longer they were exposed, the more likely an encounter with the law.

"How did he get enough support on the council?"

Connor sighed mightily through the phone. "You know how it is. Success breeds favor. String a few together, even if they're mostly symbolic, and Flanarty has them eating out of his hand. I only have one mate to count on in the best of times. Right now, it's as though the clock's turned back and everyone is hoping for blood."

"It hasn't been like this in years," Gavin said as he backed up against a cool brick wall. Only after Harry peered around the corner did they blend in with the heavy foot traffic.

"Damn fools," Connor said. "Most of them too young to remember. Sure they say they want action, to show the crown who owns this island. But they never saw dead innocents littering the roads. They're a bunch of goddamn fools drunk on trivial victories. They have no clue what's coming."

Moving in the mass of pedestrians, Gavin felt a measure of safety. After leaving Dublin Castle, they'd taken several cab rides around the city, doubling back in an effort to shake anyone on their tail. Now mixing with the crowds headed to St. Patrick's, they should be able to slip in undetected even with Keepers nearby.

"Flanarty knows. He saw the dead, the mangled bodies," Gavin said. "How can he let this happen again after all the progress we've made?"

"Because to him we haven't done anything worth talking about in years. If we're not killing Englishmen, we're wasting time. You know how he thinks." Gavin could picture his mentor now, that hand running through his silver mane, one of the few people standing between England and an all-out resumption of war with the IRA. If the Queen realized that, perhaps she'd be more receptive to the idea of a free Northern Ireland.

"Don't worry, QM. Whatever's at the end of Anne's trail may help us stop this madness."

"I hope you're right. I'll take any help we can get right now. First, though, you need to stay out of sight."

Connor outlined the rest of Arden's plan, and Gavin found no weakness to exploit. He wasn't about to call MI5 and warn them, but if his current search derailed Arden's plans, so be it.

"Stay in touch," Connor said before ringing off.

"You too, QM." Gavin had a ball cap shoved against his chest.

"Put this on," Parker said. A street vendor shouted beside them, fists clutching a bevy of headwear. "It'll have to do."

"What did your boss have to say?" Parker walked to one side, Erika on the other as they followed a narrow path Harry cleared through the sidewalk traffic.

"Our nemesis is up to his old tricks," Gavin said, loud enough for Harry to hear.

"Who?" Erika asked. "The Keepers? I assumed losing a man and having a statue blown up in the past hour bought us some time."

"No, not the Keepers. Arden Flanarty is who I'm talking about." Gavin gave them a brief overview of Arden's tactics and his battles with QM Whelan.

"Why is he such a maverick?" Parker asked. "Doesn't the guy care about the IRA's mission?"

"Keep it down." Gavin said, glancing around. "No telling who's listening." Once the Americans edged in closer, he answered. "Arden plans to build on what he's done so far. He has momentum, and now the support to do as he pleases. It's his best chance to wreak havoc. And this latest plan is bold, even for him." A woman brushed past, lugging a baby on her hip. "He's going after the Tower of London."

A step later he slammed into Harry, who'd stopped in his tracks. "Say that again."

"You heard me," Gavin said. "Our technical team rigged a commercial drone with explosives. Arden wants to attack tomorrow morning."

"Is he trying to kill tourists?" Erika asked, one hand covering her mouth.

"No, he wants to destroy the Tower. Or so he claims. Arden assured the QM every precaution would be taken to minimize casualties, but given that only certain windows are open during the day, his choices are limited."

"A most altruistic man," Erika said.

"He has a point," Harry said. "Wouldn't do much damage blowing it outside the walls. Probably can't pack more than a pound or two of explosive on a drone like that."

"I'm sure it will do plenty of damage no matter where it's detonated," Erika said through clenched teeth.

"Not really," Parker replied. "Think about it this way." His hand went out, open palm toward the sky. "Imagine I have a firecracker in my palm. If it goes off, my hand will be injured, correct?" Erika nodded. "Now," and he rolled his fingers into a fist. "Think about what happens if my hand is wrapped around the firecracker when it explodes. Then I may not even have a hand left, just mangled skin and bone. Do you see?"

"If that drone is inside the Tower when the explosives detonate, the destruction will be much greater." Erika turned to Gavin. "Can you stop him?"

"It's not that simple," Gavin said. "We're supposed to be on the same team. We can't interfere, not once a vote's taken."

As they approached a main intersection the foot traffic began stalling, everyone waiting for the light to change. Peering underneath the bill of his new cap, Gavin spotted several black orbs hovering above the masses, hanging from the side of the streetlight poles.

"Keep your heads down. Now that Arden's basically declared war on everything sacred in this city, the Keepers will likely access local Dublin Garda resources. Including those surveillance cameras overhead."

Parker and Erika could have been searching for buried treasure, so intently did they study the asphalt. St. Patrick's Cathedral lay a short distance ahead, but Gavin barely saw the structure. These Americans were their allies, for better or worse, and their questions weren't going to go away. Even as these thoughts flashed through his mind, Erika spoke up.

"Why can't you fight back against this Flanarty guy? You're crafty, smart, all of that. And you certainly aren't afraid of much. What's so scary about this guy?"

The hell with it.

Gavin took a deep breath, the sun warm on his face, shadows growing as it fell toward the horizon. "Let me tell you a story."

Gavin Rooney didn't waste words, a trait Parker appreciated. And now it seemed they'd finally get some answers. Parker glanced at Erika, pulling her in close as they walked, her soft hair flitting on the breeze and tickling his ear.

"Arden Flanarty was one of the best," Gavin started. "He and QM Whelan grew up together in Belfast. Joined up at the same time, spent years in the field, first as a team member and then as team leader."

"Is that the career ladder for people who join the leadership council?" Erika asked.

"Throw in a great big heaping of politics and a dash of luck to stay alive long enough, and yes, it is," Harry said from ahead. "However, lots of good men never get on the council because they're either too smart or too mouthy."

"Only men who toe the line attain council status," Gavin said. "But recently it's become harder to tell where the line is."

"So what worked in the past isn't necessarily the best way to achieve your goals now," Parker said. He knew little about the strife in Northern Ireland during his lifetime, but tales of this kind littered the history books.

"That's right," Gavin said. "Thirty years ago to get attention and garner support you set off a bomb or threw a Molotov cocktail. I'm not saying that's right, but it's how things were done. For years we attacked, shot, killed, and bombed our way to independence. And many believed those actions justified."

"Killing British soldiers?" Erika said. "You can't believe that."

"I never said it's right," Gavin replied. "Merely that some in our party felt it was the only thing to do. Killing is a last resort. Arden and Connor were no different than other soldiers, and while that's not an excuse, it may help you understand where each man came from and how their past shapes our current situation."

For being what you'd call a terrorist, Gavin Rooney certainly had a level head. Parker noted, each word delivered matter-of-factly, as much history lesson as propaganda.

"Arden and Connor progressed to field team leaders after a short time, both gathering support and credibility with the membership. And for a time, both held similar views. Attack the English when needed and do anything necessary to achieve their goals."

"Where did you learn all of this?" Erika asked. "It's before your time. I have to wonder if you heard both sides of the story."

"A logical question," Gavin said. "My education came from Connor Whelan. Is it biased? I don't believe so, but you may judge for yourself."

A fair answer. So far Parker didn't think he'd slanted one way or the other, sticking to facts.

"Their differences came up in the past decade," Harry said. "Before that, when Gavin and I started in the field, everyone read from the same playbook."

"As far as we knew," Gavin said. He tugged his hat lower as another camera loomed overhead. "But I'll get to that in a second. I joined a field team not long after my father died."

The stony gaze never wavered, enough to make Parker glance away. His father died not long ago, killed in a hunting accident. The void left behind never truly healed.

"It happened not long after Connor Whelan became QM. He and my father were tight, and my father told me of the rift developing within the IRA, with Flanarty the de facto leader of one side and Connor Whelan, along with my father, heading the other."

"This is the philosophical difference you've mentioned?" Parker asked.

"It is. Flanarty and his cohorts believe the IRA is straying too far from our roots. They think we've grown soft. If we're not blowing something up or if we aren't in the headlines, Flanarty thinks people will lose their faith."

"It's bollocks," Harry said. "As though we suddenly don't want our freedom if there aren't bodies on the street."

"Bollocks it may be, but a large number of our men feel that way," Gavin said. "To them there is only one path forward, and if we're not moving ahead, we're losing the war."

"Sounds as though these men need to understand that your struggle isn't simply black and white," Erika said. "Subtle movements, the gray parts between. Those are the areas where most progress is made."

"True," Gavin said, nodding. "I hope you teach your students that. Bullheaded determination to kill every last one of your enemies may have been the approach centuries ago, but the world's evolved. Diplomacy is the best method to achieve our goal. I believe it, as did my father and QM Whelan with him."

Parker saw a more practical reason for the approach. "Your adversary is the British government. I don't care how many bombs you have. The IRA will never out-muscle an army."

"If our colleagues could grasp that notion, we may free ourselves of this internal divide." Gavin's voice grew soft, hard to catch as they neared St. Patrick's. "Instead of fighting the British, we fight each other. And right now Connor Whelan doesn't have the votes to stop Arden."

"Why not?" Erika asked. "He's the boss. He shouldn't have to answer to a subordinate."

"A problem your government faces every day," Gavin said. "Our organization is a democracy of sorts. There are five seats on the leadership council. Members are elected for life, with vacancies only occurring upon the death or retirement of a sitting member. And as far as I know, no one's ever retired."

"Never had to in the past," Harry said. "What with most of them getting killed off, half the blokes on there didn't have a gray hair in their beard."

"Turnover stayed high for some time, and most of the men were of the same mind. Keep fighting. However, with the Good Friday Agreement, which ended open hostilities between the IRA and the Crown, board members started to live longer. We've had the same five on the council for nearly a decade now."

"Long enough for minds to change and differences to crop up," Erika said.

"Right you are, Dr. Carr. Not enough action leaves our men with precious little to do. Men who aren't in the field spend their time drinking and arguing. There are few more dangerous situations in Belfast than a man with plenty of whiskey and too much time to think. All of a sudden every man believes he knows what's best for us, what we should do to finally throw off England's yoke."

"And Arden Flanarty plays on these thoughts and fears to gather support," Parker said.

"That he does," Gavin replied. They waited at another intersection, Harry still in the lead. Each Irishman's head never stopped moving. Parker tried to follow suit, but short of someone pulling out a gun, everybody looked the same. Distracted and in a hurry.

"Does Arden get most of his support from younger recruits?" Erika asked. "I suspect they're more impressionable than the seasoned fighters."

"Not as many as you'd suspect. It's a mix of old and young. The new recruits are a brighter bunch overall than when I came on board. Most have a greater understanding of the world as a whole and realize it's shrinking every day. We're no longer an isolated island, hidden from view in our highlands, beyond the concern of other nations."

Parker looked up, and up and up. Stretching nearly fifteen stories toward the sky, the dark and wondrous spire of St. Patrick's Cathedral shot from the ground like a missile at the ready. Even in a world of skyscrapers and undersea tunnels, the Gothic structure's elegance grabbed hold of you and didn't let go.

"So it's become a struggle of ideas between our two camps. One led by Arden Flanarty, advocating destruction and mayhem, with the opposing side headed by Connor Whelan, while Harry and I support the QM. However, if force is needed to achieve our goals, we will provide it."

"Which means a field team is the first to go in harm's way," Erika said.

"It does. Although we keep risk to a minimum, too many good men died for us to throw lives away. Will there be casualties? Yes. But we owe it to ourselves, to everyone who wants a united and independent Ireland, to stop rushing headlong into war. If we're ever to win, our weapons must be words, not bullets."

They now stood at the edge of the cathedral grounds. Through a low-slung metal fence resided a vibrant rainbow of flowers, deep reds and sun-drenched blues forming a floral ring around the manicured lawn. Toward the cathedral, a stone fountain burbled inside a surrounding pool. Worshippers and tourists walked populated paved walkways, some clutching bibles, others selfie sticks. More than a few cameras captured the iconic building from all angles.

That's what they should be doing right now. They'd come here on vacation, one signifying the next step in their lives. Though on a certain level Parker realized he and Erika had been robbed of a wonderful experience, the matter of staying alive gave this journey of theirs an unforgettable edge.

"Stay here," Harry said. "I'll do a quick scan of the area, see if anything jumps out. Keep your phone handy."

Gavin nodded, Harry getting lost in the crowds. Gavin continued to watch their surroundings, one hand in his pocket where he'd earlier secreted a pistol.

"Your father and Connor Whelan. Were they always close?" Erika asked.

"Yes. Our leadership wasn't always so contentious." A group of school children raced between them, all tinny screams and tiny backpacks as they scampered toward the cathedral. "He kept the counsel of Whelan and Flanarty both, though after his death Connor took me under his wing, made sure I finished my education. I went into the field against his wishes."

"What about your mother?"

The words seemed to hit Gavin like an icy wind, sending him back a step, the hardened soldier shrinking into himself.

"She's the reason I went into the field. Most people think my father's death did it. That I wanted to avenge his murder." A dry laugh, devoid of humor. "Maybe that's part of it, sure. But you want to know what really drives me now, even more than wanting to live in a free country?" When he looked at Erika, his jaw clenched the same as his closed fist. "It's what happened to her."

"I'm so sorry." Erika said, averting her eyes.

"You have nothing to be sorry for." Gavin flashed a grin. "The memories always upset me. It's been a long time, but her death never gets easier."

Pain ached in Parker's gut, empty of hope and full of anger all at once. He too knew how losing both parents forced you to grow up long before your time.

"My mother died when I was young, killed in a raid meant to catch my father and his friends. They were in a pub. Somehow the English got word that a new crop of IRA recruits were there with a few of the old guard. It was later in the night, and of course when you have an Irishman in a bar that long, chances are he'll be drunk. Most of them were, pissed and full of fight. When the Brits burst in, the shooting started." Gavin kicked the ground, his boot scuffing across asphalt. "Only two people died. My mother and the bartender. Not a single one of our men or any of the Brits had anything worse than a broken nose. You want to know the worst part? The Brits claimed *she attacked them*. My mother, a twenty-something girl out for a drink. That's what drives me more than anything, what keeps me going even today. She will not have died in vain, and neither will any of my ancestors who've fought this battle."

Parker thought he caught a hint of pride in those words, alongside an opening.

"Has your family been affiliated with the IRA for more than two generations?"

"Much longer than that," Gavin said. The thunderclouds left his face, and a spark of something else, something better, took their place. "As far back as anyone knows we've fought for this cause." One hand went into his shirt, and from underneath a metallic pendant appeared. "The men in my family have worn this for centuries, passed down from father to son. My father believed it was our crest at one time, though I think that's more of a family legend than anything else. For as long as my father or his father could recall, the Rooney men fought for the IRA. It's been over three centuries now."

"There are far worse things to do than fight for what you believe is right," Erika said. "And there's no need to start dying now. Once we reach the end of Anne's journey, I hope you can go back to your boss and calm things down."

"I hope so too, Dr. Carr. But first thing's first. It looks like we're clear," Gavin said as Harry slid out from the crowd. "We need to keep moving."

"Nothing I could spot," Harry said. "We'll use the main entrance. More people to hide behind that way."

A short walk later they faced a pair of wooden doors, darkened with age. Once they purchased tickets and made it inside, Parker found himself staring up at enough stone to build a mountain.

Soaring overhead, hand-hewn flying buttresses supported smooth stone walls, the light rock polished to a luminescent shine. Dozens of intricately stained glass windows brought warming light into the space, colors splashing through the interior to bring the tiles under his feet to life. Geometric designs filled the squares, and above, pillars on either side curved to meet their neighbors, a second floor visible from where they stood.

"That roof is hundreds of feet high," Parker said. "I couldn't throw a baseball anywhere near it."

"It's a fine building," Gavin said. "But we can't do any sightseeing right now. Dr. Carr, where do we go?"

St. Patrick's worship area stretched before them, the central area laid out east to west. Further on north and south chapels branched off on either side of the choirstalls, directly in front of a high altar. Beyond this he spotted an additional chapel, hidden from view by a dais upon which the services were led.

"The sword clearly pointed us to St. Patrick's, an enduring symbol in Dublin. However, beyond the engravings on her uncle's sword, we don't have much to go on."

She slipped into lecture mode, but fortunately for them all, Parker recognized the signs.

"Erika, if you have an idea of where to look, we need to know."

And here came the obligatory glare. At least it got her moving. "As I was saying, we don't have much, but there is something. The sword had four distinct engravings. A snake, a cross, and the roman numerals three, one and seven. Taken together, those indicate St. Patrick's Cathedral. The fourth, however, doesn't appear to relate to the other three."

"The candleholder," Gavin said. "Do you think Anne's directing us to it?"

"I don't have any proof beyond what you've seen, but that's my guess. There's no other reason to include it on the sword."

"We should ask a staff member if they have anything here fitting the description," Harry said. "I'll grab someone."

"I wouldn't do that," Erika told him. "At least not right away. We may have gained a step on the Keepers, but that guy you knocked out will eventually escape or be found, and once that happens, every Keeper in Ireland will be looking for us. So the fewer people who remember our faces, the better. If we can't find anything on our own, then we ask for help."

Gavin nodded. "Not bad, Dr. Carr. You're starting to think like us."

"Let's split into pairs," Parker said. "We can cover more ground that way. I'll go with Harry. Gavin, can you keep an eye on Erika?" In truth, Parker had no interest in letting Erika out of his sight. However, Gavin and Harry carried guns. If things got hairy, better to have at least one armed man with each of them at all times.

"I'll do my best," he said. "You take the south side, we'll take the north. Meet you behind the altar. If we don't find it here, we move on to the upper floor."

Gavin turned, and found Erika already on the hunt. Now he had to keep up with her.

"Let's move," Harry said. His eyes never stopped moving, from the people around them to the walls they were supposed to be searching.

"What's going on?" Parker asked. "Is something wrong?"

"I don't like this," Harry replied. "That bomb makes this different. I can't believe those bloody bastards are so stupid. Blowing up a damned statue while there's an active mission in Dublin is as daft as it gets." A red wave swept across his cheeks. "Now everyone's on alert. Throw in that fella I left in the boot and we're asking for trouble."

"I don't think Arden knew we'd be in Dublin when he planned the bombing." An excuse, and a flimsy one at that.

"Fine. But once he did know, it should have been called off." The words bounced off the walls, far too loud in this quiet church. "Sorry," Harry said. "Gets me fired up. That's the first thing they teach you. *Never* put your own in danger. Arden Flanarty just threw petrol on this fire, and we're the ones who will get burned."

"Then let's find the candleholder and get the hell out of here," Parker said.

Rubbing his face, Harry sucked in a deep breath. "You're right. Sorry. Won't happen again." And with that, the business-like demeanor came back. "What have we here?"

Perched atop a marble pedestal, one of the foremost Irish authors who ever lived looked over the masses, his weathered face bathed in soft light.

Parker read the surname inscribed beneath. "Swift. Wait a second. This is Jonathan Swift's grave?"

"The very same," Harry said. "Every kid in Ireland read *Gulliver's Travels*. Not that I remember a damn bit of it."

Plenty of artifacts adorned the nave, but none held candles. In fact, Parker couldn't see a single candle burning anywhere. Not that any were needed with the sunlight falling all around them. The second alcove they tried offered more of the same, and still no candleholders. Not until they reached the south transept that Parker found a relic worth investigating.

"What about that one?"

Tucked into a recessed shelf in the stone wall, a golden device for holding candles. Arrayed in a circle around one center spire, unlit wax sticks protruded from circular holders.

"Hold on," Harry said, finger dotting the air. "I count twelve of them in that circle, with one more in the middle."

"Which is too many. The drawing had four candles surrounding a fifth."

A crack ripped through the air, heavy as a shotgun blast in the quiet church air. Parker spun around, searching for the source.

"Easy," Harry said. "Just an old pew over there, protesting that big fella."

Not ten feet away a portly visitor settled onto one of the wooden pews, the wood protesting again, bouncing off the stone walls.

In and out of each succeeding alcove, they found plenty of relics and more than a few candleholders of all shapes and sizes, but none matched the engraving on Laurence Hyde's sword. A service deep within the cathedral ended, the exodus of worshippers now another obstacle to navigate.

"That's the last one," Parker said. They'd inspected the final alcove and now faced a small chapel situated behind the high central altar. A few final worshippers straggled out, moving to muted organ music, the steel pipes above them tucked beneath stained glass windows.

"Gavin and Erika must still be searching," Harry said, pulling out his phone. "Hold on, this is him now."

Parker slipped away, back toward the high altar. Red ropes discouraged visitors from ascending the platform, the soft velvet tickled his palms as he leaned over them. Damn, but that was one big block of marble up there for the priests to do their thing on. Golden goblets and shining silver chalices were arrayed on top, next to a pair of Bibles and other religious symbols Parker knew nothing about. The bowl of water—*baptismal bowl, that was it*—stood next to the enormous block, all polished wood and more velvet. Parker wasn't much for church, hadn't been since his younger days when his Dad dragged him along. Even so, you didn't have to be the most pious man to appreciate this place. St. Patrick's stood the test of time and still dazzled today, perhaps even more so because of its imposing, majestic and lasting beauty. A stark contrast with the modern world.

One worshipper using a walker brushed past him, and Parker leaned further over the rope, giving the lady room to pass. Behind the altar, even the embroidered images of Biblical scenes were probably hundreds of years old. Thick silk and heavy cloth draped over a stand-alone wall, a serene yet stoic backdrop for the congregation to study as they sat. Even the candleholders gleamed golden—

The candleholder.

He hadn't seen it until the old lady bumped him further over the ropes. There were two of them, one on either side of the tapestry. The furthest one had five candles arrayed in a circle around an empty center spire. The closer one also had five candles in total, but configured differently. Four of them boxing in a fifth. Is that how the etching looked? Eyes closed, he traced the contours in his mind.

"Harry. Harry, come here." Where did he go? Looking back toward the rear chapel, Parker couldn't find him.

An iron shackle clasped Parker's arm. *The Keepers.*

"Whoa, take it easy." Harry grabbed Parker's other arm, locking on as he tried to pull free.

"Damn you," Parker said, suddenly out of breath. "Don't sneak up on me like that." Once he got it together, he twisted Harry around. "You have to see this. Look what—"

"There's a Keeper across the room," Harry said. "Probably more than one."

"What?" His mind flipped again, back to panic. "Are you sure?"

"I have no idea how, and yes I'm sure. Gavin saw a guy who stuck out, so he walked behind him and guess what's on the guy's phone?"

He'd heard this one before. "Pictures of us?"

"Not *us*. You. And Erika, to be exact."

"But that means they know we're here," Parker said, trying and failing to identify the Keeper. "Where's Erika? We have to find her."

"She's headed to the ladies room for now, until Gavin and I figure out how many Keepers are here and how to avoid them. I need you to hide too."

"I can't."

Lines creased Harry's forehead. "What do you mean, you can't? Get your ass to the men's room until I come get you. At least you'll be out of sight."

"No, you don't understand. I found it."

"Found what?"

"That." He pointed toward his discovery. "The candleholder. It's right there."

"I'll be damned," Harry said. "Sure does look like it." His head shook. "That has to wait. Right now you're hiding while we figure out how to get out of here. That candleholder won't do us any good if you two are in jail."

"Actually," Parker said. "It would. You'll be better off if we get caught. It would take the heat off you."

Harry favored him with a sidelong glance. "That might buy us a spot of time, but it wouldn't be long before the Keepers overran this place. And that's beside the point." He tapped Parker's chest. "You're part of the team now. And we don't hang our own out to dry. So you're going to hide, right now."

As tourists and supplicants shuffled past, a memory jumped up and grabbed him with both hands.

"Listen to me," Parker said. "What if we can get out of here undetected *after* we inspect the candleholder?"

"What are you talking about? Go to the restroom," Harry said. "No arguing."

"Hear me out. Believe it or not, I've been in a tight spot like this before."

Harry looked around, and apparently didn't find anyone coming their way. "You have thirty seconds."

Twenty-seven seconds later, Harry agreed to his plan.

Chapter 43

St. Stephen's Green
Dublin, Ireland

Green leaves flitted on the warm evening breeze, lending a soft glow to the luscious trees. Though the area remained cordoned off by endless strings of yellow tape, the scene had grown quiet in the past hour.

Ensconced in the mobile command center, Logan Rose could have killed someone. Not only had his technical experts lost sight of the terrorist group, the field teams reported zero progress. Every man knew that with each passing minute, their chances of capturing the four criminals diminished.

"Play it again."

Logan fumed above the lead tech, staring at the computer monitors as though he could extract an answer by sheer force. For the fifth time, the scene reverted to Erika Carr leaving a parking garage.

"Focus on the woman. Her height stands out." You wouldn't know by looking at him, but Logan's chest burned, his heart racing. They couldn't afford to lose these terrorists again.

"They get in the taxi," the tech said, finger on the screen. "Which we follow to an intersection." The view shifted, changing from one surveillance camera to another. "Now, unless they jumped out of a moving car, they're still inside when it arrives at this plaza." What appeared to be their four targets exited the cab, making their way into an open air plaza adjacent to a marketplace. "All of them enter the building."

"What's in there?" Logan knew the answer, but wanted everyone to hear it.

"Several dozen shops, sir. With no public surveillance. We're working to retrieve any interior footage right now, and our men are interviewing every shopkeeper. Nothing yet."

"Keep moving," Logan said.

"This is where the trouble starts," the tech said as footage rolled. "We *think* this is the female exiting." According to the time stamp, five minutes elapsed before the figure walked outside into the plaza. "But we're not certain. This person is wearing a hat and a different colored shirt, but the shoes and pants are the same color."

"Dark, like half the other people we see." Logan shook his head. "This is the best resolution you can give me?"

"Afraid so, sir. These are public cameras. They're good for covering lots of ground, but not for details."

"And the other three, the men?"

"We believe the man who gets into a cab with our target female is one of them." Onscreen the person they suspected to be Erika Carr slipped into a taxi with a man, also wearing a baseball hat. "As for the other two, we don't know. It's very difficult to determine when they exited the market as they could have changed clothes or put on a cap. Also, no one who looks toward the cameras resembles any of our targets. Even if we had facial recognition software, it would be useless."

"Now we're down to two targets," Logan said. "Keep going."

"The cab goes to a train station, where the occupants exit." Here the two targets virtually disappeared onto a bustling platform, hundreds of travelers milling about. "We believe they board this train which travels into the city on a southerly route, but we're not certain, because we lose visual contact with them several times as they walk through the station." The tiny figures his tech indicated could have been Dr. Carr and her companion, but then again, they easily could be someone else. "And this train has eight stops before it reverses course and comes north on the return trip."

"Any report from our men at the station?" Logan asked.

"Nothing yet, sir," One of the junior Keepers spoke up. "Our men are headed to the railcar in question, in case the two targets are still on board."

"And we're gathering surveillance footage from all stations where this train stopped," the tech offered.

So they had nothing, and everyone knew it. "Stay with it, lads. We'll find these bastards."

Keyboards rattled and phones rang as Logan stepped outside. Even he didn't believe his own bluster. Dr. Carr and her friends were gone, vanished from under Logan's nose into the anonymous safety of Dublin. Unless his field teams caught a break, they may as well wait for the next attack.

Which Logan knew had nothing to do with Erika Carr or Parker Chase. Warm air lifted his spirits, a welcome reprieve from the claustrophobic command center. The men would work tirelessly in their search, believing they might prevent another attack. However, unbeknownst to them, they truly worked to stop another type of disaster, one Logan knew posed a greater threat to their nation's security than the IRA.

As the sun warmed his face, Oliver Moore burst through the police cordon, stooping low to slide under a string of fluttering crime scene tape.

"Understood. Send it over immediately." Oliver put his phone away. "I have news, sir."

"Please tell me you've captured Dr. Carr and Mr. Chase." Logan closed his eyes and let the falling sun wash over him. If everything went to hell, at least he'd enjoy this wonderful weather.

"Negative, sir. No developments from our field teams, though we are confident that should Dr. Carr or Mr. Chase show their faces at any major monument, we'll find them."

"Then you have bad news." Logan never opened his eyes.

"Not exactly." Oliver cleared his throat. "We've intercepted a communication from the IRA. It suggests there will be another attack."

"I could have told you that," Logan sighed. "Any details?"

"The message implies it will happen within twenty-four hours and will occur on English soil."

His eyes snapped open, directly into the sun. With spots flashing on his vision, Logan held out his hand. "I want to see the message." Oliver handed his phone over, and Logan studied a single line of text.

"We took it from a Celtic football online message board often used by the IRA. One of our men ran it through a decoding algorithm he cooked up, and this is what came back."

Logan read the message aloud.

"Those Keepers in her backyard are in for a surprise with the sun. Bloody Brits won't be ready for this one! They won't see it until the stones are falling."

"How certain are you this came from the IRA?"

"Very," Oliver replied. "The message board is run out of Ireland, and multiple confirmed IRA sympathizers have been tracked on it. Also, the encryption program used to decode this message has broken other IRA messages before, intelligence which led to three arrests. Before we ran it through our program, it was a bunch of nonsense written in Gaelic." Oliver shrugged. "To be blunt, I'd say we ignore that at our own peril, sir."

Exactly what they didn't need. "Right now we don't have a single man to spare. If you're convinced this threat is legitimate, that's enough for me." Logan took one last breath of fresh air before heading to the command center, Oliver at his side. "We'll have to make our CCTV cameras do the work of a few field teams. Head back to London, and I'll join you shortly. There will not be another seven-seven on my watch."

The mere thought of the 2005 suicide attacks on the London Underground set Logan's blood to boiling. That may have been Islamic extremists, but these IRA bastards grew bolder every day. He wouldn't put it past them to plunge the United Kingdom back into another round of The Troubles.

"We'll need increased patrols around all major landmarks and public transit locations in London," Logan said. "You know the drill. We can't—"

The command center door burst open as Logan reached for it. The head analyst nearly ran headlong into his boss, jerking to a halt so quickly the glasses perched on his nose clattered to the ground.

"Chief Warder, I'm sorry." He accepted the spectacles from Logan, hands wringing as he fumbled with them. "You're needed inside, sir."

"What's happened?"

"There's an ongoing incident at St. Patrick's Cathedral. The fire alarms are active."

Chapter 44

A moment before he gave the signal, Parker breathed deeply, sucking air until it hurt. *You've done this before. Easy stuff. Same as last time.*

A pilfered black raincoat fell over his shoulders, not long enough to hide his sneakers, but it would do. Moments earlier, Harry tried the handle on a supply closet and found it to be unlocked. In a stroke of luck, it contained rain gear which, if you didn't look too closely, resembled the priestly robes every holy man wore throughout the cathedral.

Hands resting lightly on the red velvet ropes, Parker stood twenty feet from the candleholder they sought. Gavin waited at the south transept, Harry at the north, and Erika behind him, her fingers on a fire alarm. When Parker flipped the hood over his head, she would trip the alarm. They suspected to hear an ear-splitting siren, hopefully with flashing lights and any other special effects the fire department mandated, all to heighten the confusion. With Gavin and Harry shouting and screaming, there should be enough going on so no one noticed a hooded monk on the high altar. Back over the felt rope, and then Erika had ninety seconds to examine the candleholder. If she failed to uncover Anne's next clue, Parker planned to smuggle the piece through the front door under his new coat.

He hoped it didn't come to that. As soon as this alarm went off the fire and police departments would come racing, and the candleholder looked heavy. For all he knew it weighed a hundred pounds, solid gold. He'd look like Quasimodo shuffling along at a snail's pace, trying to carry the thing. Over his shoulder, he spotted Erika, ready to rock. Parker winked.

Go time.

For a beat, time slowed. And then she touched the alarm. As it fell, an image of the diamond ring in his pocket flashed across his mind. He still had it, planned to give it to her before they left. Just after they finished this.

With a piercing wail, the world came back.

"Fire! Everybody out!"

Even from across the chapel Parker heard Gavin scream. Everyone froze. Everyone except for Parker, who made it halfway to the candleholder before the dam broke loose. A confused buzzing came first, though he barely registered the din. *Damn, this thing is huge.* He could barely lift it with one hand. Most likely gold plating over some other metal.

The shouting started. Far away, some part of his mind registered people in full-on panic mode, rushing toward any exit they saw. Staff members jumped into action, throwing the fire exits open, one after another.

Each candle slid out with ease, wax bolts you could buy in any store. Nothing inside the empty sockets. No broken metal, rough edges, anything to suggest a hidden compartment. Neither did he find any markings or engravings.

Erika believed that if this truly contained a message from Anne, it would either be an engraving or a hidden compartment like they'd seen before. Anne hadn't strayed far in terms of hiding places, and if she'd crafted this candleholder specifically for the cathedral, that gave her ample opportunity to install any type of hidden feature needed.

Parker ducked behind the altar and upended the metal object, fingers caressing the gold for any tiny crevices or lines. It took a second for him to realize that two letters stared him in the face, engraved in the underside.

A S

He didn't need Erika to tell him what those meant.

Lots were shouting now. Parker looked up, saw an elderly worshipper slide to the ground, her cane twirling away. Two men exiting behind her scooped the old lady up and carried her to safety. A priest followed them, stopping to retrieve the lost walking aid. When he bent to pick it up, his eyes met Parker's. The man's bald head gleamed as he stared, eyes falling to the candleholder cradled in his arms.

He knows.

Then the priest raced after the elderly woman being carried out, the monk's guise passing its first test. As sirens wailed, Parker realized he'd been over the metal piece completely. No lines, no marks other than the initials, nothing.

Think, Parker. Use your head.

A few moments longer and he'd have to lug this thing out with him, a felony he wasn't eager to commit. He set it down, took a breath, and really looked at the thing.

Four holders jutted out from the base to form an X. From the middle, a single spire to hold the fifth candle, elevated above the rest. Only a few notches decorated the remarkably simple design. In fact, only two of the four holders had any decoration at all, just a row of ridges along the top.

Why did only two of them have designs? They almost looked like bottle caps, the ridges meant for purchase while twisting off lids.

It couldn't be the same here. Right?

The chaos slowed, shouts dying as the sirens blared. No one else paid him any mind yet, but his internal clock hit zero. If this didn't work, the damn thing came with him.

"Come on," he said, muscles bulging as he twisted. The metal didn't budge. "Maybe it's the rust." One ridged holder slammed on the ground, a dull thunk which actually chipped the marble floor. The other went down just as hard, though this time the floor held.

"Last chance." Arms straining, teeth gritted so hard he thought they'd break, Parker twisted on each holder with all his strength.

Without warning, the candleholder flew from his hands. *How'd that happen?* I didn't drop it. It was almost as though it...

From where he crouched the holder appeared to be unchanged. Only when he retrieved it to stuff the infernal thing under his coat did he realize.

An opening at the base of the support stem. A tiny doorway, slid open to reveal a compartment. And inside? A slender scroll.

"I'll be damned. Nice work, Anne."

The scroll disappeared into his pocket. The candleholder went back on the altar, Parker dipping under the velvet rope. They'd been right, and if Erika's theory held true, this should be—

He never finished the thought. It's surprisingly hard to keep the ideas moving with a gun jammed in your face.

"Parker Chase, you're under arrest."

A different guy, not the one Harry spotted. Hair graying at the temples, his face a mask of calm, and Parker didn't doubt for a second he'd shoot if Parker resisted.

"Who?" Parker said. "I have no idea what you're talking about."

"Your name is Parker Chase. You're an American, and you're wanted for aiding and abetting terrorists, and for questioning in several murders. Put your hands in the air."

One mistake amateurs make is getting too close to their targets. This guy stood inches away, his gun practically touching Parker's face, begging for Parker to take it away. And Parker planned to oblige him. At least he did, until the guy took a step back into the aisle.

"Hands up or I shoot you in the knee."

The guy meant business. Parker complied, hands in the air, stepping further into the aisle. Directly into the path of an overweight man racing toward the front door.

Big and clumsy, when he tried to hit the brakes, several hundred pounds of flab failed him and he crashed headlong into the gunman.

Just as Parker planned it.

Before the guy landed, Parker had both hands on the gun. First, aim it away from you. Second, leverage your opponent's wrist. It took surprisingly little pressure to snap the small bones. One second the guy had Parker dead to rights, the next he lay on his back, disarmed and with only one good hand. For most people, that would be enough. Parker only wanted to get away, not kill anyone.

But not this guy. He barely grunted as his bones shattered, not panicking and instead smashing his forehead into Parker's nose. However, Parker knew that trick and tucked his chin down just in time, opening a gash on both their foreheads.

Blood spurted everywhere. Parker's vision grew foggy, clouded by the flowing red liquid. Head wounds bled profusely, but looked far worse than they actually were. On top of his opponent, Parker rolled and lashed a kick at the guy's head.

Or at least where his head had been. His sneaker whistled through the air, connecting with nothing. The Keeper twisted to his feet, the broken wrist tucked under an armpit, giving him an elbow to fight with.

Parker feigned a charge, got the guy to drop low. His knee shot up, smashed into the Keeper's arm. The broken wrist one, which he'd managed to get up in time to block the attack. Parker didn't stop, slamming his fist into his nose.

All the blood made things slippery, and the blow glanced off. In a flash, Parker fell flat on his back, staring at the ceiling. Before he hit the ground the guy stood above him, raining blows with his good hand.

Parker twisted, face going left and right. Minimize the damage, press any advantage. His knee went up, found the solar plexus.

And that worked every time. With an inhuman squeal, the man balled up. Parker rolled away, tried to stand, but got tangled in the oversized coat and fell down. When he finally gained his feet, death stared back.

The Keeper, who he'd just kneed in the family jewels, had somehow found his gun, now aimed at Parker.

"Last chance," he said, his voice two octaves higher. "You move and you die."

Movement behind the man caught Parker's eye.

"Tell your boss we didn't ask for any of this," Parker said.

His eyes narrowed. "What—"

He never finished. Eyes rolling back, he fell to the ground, the gun clattering away. Erika stood over him, a bloody candleholder grasped in both hands.

"I had him right where I wanted him," Parker said. "But thanks."

"Get up," Erika said, all business. "Harry and Gavin are out that way. This guy's partner is going to show up any minute."

"I found it."

Her eyes darted back and forth like a trapped animals. "They'll find us. They have our pictures, our names, everything."

"Did you hear me?"

She grabbed his hand, pulled him away. "Not now, we have to… What did you say?" Erika stopped dead in her tracks as the words finally made it through to her brain. "Where?"

He led her toward the open emergency exit. "In the base of the candleholder. A hidden compartment. You had to twist two of the holders to get it open."

"What did you find?"

He pulled her close as they jogged outside under blue skies and into the blessed embrace of a massive crowd. "A scroll. We're almost there."

Chapter 45

St. Stephen's Green
Dublin, Ireland

Logan Rose glowered at the technician in front of him, the young man's face taut, eyes wide.

"Where is he?"

"I don't know, sir. His partner can't find him, and he's not answering his phone."

"Then send our man back inside," Logan said. "I don't give a damn what the fire department says."

"We *can't*, sir. It's an active fire scene and no one is allowed inside until the fire chief says so. Not the police, not us, nobody."

Cursed bureaucrats. Answers were inside the cathedral. Every minute they waited should be spent chasing those two Americans and stopping an assault on England's very core, not bending to the will of some fire chief.

"Keep that line open," Logan ordered. "And tell him to keep badgering them until he's allowed inside or thrown in jail."

Outside the command center, Logan found Oliver Moore studying a laptop, one arm resting on a police cruiser's boot. The intercepted threat couldn't be dismissed, not even in the midst of this Queen Anne debacle. Logan finally caught his eye, motioned for Oliver to join him.

"What's your assessment?" They stood under the center's air conditioning unit, the soft thrum masking their conversation.

"This is as credible a threat as I've seen in some time," Oliver replied. "The actual message is only one factor. We also traced it to an IP address in Belfast."

Not what Logan wanted to hear. "If that's the case, then we must meet this head on." Oliver wasn't going to like this, but there was no way around it now. "You'll coordinate our response from London."

"Yes, sir."

A hand ran through Logan's hair, sliding it behind his ears. "I realize dividing our efforts isn't ideal, but we can't take this lightly. You and I are the only ones who know why it's vital we locate the Americans before they reach the end of Anne's journey. So right now I need you on a plane back to London."

"When will you be returning?"

"I'll decide once I find out what happened in St. Patrick's. For now you'll take the reins. Do your best to use only the men we have on hand in London. Don't call in any outside assistance unless you must."

"I'll take care of it, sir."

"I know you will," Logan said. He clapped a hand on Oliver's shoulder. "Once you get a handle on our response, call me. I know we'll soon have those four in custody and we can put this behind us. Until that happens, our Keepers can best help the cause by continuing their search here."

Never one to waste time, Oliver nodded and moved out, bound for a military transport to London. Logan checked in with his technicians, though he suspected their story hadn't changed.

"No, sir. We haven't been able to locate any of the targets." The lead tech looked exhausted, dark circles under his eyes. "Surveillance footage at the train stops proved inconclusive. None of our field teams reported sighting either of the tourists, and our electronic monitoring hasn't captured any credit card transactions or official use of their passports."

"Check any stops near St. Patrick's Cathedral." This fire alarm couldn't be a coincidence. "And what about flights or train tickets?"

"Nothing, sir. No airlines have Parker Chase or Erika Carr on their manifests, and unless they use a card to pay for their train tickets, we won't catch them there either."

It wasn't their fault the task bordered on impossible. "Keep searching," Logan said. His voice lost the hard edge. "Your efforts will bring these terrorists to justice. Nobody said it would be easy, but that won't stop us, will it?"

Fists pounded the tabletop in salute. Even now, his men carried on. They'd find them, but Logan needed to catch a break.

Five minutes later, it arrived.

"Chief Keeper!" A harried young man burst out of the command center. "You should come in here, sir."

Logan bounded up the steps, nearly knocking the slow-moving warder to the ground. "What is it? What've you got for me?"

"It's our man from inside the chapel," a tech said. "He saw the Americans."

Logan grabbed the phone. "This is Chief Keeper Rose. Provide a report."

"This is Keeper Asprey, sir." The missing man from inside St. Patrick's. "I saw Parker Chase in the cathedral immediately after the fire alarm activated."

"Where is he now? Did you see Dr. Carr or either of the Irish terrorists?"

"Negative, sir. However, I strongly believe at least one of them accompanied him."

Strongly believe? "Why do you say that? You didn't see them."

"No, but someone nearly brained me with a candleholder while I fought Chase. One of his companions is my guess."

"Did you say *fighting?* Give me the full story."

Logan put the call on speakerphone for all to hear. The man relayed how he'd spotted Parker Chase inside St. Patrick's after the fire alarm activated.

"He dressed like a priest, securing the artifacts. But once he slipped under the rope I saw his face, and there's no doubt, sir. It was him."

"Wait a second," Logan said. "He's in disguise?"

"Only a long raincoat, but from far away and with all the confusion, he looked like a priest."

"What did you see him doing?"

Another voice came on the line, one of the medics telling their man to lie down. "I'm fine, doc. Sorry about that, sir. My partner and I conducted patrols of the cathedral, and on a pass through the interior alarm activated. From what they're saying it sounds as though there's no fire."

A distraction.

"I spotted Chase by the main altar, holding a large candelabra, trying to pull it apart. That's what caught my attention. I walked over, and when he ducked under the rope, saw his face and drew my weapon. However, in the chaos, I lost control of my gun and engaged Mr. Chase unarmed."

"What happened to your partner?"

"He was keeping watch near the entrance on people leaving the building. Permission to speak plainly, sir?"

"Out with it."

"Parker Chase knows martial arts and can really fight."

"And you are defenseless?"

"While I had my gun on him, someone hit me in the back of the head. Ten stitches."

Logan could hardly blame the guy for getting whacked from behind. But that didn't matter. What did is that no one else blinked when he mentioned the candelabra.

"Stay at the cathedral with your partner, and keep an eye out for Parker Chase or Dr. Carr. I'll be there in five minutes." Logan needed the Cathedral's security footage, which should give him an idea of which direction the Americans had fled. "You and you," he pointed at the two senior technicians. "Come with me. You'll be retrieving anything their surveillance cameras captured. The rest of you, go over every inch of St. Patrick's. Find them."

Logan grabbed a local Garda officer in case the firemen gave him any trouble and took off. Blue lights flashing, they ripped across town, skidding to a halt in front of St. Patrick's Cathedral. A long shadow fell from the towering spire as people milled about the grounds, emergency responders herding everyone to safety. Amid the confusion, their man sat on the back of an ambulance, an ice pack pressed to his head.

"Where exactly did you first see Mr. Chase?"

"Near the main altar," the Keeper said. "Crouched down behind it, fiddling with a candleholder until he ducked under the rope."

Logan stood closer, turning to shield his words from the other Keepers. "Did he leave the item behind?"

The man's face screwed up. "I believe so. Actually... no, he didn't. I think he dropped it when I drew my weapon."

"Did you see it after you were struck in the head?"

"No, sir. One moment I had him in my sights, and the next I'm lying on the pavement with a torch in my eyes. I don't know what happened to it."

"No matter." A pen and paper went into his hands. "Draw it as best you can remember. I need to confiscate this evidence and retrieve any prints he left behind."

The dutiful Warder never questioned Logan's order, and a rough outline took shape. A four-sided holder, one in the center.

"Good work. And until I secure this, don't breathe a word to anyone. The last thing we need is to have the locals claim jurisdiction."

Total horseshit, but the man didn't blink. Under the tent flap and up the front steps, Logan didn't even glance at the patrolman standing watch, his royal protection badge flashing in the officer's face, a scowl daring him to argue.

The cavernous space appeared even grander with the crowds driven outside, replaced by a smattering of officers and firefighters, inspecting the building and chatting on radios.

Logan moved toward the altar, an enormous block of stone in front of a backdrop draped with flowing cloth tapestries. But what happened to the candleholder? He found a different one on the far side of the altar, larger than what he needed. The one he sought had five candles in total, four deployed in an X-shape around the center.

Logan headed to search behind the altar when the floor rushed up to greet him. One arm shot out, scraping his knuckles but breaking his fall. Pain pierced his shin, a second punch landing on a knee. What the hell happened?

Only when he rolled with the fall did Logan realize he'd tripped over the candleholder.

"Sir, are you hurt?"

A priest touched his elbow, reached out and hauled him upright.

"I'm fine. Thank you." Logan stopped the man when he bent down to retrieve the tripping hazard. "I'm a member of her majesty's government. This candleholder is evidence, and I'll have to ask you to leave it there."

The kind expression never faded. "As you wish. Have a blessed day."

Once the helpful clergyman moved off, Logan knelt, examining the metal object. Larger than most, likely gilded, it rested on one side.

A red streak ran along one ridged holder, several blonde hairs mixed in the blood, the same color as his injured man's.

What drew Parker Chase to this piece? Had Anne led them here?

Logan had sparse notes from her time in Dublin. The Keepers charged with "guarding" Anne left little for him, remarking more on the foul weather than their captive's activities. Now left to his own devices, Logan had a poor chance of anticipating her next stop.

So what did Parker find? Perhaps nothing, and this candleholder didn't have anything to do with Anne's search for Prince William. A weapon at hand when the Keeper appeared.

Logan tipped the candleholder over, shirtsleeve covering his hand to keep any prints intact. In an instant, his world became crystal clear.

A hidden compartment in the base. An *empty* compartment.

Chapter 46

On approach to Heathrow Airport

Thousands of lights glittered below as the floor fell from beneath Parker's feet, their plane descending into London.

"Remember, we have nothing to declare at customs. And we're from Toronto."

The whites of Erika's eyes showed in the dim plane light as she spoke.

Anxiety again. Flying did this to her. That and a lack of sleep.

"Erika," Parker said. "Ireland and England are both in the EU, so the customs process shouldn't be more than checking our passports and asking a few questions. Also, Gavin's guy altered our photos just enough to avoid them getting flagged by facial recognition software, *if* they even use it. You need to relax." Cool as could be in all other facets of her life, something about travel made her an anxious, fiddling wreck.

"Oh, right."

Ever since Gavin slipped a dark blue Canadian passport into her hands, Erika studied the document like it was her dissertation defense. Gavin's counterfeiter in Dublin assured them these were top-of-the-line documents, enabling them to slip out of Ireland like ghosts.

"Are you sure we're safe?" Erika whispered, looking over his shoulder to the horizontal strip of lights below, the runway at Heathrow airport rising to meet them.

"Gavin got us out of the country, didn't he? I'm sure he wouldn't take us to a safe house that wasn't safe. If this place hides the IRA in the middle of London, we'll be fine for one night."

"I assure you we will be safe, Dr. Carr." Gavin said, yawning. The Scotland cap which covered his eyes slid up. "I've used this house before."

Erika actually smiled. "Thank you, Gavin. We'll need to be up and moving as early as possible."

"As soon as the Tower opens," Gavin said. "Based on what Erika read, we have to wait until then. Sleep will help, and once we get there, Harry and I will reconnoiter the area, but I don't anticipate any issue. It's one of the city's most popular tourist destinations. If there's one place the Keepers won't be looking for us, it's their own back yard."

The cabin rattled, tires chirping as they touched down on English soil.

Outside the airport, Harry hailed a cab. Traffic filled the motorway as they traveled east through the city, hundreds of black cabs joining them, burrowing into the heart of London on this late summer evening.

"Drop us at the corner." Harry passed a wad of notes to the driver, the money vanishing as though Houdini drove them.

"Two blocks ahead," Gavin said once the cabbie motored away. "It's a single level flat, what you'd call the second floor." With their luggage left behind in Dublin, Parker and Erika strolled unencumbered over the sidewalk. For the thousandth time, Parker brushed his fingers over the soft felt box in one pocket, the only thing other than his wallet that he'd managed to keep this entire journey, having also ditched their phones in Ireland.

The building had no elevator, so they climbed a narrow staircase. A woman slid past them, murmuring into her phone.

"You and Dr. Carr take the far room," Gavin said, bolting the steel front door behind them. Three separate locks secured the reinforced door, enough to stop anything short of a battering ram. "Harry and I will be in here." The rooms faced each other, an impossibly small bathroom sandwiched in between. Despite occupying roughly the same area as a large postage stamp, Parker knew this rental could easily bring in over a thousand pounds monthly. West of Regent's Park, this revitalized neighborhood teemed with young professionals, a fantastic hiding spot. Everyone here worked in one of London's finance factories, manipulating currencies to print money out of thin air. These people barely had time to sleep, let alone get to know their neighbors.

"Everything's in order," Harry said after checking each room in turn. "I'll grab some takeaway for us, and then we can get some sleep."

Erika slid behind the small dining room table, removing the folded plastic sheath hidden under her shirt as Parker and Gavin joined her.

"I need to review this before I call the QM," Gavin said. "He'll want to know anything you can determine from Anne's message, even if it's an educated guess."

"He's trying to stop Arden Flanarty's drone attack, isn't he?" Erika asked. "It's not right, blowing up a national landmark. And the man doesn't care if he kills civilians."

"Often what's right can be very different, depending on your perspective," Gavin said.

The scroll unfurled, smaller than a sheet of modern note paper. Stored inside the candleholder, it hid in plain sight for centuries, used in countless ceremonies and masses.

Dearest Laurence,

William still lives, and stayed here only a fortnight past.

He accompanied the group of Irish travelers passing through St. Patrick's scarcely ten days past. How do I know? One of his captors laid bare his soul in confession, his words overheard by my handmaiden.

He said that William endeared himself to his captors with his bravery, causing them to question their mission. These Irishmen are now afraid, so close have we come to finding them. To conceal their path, the Irishmen have chosen an unusual course. William is being taken back to London, to the site of my power and my curse. I will pray that you find me where there are no martyrs who witnessed Anne's final day.

A.S.

"Anne's message is straightforward until the end," Erika said. "William is alive and headed back to London."

"If William survived, there would be a record of it somewhere," Harry said.

"Not necessarily," Erika replied. "History is written by the victors."

"Winston Churchill," Gavin said.

"And he's right. William may have survived, may have even been reunited with his family. If King George wanted to erase any record of William's survival, he could do it. We'll find out soon enough. Anne says her son is being taken back to *'the site of my power and my curse'*. When your Quartermaster asks, repeat that line verbatim. That's the key."

"Because there's only one place which fits both descriptions, which you recognized at once," Gavin said. "The Tower of London."

"A fortress built to terrify citizens and enemies alike. Look at it as a Londoner of the day would. Executions outside, the Crown Jewels kept inside. The place exudes power."

"And it's home to the Beefeaters," Gavin finished. "Who were blocking Anne in her search for William. They were her curse."

"But where do we look once we're actually inside?" Parker asked. "It's not just one building."

"I'm working on it," Erika said. "The final line is tricky."

"*Where there are no martyrs who witnessed Anne's final day,*" Gavin quoted. "Plenty of martyrs spent their final day in the Tower, so we need to find a building or location in which *nobody* died."

"Could she be referring to a location Laurence Hyde would know?" Parker asked. "A place special to the two of them?"

"We may never specifically know," Erika said. "We need to focus on our strongest lead, which is William in the Tower of London. Let's split into pairs to cover more ground."

"Avoid the guided tours," Harry said. "They're led by Yeoman Warders. We've never heard of Beefeaters working with the Keepers, but it's best not to chance it. The Keepers may have taken them in to their confidence and shared your pictures."

"We'll be careful," Parker said. "I'm starving. What's the word on food?"

"Good call." Harry jumped from the table. "You're in for a treat."

Twenty minutes later they were elbow deep in grease, a delicious fish and chips platter spread out on yesterday's papers. After gorging himself, Parker pushed back from the table, his eyelids heavy. "Good stuff, but damned if I'm not tired. Let's set out a plan and then I'm hitting the sack."

A short while later they had a rough plan and a flash of hope this might be the end. *After tomorrow, I'm never coming back to Ireland again unless it's for a real vacation with Erika. And to give her a long-delayed gift.* As his head hit the pillow, he tucked the soft little box into his shoes.

Parker rose and looked outside, finding a soft blue sky overhead, a scenic London morning complemented by the stench of exhaust wafting on every breeze.

Once they'd eaten and headed outside, Gavin touched two fingers to his lips, and the shrieking whistle knifing through Parker's ear, the cab peeling up an instant later.

Erika tucked her blonde locks under a baseball cap. "Search for anything related to Anne." She slipped into the rear seat beside Gavin, Harry once again taking the front. "And keep your mind open. Whatever connotation the phrase had for Anne may be completely lost on us."

Cabs comprised most of the traffic as they darted through the morning rush. Parker reviewed the plan as they drove, hammering every detail into his mind. He and Harry would take the north side while Erika and Gavin searched the south. Covering nearly twelve acres and divided into three separate areas, the Tower hadn't changed much since Anne's time. A grassy field now covered the original moat, and Erika considered it the least likely location for Anne to secret a message. Their search would begin past this field, in the outer ward, hidden behind stone walls ten feet thick.

"If we don't have any luck in the outer ward," Parker said, watching the cab motor away. "We'll start on the inner ward with the White Tower." In front of them, the Tower stretched nearly one hundred feet toward the sky, a height unmatched in its day. Four floors of pristine Norman architecture dating from 1078, the king or queen stayed within these walls while in residence. "I'd rather not search the Waterloo Barracks."

Considering the crown jewels were housed there, security would make a thorough inspection impossible.

"When did your Quartermaster say the attack is happening?" Parker asked.

"Around lunch," Gavin said. "That's when most employees are on break and the chances of avoiding detection are best. It's not far from the public roadway onto Tower grounds. All they'll need is thirty seconds, tops."

A bustling thoroughfare sat east of the Tower, no distance at all for a drone to cover. At noon, with most people eating lunch, the small machine could fly over and launch an attack before anyone knew what happened.

"I picked these up out last night," Harry said. "A guy I know just happened to be in the area."

He held four hands-free earpieces, the kind used to talk on a cell phone while walking.

A whole lot of good that did them. "Erika and I don't have cell phones," Parker said. "We ditched them in Ireland."

"These aren't Bluetooth headsets. They're communication devices, like walkie-talkies." Gavin hooked his over one ear. "Go ahead, put it on." It fit his ear snugly, and Parker jumped when Gavin's voice filled his head. "They're already on," the Irishman said, grinning. "We can talk to each other as we search. If either group runs into trouble or finds a lead, let everyone know and we'll rendezvous."

Each of them tested their earpiece, the tiny microphones picking up everything they said, even a whisper.

Gavin raised an eyebrow. "Ready?"

Parker looked to Erika, found the steely glare he'd come to know. "Let's go," he said.

Down a narrow bridge past the ticket office, under an arched stone entranceway and face-to-face with a Yeoman Warder. The man fiddled with his top hat, waiting for enough tourists to form a group. A weekday, and Parker guessed they were the first visitors of the day.

"Keep sharp and let us know if you see anything." Gavin didn't look at Parker as he spoke, his back turned, he and Erika walking away. "We'll meet you in the rear."

Parker fell into step with Harry. Devoid of tourists, the place seemed to hover around them, stone walls reminding him the castle didn't only serve to keep people out. Once inside, you only left if permitted.

"So how long have you two been together?" Harry asked.

Parker glanced over. These IRA hadn't been much for small talk.

"Since college," he said. "Nearly a decade now, but we took a year off not long ago."

"You going to make an honest woman of her?" A wink softened the words.

"Maybe one day," Parker said. He wasn't about to show him the ring in his pocket. Not yet. Maybe once this mess ended.

"Doesn't everyone?" Harry nodded to a camera above them. "Keep an eye out for those. But she seems like a good one. Shouldn't keep her waiting."

"What about you? Any lucky ladies waiting at home?"

"A few, but that's the problem." Harry scuffed a shoe across the ground. "My job isn't much for relationships. Hard to explain what I'm doing if I have to leave for weeks at the drop of a hat. Most of us aren't the type to settle down." He met Parker's gaze. "Or if we are, the opportunity's not there."

"Look at that." Parker nodded to a custodial worker passing by carrying a bucket with red liquid dripping down one side. "Is that *blood*?"

"It is," Harry said. "For the ravens. They keep a half-dozen or so of the bloody things around. Brings good luck or something."

As they walked, one of the black birds whistled overhead and perched on an outer wall. Beady eyes fixed on the bloody bucket, he cried out before taking flight once more.

"Traitor's Gate," Harry pointed toward the river. "Important part of this place, what with all the people coming to be executed entering through it, but if we're looking for *no martyrs* I'd say it's not for us."

As Parker noted the metal gate, a blurb from Erika's research last night came to him. "They used to hang heads above this entrance, didn't they?"

"Too right. Imagine that." Harry shook his head, and Parker couldn't help but note a hint of admiration in his words. "Coming into this place on a boat and the poor bastard who had your seat yesterday is hanging right above you. Or at least his head is."

Past the gate, around several smaller towers jutting above the stone wall, and Parker heard vehicular traffic rumbling outside the stone walls, the area from which Gavin suspected the drone attack would come, a short distance from Tower grounds.

"Hold steady," Harry said, tapping his earpiece. "Gavin, you there?"

"Here," Gavin said. "You find something?"

"Might have. Might be nothing. You notice anything about the tourists around here?"

"Other than the fact there aren't any?"

"Right," Harry said. "We're practically the only ones here."

"Quiet as can be on our side," Gavin said. "The fewer civilians, the better. Although we have nothing so far."

"We're almost done with our half," Harry said.

"Erika," Parker said. "Anything jump out at you?"

"Not exactly. There's something that's been bugging me. The way Anne referred to herself in the third person."

The same linguistic quirk he'd noted as well. "Makes you wonder if there's another Anne involved," Parker said.

"And who might that be?"

A test. "Anne Boleyn."

As Parker spoke, he caught sight of Erika ahead, her lips moving. "Not bad. I suspected as much."

"Usually the simple explanation is the correct one," Gavin said. "Now turn off these headsets before we're all standing together."

Gavin and Harry looked everywhere but at each other when they met, finding nothing.

"Same thing on the inner portion of the Tower," he said. "Erika and I take the White Tower. Harry, you and Parker search Waterloo Block."

"Don't bother with the crown jewels," Erika said. "That room's been redesigned for security upgrades. Anything in there is long gone."

"Not to mention all the guards who'll be hanging around," Parker noted. "Letting them get a good look at our faces is not what I'm trying to do."

"Now you're thinking," Gavin said. "Sweep the remaining buildings on the west of the inner compound. Erika and I will take the east."

And if that failed, then what? If Erika had any other ideas, she kept them to herself.

"Be safe." Parker put an arm around Erika, his lips brushing atop hers. She never blinked. This wasn't like him and they both knew it, but what the hell. Maybe all the death hanging over this place made him realize how much he appreciated her.

"See you soon," she said. Her eyes lingered a moment longer, a halted step as she turned.

Harry clapped a hand on his shoulder. "Don't worry. We'll find the next message and be out of here. Now, keep your eyes off her pretty behind and help me find whatever the hell Anne left behind."

The feel of Parker's kiss tingled on her lips as she turned. *What had gotten into him?*

"What can you tell me about the White Tower?" Gavin asked.

It took a second to get back to reality. "Well, it's four stories tall," she said. "Built by William the Conqueror after the Norman conquest in 1066, this place has seen it all. Murdered children, usurped thrones, beheaded queens and captured kings."

Signs pointed them to the entrance, an attendant waving them inside. "First visitors of the day, you two. Enjoy the sights!"

Harry leaned in close to Erika. "Fascinating information, but I'm not sure how that helps us. The QM is going to text me thirty minutes before the drone takes off. Should be plenty of time to get out of here, but I'd rather not cut it close."

"Right," Erika said. "Sorry about that. I believe the final line of Anne's message, where she discusses the martyrs, is most relevant."

"There's no shortage of martyrs here," Harry said. "Scores of people have been killed in the Tower."

"True. And I don't like the idea of Queen Anne using the third person. It's different from her other messages."

"So you think she's talking about another Queen Anne? The one named Boleyn?"

"I do," Erika said. "She died just outside these walls. As a queen, they likely took pains to keep her death hidden from any citizens, servants, or other common folk."

Suits of armor lined the walls on either side, fully armed metallic men staring vacantly as they passed. Behind protective glass stood a gilded suit belonging to Charles I.

"Could Anne be speaking literally?" Gavin asked. "She refers to witnesses, perhaps people who saw Anne Boleyn die. We need to find a room with a view of that execution."

Valid points, all. Except right now something else grabbed her eye. A plaque, hanging across the hall.

"Hello?" Gavin sidled next to her, not realizing what had her eye. "Are you listening?"

"There it is." Right in front of them, hidden in plain sight. Fitting, given how Anne's clues were obscured in much the same way.

"What in the world are you talking about?" he asked.

Instead of answering, she tapped the plaque hanging in front of them. Nondescript, a wash of gray and brown hues, you really had to get close to read it. And once she did, Erika's nerves tingled with electricity.

Ahead lies St. John's Chapel, the Tower of London's parish church. Smaller confines give visitors to this lesser known chapel an intimate opportunity for worship, and offers an unparalleled view, though it is not as unspoiled as visitors may believe.

Overlooking the hill upon which numerous royal executions took place, including that of King Henry VIII's second wife, Anne Boleyn. Given Saint John was the sole apostle not to be martyred, it is interesting that a holy site such as his oversaw the death of so many.

An instant later, Gavin had Parker and Harry on the line.

"We have something," he said. "The White Tower. There's a chapel on the second floor, St. John's. Meet us there."

"Are they coming?" Erika asked.

"En route now." Hard lines accented his jaw. "Let's get up there and find a lost prince."

Down the hallway from Erika and Gavin, a Keeper stood still as could be, his eyes locked on the pair. They never turned around as they walked toward a staircase and disappeared up the curving stone steps. He glanced at the photo in his hand, distributed at the start of his shift.

No doubt about it. The girl he'd seen stared back from the photograph.

"Deputy Chief Moore," the Keeper said, tapping his radio. "Come in."

The receiver squawked, hissing static. "This is Oliver Moore."

"I just found Erika Carr."

Chapter 47

Tower of London
London, England

Inside the Tower of London tactical command center, Oliver Moore stared at the radio in his hand like it might explode.

"Do you copy, sir?"

"Say that again."

"Erika Carr is in the White Tower, sir."

They'd come *here*? "And Parker Chase?"

"No sign, sir. She's with a man, one I don't recognize."

Coming to the Keepers' stronghold, the very people chasing after them? So foolish as to almost be brilliant, the last place Oliver expected to find them.

"Where are they?"

"Leaving the ground floor at the end of the armor and weapons exhibit. They're headed upstairs on one of the north staircases."

"Do not follow them."

"Copy that. I'll return to the command center."

This isn't what he needed right now. Short-staffed, with another unidentified terrorist threat hanging over his head, in no position to mount a significant defense. If Dr. Carr and her associates proved as resourceful as suspected, capturing them alive would take all the men at his disposal. Which left them unprepared should this mysterious threat materialize.

First thing, bring Logan Rose up to date. His boss answered on the first ring. "Rose here."

"Erika Carr is here."

"They're *in the Tower*?"

"Visually confirmed less than a minute ago."

"What about Parker Chase?"

"We haven't identified him yet, but the men are reviewing security footage. I've ordered them to begin escorting visitors from the grounds. It's still early in the day and there aren't many people here yet."

As Oliver spoke, live surveillance footage showed most guests making their way toward an exit. Fortunately, Dr. Carr chose a weekday to appear. With so few visitors inside, Oliver might be able to empty the place before Erika and her friends noticed.

"I'm on my way now," Logan said. "I'll take a helicopter from the airport and be back within the hour. Do not let them leave the premises."

"I'd suggest allowing them to continue their search until we determine why they risked coming here. If the man with Dr. Carr is IRA, he knows the risk in coming here."

"Agreed." Logan said. "Whatever motivated them to come to London must be important. Those Irish bastards won't say a word once we take them in. Let's see if they'll show their hand when they don't know we're watching."

"Understood, sir. Surveillance until you arrive."

"Any word on the other threat?"

"No, sir. Everything is quiet."

"I'll call when I board the chopper."

As ten camera angles played out on the wall-mounted monitor in front of him. Oliver studied each one, searching for Erika Carr. A single screen played in reverse, following the path of Dr. Carr from the armor exhibit back to wherever she'd started her journey.

"Stop." Oliver jabbed the screen. "Right there."

In the open walkway between the White Tower and Waterloo Barracks, a group of four people gathered, including Erika Carr. All wore hats, never looking skyward.

"Let it play. But follow those two after they separate from the woman."

Two men hustled toward the Barracks as Dr. Carr and her companion headed to the White Tower.

"What about a view from the doors?" Logan said.

Cameras covered most of the exterior doorways on the grounds, and when the two men veered close to one, Oliver got lucky.

"Stop it there. Can you zoom in?" A tech manipulated the image, the grainy pixels coalescing.

"I'll be damned. They're both here." Just to be sure, Oliver pulled out the photo given to each Keeper.

A match. Erika had brought Parker with her to the Tower.

It might prove to be the last mistake either of them ever made.

Chapter 48

Tower of London
London, England

Footsteps echoed off the narrow staircase as Erika raced toward the second floor, Gavin one step ahead. Down the hall, light spilled from the open chapel door, dust mites flitting through the sunlight, dancing as a breeze carried scents of freshly cut grass and a distant hint of exhaust fumes.

Gavin reached the door first. "Damn. This Chapel has two levels. More to search."

"You mean more opportunities to find what Anne left behind," Erika said. "This is a good sign. Most chapels from her time have galleries. A lower level for the rich and powerful, and a gallery for the masses. The nave is reserved for the royal family, while anyone else fortunate enough to worship with the monarch would likely be relegated to the level above."

Constructed of white stone, thick columns ringed a curved room fronted by a vaulted apse, with rolling arches supporting the gallery level. Stained glass windows colored sunlight, several of them open, the breeze soft on Erika's cheeks.

"Not much to it, really." Several rows of chairs sat facing a stone altar, though the candleholders on either side drew her gaze.

"I thought of that too," Gavin said. "But nothing points to candleholders again, does it?"

"Not based on her message." Erika walked to the closest column, the stone smooth under her touch. "Don't let that stop you from checking. Look for anything suggesting royalty or... you know the drill by now."

Gavin went to work on his side of the room. When the first column revealed nothing but stonework, Erika had a thought.

"If anyone walks in here, try not to make our search obvious. Sooner or later someone's going to wander through."

"I'll have Harry keep an eye out when he gets here."

Goosebumps dotted her arms as they searched. The final truth behind Prince William's fate could be here, close enough to touch. Unless Anne never learned the truth herself. Erika hadn't considered that. Perhaps she'd only allowed herself to imagine this story with a happy ending.

A shiver knifed up her spine. In the middle of so much death, how could William have survived?

"Any idea why they're so interested in a chapel?" Harry asked.

The pair hurried along deserted streets toward the White Tower.

"Beats me," Parker said. "But anything grabbing Erika's attention is a good sign for us."

A black raven floated overhead, cawing as it settled on a low-slung wall. The birds pretty much had the run of this place, unafraid of humans.

"Is it just me, or does this place seem quiet?"

Harry looked around. "Sure aren't many people around. If anything, I'd say it's gotten emptier since we walked in. Maybe the crowds don't show up until later on a weekday."

Parker nodded, but couldn't shake the feeling. *I'm in the Tower of London, one of the most popular tourist attractions in the city. Where's everyone else?*

Wispy clouds cast fleeting shadows across the White Tower as they approached, but something else caught Parker's eye.

"Harry, whatever you do, don't react."

To his credit, the Irishman nodded, looking at the ground. "Sure, I understand."

"Those two ahead, the guards. Does it look like they're interested in us?"

What caught his eye were the two men clad in Tower uniforms. Huddled together near the White Tower entrance, one kept his back to them, while the other couldn't seem to keep his eyes off Parker. His gaze flitted away for a moment, only to return an instant later.

"That one sure does. Maybe it's nothing. I think I know how to tell."

Harry never broke stride as he approached the two men. Parker glanced around, his gut feeling growing with every step. This place was deserted. And the only other tourists in sight were *leaving* the grounds, a trickle of people exiting under the open front gate, none coming in.

"Good morning!" Harry gave the guards his best smile. "Can you gents help me out?"

The one staring Parker down went white, his lips sealed shut. The other one kept his back turned, never facing either visitor.

"What's the problem, sir?" white face asked.

"Why isn't anyone here today?" Harry asked, arms waving around the empty streets. "Is this place closing? I thought it would be *packed*."

The man didn't respond. One arm slipped inside his jacket and didn't come out.

"Nothing you missed," the other finally replied. "Just a slow morning is all." As he spoke, the man never faced them.

"I hope so," Harry said. "My friend and I are excited to see the White Tower here."

When neither guard responded, Harry went in for the kill. "You mind if we get a picture?"

He threw an arm around the guard who wouldn't face them. When he did, two things happened. First, the man jerked like a marionette, shoulders bouncing as though Harry's arm was on fire. Second, a picture fell from inside his coat. As it fluttered to the ground, all four men couldn't look away. It landed face up. In perfect position to display the four photographs it contained, spaced evenly in each corner.

Parker, Erika, Gavin, and Harry.

When a gun came out, Parker didn't blink. His fist caught the guard square on his chin and sent him sprawling to the ground, out cold. Harry elbowed the man in front of him, and a second blow slammed home, rendering the man unconscious.

"Get them inside," Harry said, dragging his man through the White Tower's front door. "Hurry, before anyone else gets here."

Parker grabbed a pair of ankles, pulling his opponent through the door Harry kicked open. As the wooden door slammed shut, Parker didn't note any sign of alarm.

"Safe to say our cover's blown," Harry said. "Why do you think they didn't do anything? They had to know it was us."

"Maybe they didn't want to take us in yet," Parker said, pulling chairs in front of the two bodies. Now at least they weren't in plain sight. "They might figure we're basically trapped in here. After all, it is their headquarters."

"Or maybe they had no idea we were here and didn't know what to do." Harry pulled a tablecloth off the visitor's desk and draped it over the two men, but only after liberating each of his firearm. "There's a chance they haven't raised the alarm."

"Either way, we need to move," Parker said. "Those two will be missed, and when they are, I want to be as far outside these walls as possible."

Harry ran up the stairs, two at a time. "Let's see what has Erika and Gavin so worked up."

Up the rounding staircase and down a wide hallway, Parker darted through the open chapel door to find Gavin and Erika on opposite sides of the narrow chapel, noses nearly pressed to the white stone walls.

"It's about time," Erika said. "Parker, you take the gallery. Harry, I think you—"

"We have to leave."

"What are you talking about?" Erika didn't even look at him, engrossed in her search.

"We just knocked out two guards," Harry said.

"You *what?*"

Parker recapped how the two guards took an unhealthy interest in him and Harry, and their ensuing ruse. When he mentioned the paper with their photos, Erika's hand flew to her mouth.

"How do they know we're here? This should be the last place they'd be looking."

"Either Harry surprised them," Parker said. "Or they knew we were here but didn't want to stop us."

"If they already know we're here, we may as well keep searching." Gavin's tone left no room for dissent. "We still have some time. Harry, you watch the door." He turned to Parker. "Do whatever Erika tells you."

He still didn't know what had drawn them here. "What are we looking for?"

Erika explained the connection between St. John and Anne's reference to *no martyrs*, as well as the fact the chapel windows overlooked the spot of Anne Boleyn's execution.

"Any idea what she left behind?" Harry asked.

"Anne apparently moved on from the candleholder theme," Parker said. A pair of the accessories, each as tall as he, lay on the floor, devoid of hidden drawers.

"This is her chapel," Erika said. "As Queen, Anne could do anything to this room. My guess is we're looking for a permanent marker, perhaps a design or series of letters which blend with the décor."

"Hidden in plain sight," Parker said. So far her tricks stood the test of time well enough. "It would've needed to be significant to her uncle."

"We're at a disadvantage there," Erika said. "Search everywhere and if anything catches your eye, let me know."

Parker started upstairs, searching every step as he went. For such a small chapel, there were any number of nooks and dark corners. Every minute spent searching heightened the risk of discovery, but he dared not hurry. Not if it meant overlooking Anne's message.

Cool stone ran under his fingertips, rough at the edges. As Parker searched, the chapel floor rumbled beneath his feet.

He must be losing it. "Do you feel that?"

"It's a helicopter," Gavin said. "It sounds like it's landing outside."

As long as it wasn't a team of British commandos descending on them, Parker didn't care if the pope had come to visit. They needed to find this clue and get the hell out of here.

"Not to alarm you," Gavin said, eyes on his watch. "But we need to be out of here in fifteen minutes. Arden Flanarty gave the final go-ahead. The drone takes off in thirty."

Logan Rose bent over as he ran, hair swirling in the downdraft. Rotors buzzed above, and the helicopter barely settled onto the Tower's landing pad before he bolted from the cockpit, running to where Oliver Moore stood at attention.

"Welcome back, sir. Follow me."

Once inside the control room, Oliver tapped one of the over-sized viewing screens.

"Dr. Carr and her associates are in the White Tower," Oliver said. "Likely in St. John's Chapel, though we haven't confirmed that."

"Why not?" Logan didn't have any time to waste. If he could wrap this up now, they needed to act.

Oliver lowered his voice so only Logan could hear. "I presumed you want to see what Dr. Carr is after. All visitors were told there is a problem with the utilities and the tower must be evacuated, so we don't need to worry about civilian interference. The Americans and their Irish guides aren't going anywhere. If there *is* something hidden in the chapel, we haven't been able to locate it. Perhaps Dr. Carr will find it for us."

"Alright," Logan said. A damn good plan, actually. "How many men are here?"

"Seven, including you and me." Oliver tapped a button, and on-screen the rapid takedown of two Keepers outside the White Tower played out. "Though only five are in fighting shape. The rest of our men are still in Ireland and won't return until this afternoon."

"Get everyone together," Logan said. "We'll surround them and move in. Make sure the men know this isn't a drill. Live ammo, and they have the green light to fire if fired upon."

"I'll get them ready."

"Any word on the terrorist threat?" Logan asked.

"None," Oliver said. "We haven't heard any chatter, and all appears to be well within the grounds. Except for the White Tower."

"We'll fix that shortly." Logan walked toward his office. "Have the men ready in five minutes."

"You don't want to wait, sire?"

"We've pissed around long enough. We're going in through the front door, and we'll give them a show."

Parker stood on the gallery railing, one hand poking a smooth stone pillar for any sign of Anne. Finding nothing but stone and mortar, unmarked in any way, the cold knot in his stomach migrated to his throat.

They'd failed.

Erika and Gavin stood by the open window beneath him. Harry leaned around the front door, bouncing from one foot to the next. They'd been over the entire chapel and found nothing.

"We're out of time," Gavin said. "The attack will begin in ten minutes. Unless we leave now, we won't make it outside the gates before the drone explodes."

As much as he wanted to stay, Parker couldn't argue. Death by bombing made for a persuasive argument. "We can always come back," he said, looking to Erika.

"But it has to be here," Erika said. "Nothing else makes sense. We must have missed it."

Not used to being wrong, Parker knew even the threat of an explosion didn't guarantee she'd agree to leave.

"Use your head," Parker said, descending from the gallery. "Gavin's right. We're no good to anyone dead. You want to finish what Michelle

250

started? You can't do that in a coffin."

Mentioning her murdered friend finally did it.

"You're right," she said, her eyes on the floor. "We'll come back."

"Follow me," Gavin said. "And keep your heads down. We're headed straight for the exit. No matter what happens, don't stop until you're beyond those gates."

Harry stepped through the door, waving for them to follow him down the hallway, single file. Both IRA men kept one hand in their coats, next to the pilfered Keeper weapons. Down the winding staircase, and Parker saw the first floor stretch out below.

Harry reached the last step and turned to face them. "We'll take—"

The shot sounded like cannon fire bouncing off the walls. Harry spun around, blood splattering on the wall. Before he landed, Gavin returned fire, holding Harry's arm and dragging him up the stairs, stone chips flew as round after round smacked into the wall.

"Get back!" Gavin threw Harry up the stairs, Parker grabbing his arms and pulling. Erika hadn't moved, but one look at Parker racing toward her with a bloody Harry in tow got her moving.

"Keepers," Harry said between gritted teeth. "With assault rifles. They came in when we turned the corner."

"I clipped two of them," Gavin said between shots. "But there's three more. We need cover."

A breeze blew through St. John's Chapel as Parker brought Harry inside. Maybe they could jump.

"How far is it?" Parker asked, leaning Harry against the wall, putting pressure on the shoulder wound.

Erika looked out over the ledge. "No good. It's more than twenty feet down. You'll break your ankles – if you're lucky."

Which left the gallery's roof access as their only option. He'd seen it during their search, but hadn't opened the door for fear of triggering an alarm.

Gunshots rang out from the hallway. Gavin appeared, striding backward with his gun pointed ahead. "Can we get out of here?" A bullet clipped the ceiling above his head. "Now, please."

"It's too high to jump," Parker said, pointing to the window. "But there's a roof access door."

Gavin leaned out the door and fired, ducking back as bullets sparked on the frame. "Only two left now. I'll hold them off while you get him upstairs," Gavin said, nodding to Harry. "Getting lost in the streets is our best option, and then we can get him to a doctor."

Grunting as he stood, Harry pulled himself upright, a tapestry of red left on the wall. One step, and the gun slipped from his grasp. A bullet fired when it landed, shattering a part of the altar across the room.

"Sorry about that." Stumbling, Harry leaned against the wall as Parker retrieved his weapon. "Bit slippery now."

"Hang on," Parker said as they limped to the stairs. Erika ran through the gallery, her feet disappearing toward the roof exit.

"I think I'll be needing a pint or two when we get out of here."

Damned Irish. The guy gets shot and starts cracking jokes.

"I'll buy the first round."

The shooting stopped below them, and Gavin hadn't been hit. He stood inside the doorway, watching their progress.

"Almost there," Parker said. "One more flight and we're out of here."

Ahead, he spotted Erika's feet on the stairs.

"Is it open?" he asked. This didn't look good. Harry could barely stand. One arm draped over Parker's shoulders, he still held the pistol, drops of red glistening on the barrel.

"Almost there," Parker said, looking upstairs. Wait a minute. What's Erika doing? Her feet now moved *backwards*, down into the gallery. "Erika, we're running out of time."

And then a pair of black boots descended in front of her retreating frame. A Keeper, waiting for them on the roof. And he had an automatic rifle aimed at Erika's chest.

"Drop the gun or she dies here."

Logan Rose took no pleasure in saying it. He'd seen enough bullet wounds to realize the guy draped across Parker Chase probably couldn't even aim his gun, much less hit anything. Blood dripped from his arm, pooling on the floor.

"Drop the weapon."

The pistol clattered on stone, and the wounded man kicked it away.

"Downstairs," Logan said. "Into the chapel. Keep your hands where I can see them."

Logan caught sight of the second Irishman. Noting the rifle aimed at Erika's chest, he dropped his gun.

"Oliver," Logan shouted. "Come into the chapel."

Boots pounded as Oliver Moore came around the corner, his rifle leading the way. The lone unwounded Keeper followed. His other two men were downstairs, wounded but alive.

"Dr. Carr," Logan said. The four intruders lined up by the altar, the wounded man wobbling. "We finally meet. And Mr. Chase."

Pure hatred met his gaze.

"You killed my friend," Erika said. "Over a letter."

Logan glanced at the third Keeper. "Secure the ground floor," he told the man. "Check on your injured colleagues."

"Yes, sir." The man disappeared out the door, though his gaze lingered on Erika Carr.

"An unfortunate necessity," Logan said. "I took no pleasure in ordering her death."

"You murdered her," Erika said. "For what? So some musty old secrets about a kidnapped prince don't get out? It happened three hundred years ago. It doesn't matter anymore."

"You're wrong, Dr. Carr." Logan needed to know what they'd discovered. Something led them back to the Tower, a loose end in need of securing. "What you've uncovered could destroy our government."

Parker Chase spoke up. "What the hell are you talking about? We know people kidnapped Prince William and Anne chased him all over the kingdom. Some Irishmen wanted their freedom and tried to force her hand. They didn't count on Anne's cousin stealing her throne. So what? It's buried history."

They really didn't know.

"Those kidnappers founded a terrorist group that continues today, killing civilians and destroying any hopes of peace. Two of them are standing here." Logan tipped his gun toward the two Irishman.

Before they could respond, a phone chirped. The uninjured Irishman reached into his pocket.

Oliver jammed his rifle into the guys' chest. "Keep your hands where we can see them."

"I assure you, I'm unarmed." The man removed his phone, holding it out. "You'll want to read this."

Gavin studied Logan Rose and his associate, the cell phone clenched in his hand. "Yes, we belong to the IRA." These Keepers had no intentions of letting them live. So he played his only card. "An attack is happening right now. Here. A drone is going to fly into the Tower in sixty seconds. Attached to that drone is a bomb, and it's going to blow this place apart."

"You're lying," the Chief Keeper said.

"You've been warned." Gavin shrugged. "You have access to the anti-terrorism alerts. Hear anything about an attack today?"

He'd guessed right. Rose blinked, eyes darting to the bald man.

"What's the target?"

"I only know it's here, at the Tower. They plan to use the drone to deliver a payload inside for maximum destruction."

Footsteps behind him. Gavin turned, saw the man with his head stuck out the open window.

"I don't see anything," he said. "There's no way a drone can get close enough to the Tower without our men detecting it."

"What men? You have five downstairs, four of them wounded. I'm guessing most of the Keepers are still in Dublin, searching for us."

Right again. Rose walked toward his associate, giving the four of them a wide berth. Gun aimed at Gavin, he glanced outside. "Where's the attack coming from?"

Harry pulled himself to the window and raised an unsteady hand. "East, across the river. Brilliant plan, actually."

"You need to evacuate immediately," Gavin said. Right now he actually hoped for an explosion. He'd take all the destruction Arden Flanarty could muster if it got Harry out of here. "The civilian casualties could be tremendous."

"Why are you waiting in here?" Gavin asked. He gestured toward the roof. "Do you have sharpshooters? There's a chance you could take the drone down. If you destroy the machine, the bomb won't detonate."

Just as the Chief Keeper headed upstairs, the bald man's voice rang out.

"Here it comes!"

Parker's stomach nosedived.

"Parker." Erika whispered his name, crouched down behind the altar. "Parker!"

"What?"

She pulled when he grabbed her arm, ripping him down to her level. "Look at this."

White powder coated her hands.

She didn't seem to get it. "Didn't you hear him? The drone's coming."

"This is it," she said, a chunk of white rock in hand. "I found it."

"Found what?" The two Keepers stood at the window, crowded around Harry. With death bearing down, maybe they'd let Parker and Erika run and not shoot them in the back.

"Anne's message."

For the first time, he actually looked at her. "*What?*"

"Here, in the altar."

She indicated a jagged opening in the massive stone block.

"The altar's hollow," he said.

"At least this portion is. It's a drawer," Erika said as Parker kneeled on the ground. "Look, you can see the edges. We missed it."

Gunshots rang out.

"You didn't check the altar?"

"No," she said. "Gavin started to, but then all *this* happened."

This meant the bomb. Coming right for them.

"Is anything inside?" he asked.

Her arm disappeared into the depths, chunks of stone scattering as she groped. "There's something round, and it... feels like metal. It's *heavy*."

She pulled her hand free, holding what looked like a relay baton.

"Is that gold?"

"Feels like it," she said. The full weight hit his chest. "You hold it."

"How do you know it's from Anne?"

"I didn't," she said. "Until now. Look at the end."

Two letters, scratched into the top end of the gold tube.

A. S.

"But why in here?" he asked. A simple cross dominated the front of the altar, strange words inscribed above and below. Nothing to indicate a royal missive was protected inside.

Finally on their feet, Parker glanced out the window.

A black dot bearing death steamed their way.

Logan saw it. The black bird, still at a distance, whizzing toward them.

"Get back!" Logan leaned out the window and started firing.

The bird didn't stop. The hammer fell on an empty chamber, and Logan grabbed the wounded Irishman's gun and blasted away. Sparks flew, the drone bobbing, but it didn't stop. Beside him, Oliver Moore unloaded his assault rifle.

"You told me there's a camera on it," Logan said. "They can see you.

They know you're still in here."

"That won't stop them," the uninjured Irishman said. "We're expendable."

What kind of commander killed his own men?

The bird dropped, correcting course and making a beeline for them.

"Get out," Logan said. "All of you."

Oliver turned and ran, but stopped when he looked back to find Logan at the windowsill.

"Come on, Chief."

Except sometimes an Englishman didn't run, even when he should. "Take care of yourself, Oliver. You'll be a fine chief."

Before Oliver could react, Logan jumped onto the window ledge, the drone barreling toward him.

Twenty feet.

The nose stayed down, on course.

Ten feet.

Logan saw the camera, a tiny red light blinking beside it.

And then it stopped. Hovering outside the building, frozen in mid-air. Maybe the operator knew.

So Logan jumped.

One rotor bit his hand, slicing through flesh as he dropped, grabbing hold of the metal beast. For an instant, it held, supporting him.

Then they dropped as one.

The ground raced to meet him. An instant before they landed, the light flashed, and the world burned.

Chapter 49

Parker stood rooted to the ground, his eyes on the window. That crazy Englishman had jumped.

Then it happened.

A flash lit the ground, blinding him as it rose, wiping the landscape from view. As Parker stumbled back, Gavin made his move, fist slamming the bald Keeper's jaw, sending him down and out.

"He'll live," Gavin said as Erika stared. "Help me with Harry."

Parker handed the slender golden cylinder to Erika, turning to find Harry crumpled on the ground.

A long smear of crimson marred the white stone wall behind him.

"Harry, get up." Gavin grabbed an arm, Parker moving to taking the other, his grip slipping with each try.

Why couldn't he grab hold?

"Gavin." The Irishman looked up at Parker's blood-covered hands.

"No." Gavin turned Harry's unresisting frame over, the glazed eyes staring back, unseeing.

Gavin knelt, Harry's hand clasped in his own. Parker caught a hint of Gaelic before Gavin gently laid his friend's hand down and closed Harry's eyes, eyes which sparked so brightly now dimmed forever.

"Let's move." Gavin walked out and didn't look back.

Pulling Erika, Parker looked back at the young Irishman.

If not for him, they'd be dead now. A stranger only days ago, he'd become so much more.

Thank you, my friend.

Chapter 50

Outside the Tower of London, horns and sirens blared. A fire engine raced past, nearly clipping a row of parked cars as it barreled toward the rising pillar of black smoke below St. John's Chapel.

Parker tucked his chin down. Long, loping strides ate up the ground, the trio putting as much distance between themselves and the Tower of London as possible.

It took a moment's work to slip outside, dodging through the front gate as crowds gaped at a scorched wall on the White Tower, the stones blackened and charred. Had the drone made it inside, the blast could have taken down an entire side.

The Keeper had saved them. All of them, IRA or not.

"What about using the Underground?" Erika asked, the golden cylinder clutched tightly in her hands.

"Can't risk getting stuck if they shut them down." Gavin eyed the yellow tube, though that's all he did. "We'll take multiple cabs, get close to the safe house. I have a car to get us out of the city."

Three black cabs and one circuitous route later, Gavin rummaged under the wheel well of a dinged-up Toyota Land Cruiser.

"Got it," he said, displaying a key. "Let's get the hell out of here."

They rode in silence. Eventually Gavin maneuvered onto a motorway, staying just below the speed limit.

"Looks like you found something." Gavin turned toward Erika, riding shotgun. Parker looked up, catching Erika's gaze in the rearview mirror.

"I found it in the altar. A bullet damaged the front stone so I could see the compartment."

"I missed it?" Gavin asked. "I didn't see any drawers."

"I wouldn't have either," Erika said. "Even with the damaged front I

258

could barely find the seams. And unless you could read Middle English, you'd miss the clue." She shook her head. "That one's on me."

"Forget it," Gavin said. "Focus on what you're holding."

Erika held out the cylinder. "It's made of gold."

Gavin ran a hand over it, whistling. "I'll be damned. Thing must be worth a fortune. And what do you mean about knowing Middle English?"

"You'd be right," Erika said. "It's a container. Look, you can see where it opens in the middle."

Parker leaned over, his fingernail clipping the minute line running the width of the tube, splitting it down the middle. "Does it unscrew?"

"First, the language." Erika laid the container in her lap. "The decorative cross on St. John's chapel altar is unremarkable. Taken alone, the Middle English inscription isn't noteworthy either."

"What did it say?" Parker asked.

"*Sainted Patrick who drove the serpents away.*" She turned to face Parker. "And at the base of the cross, the numbers three, one and seven."

"Just like the sword at Dublin Castle," Gavin said. "A clue only Laurence Hyde would recognize."

"Nearly verbatim. And directly below the numbers, this hidden drawer. From what I could see it operated on a hinge mechanism of some sort. Perhaps a button or lever hidden in the cross activated the drawer, releasing the lock so it slid out."

Gavin's eyes remained on the road. "If I found it sooner, we might have been able to escape."

"Don't think that." Parker had been down this road before, blaming himself for events out of his control. "We were caught long before you laid eyes on the altar."

"He's right," Erika said. "There's nothing anyone could have done."

And then she looked at Parker. "Go ahead," he said.

She twisted, and the gold cylinder unwound without a sound. "Amazing. Three hundred years and it's as smooth as when they made it."

As the halves parted, two objects fell to her lap. Parker glanced down to see a scrolled paper wound tight. "What's in your lap?"

Flat across the top, with two sloping edges, it had the appearance of a miniature gold shield. On the surface a line ran horizontally, and another vertically, bisecting each other in the center.

"A pendant or charm of some sort," Gavin said. "With something in each of the corners."

In the lower right, Parker noted scratches. Only when Erika held it in the sunlight did the marks become clear.

"It's a drawing," she said. "It looks like a tiny *harp*. But look at this." She squinted, the piece barely larger than a quarter. "The hypotenuse, the longest side, is a straight line. The other two sides look like an angel with her wings stretched out behind her."

Parker peered over her shoulder. Small, and tough to see, but once she stopped fiddling with it, Parker couldn't argue. A harp in one corner, and angels in two others.

"Have you ever seen that before?"

"Never," Erika said. "I have no idea what it means."

"Maybe the paper will tell us," Parker said.

Scratching as it unrolled, the silk knot binding it fluttered to the floor. Parker noted the familiar elegant quill strokes as the royal missive unfurled.

"It appears to be the right age, and this certainly looks like Anne's writing based on what we've seen."

Parker couldn't glimpse the body of text. Erika held it close to her face, tilted away from him to catch the light.

"Please move it along, Dr. Carr."

Erika looked ready to argue, but Gavin's face brooked no argument. One hand on the wheel, one scratching at his shirt, he stared out the windshield, waiting.

Erika gave voice to the final chapter of Anne's unusual journey.

Dearest Laurence,

The fates have not smiled upon me, though if you read this letter, hope yet remains. I sit here, a prisoner in my own tower. For though I know William lives, I cannot retrieve him.

Upon returning to London, one of my retinue was approached in the gardens by a simple priest from the parish of Saint Paul. This godly man gave voice to a tale that sets my heart beating while crushing my soul in one breath. The priest was visited by a man and a young boy not one week past. The man asked that this priest deliver a message to me. Through the grace of our Lord, one of my ladies attends mass in Saint Paul's and is known to the priest.

The man who visited this priest is of the Irishmen who kidnapped William. The boy in his care is my own son. William, the future King of England, was not a mile from where I now sleep. And yet I cannot save him. The Irishman's message? Free Ireland from English rule and William will be released unharmed. Fail to do so, and William is to be raised with the Irish, never to return.

I cannot rescue my son. George has stripped me of all power. Gone are my allies, those who would defend the crown. The royal physician is murdered, replaced with a man of George's choosing. This man has declared me incompetent. For my own safety, I am told, departure from the castle walls is impossible except to pray. It is through this small privilege that I have been able to secret this letter which I hope you will retrieve.

A pendant identical to the enclosed was around the neck of my son when he visited St. Paul's. The Irishman made the priest take special note to prove it was William. I would know it anywhere, for there are only two in the world, one of which belonged to my departed daughter Mary, and which I now give to you. The other hung around William's neck when he was taken.

Find my son and destroy the imposter King George. His unjust reign must end.

Godspeed,
Anne

A thought buzzing at the back of Parker's mind finally came to light. He'd seen that pendant before, the little gold shield. But where?

He didn't have to wait long to find out.

Gavin reached into his shirt. Erika gasped, Anne's priceless letter falling from her hands.

"This belonged to my father," Gavin said, pulling at the leather string around his neck. "And his father before him." It caught on his shirt, finally coming free with a jerk.

"It's the only thing I have left of them. They could never tell me where we came from, what lands we'd tended in Ireland's long past. Now I know why."

Hanging from the leather string, hidden in plain sight during their entire journey, Gavin held Prince William's matching shield.

Epilogue

One week later
Blarney Castle
Cork, Ireland

"So what do you want to do now, *future husband?*"

They'd been engaged for an hour and he'd already had enough. She must have called him that fifty times. In one hour.

"I think this calls for a few pints," he said, his lips pressing hers. "And then a few more. And after that, who knows? I have a couple of ideas."

She didn't even listen, the sparkly bauble on her finger the only thing she had eyes for now. He'd gone for the classic look, a round stone with a simple band. Well, maybe it was a *little* big. So what?

"I can't believe we're *engaged!*"

Erika jumped into his arms, and more than a few of their fellow tourists at Blarney Castle clapped. It had been even worse at the top of the tower, when he'd tipped a guard to his plans. The attendant lowered Erika to kiss the famed stone and cleared out the upper level to give them a bit of privacy.

When she'd come back up from the inverted good-luck smooch, Parker had been on one knee. Of course, she'd nearly killed them both by jumping into his arms, which sent the ring flying. Parker darted after it, slipping on the damp stone and crashing into the battlements. Not much higher than his waist, he'd been a few inches from toppling over. Fortunately, disaster had been avoided, and the ring found not far away.

"A story for the ages!" the attendant exclaimed. "Would have been sad to see you go, young man. Mighty close call."

Only after they navigated the treacherously narrow stairs did his heart slow. As they descended, of course, the story of their engagement followed by word of mouth, every person in line offering congratulations. Today, they celebrated.

Goodness knows they'd worked hard enough to get here. After their discovery of Gavin's potential royal lineage, which Erika quickly pointed out was far from confirmed, events happened quickly. Parker and Erika spent the next few days in Belfast, eating breakfast and playing cards with wanted criminals. Arden Flanarty, as crotchety and crafty a bastard as Parker had ever seen, immediately lost all internal support when the IRA rank and file learned Arden's bomb nearly killed two of their brothers. Harry's death weighed heavily, and Connor Whelan used backdoor diplomatic channels to discuss terms with the Keepers.

With the former Chief Keeper dead, his replacement turned out to be the second man from inside the chapel. After several tense days he agreed to erase all records of Parker Chase and Erika Carr from their database, but only if Connor agreed to return the golden cylinder and its contents. Fully in control of the IRA once more, Connor agreed, his belief that cooperation and negotiation would ultimately end their war winning out. No one other than Quartermaster Whelan knew of the find, and Parker swore he and Erika weren't telling anyone. Who would believe them? Absent any proof, which the Keepers likely destroyed, they had nothing more than a fantastic tale.

And so they'd been able to travel freely, albeit using their Canadian passports to leave England. After all the excitement, Parker figured they'd earned time to relax, and a chance for him to make good on the promise he'd carried every step of the way.

"Oh my goodness," Erika gushed, dancing about. "I have to call my friends, my colleagues – did you tell anyone – we need to pick a date, make an invitation list." Both hands waved in front of her face. "This is too much. I can't handle being engaged."

"Relax," he said as they passed through Blarney Castle's front gate. "There's no need to hurry. Just enjoy it." He didn't have to ask about the tinge of guilt in her eyes, a sadness even this joyous day couldn't erase. Michelle's death was a cloud in their bright blue sky.

Warm rays hung like a reddish curtain as they hit the horizon, dull streaks riding the wind, carrying the unmistakable scents of luscious green hillsides. In his hand, the keyless entry beeped, lights flashing on the Range Rover he'd rented.

"After you," Parker said, holding the door. As she slipped by, Erika

263

grabbed him with both arms, pulled him close, and whispered in his ear.

"Thank you. For the best gift I could ever receive."

For a second after she turned, the lump in his throat didn't move.

Damn. No time to get soft now. They had an entire life to enjoy.

"How about we take a walk through town and see how many pubs we can find?" Parker slid behind the wheel, which still felt funny on the right side.

"That sounds great," Erika said. Held out like a strutting peacock's feathers, she flipped her ring every which way in the sunlight, the fire inside breathtaking.

"Oops." As he turned the key, the ring box slipped from his hand. She'd need it, would want somewhere safe to keep the ring at night. Parker ducked out of his seat, crouched low on the ground. *Where did that thing go?*

Under their car, a red light blinked behind the front tire.

That shouldn't—

White light flashed. And then the noise hit. The loudest he'd ever heard. For an instant, Parker floated.

Then, nothing.

London, England

"It's done."

Oliver Moore ended the call, his phone splashing into the Thames.

When he'd come to on the floor of St. John's chapel, the two Yanks and their Irish friend were gone. Soon after, when the IRA Quartermaster revealed what had been found in the altar, Oliver knew what must be done. Yes, he'd promised them their freedom. But it couldn't be.

Two IRA terrorists? No one would believe them. But two Americans who'd witnessed it all firsthand? No. Not when so many gave their lives to protect the crown.

A soldier did what must be done to protect Queen and Country. There were always casualties.

The true king may not be dead. But again, as always, Oliver Moore would do anything necessary to protect the crown.

Long live the Queen.

GET THE ANDREW CLAWSON STARTER LIBRARY

FOR FREE

Sharing the writing journey with my readers is a special privilege. I love connecting with anyone who reads my stories, and one way I accomplish that is through my mailing list. I only send notices of new releases or the occasional special offer related to the Parker Chase or TURN series.

If you sign up for my mailing list, I'll send you a free copy of the first Parker Chase and TURN novels as a special thank you. You can get these books for free by signing up here:

DL.bookfunnel.com/L4modu3vja

Did you enjoy this book? Let people know

Reviews are the most effective way to get my books noticed. I'm one guy, a small fish in a massive pond. Over time, I hope to change that, and I would love your help. The best thing you could do to help spread the word is leave a review on your platform of choice.

Honest reviews are like gold. If you've enjoyed this book I would be so grateful if you could take a few minutes leaving a review, short or long, on this book's Amazon page.

Thank you very much.

Author's note

During the seven years she spent on the throne, Anne, Queen of Great Britain, experienced an unusual amount of strife and heartache, even for a monarch. Despite seventeen pregnancies by her husband, she died without any surviving children, and took the House of Stuart with her to her grave. Her second cousin George, a Protestant, succeeded her on the throne, his accession made possible by the Act of Settlement passed in 1701 which disqualified any Roman Catholics from inheriting the throne. At the time of Anne's death in 1714, over fifty Catholic claimants more closely related to Anne were excluded from the line of succession.

Prince William died in 1700, aged 11. A sickly boy, his symptoms were consistent with hydrocephalus, a condition in which cerebrospinal fluid accumulates in the brain. His kidnapping at the hands of Irish revolutionaries is my invention.

Laurence Hyde was Anne's uncle, and he served as the Lord Lieutenant of Ireland from 1700 until 1703. In truth, they were not close, and Anne dismissed him from office in 1703 owing after a series of disagreements.

The wishing steps at Blarney Castle are real, and legend has it that if you walk down and back up the steps with your eyes closed while thinking only of a wish, that wish will come true within a year. Of course, the wish is supposedly granted by the Blarney Witch, who steals firewood from the estate for her kitchen and grants any wishes as payment. So if broomsticks and black cats make you nervous, maybe give this one a pass.

In Waterford, Reginald's Tower still stands, and though it is not so lustrous as to outshine the world-famous crystal produced there, the oldest civic building in Ireland has quite the story to tell. Aoife's father, one of Ireland's many kings in the 12th century, orchestrated a Norman invasion of his own country, and the price he paid for this invasion army was Aoife's hand. When Richard "Strongbow" de Clare invaded Ireland, he gained land, title, and a wife.

Kilkenny Castle stands today, though the painting of Anne is my creation. Of note, the first building raised on the present-day site of the castle was a wooden structure built by Richard "Strongbow" de Clare.

Leap Castle is now in private hands, though in the 16th century the O'Carroll clan kept it as their seat of power. One brother truly did kill another in a fit of rage, slaying the priest while he was holding mass for their family, and ensuring the Bloody Chapel would forever be known for this infamous deed.

Bram Stoker's alma mater, Trinity College in Dublin, is the oldest university in Ireland. Trinity College Library is a legal deposit library, which means it is legally entitled to a copy of every book published in Great Britain and Ireland. Every year the library receives over 100,000 new items, though the most famous resident is the Book of Kells, which is widely regarded as Ireland's most wonderful national treasure. However, to my knowledge, no hidden writing exists in its pages.

Dublin College and St. Patrick's Cathedral are similar to what is depicted in this book, though the clues left by Anne are fiction. The Tower of London is a fascinating place, and the ravens described in this tale are real, and they are well-fed, sustained by a diet of meat, fruit and cheese. Eight birds in total, they are vital to England's well-being, for superstition holds that if the ravens are lost or fly away, the Crown will fall. Anne Boleyn's execution took place on the north side of the White Tower, away from the site of the memorial commemorating her death. St. John's Chapel is in the Tower of London and is as described, this second chapel often taking a back seat to the parish church of the Tower, St. Peter ad Vincula. As far as I know, however, the altar does not contain any hidden messages from Anne.

Acknowledgements

A special thanks to everyone involved with the production of this work. Without your dedicated efforts and generous gifts and of time and insight, none of this would have been possible. My mother, Rob, Sav, Mike and Kevin, your contributions are invaluable.

To the wonderful artisans who helped craft the cover work, proofed and formatted every line, and helped move my manuscript from start to finish in the best of shape, thank you. And to Kelsey...wow, we did it.

Dedication

For Kevin and Emily.

You help me be a better person every day.

Also by Andrew Clawson

Have you read them all?

In the Parker Chase Series

A Patriot's Betrayal

A dead man's letter draws Parker Chase into
a deadly search for a secret that could rewrite history.
Free to download

The Crowns Vengeance

A Revolutionary era espionage report sends Parker
on a race to save American independence.

Dark Tides Rising

A centuries-old map bearing a cryptic poem sends Parker Chase
racing for his life and after buried treasure.

A Republic of Shadows

A long-lost royal letter sends Parker on a secret trail
with the I.R.A. and British agents close behind.

A Hollow Throne

Shattered after a tragic loss, Parker is thrust into
a race through Scottish history to save a priceless treasure.

In the TURN Series

TURN: The Conflict Lands

Reed Kimble battles a ruthless criminal gang
to save Tanzania and the animals he loves.
Free to download

TURN: A New Dawn

A predator ravages the savanna. To stop it, Reed must be
what he fears most – the man he used to be.

Check my website AndrewClawson.com for more details,
and additional Parker Chase and TURN novels.

Praise for Andrew's Novels

Praise for *A Patriots Betrayal*

"A Patriots Betrayal had me hooked from the first page!"

"The characters were well developed and authentically true to life. The story was incredible, realistic, and historically intriguing."

"The mystery and suspense had me so intrigued that I had to keep reading."

Praise for *The Crown's Vengeance*

"Moments of sheer intensity make it hard to put this book down."

"This one is just as exciting and fast paced as the first, with new adventures flying at the couple in every turn."

"Be sure you set aside enough time to finish this one, you'll not want to put this one down until you read the last page."

Praise for *Dark Tides Rising*

"Yet another gem-filled yarn weaving fact and fiction."

"A story that is so well written it keeps you from putting the book down."

"Very fast and action-packed. Can't wait for the next amazing tale."

About the Author

Andrew Clawson is the author of the Parker Chase and TURN series.

You can find him at his website, AndrewClawson.com, or you can connect with him on Twitter at @clawsonbooks, on Facebook at facebook.com/AndrewClawsonnovels and you can always send him an email at andrew@andrewclawson.com.

Made in the USA
Monee, IL
17 October 2020